Broken Bond

By

Kerry Barnes

Dedication

To my handsome and beautiful cousin, Lee, who was sadly taken far too soon. You were the funniest man I knew, always making me laugh – even at my book signings. May you be up there catching the biggest fish, with that unforgettable smile on your face.

Copyright

Broken Bond by Kerry Barnes ISBN 978-1-7393019-3-4

This is a work of fiction. Names, characters, places, and incidents either are the product of the author's imagination or are used fictitiously. Any resemblance to actual persons, living or dead, events, or locales is entirely coincidental.

ISBN 978-1-7393019-3-4

Broken Bond by Kerry Barnes

For more information, address: kerrybarnes999@gmail.com.

Publishers Once Upon A Book

www.authorkerrybarnes.co.uk

Warning

This book contains graphic details of murder, kidnapping, violence and profanities.

Other works by Kerry Barnes

Ruthless

Ruby's Palace

Raw Justice

The Hunted

The Rules

The Choice

Deceit

Cruel Secrets

Wicked Lies

Ugly Truth

Raising A Gangster

Outcast

Voice of Reason

Voice of Rage

Trusted

Taboo

Torment

Nemesis

Malice

Callous

Needs Must book 1 of the Carrie Verne Series

Bitter Enemies is Book 2 of the Carrie Verne trilogy

Broken Bond book 3 of the Carrie Verne Series

Acknowledgements

Thank you to my editor, Robert Wood, for your keen eye and invaluable insights. Your guidance and expertise have been instrumental in shaping this story into what it is today. I truly appreciate your dedication and hard work.

Having worked together for eight years, starting with *Ruthless*, and now, twenty-three books later, I'm grateful that we're still on the same page. I believe it's our opposite personalities that make the process work – I'm laid-back, and you're thorough and particular. It's a balance I wouldn't change for the world.

I would also like to thank all my readers – both the loyal ones who have been with me from the beginning and the new readers who have taken a chance on my books. Without your support, I wouldn't have been a finalist in the Kindle Storyteller competition this year. So, thank you from the bottom of my heart for your encouragement and belief in my stories. It means so much to me.

PROLOGUE

December 1955

Sandra O'Malley was in the kitchen rolling out a thick slab of pastry while listening to the radio. She was shocked by the news that the Barnes rail crash in London, which happened the previous evening, had killed and injured so many people. As she was about to turn the volume up, the phone rang in the hallway. It made her jump because no one rang. Not many people had a phone, and *they* only had one because of her husband's work. Her heart raced as she hurried along the hallway, brushing her flour-coated hands on her apron.

***

Ten minutes earlier

The playground was dull and dismal, the ground was wet, and the cold bit through her oversized hand-knitted cardigan, which had stretched in the wash, and through her thin cotton dress that was a size too small.

With the sky threatening rain, Shirley, for the first time, wished fervently that the heavens would open quickly because then someone would ring the bell. It was Mary Brown's turn this week. Then, of course, they would all be ushered back inside.

Her eyes momentarily flicked from the two school dinner ladies dressed in pink tabards, who were engrossed in exciting gossip, back to the jagged edge of the corned beef can that the boy waved in front of her. He laughed, followed by a sickly evil chant, 'I'm gonna make you bleeheed, I'm gonna make you bleeheed.'

The dinner ladies, with their legs-of-lamb arms folded across their chests, putting the world to rights, couldn't see what he was doing. The other children had no interest either. They were all playing British bulldog. She wasn't included, and neither was he. They were the two misfits, so everyone said. At least, she thought they had that in common.

Now with her back pressed against the school wall, every muscle and every sinew in her body froze with fear, as a warm sensation spread down her leg, followed by the sound of water trickling and filling her Clarks T-bar shoes.

She didn't dare look down, too afraid that any movement would set him off. In her seven-year-old mind, she imagined that as long as she kept her eyes locked on his, he wouldn't strike. But his grin – and those stubby teeth set against his red gums – was unsettling. His beady eyes were cold too, slotted into his fat medicine ball-shaped head of his.

She wished she'd listened to her mother. 'Don't you play with that boy,' her mother had warned, finger-wagging, with that wild look in her eyes. 'I'm telling you, Shirley O'Malley, he's not right in the head. There's talk of him being carted off to the funny farm.'

But he'd seemed all right to her. He'd sat next to her in the classroom when the other children wouldn't, all because she sometimes wet herself. A weak bladder, the doctor had said. She would grow out of it, eventually, or so she'd been told. But now, she'd done it again.

Darting her eyes to the gap in the wire fence, she wondered if she could make a run for it before he hurt her –

and before the other kids realised she'd wet herself and ribbed her until she cried.

The bullying was relentless, and if she had the guts, she would fight back by screaming at the girls for poking fun at her.

She should, if she was brave enough, be yelling at him now, although she didn't want to because he seemed to be the only friend she had. But today, it seemed he wasn't her friend. Perplexed, she whispered, 'Why are you doing this?'

He leaned in closer, grinning wider. 'Because I can,' he sneered. 'And I want to see you bleed.'

'But I haven't done anything to you,' she pleaded, her eyes filling up.

'So?' His face twisted into a snarl as if she spoke an unfamiliar language.

'I thought we were friends.'

'Friends?' He looked her up and down and laughed. 'I don't need friends.'

Focusing on the jagged edge of the can now, with her stomach churning, she began to sway as her legs turned to jelly beneath her. Suddenly, she saw stars dancing in her vision as the world around her blurred. With no clue as to what was happening to her, she slid down the cold, damp wall and lay lifeless on the concrete playground.

***

'Please, Mrs O'Malley, please keep your voice down,' the headmaster insisted, as he wiped the sweat covering his forehead. He wished he could have removed his woollen jacket and his tie, but he was the head of the school and so he felt he had a reputation to uphold, starting with his attire. However, Mrs O'Malley had every right to scream and shout. The hysterical shrill in her voice along with her finger wagging, which put him on edge, were entirely justified in the circumstances.

‘Keep my voice down?’ She slapped her hands on her skinny hips, her face contorted with absolute rage and her eyes wide. ‘How dare you! You, the headmaster of this school, have allowed that animal to run freely around the playground with an opened corned beef can! And my little Shirley is in with the nurse because that reprobate has cut her arms to ribbons. And why – do tell me – is a bloody *nurse* trying to bandage my daughter’s arms when she clearly needs to go to the hospital?’

‘I can assure you—’

‘You cannot assure me of *anything*. My husband will be talking to the authorities, I can assure you of *that*.’

About to go further with her rant, she suddenly stopped when the boy’s parents entered the room, their heads bowed in shame.

Mrs O’Malley was about to launch herself at the woman when she saw the tears streaming down her face. She stopped and shook her head. ‘That bastard child of yours should be—’

‘I know, I know. He shouldn’t be here. He should be in a special facility.’

Mrs O’Malley stared at the woman, her woollen coat frayed at the bottom, her giant gold earrings hanging from her ears, and a long black plait down her back. She would have looked quite beautiful if she hadn’t appeared worn down, clearly by her son.

‘No, that’s not what I was going to say.’

The boy’s mother lifted her head to meet Mrs O’Malley’s eyes.

‘He should be put down like any farmer would their vicious dog.’

The boy’s father shook his head and guided his wife out of the room, leaving Mrs O’Malley with the headmaster.

‘I’m taking my little girl to the hospital, and you!’ – she pointed a sharp finger in his face – ‘had better hope the doctor doesn’t say she will be scarred for life or this will come down on you and this school. My husband will make you accountable for this, you mark my words, he will.’

Hoping the chair would swallow him up, he replied, ‘I’m sorry, Mrs O’Malley, but we had no idea, and before the dinner ladies could stop him, he had cut her.’

‘Cut her! Cut her? He flaming well *butchered* her. Have you not seen the state of her tiny little arms? And you dare suggest it was anything less, you stupid, pompous man.’

Storming from the room and slamming the door behind her, she marched along the corridor back towards the exit doors. The sound of her heels echoed angrily, matching her mood, as she stomped along the wooden floor that reeked of beeswax.

Suddenly, something caught her eye. What she saw through the wired glass door made her stop dead in her tracks. And the hairs on the back of her neck stood on end.

Sitting with his head held high was the boy who had violently wounded her daughter. Beside him was his mother with her arm around his shoulders. But utter despair had dragged the corners of her mouth down. Her cheeks were blotchy compared to her pale pallor and unspent tears glistened her eyes.

Mrs O’Malley couldn’t help herself. Throwing the door open, she yelled in the boy’s face, ‘You ought to be shot!’

But as she straightened up, she saw the look in his eyes. He didn’t care. He was fearless and mocking her. A subtle twisted smirk curled his lips. It was too restrained to be playful, and yet way too sinister to be innocent. The child’s smile widened just a fraction as he almost mimicked her expression. She felt as if it was a pantomime, like the sudden appearance of a creepy clown. Perhaps it was his bow tie – *what child wears a bow tie, for Christ's sake* – and the blood splattered over his white shirt. His eyes bulged as his mouth opened even more into a mimicking gasp. He held the pose for a moment, for effect. Then he raised her anger by releasing a quiet breathy chuckle as if savouring a private joke that only he understood. For a moment, she was rooted to the spot. Was she staring at the Devil himself?

CHAPTER ONE

March 1995

Cas Ferrier drove the stolen car to the rear of The Old Bull's Head, its headlights already switched off to avoid drawing attention. To any passer-by looking for a quiet pint, the pub from the front exterior looked like an old spit-and-sawdust joint. The small bar was tired and worn, the old black beams were full of woodworm, and age-old hops tied to the beams were gathering dust. But it was a great backdrop for one of the many covers of the classic cult song 'I Put a Spell on You', or a Halloween party.

Beneath that rough exterior, it was a business hub for drug dealers and gamblers. The rich, the dangerous, and the nasty gathered in the basement. It was accessible via the back door, which led from the rear alleyway. The large room was modern and fresher, with a sleek well-stocked bar and clean tables for the customers' card games. The clientele played high-stakes poker games – not throwing the odd tenner on the table but thousands of pounds – and sometimes they wagered on the turn of a card.

Cas cut the engine and turned excitedly to wink at his wingman Keith Purdy. 'Let's have it right off, mate. You got the bag?'

Keith lifted the holdall. 'Check.'

'The shooter?'

Keith lifted his jumper, revealing the gun tucked beneath.

'Rope?'

Keith opened the bag and pointed to the nylon reel.

'Right. All we're waiting for is Vic Slade and his brother. Haven't met the bloke, but Vic says he's as sound as a pound.'

'Why'd you bring them onboard, Cas? I can't stand the prick myself. He's a pikey, and he ain't got much going on upstairs.'

'See, Keith, that's why I do all the planning.' He chuckled. 'With a bit of help from you, of course.'

Keith rolled his eyes. He knew Cas was clever – there was no denying that. The man had made a lot of money from pavement jobs, robberies, and drugs. Anything, in fact, that brought in quick cash. But, sometimes, Cas could get either hotheaded or overexcited, where he would go in like a bull in a china shop, and that was when mistakes happened. Unlike the old days, crime was very different now. It was so easy to get caught. With CCTV cameras popping up at every corner and the use of DNA, those on the take had to be doubly clever.

'Listen, Keith, don't look so worried.' Cas tapped the man's chest. 'It's a straightforward job. Vonny reckons Georgie hasn't changed the safe combination in six months, so all the numbers are up here.' He pointed to his forehead, grinning away, as if this gig was a piece of cake. 'He's hardly likely to have changed it today.'

Cas could have gotten the combination directly from the landlord with a little physical persuasion, but he was older now. And a little wiser, he liked to think. Also, he didn't feel the need to cut off bits of a person just to prove a point. His reputation for violence was still intact, but tonight, he was aiming for a smooth transaction. A few well-placed threats before they tied up Georgie Stubbs, the landlord, and Veronica Webster, the barmaid in her fifties, to a couple of chairs in the basement and grab the cash without interference. It would be so clean and effortless, almost like taking candy from a baby. And no mess.

Cas had no doubt the heist would go to plan because Veronica had meticulously studied the goings-on in the pub. She knew the clientele, the business flow, and exactly how much money passed through the tills. She'd told him when Georgie made his bank runs and when he paid off the dealers. So, tonight, he knew the safe would be piled high with cash.

The heavies wouldn't show up until tomorrow's collection, meaning Cas had the night to himself. Sunday was quiet anyway, and the money Georgie needed to deposit to keep up the appearance of a legit business wouldn't hit the bank until Monday. Everything was lining up perfectly.

'I still don't get why Vic Slade of all people,' Keith muttered. 'You've got your own lads – Dennis the Menace, Walter Whistler. Why the pikey, for God's sake?'

Cas sighed. 'Look, mate, years ago, me and Vic did a job together. We both got caught – I got two years, he got four. So, yeah, I feel like I owe him. This job's easy enough, but I thought he could take a cut and stop banging on about serving longer than me. The fucking bloke's a right pain in the arse. If I see him in the pub, he's always half-cut, and, Christ, he moans and groans. The truth is, he does push his luck, at times. Maybe, the booze gives him Dutch courage. And . . .' he said, laughing, 'I've nearly glassed him a couple of times. But the fact is, he did get a nasty judge who banged him up for longer. Me, well, I got lucky. Another judge who sentenced me on appeal had used my stables once to house his horse, just before Christmas one year – a surprise for his daughter.'

Keith wondered if Cas was going soft. 'You're not gonna split it four ways, are ya?'

'Don't be stupid, Keith.' Cas shot him a look. 'I might feel a bit guilty about Vic doing extra time, but I ain't carving this up four ways. Besides, he won't know how much is in the safe, will he. He's got another job to do.' Cas smirked. 'He'll take care of Georgie and Veronica. Vonny's all right with being tied up.' He grinned like a naughty schoolboy. 'Yeah, good ol' Von. Bless her.'

Keith's eyebrows shot up. 'You and Veronica?'

Cas's expression darkened. 'Mind your own business, Keith. Me and Vonny are mates. Good mates. I won't have a bad word said about her, or her . . . favours.'

Keith chuckled. 'I'll ask no more, then.'

'Right an' all,' Cas said, a subtle reminder to Keith that while he might be the right-hand man, he wasn't a partner. Keith was on the payroll, and that was that.

A beaten-up old car pulled in behind them. 'That's them,' said Cas, pulling his balaclava down over his face before he got out of his car.

Doing the same, Keith swung the holdall over his shoulder and kept his hand on the gun. He didn't like or trust the pikey.

Cas watched the two men clumsily get out of the car behind them and wondered why on earth he'd even bothered about getting Vic on board. He must have been a bit pissed when he asked the man. *And come to think of it*, he thought – *yeah, he had been pissed.* Still, they were here now.

All four men stood together in the alleyway, where it was dark and the place was dead quiet.

Cas eyed Vic and gave him a confirmative nod, but as soon as he clapped eyes on Vic's brother, his blood ran cold. The man looked as though he was on serious drugs. He'd only seen that look once before, and that was on the hospital wing in prison where they'd had to sedate a patient because he was a nutjob. Even after giving him a tranquilliser, which would have brought an elephant to its knees, the guy didn't do anything except make his eyes look dead – just like Vic's brother's eyes were doing now.

'This is me bruvver, Irvin. He's as strong as an ox.'

'He ain't ploughing a fucking field, Vic! Has he got brains?' He looked the brother up and down.

Irvin took a few steps closer, standing right in front of Cas, his grin menacing.

Without hesitation, Keith sidestepped, positioning himself just in front of Cas. His prime job was to protect Cas and take on whoever needed sorting out.

Ordinarily, Cas could handle himself, but even he needed backup sometimes, and there was no harder man than Keith.

'I have got brains, you mug,' came the rejoinder, which actually surprised both Keith and Cas.

But Keith was getting edgy now. 'We ain't got time for this. Now, are we gonna earn some money or what?' he growled.

It had crossed Cas's mind that he would almost certainly need support if any of the heavies returned to the pub. He and Keith could handle a couple of geezers – no problem – but if they came mob-handed, they could be in trouble.

As he eyed Irvin – who was built like a brick shithouse and had that wild, deranged look – he knew which side he would rather be on. Irvin was dangerous, but Cas trusted Keith to handle him, if needed.

Suddenly, the back door creaked open. As planned, Veronica appeared, pretending to take out the rubbish. Cas flicked his head towards Vic – it was his role to handle this part. The penny dropped a second later, and Vic darted towards Veronica, grabbing her roughly, his hand clamping over her mouth, as he dragged her back inside. Irvin followed closely behind.

Cas flared his nostrils. He'd already warned Vic to be gentle with Veronica. She was a tender-hearted woman, but while she was part of the plan, Vic didn't know the full extent of her involvement.

In fact, Cas had kept that part quiet. He didn't want anyone to know that Veronica had helped plan the heist. The last thing he wanted was her name being put forward to the wrong firm, or her body parts would end up being posted all over London.

Keith hissed under his breath, 'Fucking bully,' but he said no more, as he hurried after them.

Inside the basement, they were met by Georgie. Now pushing towards the big five-o, he was no fighter, despite being stocky. As soon as he saw the four men, who were all wearing balaclavas, his insides churned, his mouth dried up, and his legs felt like jelly.

Panic set in, and just as he was about to scarper, Keith yanked him back and shoved the gun under his chin. 'Not so fast,' Keith snarled, gripping the trembling man around his neck.

Georgie looked as though he wouldn't even make his fiftieth birthday. Now ashen-faced, he shook uncontrollably.

But Cas had no intention of hurting him or Veronica. It was the money he wanted.

Cas sprinted up the stairs with Keith hot on his heels, leaving Vic and Irvin to tie up Veronica and Georgie, as planned.

Once the cash was in the holdall, they would slip out the same way they came in. Finding the safe was easy. They entered the room at the top of the building. Larger than any room downstairs, it was fairly tidy and clean. A cream carpet covered the floor, and the double bed was made up with a blue striped cover. Apart from the bed, the only other furniture was the built-in wardrobe, which stretched across one of the walls. Everywhere looked spick and span, much like the landlord himself.

Veronica had told them that the safe was hidden in Georgie's bedroom wardrobe. But as Cas fumbled with the lock, it was clear the safe wouldn't open as easily as expected. There had to be a knack to it, one only Georgie knew.

Keith rolled his eyes, wiping sweat from his brow beneath the balaclava. 'Let me try.'

Cas stepped aside, now really irritated. 'It'll be daylight by the time we get that fucker open. I knew it. I should have brought some jelly!' He huffed. 'Well, go on, then, *Mister I know better*.'

'I wasn't saying that, Cas. Just . . . sometimes a change of hands helps, yeah?'

'Jesus, they say that about stopping a baby from crying, not cracking a bloody safe,' Cas muttered, but with few options available, he let Keith take over.

Moments later, Keith grinned. 'Done.' The safe door swung open, and just as Veronica had said, stacks of cash in used notes stared back at them.

The men stuffed the holdall full and hurried back down to the basement, eager to escape. But when they reached the bottom, horror gripped Cas. Although both Veronica and Georgie were tied up as planned, the first thing they noticed was that Georgie's head was slumped forward.

'The cunts,' Cas growled, through gritted teeth.

Then, when his eyes landed on Veronica, rage surged inside him. He ripped off his balaclava and rushed to her side. 'Vonny! What the fuck happened?'

Vic and Irvin had gone. Cas's first thought was that the heavies from the protection racket must have shown up and dragged both Vic and Irvin outside, but he couldn't have been more wrong.

Veronica slowly lifted her head.

Cas then saw the bruise spreading around her eye and the swelling on her chin. Her usually neat ashen bob was a mess. It was as though someone had tried to tear it out. But that wasn't the worst part. Her shirt had been ripped open to expose her deeply scratched and hideously bruised breasts.

He couldn't help but stare for a moment while taking in the state of her. His eyes settled on what appeared to be bite marks. When he frantically tried to untie her, she shook her head. 'No.'

Cas glanced at Keith, who was checking Georgie's pulse. 'He's just been knocked out, that's all,' Keith confirmed.

Cas turned back to Veronica, his voice trembling with anger. 'I can't leave you like this, Vonny.'

'Just cut me in for a slice of that money and get outta here,' she whispered, her voice broken. 'Take those two bullies with you, yeah.'

'Who? Vic and Irvin?' Cas's eyes widened.

Her voice lowered, barely audible. 'Yeah. You said I wouldn't get hurt, Cas. I didn't sign up for this, not for a beating, just to make it look real.'

'Who did this to you, babe?' Cas asked, his heart sinking.

'The big one. Before he ripped my shirt . . . I thought he was gonna tear me tits off. And I paid a lot of money for this shirt, Cas.' Her voice cracked.

Cas glanced back at Keith, concerned that Georgie was still unconscious.

'He'll be okay.'

Cas sighed with relief, but it did little to quell his anger. He turned back to Veronica. 'I'll call the police from a phone box, love. I won't leave you in here long. In fact, fuck it, I'm not going to leave you.'

Smiling weakly, her battered face so swollen, she looked as though she'd been in a ring with Nicola Adams. 'I don't want you to stay, Cas. Go on. If you don't go now, all of this will have been for nothing.'

Cas hesitated. It was obvious to those present that the guilt was gnawing away at him. 'But I don't wanna leave ya.'

'Leave off, Cas. I've got me big girl knickers on,' she urged, while fighting back the tears. 'Go on.'

Cas gently pulled Veronica's shirt closed, giving the woman her dignity by covering her exposed chest. He then kissed her on the forehead. 'I'm gonna kill him,' he hissed, through clenched teeth.

Storming outside, with Keith close behind, Cas clocked Vic hovering nervously around his car, but Irvin was nowhere to be seen.

Fury surged through Cas like an inferno. 'You dirty fuckin' cunt! I told you not to hurt them!' he roared, as he charged like a rhino at Vic.

Before Vic could react, Cas grabbed him by the ears and viciously yanked his head down. With so much force, he almost ripped the man's ears off. Savagely, he raised his knee and cracked Vic hard across the nose. Blood instantly spurted over Cas's shirt. This was the last straw. Cas threw a brutal uppercut that sent Vic sprawling onto his backside.

Vic curled into a ball, trembling and begging Cas to accept his apology. 'It wasn't me, Cas! It was me bruvver, I swear! He didn't know – I mean, he thought he was supposed to make it look like a . . . I'm sorry. I swear, Cas . . . I swear! I couldn't stop him. I'm really sorry.'

'Sorry doesn't cut it!' Cas growled, stooping and grabbing a fistful of Vic's hair. He rammed the man's face onto the pavement, tearing the skin from his cheek.

Blood poured down Vic's face as he desperately tried to scramble to his feet, knowing that another strike like that and he might not recover.

Cas was unforgiving, and Vic knew he had to get away before the man beat him to death.

Keith stepped forward, ready to pull Cas away, but before he could, Cas ripped the gun from Keith's belt and pointed it at Vic.

Both Keith and Vic froze. They knew Cas wouldn't think twice about pulling the trigger. If he wanted Vic dead, he would do it in a heartbeat. And in that moment of angry recklessness, Cas's finger tightened on the trigger. He was ready to blow Vic into the middle of next week.

But the sound of a police siren snapped Cas out of his rage. 'You're lucky, you cunt, you're getting away alive. But you can kiss my arse for the money. It's going to that poor cow in there that you and your troll of a brother fucked up,' he growled, before he scooted towards the stolen car.

Keith jumped into the driver's seat, and within seconds, he and Cas sped off.

Still shaking, Vic struggled to get his keys into the ignition. His heart pounded in his chest as he wiped the blood from his face. Cas had nearly killed him. He'd never been so scared in his life. In fact, he couldn't believe he was still alive. But alive he was, as he let out a high-pitched nervous laugh to celebrate the fact.

With trembling hands, he gripped the steering wheel, torn between fury and fear. He didn't know who he was angrier with – Cas or his brother. Irvin was only out of the nuthouse for the weekend, but, clearly, he needed to be back inside. He definitely needed a good dose of the liquid cosh. But with Irvin having vanished, he couldn't shake off the feeling that his brother had enjoyed that taste for violence and was off, very probably causing even more mayhem. He could only hope he was wrong.

***

Cas pulled up outside Veronica's one-bedroom flat in Downham three days later. The building was a dump, but her place was immaculate, just as he remembered. Having known her since they were kids growing up in care, he'd always felt protective of her.

When Veronica opened the door, Cas was aghast at the sight of her. Seeing the bruise still lingering on her face, he lowered his head in shame. She quickly ushered him inside. 'Hurry, before the neighbours see us and start wagging their chins, the nosy bastards.'

'How are ya, babe?' Cas asked, his voice softly spoken, although he could have kicked himself for asking such a dumb question. The woman was definitely not all right.

'Well, I'm not gonna be modelling for Versace anytime soon, but I'll live, Cas.' Her eyes flicked to the holdall he was carrying. 'So you've brought me my little cut, I see.'

She smiled, and for a moment, his heart melted. With her tiny frame and big blue eyes, Veronica had always been something special to him, even with the thick layer of mascara she liked to wear.

'Here ya go, girl,' Cas said, dropping the holdall on the table.

'Was there a lot?' she asked, excitedly.

'Yeah, there was.'

'How much?'

He shrugged. 'We never counted it.'

She looked at him, puzzled. 'What do you mean? Is something wrong with the money? It wasn't fake, was it?'

Cas stepped closer, gently brushing his hand down her cheek. 'They should never have touched ya. I should never have trusted them.'

‘Never mind that, Cas. Why didn’t you count the money? I was supposed to get ten per cent, right? How will you know how much that is if you haven’t counted it?’

‘Because it’s all yours, Vonny, love. My cut, Keith’s, and those two ugly bastards’ cut.’

She gasped, throwing her hands over her mouth. ‘What? No! I can’t take that.’

‘Yes, you can, darling. See, I’m all right for money. Keith is, too. And as for Vic and Irvin, well, that’s compensation. Me and Keith circled the place until we saw the ambulance, and we both agreed: you deserve it all.’

Veronica peered into the holdall, her eyes wide, and noticed a Harrods bag lying on top of the money. Slowly, she pulled it out to reveal a beautiful box inside.

‘Go on, open it,’ Cas urged, excitedly.

Her face lit up. ‘Is this a present, Cas?’

He nodded. ‘Well, kind of . . . not exactly.’

‘I never get presents,’ she said, her voice barely carrying, as she carefully opened the box. Wrapped in tissue paper was a stunning silk blouse. She ran her fingers over the smooth fabric, her eyes glistening. ‘It feels like silk.’

‘It *is* silk.’

‘Aww, Cas, it’s beautiful. I dunno what to say.’

He wrapped an arm gently around her and kissed her forehead. ‘You can buy yourself hundreds more of those blouses with that money. The bag’s heavy, so there’s probably a good few grand in there. Hide it away, love, and if you need anything, call me. You’ve got my number.’

She nodded, a lump forming in her throat, unable to speak. She watched him walk out, the door closing quietly behind him.

Cas was the only man – the only boy, in fact – who had ever looked out for her. She opened a drawer in the sideboard and pulled out a battered old dress ring. It was one that Cas had given to her on her thirteenth birthday. She still treasured it, just like she would the blouse he'd bought for her today.

CHAPTER TWO

10 July 1998

Billy walked up the drive of a magnificent six-bedroom neo-Georgian home. Stopping at the large imposing high-end front door, he used his fingers to comb his long fringe away from his eyes. He pulled his shirt cuffs a centimetre away from the sleeves of his crisp dark-blue jacket and looked at his brand-new leather shoes to check they were clean. Then, he smiled. Glancing at his gold watch, which was inlaid with diamonds, he wore this with pride, since he had bought and paid for it himself. The only niggling issue that didn't match his overall look was the taxi idling outside the gated driveway. He wished he was old enough to drive legally, but he would have to wait at least one more year. He already had his heart set on a car, an Audi Cabriolet. As soon as he could drive, he was buying it. He snatched a dog hair – no doubt Duchess's – and swiftly plucked it from his jacket.

After confidently knocking at the door, he stood back, waiting for Laurence, or Lolly, as he was known, to greet him. The door opened within three seconds, and Cas Ferrier, Lolly's father-in-law, stood there with his hair tied back in a thin ponytail and with a beaming grin on his face.

Billy had always had reservations about the man, ever since the time he'd first come across Cas over an incident involving a briefcase that he'd found in the woods. But even though the matter was all dead and buried, he remained cautious. He should thank him for the very generous payment for his injuries, which he had shrewdly invested. Hence he could afford a few luxuries.

'Looking smart, Billy. Gold watch, classy shoes, and expensive aftershave, I see. Trying to impress my Willow, are you?'

Billy peered up through his long black eyelashes. 'Good evening, Cas.' That was all he said.

It immediately made Cas smile.

Cas liked the boy – a lot.

'She's getting ready, and she'd better look a million dollars an' all, considering she just tapped me for a hundred quid for a dress.'

Billy remained poker-faced, while he waited on the doorstep to be invited in.

'So if you're taking my granddaughter out, make sure you keep her safe,' Cas said, half jesting, because he knew that Billy, of all the teenagers, would be the one who *would* take care of his granddaughter.

'You insult me, Cas,' Billy replied, with a well-modulated tone. His eyes remained steady, exuding a self-assured demeanour.

Cas grinned again, knowing that Billy was no pushover. As a kid, he behaved way older than his years, and now, at nearly sixteen, the boy was like a man, with a silent confidence about him.

'Gotta be said, though, son.'

'No, it doesn't, Cas. You know I would look after her.'

'So, how long have you been courting?'

'Dating, you mean.' *Courting was straight out of the ark*, he thought. 'We haven't been dating.'

'So, then, what's tonight about? 'Cos old Britney Spears up there is stinking the house out with her mother's perfume and slapping on a ton of make-up.'

Before he could answer, Lolly appeared. He had clearly been working out in his well-stocked basement gym. He was rubbing his face with a towel, still in his shorts and sweaty vest. 'Cas, don't leave the boy on the doorstep.' He smiled at Billy. 'Come on in, Billy. Willow's still getting ready.'

Billy glared at Cas and stepped inside the house. The hall was vast with tiled flooring and black metal bannisters. He noticed that there were no longer any photos of Tara and the family on the hall table. In their place, there was a photo of Lolly and Willow in a speed boat. The location looked unfamiliar. But he assumed it was in some exotic country. The family knew how to splash the cash all right.

Cas watched as Billy walked through the hallway into the lounge, where he stood, evidently very comfortable in his own skin. Cas couldn't help but stare, wishing he was young again and also wishing he could say he'd been a lot like Billy when he was a teenager. But he couldn't. Although he'd been cocky and wild, he'd never held himself the same or had the balls to stare into a man's eyes and not twitch a muscle. The kid's level of self-control was off the charts.

'Billy, a word of warning, mate,' said Lolly, wiping the sweat from his neck. 'She's still a little bit down in the mouth—'

'Down in the mouth,' interrupted Cas. 'She's been a right fucking mare, if you ask me.'

Lolly shook his head and glared at his father-in-law. 'Cas, I *didn't* ask you. Look, give the kid a break, will ya. After all, her mother's only gone off with some wannabe mafia guy all 'cos he's loaded and has a lot of clout. So how would you expect her to feel? Now, I know Tara's your daughter, but she is still a bitch, and what she did was a proper cunt stunt.'

Cas pointed a finger. 'Oi, don't push it, Lolly.'

Lolly threw his hands in the air. 'All right, so what would you call it, eh?'

Cas rolled his eyes. 'I know what she's gone and done, don't I. But you can't call her names and get away with it. She's my daughter, and that's fucking that.'

This was all common knowledge as far as Billy was concerned. Of course he knew about Tara's situation because Willow had called him and filled him in. He'd guessed she'd needed a listening ear or a shoulder to cry on, and so he'd been there for her. He hated hearing her break her heart over the phone.

Cas ended the argument with a tut and a face like thunder.

At that moment, Willow emerged, and Cas spun around to see this dress that she absolutely had to have. 'Is that *it*? Is this the hundred quid's worth of frock?'

Willow had grown a good two feet and was almost as tall as Billy now. Having piled her tight black curls high and away from her face, she had lost a lot of her rounded cheeks and was now slimmer, with high cheekbones and almond eyes. In fact, she was blossoming into a young woman. And a beautiful one at that.

'You look lovely, Willow,' said Billy, ignoring the men in the room. He didn't care about them anyway because he was only here for her. Cas and Lolly could argue the toss all they wanted.

'Lovely? Lovely?' snapped Cas. 'Surely, Willow, that didn't cost a ton, girl. There's as much material in that dress as I've got in my pocket-handkerchief. God almighty, they bloody saw you coming.'

'Grandad, do you mind. If there were conditions to you giving me the money, then you shouldn't have given it to me. Now, you've proper ruined my mood.'

'Willow, come on, love, don't be like that,' said Lolly, trying to reason with her. 'You know your grandfather has a warped sense of humour.'

Stamping her foot, almost like a spoiled brat, she turned to face her grandfather and replied, 'Well, go and buy a new sense of humour because yours is getting on my nerves.'

Pivoting around on her high heels, she grabbed Billy's arm. 'Come on, let's get out of here.'

Billy was as stunned as the men were. Even though he wasn't too keen on Cas, he thought her tone was highly disrespectful and actually bloody unfair. After all, it was plainly obvious that Cas doted on Willow. Everyone knew that, and she was lucky to have him. He looked over his shoulder and gave a sharp nod, indicating he would take care of her.

Willow slammed the front door behind her and stomped towards the gate, leaving Billy stunned by her stroppiness. But before she could get in the back seat of the cab, he grabbed her arm and pulled her back. 'Now, before we go anywhere, tell me what's the matter.'

Her green eyes clouded over as she shot Billy a dark look. 'It's Grandad. He's always sticking up for my slut of a mother.'

'Hey, stop there, Willow!' He paused and waited for her to slow down her breathing and take the wild look off her face.

'Now, no matter what she did, she's still your mother. Christ, if I ever called my mother a slut, I'd be picking my teeth out of the gravel.'

Willow folded her arms and tapped her foot. 'Are you sticking up for her now, as well?'

Billy shook his head. 'No, I'm not getting involved, but throwing names like that around doesn't make you look good.'

Her eyes scolded him until her shoulders slumped, and she tenderly offered a sorrowful smile. 'I'm sorry, Billy. I'm just so . . . so . . . *hurt.*' Her voice quivered, and a tear plummeted down her cheek. 'She left not just my dad but also me. It was like she never really cared. As if it was all a lie. Well, maybe it *was* a lie. Maybe she saw me as just an accessory that she could dress in frills and lace.' Her hands flew to her face, and her head drooped.

But Billy quickly wrapped his arms around her and held her for a short while until she stopped crying.

'Let's get in the cab and go. You'll be okay, Willow.'

She stamped her foot again. 'And now, all my make-up has smudged.'

Lifting Willow's chin to inspect the mess, Billy smiled. 'Willow, you look better *without* make-up.' He leaned into the car. 'Sorry, mate. Have you got a wipe or a tissue?'

The driver opened the glove compartment and handed Billy a packet of baby wipes. 'There you go. I have to warn you: the clock is ticking, mate.'

'Don't you worry about that,' Billy replied, as he helped Willow remove the black circles of messy mascara. 'Now, that's better. The natural Willow. That shit don't do you any favours, anyway.'

Willow smiled and climbed into the back seat. 'So where are you taking me, Billy?'

'I thought we could go over to Bluewater. Maybe have something to eat and go to the cinema.'

She gazed out of the window nonchalantly as the cab pulled away.

'Willow, what's up? Don't you fancy that? I thought you wanted to take your mind off everything?'

She shot him another one of her fierce looks. 'Yeah, but *Bluewater? Seriously?*'

'Where would you like to go, then?'

'Into the City, to a fancy bar.'

Billy frowned. 'Willow, listen to me, we're not old enough. Also, I don't know London that well, and Bluewater's got some decent food places and . . .' He sighed. 'I was going to treat you to something nice for yourself.'

Her expression changed faster than an express train. '*Really?* What, like jewellery, diamonds?'

For a moment, Billy paused, now stunned by her reaction. He'd known Willow for three years now. Recently, they'd been talking to each other daily on the phone late at night for hours. Previously, they'd probably spoken at least once a week and had met up when they had family gatherings, so he thought he knew her well. And he was developing feelings for her. In fact, it was a bit of a theme in their house that he would end up marrying Willow. However, right now, this wasn't the Willow he had feelings for.

'Well, come on, Billy, don't keep me in suspense. What were you going to buy me?'

He would have bought her a diamond. He had the money now. But the idea was slivering away faster than an adder on cocaine.

'Why are you looking at me like that, Billy?'

'I'm not looking at you like anything. So what are you after, then?'

Her face was glowing and she suddenly became animated. 'Well, there's a new Louis Vuitton range, and I also like the Burberry quilted coats. All me mates have one, and . . .'

'And? . . . Look, just stop it, Willow. I'm not that rich.'

'Oh, come off it, Billy. I know you've got money. All that stocks and shares stuff. The Netscape deal you did.' She glanced at his wrist. 'The watch, the clothes. You're rolling in it.'

The idea of having a fun evening was now fading fast. Billy struggled to understand her personality change. He presumed it was all because her mother had run off with another man and left her behind, so he decided not to jump on her attitude. Not yet, anyway.

As they arrived at the massive shopping centre, Billy had all but switched off. All her chatting about all the things she wanted was really doing his head in. It was all bags, shoes, dresses, and make-up. In his fifteen-year-old brain, he was deciphering that maybe he'd been so attracted by her looks – and she was stunning – make no mistake about that – that he'd failed to see her lack of substance. Or was it her way of reacting to her mother running off? He wondered if Willow was now imitating her mother's personality. He'd guessed Tara was a materialistic woman and very much focused on her looks because you would have to be blind not to see that her tits were out of all proportion with the rest of her body. Her teeth, which were brighter than brilliant white, had to be veneers. And her nails were always perfect, as well, although they resembled a set of samurai swords to him.

He paid the driver and was about to reach for Willow's hand when he saw her walking off in the distance and marching towards the entrance doors.

'Cheers, mate,' he said, as he handed the driver a tip.

He scooted towards Willow, who hadn't even bothered to hold the door open for him. She was inside the Centre on her own mission, clearly expecting him to follow her like a lapdog. However, had she known it, he was anything but.

'Willow, wait for me, please.' His voice was sharp and deep.

She stopped and spun around. 'Sorry, Billy. Right, the shop with the new Burberry jackets is just up there.'

He wanted to put his foot down and stop her, but, suddenly, she gave him such a sweet smile, she was like the Willow of old. When she squeezed his hand, he mistook her excitement over shopping for her elation at being with him.

Just then, on the other side of the escalators, came the unmistakable voice of Joey Carson. 'Oi, oi, if it ain't me cousin, Billy boy, with his new tart, if I'm not mistaken. Ain't ya gonna say 'ello, Billy boy?'

Billy turned to face Joey and noticed that the lad wasn't alone. Not only had he his wonky-eyed brother Stuey with him, but another guy, who looked roughly sixteen years old and was big – built like a truck – and stood square-shouldered, was there as well. He had an inkling that he knew of him, although he'd never seen him before. But the lad had a canny resemblance to someone he had once seen. He thought it might have been on a prison visit.

The large stockily built lad was staring at him and Willow, and not in a friendly manner either.

Billy saw Joey whispering in the lad's ear, which seemed to escalate his hostile stance. He began to sway from side to side, repeatedly punching his clenched fist into his cupped hand.

Dressed in his new clothes and eager to treat Willow to a lovely evening out – even if he had to buy her some Burberry coat – Billy decided to ignore Joey and his sidekicks and walk on. He straightened his jacket, took a deep breath, and focused on the night ahead. Despite the looming threat, he was determined not to let them ruin his plans. Willow deserved a special evening, and he was set on making that happen.

'Who were they?' whispered Willow.

'Scum, just scum.'

'But he said he was your cousin.'

'Ignore them,' he said, as he gripped her hand more tightly and marched on.

'Billy boy, don't be like that, you ignorant wanker! Come on, introduce us to ya bit of skirt. Good in the sack, is she? I bet she gives it out!' hollered Stuey, who looked as though he was a by-product of inbreeding.

Billy wasn't going to bite. He didn't want to fight because he wasn't here for that.

'Are you going to stand for that, Billy?' said Willow, rolling her eyes, as she stopped dead and looked Billy up and down as though he was a coward. 'I thought you were supposed to be able to handle yourself, Billy Murphy. Seriously, are you going to let him speak about me like that?'

By now, a few other teenagers were gathering. They regularly used the Centre as a meeting place to hang out, where they used the food halls and generally got together. All eyes were on him.

'Just ignore them, Willow. They're not worth the aggravation.'

'Oh, I see, so I'm not worth it, then? Is that right? I mean, not even my grandfather would stand for that, and he's an old man.'

Billy glanced back at the big lad, who had come closer to them. He looked like a raging bull, his neck being the size of his head.

'So you're Billy Carson,' said the big lad.

'And you are?' asked Billy. But he'd already guessed who he was.

'I'm Atlas Carson.'

Atlas Carson was the son of Atticus Carson.

Not only had Billy's mother stabbed Atlas's father through the hand with the heel of her shoe but his Uncle

James had almost killed Atticus during a prison visit three years earlier.

Their eyes locked before another teenager came bowling over. He was older – probably seventeen or eighteen – tall, athletic, and with a blond buzz cut.

Billy didn't recognise him. He seemed to have an entourage, and now they were surrounded.

The blond lad stepped forward and winked at Willow. 'Nice dress ya got there, babe.'

Billy wanted to punch the cocky look on his face, but he would never show he was jealous. It wasn't who he was. Instead, he gripped Willow's hand even tighter and turned to walk towards the shop that she'd been so eager to go to.

'Fucking chicken.' Atlas laughed and proceeded to make chicken noises while a few others joined in, but they stopped when Billy released his grip on Willow's hand, spun around, and took a few steps towards them.

'Chicken? Are you telling me I was walking away from a fight? Because I never heard anyone call it on. So, tell me, Atlas, are you saying the feud between the Murphys and the Carsons is still ongoing? Only I understood that my father, *Sunny Murphy*, beat the granny out of Jimmy Carson, and they agreed this pointless feud was over.' He grinned sarcastically and raised his brows for an answer. 'Just a yes or a no will do.' He tilted his head but remained still, his eyes locked on the lad in front of him, until he clocked Atlas hesitating.

Atlas shifted uncomfortably from foot to foot while his right eye twitched nervously, and he repeatedly licked his lips. Now uneasy, he glanced at Joey and Stuey as if he was awaiting some backup.

But they looked at each other, both realising they had probably not thought it through. After all, it had only been by chance that they'd bumped into one of the Murphys. As

Joey saw it, perhaps Billy was the more dangerous one of the brothers. Although he wasn't so sure his brother Stuey would agree. Not after the kicking he'd had from Jesse not so long ago. They thought that being in a gang would up their confidence level because they sure as hell wouldn't gob off to either Billy or his brother Jesse if they were alone with them. The end result would be one of two things: they would either be carted off to the hospital or have a road sweeper cleaning up their remains.

'I see. No answer? Right, well, the conversation is over.'

But now curious, Billy glanced at the tall blond guy. 'And you seem to be sticking your beak in, so who are you?'

'Danny Slade. And you, I reckon, are Billy Carson.'

Billy shook his head and then gave Atlas a mocking grin. 'Nah, Danny, I'm Billy Murphy, or are you being funny, mate, because you heard me say my father is Sunny Murphy? Anyway, excuse me, I'm not here in anyone's company other than hers,' he said, pointing towards Willow, as he walked away.

But then, when he heard the imitation chicken cluck sound again, he spun back, his head nodding as he stood nose to nose with Atlas. He made it clear by his firm demeanour that he was never going to back down. 'If you want to have a proper tear up, I'm all for it . . .' – he said, pointing around him – 'but this, in case you haven't noticed, is a fancy shopping centre with security guards and cameras. Now, if you're serious and you want to throw your fists around and have a good ruck, I'll have it with you. You and me – bare knuckles – but not when I'm suited and booted and on a date. I don't fancy getting nicked, or having my jacket ripped, so if you want to act like a big man, by all means go for it, but not here, like a couple of backstreet scrappers. In fact, Atlas, I reckon we should have it in a ring, with bets and witnesses and a fair fucking referee.'

Atlas's eyes flicked about. He had never expected Billy to talk, walk, and carry himself like a man. He seemed way older than fifteen, and it had never occurred to him to fight in a ring with men gambling on them. Decision made, he recoiled, going off the idea. Never having met Billy before, he had conjured up a completely different image of him. He'd been used to most lads his age running a mile, the minute he threatened them. He was too much of a size. But it was evident that this Billy guy wasn't bothered.

Stuey nudged him, but he nudged him back.

'So, Atlas, up for it, are you, man to man?'

Atlas laughed nervously. 'You'll back out.'

'Nah, not me. I just called it on. So do you want to have a proper fight, or are you all fucking mouth? See, you're all the same. Giving it the Billy big 'un when you're together. But you shit ya pants when it's one on one. 'Cos you lot of pikeys will all want to put the boot in, which' – he held up his hands – 'is all well and good, but understand this. You, Stuey, and you, Joey, if you do all jump me, I'll come for each of you, and I *will* fuck you up.'

Before anyone could say a word, Billy's new mobile phone rang. He held up his hand to stop anyone from talking, as if he was in an office. It was his brother, Jesse.

'Billy, Billy, listen. Me and Dad are watching your computer screen, right. I'm not sure what's going on, but we reckon the shares are going through the roof. What do we do?' Jesse's voice sounded so eager, he could hardly breathe.

'Okay, Jesse, slow down. What's Dad saying?'

'He says to sell them now. He reckons we'll have enough to buy our own gaffs. Fuck me, Billy, it's a lot of money. What shall we do? Dad said even though they're in his name, you have to decide.'

'Sell, Jesse. Sell all the shares, now!'

''Ark at him *fucking sell, fucking sell.* Who does he think he is? A poncy yuppie?' hollered Joey, still believing he had the backing of Atlas, if it all kicked off.

Jesse could hear the voice in the background. 'Who's that, Billy?'

Billy stepped away from the crowd. 'Joey, Stuey, and Atlas Carson. Just tell Dad to sell.'

He could hear Jesse calling out to their father to sell the shares before his brother was back on the phone. 'Where are ya, Billy boy?'

'Bluewater, why?'

'I'm coming, in case they fucking start anything, the wankers.'

'I'm with Willow. Don't worry, Jesse, I'll be fine . . .'

The line went dead, and Billy let out a long sigh. 'That's all I need.'

He pointed his finger at Joey. 'Jesse heard you, you stupid prick.'

Joey's face turned pale. 'Is he coming here?'

Billy sighed again and nodded. 'Why can't I just have a nice evening out, eh.' His lips tightened in annoyance.

But Willow gripped his arm. 'Is Jesse coming?'

'Looks like it.'

Pointing at Atlas, Willow warned the lad. 'Now you lot are fucked. His brother's on his way.'

Danny's brows furrowed. 'So what's going on? Is he supposed to be hard or something, Willow?'

Stuey suddenly bolted. Atlas looked at Joey, bewildered. 'Why's he buggered off?'

Joey leaned into Atlas and whispered, 'The two together are like a fucking tornado. I'm outta here.'

Without another word, Joey scooted away, followed by Atlas, who struggled to keep up, clearly carrying far too much weight.

Billy turned his attention to Danny. He had taken an instant dislike to him. 'Aren't you going as well?' he asked.

Danny grinned. 'I don't walk away from nuffin, mate. Do I, Willow?'

Billy turned directly to Willow. 'Do you know him?' he asked, his anger rising at the cocky look on Danny's face.

'Yeah, I do.' She flirtatiously smiled at Danny, who winked at her.

Deciding not to stand around and ask how they knew each other, Billy snatched Willow's hand and walked away, but not before noticing how she brazenly glanced back over her shoulder and smiled at the lad. Anger and jealousy got the better of him. 'Would you rather have his company tonight?'

She was stunned at Billy's firm and cold voice. 'What? No, don't be daft. Now, shall we hurry to the shop before it closes? I think maybe a beige Burberry . . .'

CHAPTER THREE

Luckily for Billy, the shop was closed, but Willow reacted like a spoiled brat, by stamping her foot yet again. 'If we had walked a bit faster—'

'Willow, never mind. Let's go and see what's on at the cinema.'

'Nah, I'm not in the mood now.'

Billy could see this date was going from bad to worse. 'What about a meal? You choose,' he offered, trying to lighten the atmosphere.

'As long as it comes with champagne,' she replied, with an air of sarcasm.

Billy took Willow's hand and led her towards the newly refurbished fish restaurant. Noticing how the soft lighting and low-level music gave it a sense of romance, he decided that this would be an excellent opportunity for them to sit down and spend some quality time together by talking the night away. For a start, he wanted to know what she thought of him. As far as he was concerned, he wanted to be more than friends, and she had already given him subtle clues that she wanted the same. Her flirty innuendoes on the phone and the cheeky text messages of encouragement had certainly spurred him on to ask her out. And now, with her mother leaving the family home the way she had, with Willow now beside herself, she had evidently seen him as the shoulder to cry on.

Willow was clearly sulking and it was easy to see why. The waitress had just shown them a little secluded bay area with a window looking out at the centre of the food hall, but the view wasn't great.

They could see teenagers, who were all hanging out, but Billy resigned himself to the notion that what was happening between the two of them couldn't be ignored. There was no romantic bubble, it seemed. Perhaps there never had been. Perhaps it had all been in his imagination.

Willow glanced around and shook her head. 'This is a bit boring.'

That was it. He had tried everything, and now she was just becoming intolerable. 'Look, I'm sorry the shop was closed. I'm sorry you don't fancy the cinema. And I'm sorry this is all boring. But I am *not* sorry for trying. So, come on, I'll get a taxi to take us home.'

'No, don't. We're here now,' she said, as she took the menu from the waitress. 'So, do you know Danny Slade?'

Billy's frustration was almost at boiling point at hearing that question, but he was determined that the evening wasn't going to be ruined by Willow's petulance, so he took a deep breath to keep his cool. 'I've heard of him, but, anyway, let's not spoil our dinner by talking about that interfering prick.'

Willow raised an eyebrow, sensing his irritation. 'Why are you so wound up, Billy? He's just a guy.'

Billy clenched his jaw, now struggling to maintain his composure. 'Because, Willow, tonight was supposed to be about *us*. I wanted to give you a nice time, but all you seem to care about is making everything difficult.'

She studied him then, taken aback by his sudden outburst. 'I didn't realise I bothered you that much.'

Billy sighed, running a hand through his hair. 'I just want us to have a good time together. Is that too much to ask?'

Willow looked at the menu but failed to actually read it.

With the tension still hanging between them, Billy took a deep breath to try to reset the mood.

'What about the seafood platter?' he suggested, hoping to steer the conversation to something more pleasant.

'If you like, but I'm not that hungry now.'

'I thought you'd like this,' he gestured at the classy restaurant.

'It's hardly entertaining. Those girls outside look like they're having more fun.'

She gazed out of the window as if she was a kid locked in her bedroom, only able to watch all the others having a good time.

Billy followed her eyeline and noticed quite a few teenagers gathered. Many were from the Irish travelling community, and there were a few Romany gypsies, including some he knew. He sighed again when Danny appeared. It seemed that the crowd of teenagers were gravitating towards him.

Billy deduced that Danny may have been selling weed because they didn't seem like they were his buddies.

At that point, the double glass doors to the side of the food court opened. Walking in with a swagger and a cheeky smile was Jesse. With him and a good foot taller was their older cousin Ross Verne. He was his mother's cousin's son, who was down from Cumbria for the summer holidays.

'Look, there's Jesse. Shall we go and say hello and see what he's up to?'

Hearing Willow's voice holding a tone of excitement, Billy realised that the thought of a sophisticated date was not her idea of a good time. And seeing her eyes light up, he knew then that she wasn't into him. In fact, she was probably into anyone other than him.

Without an ounce of finesse, she banged on the window, while dramatically waving to get Jesse's attention, which made Billy's heart sink.

Knowing the proposition of a special meal was pointless, he rose from his seat, apologised to the waitress, and began to walk out of the restaurant.

She smiled back and said, 'It's okay.'

Meanwhile, Willow had already left the restaurant, having almost fallen over the table to get outside first.

But Jesse wasn't there to see Willow. He was there to find his brother. He smiled, gave Willow a sharp nod, and grabbed his brother's arm, his face beaming. 'Me and you, Bruv, are loaded, mate. Now where's that Joey and Stuey, the one-eyed fuck-up?'

Willow was still energised at seeing Jesse. 'Ha, they scarpered when they knew you were coming. It seems they're more scared of you, Jesse, than Billy here. As soon as your name was mentioned, they all ran off, not bothered by Billy, but they were of you.' She laughed. 'And I thought Billy was the nutter. You, though, would have waded in, wouldn't you, Jesse, if they disrespected me.' She laughed again and gently pushed him, eager to get his attention.

Jesse's expression turned cold, and his eyes darkened as he turned to face Willow. 'So me bruvver didn't *wade in*, as you put it?'

Billy stood with his hands on his hips, sighing; he knew this wouldn't end well.

'No, but you're here now, so if they come with their lousy mates, they'll have a right shock, seeing you and . . .'

She looked at Ross, who was so obviously related to Jesse. They had the same thick black waves and tanned skin. She smiled in acknowledgement before she turned her attention back to Jesse. 'Your cousin, I assume. I think they will think twice about insulting me now.'

Jesse could now see the uncomfortable expression on his brother's face. He then glanced at the restaurant and knew they couldn't have eaten their meal so quickly. And he was well aware that Billy had planned to take Willow out for a nice meal.

'Me bruvver was treating you to a proper classy dinner with all the trimmings, I see. We won't keep ya. I only came in case you needed some backup.'

Willow waved her hand. 'We didn't stay for food. When we saw you, we decided to ditch the grub. It's so boring. So what are you doing tonight?'

Jesse glanced at Billy again. He knew how much this evening meant to his brother. He had spent hours in the bathroom and even longer in front of the mirror fussing over his clothes. He'd also left the house overloaded with aftershave and deodorant and taken his fat wallet, with the intention of spoiling Willow rotten.

Jesse had even patted his brother on the back and said, 'She'll be putty in your hands looking like that. That's if she doesn't choke on your aftershave.'

And Jesse recalled Billy standing in front of him. 'Do I really look all right, Jesse?' he had asked, genuinely eager to make a good impression. Underneath Billy's sometimes sultry exterior, he was a kind and gentle person, who would make the perfect boyfriend.

But all Jesse could see now was Willow trying to humiliate his brother and throw his good nature back in his face. Just as he was about to have a word with her, a slim attractive girl with dark hair down to her waist and wearing combat trousers with a crop top approached.

'Hi, Jesse, good to see you.'

Her voice was almost teasing, and her vast dewy eyes drew him in. She even caught Billy's attention, who was stunned for a moment. The girl had a figure that would stop traffic. And she clearly had a thing for Jesse.

As Jesse turned to her, sporting his trademark lopsided cheeky grin, he warmly greeted her. 'All right, Bronte? You look good, babe.'

'Bronte! What kinda name's that?' Willow mocked, under her breath.

Bronte turned her back to face Jesse, not rising to that comment, while flicking her long poker-straight hair and catching Willow in the eye.

For a moment, Billy wanted to laugh at Willow's indignant expression. She had well and truly had her nose pushed out of joint.

As Jesse walked Bronte away from Willow, he whispered something in her ear and then gently kissed her cheek and winked. Whatever he'd said, it had put a huge but coy smile on the young woman's face.

Willow was taking it all in. With her arms folded and her face full of piss and vinegar, she asked, 'Who was that pikey sticking her nose into our business?'

Ross, standing quietly, spoke up. 'I don't think she was sticking her nose in. More like saying a polite hello. Cor, I wish it had been me. She's a right good-looking girl, eh, Billy boy?'

Billy nodded. 'And she likes Jesse, and I think he likes her.'

'Yeah, well, I reckon she's a bit of a tart meself,' hissed Willow.

'Meow,' said Ross, before laughing his head off.

When Jesse returned, he scowled at Willow. 'So the restaurant wasn't your thing, Willow?'

Her eyes lit up; she clearly couldn't read Jesse. 'Nah, I like fun stuff, so what are you up to, now that the Carsons have scarpered?'

Jesse bit his lip, but being Jesse, he couldn't control himself. He leaned in and said, 'I came with Ross because I didn't want me bruvver getting nicked, 'cos, Willow, if it had all kicked off, Billy boy would've turned this place upside down and found himself in the gavvers' station before he could say Bob's your uncle and Fanny's your aunt.' He gently put his hand on her shoulder. 'When you were twelve, me and Billy shielded you from a nasty fight. We protected you. But you're sixteen now, and that level of protection has gone. You—'

'No, no, Jesse, leave it. I'm taking Willow home,' interrupted Billy, his voice firm.

'Nah, Billy, she just tried to humiliate you in front of me and Ross.' Jesse glared at Willow. 'Listen to me, girl. As much as you've been a kind of an adopted part of our family, all 'cos your farver is best mates with James, you actually ain't *real* family.' He pointed to Billy. 'But he is, and I don't care who you are or who your grandfarver is. If you insult me bruvver, you insult me and the rest of us.'

'Jesse, don't. She's not in a good place. You know her mother's gone off with some fella,' Billy said, trying to calm the situation.

Jesse nodded, his expression softening slightly. 'Fair enough, Billy, but I just had to have my say. I won't have anyone take the piss. I know what you planned.' He looked at Willow's neck, and then he laughed. 'Still, I won't say no more except you missed out there, Willow. He got you something right nice, didn't ya, Billy?'

Billy looked down, feeling a mix of frustration and embarrassment. He knew he could shut Jesse up when he was angry, but this was not the time or place.

It now dawned on Willow that despite her usual ability to attract male attention and because she was well aware of the fact that she was good-looking, there was no way she could come between the two brothers. She'd been very foolish because it looked like she'd lost them both right now. It hadn't been a secret that Billy was going places; she'd heard her father and grandfather say as much. And he had a handsome face and a fit body. They'd always got on so well. He would have been the guy she would have married if her life hadn't changed so drastically.

Hot and sweaty with embarrassment, Willow wasn't going to stand there and be humiliated. She glanced at the crowd and spotted Danny, but before she hurried over to him, she turned her attention back to Billy. 'You can keep whatever was supposed to be *right nice*. It's obvious you don't even know my taste. And you should have smashed the life out of those Carsons for disrespecting me.' With a sharp glare and a quick once-over, she was about to scoot off towards Danny.

However, Billy grabbed her arm. 'Oi, Willow, I'm taking you home.'

'Like fuck you are.' She shook him off. 'Don't ever touch me again.'

'Willow, I promised your grandfather I would look after you.'

'Oh yeah? Well, when he hears that you let them dirty creepy pikeys talk so disgusting about me, and you did nothing, I think he'll understand why I left your company. I thought you were more of a man, Billy Murphy. I guess I was wrong.'

'You wanna watch ya mouth, Willow. For Christ's sake, if me bruvver promised to get you home safe, then that's what will happen,' Jesse hollered.

'Go fuck yaself, Jesse.'

The loud voices captured Danny's attention. He peered over and smirked when he saw Willow heading his way. Instantly, he put his hand out as if he was going to hold hers. To the horror of both Billy and Jesse, she eagerly accepted it, and she even had the brass balls to look back and laugh as if it was all a huge joke.

'I'm gonna split his head wide open, the cheeky wanker,' said Jesse, glaring at Danny.

'Leave it, Jesse. Seriously, she ain't worth it.'

'Nah, Billy, who the hell does he think he is. Go and get her. She can't do that. You made a promise.'

Billy would have walked away, but the look on Danny's face riled him up. He, along with Jesse and Ross, headed over to the crowd.

Billy grabbed Willow's arm. 'You have to come with me.'

But from nowhere, she lashed out with a wave of fierce anger as if everything she had been going through had come to a head. Aiming her frustration at Billy, her nails scratched his face, narrowly missing his right eye.

He yelped and put his hand to his cheek, feeling the blood.

Having never heard his brother make a noise like that, even in a boxing ring, Jesse quickly removed Billy's hand to see what damage she had inflicted. Sure enough, there were three deep scratches from his forehead to across his cheek, which was bleeding. He wanted to punch her in the face, and if she'd been a bloke, he would have. Instead, he got up in her personal space. 'You shouldn't have done that, you spiteful bitch. Go on with ya, you're a fucking nightmare of a girl. And lucky you are a bird an' all.'

'Or what!' mocked Danny, letting go of Willow's hand and squaring up to Jesse.

But Jesse smirked. 'Want it, do ya, fuck face?'

Billy got in between them. 'You'd better leave before it kicks off in here 'cos, believe me, it will.'

Danny looked at Jesse, Ross, and then back to Billy. His eyes ping-ponged while the cogs in his brain turned over.

Something about their stance and fearless composure made him think twice about having a fight. He knew who they were; he'd only played dumb on purpose. The word going around that they were a force to be reckoned with was probably accurate. He'd noticed a few of the lads slowly siding with the Murphys, probably too wary of the consequences if there was a fight and they were on the wrong side of the argument.

But he didn't like it one little bit. As far as he was concerned, he should be the top dog. How could two lads parade around with watches that cost as much as a car and dress themselves in expensive clobber at the age of fifteen? They had to be up to illegal dealings, and if anything was going around, he should be the first to know about it. Clearly, not, though, in the case of the Murphys.

Jesse protruded his bottom jaw, his tone mocking. 'What's the matter, Danny? Did ya shit a live penguin, or is that your usual dumfuckery expression?'

Danny would have punched Jesse clean into the air for less, but he was unnerved by his calm demeanour. 'Like Billy, I don't wanna fight in the Centre. I'm not getting nicked.' Gripping Willow's hand tightly, he formulated a plan. 'I'll see her home safe, Billy,' he replied, completely ignoring Jesse.

Willow could give him the complete rundown on the Murphys. All he had to do was to take her for a spin and then drive her to the secret spot away from prying eyes. Without another word, he left the Centre with Willow excitedly clutching his hand. If she wanted fun, he would give it to her, all right – and then some. Or so she would think.

Billy watched them go, with a sinking feeling in his stomach.

Willow glanced back once more, but this time she wasn't laughing. Her face held so much sadness that even her eyes were welling up.

For a split second, he wanted to believe that that was what he saw. But the chances were that he'd imagined it.

Sensing his brother's unease, Jesse placed a hand on his shoulder. 'Don't worry, Billy. She'll see through him soon enough.'

Billy nodded, but he couldn't shake that feeling of apprehension. 'I hope you're right, Jesse. I'm only concerned about her safety, though, because I don't want her now. She's a right pain in the arse,' he said, wondering who he was trying to kid – his brother or himself.

'Go on, Jesse, I'll catch you up.'

Billy hurried through the car park, his eyes fixed on Willow and Danny as they climbed into a red Ford Escort with black go-faster stripes running down the side. He'd hoped – stupidly, maybe – that she'd change her mind, that she'd come back. But she didn't.

He stopped in his tracks, exhaling a sharp sigh, as he ran a hand across his sore cheek. The sting served as a bitter reminder of the night's mess. Shaking his head, he turned away and made his way back towards the Centre. Scanning the crowd for Jesse and Ross, he saw them eventually as they entered probably one of the only shops still open.

CHAPTER FOUR

Billy wasted no time in calling Lolly to inform him that despite his best efforts, he hadn't been able to stop Willow from going off with a lad named Danny Slade. Bracing himself for the backlash, the harsh rejoinder never happened.

Lolly was surprisingly quite calm as he replied that he had actually been expecting it.

He went on: 'Oh, for God's sake, not again . . . Listen to me, Billy. I can hear it in your voice: you're upset. But understand this: Willow is so strong-willed, especially since her mother left. I know you couldn't have stopped her, if that's what she wanted to do. But do you know where they went?'

Billy felt relief wash over him. 'No, they left Bluewater in his car, a red Ford Escort . . . I'm sorry, Lolly. I really am.'

'It's not your fault. I know my girl, and she is becoming a proper handful. But you sound as if you're sorry for more than her just going off with this Danny guy.'

'Well, actually, I am, Lolly. I won't be asking her out again.'

'Oh, I see. That's a shame because you would be so good for her. I could see you two together.'

'Honestly, Lolly, I could have too, but I'm afraid I don't have a lot of patience. I tried my best, but I'm not the kind of friend Willow needs right now.'

'I understand. Thank you for being man enough to call me and let me know that she's on one of her wild, rebellious rampages again.'

‘I feel bad because I told Cas I would look after her.’

‘Billy, Cas is so old school. He hasn’t realised that the women of today are so headstrong and independent. Anyway, it wasn’t your job to do that: it was mine.’

When Billy ended the call, he turned to Jesse. ‘It’s fine, Jesse. I’m honestly not that bothered. To tell you the truth, the minute she wanted to go into those designer shops with my money, it was a right turn-off for me.’

‘What a bloody liberty! I warned you about her, didn’t I, Billy? I said she’s gonna be a bleedin’ handful.’

Billy frowned. ‘And how would you know, Jesse?’

Jesse looked down at his feet. It was a dead giveaway that he was hiding something.

‘Jesse, I asked you how would you know?’

‘She kinda sorta tried it on with me. I don’t mean like she tried to kiss me or nuffin like that. But, she, er . . .’ He lowered his voice, in embarrassment. ‘She said we should go out sometime.’

Billy glared at his brother. ‘And you failed to tell me?’

‘No, not exactly, Billy boy. It was ages ago at Muvver’s birthday party. I didn’t think much of it until you, ya silly git, started getting all stupid over her.’

‘Oi, I didn’t get stupid.’

‘Oh, no? So what about that gold necklace you bought?’

Billy shook his head. ‘Oh, shut it, Jesse. Let’s just go home, shall we.’

‘Good idea. There’s no action, so let’s get a pizza takeaway,’ said Ross. ‘You didn’t get to eat, did ya? I can hear your stomach rumbling from here.’ He winked at Billy.

***

Feeling a tad disappointed that there wasn’t going to be a ruck, Ross set off for Billy and Jesse’s home. But even though he enjoyed a good fight, he wasn’t the type to start one. He was just more inclined to end it. He had perfected his level of control in the ring. If he continued the way he was, he could see him becoming a professional boxer. Yet, like other lads of his age, the attraction to girls captured his attention more than the pull of the boxing ring.

The evening light barely lingered as Ross navigated his Ford Fiesta along the narrow lanes heading for home. Losing his bearings, they ended up getting lost a few times, before, finally, they reached the lane that took them to Crockenhill. Despite his desire to impress, he was careful on the bends, having only been driving for a few months. He had saved hard for his car.

As they reached a particularly sharp bend, a car came hurtling around, forcing Ross to swerve dramatically. 'Prick,' he muttered, slamming on his brakes. The car stalled, and he tried to restart it, his hands shaking.

Billy didn't get a good look at the driver. The lack of daylight and the speed of the vehicle as it rounded the bend towards them made that difficult. But he was almost sure that it was Danny. It certainly was a red Ford Escort.

'Wanker,' said Jesse, sitting alongside Ross.

'Wasn't that Danny?' asked Billy.

'Might have been, the idiot. Cor, if he'd dented Ross's car, I would've stuck him in that field as the new scarecrow.'

Billy suddenly diverted his eyes to what he thought was a movement in the nearby wheat field. Nevertheless, uncertainty clouded his perception as he couldn't definitively determine if the movement, which he glimpsed from the corner of his eye, was a person running or a substantial fox. He stared into the darkness, but he could only make out the fields and a few trees.

Ross managed to start the car, and they were off again, this time driving even more slowly. He had only got as far as a hundred yards when he realised he had a puncture. The tyres must have hit a rock or something.

Although Billy would normally be more than happy to help Ross change the tyre, he didn't like the idea of getting his brand-new jacket and tailored trousers greasy, so he supervised. Finally, they were off again. However, when they reached a wider road where two vehicles could pass easily, a police car flashed them down.

'Oh, dordi, 'ere come the poxy gavvers,' said Ross, in a true to form traveller's accent.

'Oh, for fuck's sake,' said Jesse.

'It's all right, Jesse,' Ross said, suddenly ditching the accent. 'I'm all insured and taxed and everything.'

Billy was still fuming that Willow had dropped him like a hot brick in front of a crowd. His affection for her turned to hate, and his stomach rumbled again. He certainly wasn't in the mood for a conversation with any copper.

As soon as Ross pulled the car over as close to the hedgerow as possible and wound down the window, a burly officer with a torch bowled over to them.

He leaned into the car through the open window and flashed his torch directly behind Ross into Billy's eyes.

Blinking furiously, Billy put his hands up to stop the glare.

'So, what's up, officer?' asked Ross.

The officer turned off his torch and spoke directly to the driver. 'Driving a bit fast, lad.'

Jesse was about to protest, but Ross got in first. 'Sorry, officer, I didn't realise. I will make sure I drive slower in future. Thank you.'

The officer glared at Billy in the back. 'Nasty cut on your face.'

Billy shrugged. 'It's fine.'

'What's your name?'

Billy, like Ross, just wanted to get home, so with no hesitation, he replied, 'Billy Murphy.'

The officer then looked at the lad in the front passenger seat. 'And you?'

'Jesse Murphy.'

He nodded before turning his attention back to Ross. 'Do you have your driving licence on you?'

'I do, as a matter of fact.' Ross quickly leaned across Jesse, opened the glove compartment, and retrieved it. 'There you go, officer.'

The man shone the torch on the licence, gave Ross a questioning glare, and then asked, 'What are you boys doing around here, if you come from Cumbria?'

Billy could have easily gotten smart and shown the officer up for being stupid, but he didn't. He allowed his cousin Ross to answer.

'Oh, I'm from up north, but I'm staying with my cousins for a break.'

The officer nodded, his thick neck rippling with fat rolls, and his top lip coated in sweat. 'Go on then, off you go.'

They waited until the officer had reached his car before Ross gently pulled away. 'Fat cunt,' he mumbled, under his breath. 'He thought we were pissed or gonna get cocky.'

'He can't pull us over for no reason,' said Jesse.

'Well, Ross handled it the best way. At least we're not nicked for something stupid. Right, pepperoni pizza and garlic bread. What about you?' said Billy.

Jesse looked back over his shoulder. 'The same.'

'Hawaiian for me,' said Ross.

***

By the time they reached home, Billy had already called the pizza takeaway and arranged the delivery ahead of their arrival, if possible. He was starving and ordered extra pizza for his little brother Charlie and his sister Nellie, assuming they would crawl out of their beds if they smelled it.

As soon as they trundled into the kitchen via the back door, Carrie, Billy and Jesse's mother, gasped. 'What on earth has happened to my beautiful boy's face?' She hurried over, gripping Billy's chin and turning his face from side to side. 'Who did that? I'll bloody floor 'em.'

'Good news about the shares, eh,' said Sunny, looking up from his mug of hot chocolate. 'Blimey.' He stopped dead, his eyes widening as he took in the scratches. 'Cor, nasty marks. I hope the other lad came off worse.'

Billy pushed his mother's hands away, trying to play it cool. 'It's nothing, Mum, all right.'

'Well, it doesn't look like nothing to me.' She scanned the room, her gaze sharp. 'Where's Willow? I didn't expect you all back so soon. Where have you two been?' She looked from Ross to Jesse, her worry deepening.

'Mum, Willow went off with another lad, and Jesse and Ross came to Bluewater because they heard those twats Stuey and Joey making threats,' Billy explained, his voice tight.

Carrie threw her hands in the air, her frustration evident. 'So, then, you all got into a fight, did ya?'

'No, Mum, we didn't,' insisted Billy. 'I tried to stop Willow from leaving with this Danny geezer, and she scratched my face. Anyway, we've got pizza coming, and I'm starving,' he said, trying quickly to change the subject.

Carrie was already in her pyjamas, having just got out of the bath. Her skin glowed from the moisturiser, and her thick dark hair, although piled on top of her head, still had a few loose damp strands. Her eyes shone with a mix of anger and concern. 'You are too good for her.'

Sunny laughed, trying to lighten the mood. 'That's a change. You always said they would look good together.'

He put his muscular arm around her shoulders and kissed her cheek.

'Well, I don't believe so now. I mean, look at me boy's face, all clawed up like that. She needs a swift backhander, if you ask me. What a little bitch. Well, Sunny Murphy, I don't care what I used to say. Right now, the cow ain't welcome in my home.' She huffed. 'I know you like to do a bit of business with Lolly, but I can't have Willow in the same room as my beautiful boys. Look at his face, Sunny. Just look at him.'

Billy winced as he put his hand on the weeping wound. Not wanting the fuss, he said, 'I'm gonna go and get changed.'

Carrie rubbed the back of her neck as he walked away, her voice trembling with emotion. 'She's broken my boy's heart, she has. But then, I never liked her.'

Sunny laughed softly. 'Yeah, you did. You liked her a lot.'

'Well, I don't now. I mean, look what she's done to him. Unless he hit her, then there is no need for that. I'll tell ya, if I see her, I might just—'

'No, you won't, Mum. Anyway, Billy's a big boy now.' Jesse laughed. 'And a rich one.'

'Not half,' said Sunny, giving Jesse a high-five. 'He can have all the girls he likes.'

'I'm gonna go upstairs to see if he's all right,' Carrie said.

Sunny took hold of her arm. 'Listen, babe, he's getting changed. Leave him be. Christ, Carrie, he's almost sixteen and going on twenty-five. Give him some space.'

'I dunno what he sees in her, meself. There's plenty of girls who wanna go out with Billy, but he liked the gold digger,' said Jesse.

'Gold digger?' questioned Sunny, a little annoyed that his son was disrespectful to a young lady, even though she wasn't present.

'Yeah, she wanted our Billy to take her to buy a load of designer gear with his money.'

Carrie glared at Sunny. 'See! She's a wrong 'un, and I don't want her in me house ever again.'

'Oh, for God's sake, Carrie, she's just a kid pushing her luck. You were probably the same.'

'Like hell I was. And don't you dare say I was like her. I'm not 'aving it, Sunny Murphy!'

Giving him a look that told him he had gone a little too far, Sunny decided to keep his own counsel and say no more about Willow. However, he would be having a word with Lolly about the situation. Lolly would want to know what she was like outside the home because he surely would if it was his own little Nellie. Although he couldn't imagine his princess ever being that nasty. As far as he was concerned, Nellie was the apple of his eye.

***

Billy sat on his bed. He was dressed in a lightweight tracksuit and replaying the evening's events over and over in his mind. If he could only turn back the clock, there was one particular thing that he would have liked to have done differently. He wouldn't have grabbed her in the way he did.

The scene still haunted him. Not only had she well and truly shown him up, but he could still picture Danny laughing at him behind his back. In fact, he could imagine them all laughing at him. Bluewater would be a no-go area for him now. He would stay away and certainly keep his distance from Willow. He couldn't wrap his head around how sharp and cruel she'd actually been. And as much as 'cruel' was a strong description, he felt it was the right one, given the circumstances.

'Billy boy, are you all right?'

Nellie's soft and sweet voice broke through his thoughts. She'd been standing in the bedroom doorway watching him as he stared down at the floor.

Entering the bedroom, she sat beside him and gently put her arm around his waist. 'I love ya, Billy boy.' Her voice carried a hint of a traveller's accent, just like Carrie's. Sunny and Billy were the only two in the house who didn't have an accent.

Billy turned to face his pretty little sister, all of nine years old, with the biggest soulful eyes anyone had ever seen. 'I know you do, and I'm lucky to have a sister like you, Nellie Luanne Murphy.'

Her eyes widened when she saw the weeping wounds on his face, and then they narrowed. 'Did Willow do that?'

He was about to make an excuse for Willow's behaviour when Jesse also entered the room.

'Yep, Nellie, Willow scratched his face. Nasty, weren't she?'

Nellie nodded, her small hands curling into fists. 'I'll scratch *her* face if I ever see her.'

Billy smiled at the protective nature of his little sister.

'Nells,' said Jesse, 'there's pizza downstairs. Call Charlie as well.' He winked as he pinched her cheeks.

Both brothers adored their younger siblings. Nellie was the baby and was treated like one in many ways. Charlie could be a little irritating because he always wanted to join in, but he was just a little bit too young at the moment.

The door closed behind her.

'Are you all right, Billy? Really, all right, I mean? Or has she hurt ya bad?'

Billy stood up and paced the room. 'Jesse, she has really pissed me off. I'm more embarrassed than anything. She showed me up, disrespected me in public, and you know me. I can’t stand that. So, to your question, no, she ain’t hurt me. But one day, Jesse, I will get my own back. Mark my words.’

Jesse knew everything there was to know about Billy – every like, dislike, quirk, and pet hate, even his subtle expressions. But right now, his brother was wearing a look he’d never seen before: it was dark, angry, and vengeful. What Willow had done had pushed a button even he didn’t know existed. Deciding not to say another word, he flicked his head for Billy to join them for some pizza.

As Billy followed Jesse downstairs, his mind was a whirlwind of emotions. The smell of pizza filled the air, but it did little to calm the storm brewing inside him. The evening had left a mark that was deeper than the scratches on his face. It was a wound that only time – or revenge – might heal.

CHAPTER FIVE

A few hours earlier

Feeling excited and daring, knowing she was breaking every rule her father and grandfather had set, Willow ran through the car park gripping Danny's hand.

She knew she'd probably broken Billy's heart, but as much as he'd been a constant friend – and although she knew *he* assumed it was more than just a friendship – she couldn't handle that type of relationship.

She really enjoyed all the attention Billy showed her, and she was grateful that he was always there at the end of the phone or at the many family get-togethers, which were often. She'd heard the jokes about how she and Billy would probably end up married and what a lovely couple they would make. But that, she conceded, was not likely to happen. Not now. Not after everything that had happened to her. And she could see the world for just how cruel it could be.

As soon as Danny hopped into the driver's seat, Willow frowned. She noticed he was texting someone instead of opening the door for her. Billy, no doubt, would have held the door open, like the gentleman he was.

But the thing was, she didn't really want a gentleman, she wanted a bad boy. Someone she could never fall in love with but still enjoy wild and exciting times with, all the same. So here they were acting like they were escaping from a bank job. Hurriedly, she climbed into the front seat, while Danny tossed his phone into the side pocket of the driver's door and then shot off like a bat out of hell.

‘So, where are you taking me, Danny?’ she asked, twisting her hair by trying to look and sound provocative.

He chuckled under his breath. ‘I thought we’d have a little bit of fun: me, you, and charlie.’

‘Charlie?’ she quizzed.

‘Yeah, I’ve got some powder in my back pocket. Been saving it for something special, and I think I’ve got me something special right here, princess.’

She giggled. ‘Really?’ she said, turning slightly to get a better look at his profile. She liked Danny. They had met at a party she had snuck out to, and he was the one who had introduced her to cocaine. She knew it was a terrible thing to do, and she was well aware of how furious her father and grandfather would be if they found out she had been sneaking out and hanging around with boys older than her and snorting cocaine – and whatever else was shoved under her nose.

He was definitely more her type. Tall and fair-haired, he had a captivating smile. He reminded her of Jesse with his boyish, cheeky grin. To her, they were both very different compared to Billy, who was undeniably handsome. And if she was honest, she was well aware that many found his mysterious side attractive. But the problem was he was far too serious. She wanted FUN. She wanted a guy who was ready to do anything. Danny fitted the bill in spades. At least for now.

Smiling to herself, she imagined him throwing her into the back seat of his car, ripping off her knickers, gripping her hair, and bending her back. She slid her hand onto his leg, gently rubbing it, hoping for a reaction. She wanted to see his lips curl into an excited smile. But, strangely, his expression didn’t change. *Maybe*, she thought, *he was playing hard to get*. Perhaps he liked making the first move. Unsure, she pulled her hand away.

'You wanna fuck?' he asked, still looking straight ahead.

Willow felt a bit uncomfortable. She hadn't expected him to come out with something so blunt and cold. But, then again, maybe that was just his way – perhaps he was asking for rough sex, which, if she was honest with herself, was something she had fantasised about. She wanted him to throw her around a little, maybe bend her over the car bonnet, spread her legs, and go at it. She wasn't exactly a virgin anymore, was she!

She chuckled nervously. 'Do you want to fuck me?' she asked, trying to act grown up with oodles of confidence.

When he slowly turned his head, raising an eyebrow as he looked at her, she gave him her best sexy pout, but something about it seemed forced. To any other red-blooded male, she might have been a dream come true, but to Danny, clearly she wasn't.

'God, Willow, who wouldn't want to screw you? You're stunning, darling. Absolutely stunning.'

That was all she needed to hear. At that moment, she was ready to have the time of her life.

She didn't ask where they were headed. She didn't care, as long as she was having a good time. Noticing how he had slowed down when they reached the country lanes, she felt her heart thumping in her chest. So he obviously wanted to take her somewhere secluded so they could be alone. And as much as she liked to go to a club or a posh bar, being alone with Danny was probably the best the evening had to offer. After all, the secluded seat in a restaurant with Billy hadn't cut it, especially now she knew Danny had cocaine.

He turned to face her once he had pulled into a heavily overgrown lay-by with sprouting hedges growing in a curve, virtually hiding the lay-by from view.

She ran her finger down his cheek and arched her back, giving him the come-on.

'Let's get out of the car. I need a fag. I don't smoke inside. I like to keep my car smelling nice. Know what I mean?' he said, climbing out and lighting up at the same time.

She nodded but remained a little perplexed, having built a level of confidence that made her believe every lad fancied her. *But maybe*, she thought, *he was keeping it cool.*

As she got out of the car, he offered her a cigarette. Her heart sank. Why wasn't he trying to rip off her knickers? She shook her head, feeling almost rejected.

Then she saw his face light up as he slid his hand into his back pocket. 'Here, look what I've got.' He waved the sizeable bag of white powder in front of her.

She was surprised at how big the bag was. It must have cost a few hundred pounds.

'Bloody hell, we can have a right night of it. I bet it'll keep you up for hours,' she said, wondering if he was bright enough to understand the double entendre.

Suddenly, they saw flashing blue lights. Danny's eyes were like saucers.

'Shit, the cocaine. I'll get fucking nicked,' he said.

Still holding the bag, Willow didn't know what to do. Her immediate reaction was to run.

The corn was ready to be cut, and as she hitched up her dress and tore across the field, she could feel the dry sheaths grazing her bare legs. No sooner had she started running than she heard the sounds of two cars being started up. Looking back, she saw Danny's car speeding off in one direction and the police car in another. So Danny wasn't waiting for her. That was obvious. He had gone, and so had the police car.

‘Shit, shit!’ she yelled, as she continued sprinting, in the vain hope that Danny would circle around the field to pick her up on the other side. But, somehow, she didn’t think he would.

It was dark now and very eerie. There were no streetlamps, no houses – just field upon field of crops. She stopped to catch her breath and suddenly realised she was alone. A car zoomed past and screeched its brakes, but then, it kept going.

The temperature had dropped, and the darkness was becoming more unsettling. ‘Damn!’ she said, realising that she had left her mobile in Danny’s car. So, what had started out as an exciting evening had turned into a living nightmare. Her mind raced with creepy thoughts – scarecrow films and mad axemen. She stopped, took a deep breath, and looked at the bag of cocaine in her hand. ‘I’ll teach you to sod off and leave me alone, ya prick, Danny Slade,’ she said, before she decided to let the wind carry it away, which it did, and finally ditch the clear plastic bag.

As she neared the other side of the field, separated from a neighbouring one by a road, she clocked the police car.

‘Great!’ she said, aloud.

They could take her home, and without the cocaine on her, she wouldn’t be in any trouble. Waving frantically, she ran towards the car, but then she realised it was stationary. She looked back across the field, noticing how pitch black it had become. Would the officers have seen her from that distance?

‘Don’t be silly, Willow,’ she said, to herself. The car was probably just coincidentally parked there. As she walked closer, she hesitated. An officer, a large man, stepped out of the car. He had his hand on his belt and swaggered towards her like some cop in an American film. But when she got a better look at him, she noticed that there was something off about him. Fear began trickling through her like ice-cold water. As the officer came closer, she noticed not only a predatory grin creeping across his face, but the way in which he was licking his lips. He was like a wild cat, ready to devour its prey. And it nearly freaked her out.

Now, every hair on her body stood on end. Her grandfather had always warned her: if any man makes your hair stand on end, run. It was something to do with primal instinct. She hadn't paid much attention to his advice at the time, thinking he was just being overprotective and probably making things up to scare the shit out of her. But now, she could hear her grandfather's voice in her head – *run, and if you can't run, fight with everything you have*.

'It's all right. Come here, I'll take you home,' the officer said, as he stepped closer.

There was no doubt he looked like a police officer and those words should have comforted her. But everything felt wrong. Why was he holding a bin bag and why did he have a knife tucked in his belt?

Her heart suddenly beat so fast, she thought she would faint. Police don't carry knives, surely. And that bin bag? Really? Was she seeing things?

Something else didn't seem to add up. He looked far too fat to be a policeman – even by the size of some of them she had encountered. But then she realised that it wasn't just his size. He still had that strange expression and those eyes of his were taunting her. The fear became so overwhelming that she spun around to run. Still, her legs felt heavy, her heart was about to explode, and suddenly, she let out a scream.

However, her scream was stopped by the man's hand around her mouth. She could feel the strength of his fat fingers, and she could smell the stale cigarettes and whisky breath as he whispered in her ear, 'Shut the fuck up.'

She knew that if she didn't fight back, she would die. As her grandfather had said: fight with everything you have, rip their bollocks off with your teeth if you have to, but hurt them badly and run. It was as if he had a premonition.

With the man's words ringing in her ears, she gripped his hand and yanked it away from her mouth, spun around, and kneed him hard between the legs. Not just once but twice.

Their eyes met, momentarily transfixed, before he bent over.

At that very moment, she thought she could get away, but it was soon apparent, when he rapidly straightened up, what he'd just done. She gasped, her eyes filled with sheer terror. Strangely, and to her great surprise, she felt no pain. But she did when he rammed his knife into her stomach again.

'That's for bashing my balls.'

A sick giggle left his lips, and he watched the terror on her face, enjoying every minute of it. 'Well, ain't this fun?' he said, letting out a sickly chuckle.

Her eyes widened as she now realised she might die and the last face she would see would be the one belonging to the ugly fat copper.

'Oh, Billy, I'm sorry. I'm really sorry.'

If only it was Billy's face she was seeing right now: her protector – her shoulder to cry on – the only boy she had truly loved.

CHAPTER SIX

11 July

It was one o'clock in the morning. Billy must have looked at their alarm clock twenty times since climbing into bed over two hours ago. Now utterly restless, he rolled over in his bed to see if Jesse was asleep. But he should have guessed he was, just by the gentle purring followed by the random snort. Sitting upright, he rubbed his head and yawned, although he wasn't tired. Something was bothering him, and he couldn't lie in bed any longer torturing himself.

Slipping on his trousers and sweatshirt, he picked up his trainers and crept out of the bedroom, careful not to wake anyone as he tiptoed down the stairs. After gently closing the back door behind him, he entered the garage, put on his trainers, retrieved his mountain bike, and rode along the path. There was a profound silence. The stillness was so intense, it was a stark contrast to his mind, which felt like a riot going off.

The problem was that he could still picture something that he'd seen in the car on the way home. He couldn't get the image out of his head. It was the expression on the driver's face, who he was convinced was Danny Slade. He had looked scared as he rounded the bend at high speed.

But it was not so much that that was bothering him. It was what he thought he saw in the field. Was it really a fox jumping or was it in fact a person? There was a big difference between a fox and a human being. He would put his money on the latter. If so, was it Willow?

He checked his phone to see if she had replied to his text, but she hadn't. She was probably at home, safe and sound. And here he was, like an idiot, riding along the country lanes in the pitch black, on the off chance that Willow was wandering around, having escaped Danny Slade. Of course, this could all be conjecture. A figment of his imagination, perhaps? But if so, why would she be running from Danny? She wanted to go with him, and she clearly wasn't going to let anyone else get in her way from doing exactly what she wanted to do.

Shaking his head, he sighed, now wondering if he was going mad. Still, he needed to check to satisfy his mind, and, dare he think it, his conscience.

By the time he reached the bend where Danny had narrowly missed them, he stopped and stared across the field. The view was very different now. It was so much darker, now blackened by the threatening storm clouds. A few bushes at the end, which were moving in the wind, were barely visible. Was that what he could have seen – the moving trees or bushes? Not a person at all. Feeling stupid, his shoulders slumped, but all he could do was head back home and hope he wasn't missed.

Stepping on the pedals, he rode back along the road. Just as he was about to pick up the pace, he was almost blinded by piercing headlights, which forced him to stop. When he was able to focus on the car that came to a sudden halt in front of him, his heart was in his mouth.

'Fucking police! Damn,' he mumbled, under his breath.

The officer turned off the headlights, got out, and shone a torch in the lad's face. 'What are you doing out here at this hour, son?' he asked, his voice sounding fatherly.

Trying to come up with a plausible explanation, Billy's mind raced. 'Just out for a ride. Couldn't sleep.'

The officer's eyes narrowed, now scrutinising the lad. 'Bit early in the morning for a ride, don't you think?'

'Yeah, well, I've got a lot on my mind,' Billy replied, trying to keep his voice steady.

The officer stared at the lad. He followed it up with a furrowed frown. 'Hey, I recognise you. I pulled you over earlier in the evening. It's Billy Murphy, if I'm not mistaken. Yeah, you've got that mark on your face.' He pointed to Billy's cheek.

Billy decided it was best not to argue. 'Yes, you did.'

'It's two o'clock in the morning, so what are you really doing here? I feel like there's something you're not telling me, and I have a nose for this kind of thing, you see.'

Billy had to think fast. He smiled. 'Okay, I'll tell you. When we were on our way home, I threw some litter out of the car window around here, but I reckon my watch came off as well. It's worth quite a bit of money, so I thought I'd best have a look for it.'

The officer shone his torch at the surrounding ground. 'Can't see a watch,' he said, but he had replaced his fatherly voice with a menacing tone.

When he looked up and grinned, his demeanour suddenly put Billy on edge.

Billy shot a look at the police car, expecting to see another officer, but there was just the burly copper with the torch and a weird fixed smile.

'Never mind, thanks for looking. Gotta go.'

'Oi, not so fast,' said the officer, grabbing Billy's arm.

Something in the man's ogling eyes and the way he grinned made the hairs on the back of Billy's neck stand on end.

'Get the fuck off me, you perv!' Billy growled.

‘No, Billy, you are coming with me. We can go for a little drive.’

His grip was firm, and Billy estimated that the man was twice the size of his father, but how much of that was muscle was anyone’s guess. Fighting a copper was a serious offence, so he had to weigh up the risk of getting nicked against his own safety. But despite being only fifteen, he was good at reading people, and right now, this copper seemed as dodgy as fuck.

Billy’s stomach flipped over as he tried to pull away, but the officer’s grip tightened.

‘Look, I’m not doing anything wrong. I just want to go home.’

‘Too bad,’ the officer sneered, dragging Billy towards the police car.

Trying to yank his arm free, Billy shouted, ‘Either arrest me or get your hands off me because I’m warning you, I will fight back.’

Still gripping Billy’s arm, the officer stopped and turned to face him with a smirk. ‘Behave, you silly kid. You couldn’t fight me.’ His words were long and drawn out. ‘I eat kids like you for breakfast. Now, get in that car before I do nick you.’

‘For what?’ Billy asked, violently shaking off the officer’s grip.

‘I’ll find something, don’t you worry about that. I could have you locked up for a very long time. Or . . .’ He smirked. ‘I could let you go. It’s all up to you. See, you do as I say or face the consequences. It’s simple, really,’ he replied, as he licked his fat lips.

When Billy tried again to break free, this time the officer dropped the torch, pulled a knife from his back pocket, and shoved it under his chin.

Billy noticed how evil looking the knife was. One false move and his neck would be gaping wide open.

But as soon as the knife had appeared, it was back in the officer's pocket.

For a moment, every muscle in Billy's body screamed at him to run like hell away from this man. But he couldn't. He froze to the spot.

Assessing the situation, Billy knew he was fucked. There was no one else around, and here he was standing out in the sticks, with just this burly copper.

Right now, the copper seemed to have the upper hand in strength alone. His menacing eyes held an eagerness that Billy had never seen in a person before. He knew what the sick bastard wanted, but there was no way on God's earth he would allow anyone to touch him if he didn't want them to. He would rather die.

'Fuck off,' he managed to holler, even though his mouth felt like sandpaper.

Suddenly, the copper threw Billy against the car, chuckling like a deranged psychopath.

This was the moment when Billy knew he only had one choice: fight back, and then run for his life.

Adrenaline surged through Billy's veins as he felt the cold metal of the car door against his back. But fear and anger gave him a rush of strength he didn't know he even had. In a flash, he violently twisted out of the officer's grip, and then he brought his right knee up at such a speed and with so much force right between the man's legs that the copper's sick chuckle instantly turned into a pained grunt as he doubled over to clutch his balls.

Seizing the opportunity, Billy slammed his elbow into the officer's ribs, and, for good measure, he kicked the man in the face, knocking him backwards.

Billy was unsure if he had done enough to disable the officer.

But the copper was clearly in too much pain to do anything. He hit the ground like a falling statue.

Billy knew he couldn't outrun a car, so he dashed across the field, not bothering to collect his bike and not looking back. His heart was pounding like a drum inside his chest.

The officer's outraged cries rang out behind him, but Billy didn't slow down, his mind set on escaping. His breath came in ragged spurts, each step fuelled by pure horror. The vast wheat field made running difficult, but, thankfully, the darkness provided cover.

After hearing the copper start the car, Billy paused momentarily to regain his breath. He realised he was on his way to the other side of the field, where there was another road. The officer would know the lanes like the back of his hand, and so the nonce was clearly aiming to catch him on the other side.

'Shit! Shit!' Billy cried, as his lungs burned and his legs felt heavy. Dropping down below the height of the dry brittle wheat, he crawled back in the opposite direction, his ears straining for any sound.

Once he heard the car stop and the engine turned off, Billy knew he had to hurry before the officer guessed he'd done a U-turn. Keeping low was painful: his hands were sore from the harsh, dry, and gritty ground. He followed the plough lines while also being careful not to make too much noise.

Relief washed over him when the heavens opened, and the rain poured down, masking the sound of his movements. It enabled him to scurry as fast as he could without – he assumed – the officer hearing him.

Even the sound of the downpour wouldn't drown out the noise of the car engine if it started up again, so he guessed the officer was still on the other side of the field looking for him. Finally, he reached the road and saw his bike where he had left it. Wasting no time, he jumped onto it and rode like the clappers to get away. He assumed that once the officer saw his bike was missing, he would be tearing around the lanes in pursuit.

Billy's legs shook with pain as he pushed himself to the limit, but he couldn't slow down. Terror surged through him, urging him to pedal faster. The copper's sickening grin was not only fixed in his mind but so was the memory of the officer's grip and the sinister intent in his eyes. It gave him all the incentive he needed to keep going. Riding along the rain-soaked lanes, each turn and twist felt like a lifetime, but he was determined to stay ahead, no matter what.

Anyone else would have been shocked to the core that a police officer could get away with attempting to molest a child. But Billy knew better. He was sure that this wasn't the first time the man had done something like this. Evidently, he was some kind of whacko, a sick bastard, perhaps an opportunist. Who knew?

However, he wasn't going to hang around and find out. He knew the guy wasn't wired right. He had never really been afraid of men – he could handle himself and verbally give as good as he got – but this copper was on a whole other level of crazy.

And who would believe a fifteen-year-old's version over that of a copper's? As far as the public was concerned, the police were there to protect them.

But that was the thing. Billy knew differently, especially after what his family had been through when Detective Constable Brian Colt had set his father up for murder when all along Colt had been the culprit. So, nothing surprised him when it came to the power of the police.

As soon as he was on home ground, namely, the estate, he knew he only had a mile to go to reach his house. He stopped for a breather to prepare himself for someone to be up and about in the house when he returned home.

His mother was his main concern. As much as he adored her, she was a pain in the arse with all those questions of hers. He knew she was reluctant to let him and his siblings grow up by themselves.

His other mother Dottie, aka Mottie, the name he and his brother had come up with when they were very young, on the other hand, was so different. She understood him more than anyone, mainly because he had so much of her in him. It stood to reason since she was his natural birth mother.

What would she make of the situation? A sudden short smile slithered across his face because he knew exactly what she would do. She would hunt the bastard down and probably slit his throat. He was also aware of what she'd done when as a teenager she had killed her parents. So he assumed she was more than capable of exacting retribution if need be.

For everyone's sake, he thought it was probably best not to mention the incident at all and instead just put it down to experience. Nevertheless, what had happened had rankled, and it fuelled his anger towards the police. But not every member of the police force. Former Chief Inspector Ray Clarkson, who had now retired, couldn't be put in the 'bad cop' category. He was genuinely one of the good guys.

Billy took a deep breath and pushed all these thoughts aside. He needed to focus on getting home without arousing suspicion. The rain had slowed down to a drizzle, and the night was eerily quiet. He walked with his bike the remaining distance, his mind racing with everything that had happened.

When he finally reached his house, he paused at the back door, listening for any signs of movement inside. The house was silent. Very slowly, he opened the door and entered the kitchen, careful not to make a sound. He looked up at the clock on the cooker. It was now four thirty in the morning and his ears buzzed with exhaustion. He needed his bed.

CHAPTER SEVEN

Tiptoeing through the kitchen, Billy was on tenterhooks hoping that his absence hadn't been noticed. But then, he heard muffled voices, and as he stepped on the bottom tread of the stairs, his mother called out from the lounge, 'Billy Murphy, get your flaming arse in here now.'

He stopped in mid-stride, his heart thumping once again, wondering if the horrors of the last few hours were a lead-up to even more. Standing in the doorway, he tried to look confident, but probably, he thought, he appeared very sheepish. His mother was sitting in an armchair with a glass of water in her hand. On one of the many sofas were his father and Jesse, but, more surprisingly, Lolly was perched on the edge of the opposite armchair, with a small glass of some amber liquid in his hand.

'Get in here, Son, and tell us where you've been. Lolly's been worried half to death over Willow,' she said, turning to Lolly. 'Ain't ya, mate?'

And he did look pale, considering his skin was naturally dark. Maybe it was the look of fear in his eyes.

Billy glanced at Jesse, knowing that if anyone could speedily establish the facts, it would be his motor-mouth brother.

Right on cue, Jesse announced, 'Willow's gone missing. She ain't come home, Billy. Like I said to Lolly, she left with that Danny geezer, and that's the last we saw of her.'

Billy wished that his brother would just shut up sometimes. It made them both look like they were hiding something. Jesse's words were like torpedoes, and his head nodded just as fast.

Lolly glared, accusingly. 'How did you get those scratches, Billy?'

Billy's hand automatically shot to his face, but before he could answer, his mother jumped in. 'Lolly, to be honest with ya, I would have told you what a cow Willow had been. My Billy came home with those cuts, and I was fuming and would have torn a strip off her meself. But seeing as she's missing, I thought I'd keep my mouth shut. Anyway, that's what she did. Ross and Jesse told me they saw her swipe him.'

Lolly nodded, accepting the explanation, but he returned to Billy. 'Why, Billy?'

'Like I said to you on the phone, I tried to stop her. She clawed me and went off with Danny Slade.'

'D'ya know where he lives?'

Billy shook his head. 'No, I don't really know him. I know *of* him, but I got the impression that Willow knows him.'

Unexpectedly, Carrie rose from her armchair. 'Excuse me a second, Lolly,' she said, as she steered Billy into the kitchen. 'Where the fuck have you been? Ya look like you've been through a bleedin' cornfield,' she hissed, through clenched teeth.

'What?' Billy was stunned. *How the hell did she know?* he wondered. But then, when she plucked a wheat head from his T-shirt, which must have pierced its way in, it was obvious.

'What were you doing out at this time of the morning? We've been waiting ages for you to get back. You left your phone at home. Do you have any idea how scared I was? First, Willow goes missing, and then you're not even in your bed. The sheets are cold, and your bike's gone.'

'I'm sorry.'

'Sorry doesn't cut it. Well?'

'Well, what?'

'Billy, don't get me fucking started. Where have you been? Oh, and before you answer, I gotta tell ya, Mottie's on her way.'

'Why?'

'It's bleedin' obvious why,' she hissed again, trying to keep her voice down. 'I called her and got her outta bed 'cos I thought you might have gone over to hers.'

Billy sighed. 'I'm fine. Call her back and tell her I'm okay.'

But a moment later, the back door opened and in barged Dottie. 'Oh, bloody hell, Billy. I nearly had an accident driving over here. You had us worried sick.' She gripped his chin. 'Who did that to your face? And don't say it was an accident. I can spot a talon scratch a mile off.'

'Can I get a drink, please?'

Carrie looked at Dottie and shrugged while Billy poured himself a cold glass of water and drank it fast to quench his dying thirst.

'And what have you done to your hands?' asked Dottie, scrutinising her son.

Billy placed the empty glass on the draining board and slowly opened his hands, palms up. He hadn't even noticed the scratches, with the numerous small piercings, and how dirty they were from crawling along the wheat field.

However, before he had a chance to launch into the story, Lolly's mobile phone rang. They all hurried into the lounge and eagerly listened as Lolly answered the call.

'Yes, this is Laurence Price,' he said, putting his hand over the phone to relay to all the concerned faces in the room that it was the police on the line. He had reported Willow missing and given them a description of her. Still, they had advised that they couldn't formally classify her as missing until she had been gone for twenty-four hours. The call had his stomach in knots, and he could feel its contents rising.

'Why do you want me to return to my house? Please, just tell me. Have you found my daughter or what? If so, does she need a lawyer? What's she gone and done?'

Dottie glanced at Carrie, whose eyes were wide. Clearly, they had all suspected the worst. So if that was the case, why didn't the policeman on the other end of the phone put Lolly's mind at rest? The only conclusion was that the police wanted to give the awful news to him face to face.

'I'll drive you, Lolly,' Sunny said, jumping up from the sofa and snatching his car keys from the side table.

But Lolly was now angry. He raised his hand to quieten Sunny, and then he raised his voice firmly, like a sergeant major. 'Listen, officer, I will ask you again: what has my daughter done, and does she need a lawyer?' He paused, awaiting an answer, but the silence was cold and dark.

Lolly's hand was visibly shaking as the blood drained from his face. 'What's . . . going on?' he asked, not wanting to hear the truth. But the officer was obviously asking him another question.

Everyone was holding their breath waiting for an answer. 'Why are you at my house? I'm at my friend's place in Petts Wood.'

The officer's voice was so quiet that no one could hear what he was saying, only Lolly's answers. 'Why do you want their address? What the bloody hell's going on, mate? Just tell me, please.'

Everyone stared, but they now knew what the dreaded news would be. It was so obvious, except to Lolly, who couldn't even contemplate it.

Carrie couldn't hold back any longer. She snatched the phone, which Lolly didn't even try to fight her for.

'Hello, this is Carrie Murphy. Lolly – I mean Laurence – is in our company. He is with friends. We all want to know where Willow is. Have you found her?'

There was a brief pause. 'I'm afraid we believe we may have, from the description Mr Price gave us.'

'Oh, I see. My husband – he will drive Lolly home.' She struggled to get her words out. As much as she thought she could be strong and hold it together for Lolly, her sudden downpour of tears told a whole other story.

'Sunny, you have to take Lolly home. The police are there waiting.'

Sunny nodded. He knew by the distraught look on his wife's face. She was as white as a sheet.

Billy knew it too. He felt it in his bones, and while everyone stood there struck dumb, he slid away out through the back door. In the garage was his father's fishing gear. Along with it was an extremely sharp knife used to gut the fish, much to the horror of Jesse, who was now a vegetarian, except when it came to pizzas. He found the knife in its holster, slid it down the back of his trousers, and wasting no time, he headed back towards Crockenhill. The difference this time was the time of day, the sunlight piercing through a blanket of heavy mist. And the fact that he was a different lad from the one who'd ridden home in terror. Now, here he was returning to give the guy a taste of his own medicine.

He was tired, but his mind was alive with visions of how he would gut the fat copper like a fish. There was not a speck of doubt in his mind that the copper had something to do with Willow's disappearance. He wasn't stupid. He knew she was dead, and all his anger towards her for showing him up disappeared as quickly as the half-smile from Lolly's face. He could tell Lolly was saying everything to the officer on the other end of the phone except one thing: 'Is my daughter dead?' But, nonetheless, he didn't need the answer spelled out. He knew.

Suddenly, Billy felt the tears sting his face as a cool breeze threatened to blow the mist away. He wiped his face with the back of his hand while pedalling as fast as he could, determined to find the fat copper. He imagined smashing the bastard's head in with his own torch and carving up his face.

The ride was very different this morning, considering it was daylight and cars were passing him, probably on their way to work.

When one car shot around him and slammed on its brakes, he recognised it. It was Dottie's. As she clambered out less than gracefully, unlike her usual self, she stomped towards him, her face like thunder. She didn't ask anything. She merely said, 'Put your bike in the back and get in the car!'

Reality hit him like a punch in the gut. What was he really doing? Clearly, his rage had taken over his body, and the sense of danger, or even the consequences, had vacated his brain.

Dottie didn't hug him or offer words of comfort. Her expression was cold. 'Hurry up, Billy.'

As he removed the front wheel of his bike, he turned to look around. In the distance, he saw blue flashing lights. Suddenly, a long convoy of cars passed by, clear evidence that the road further on had been closed and the traffic diverted. Hurriedly, he threw the bike in the boot and hopped into the front seat.

Dottie made a U-turn and joined the diverted traffic.

'Her body is over there, isn't it, Mottie?' Billy asked.

Dottie didn't turn to face him. She kept her gaze straight ahead. 'Quite possibly, but, Billy, how would you know that?'

Shocked, he threw her a fierce look. 'I never killed her. Fucking hell. I . . . I . . . *loved* her.'

'I didn't say you killed her. In fact, we don't even know if she *was* murdered. They've not even confirmed it's her or that she's even dead. All we know is that the police have found a young girl who they *believe* is Willow.'

'That's just covering their arses, that's all that is. She's dead. I just know it.'

'And what makes you say that?'

'It doesn't matter. No one would believe me.'

Unexpectedly, Dottie pulled over into a lay-by. She spun to face him. 'Right, Billy, have I ever *not* believed you?'

He shook his head and looked down. 'No, I guess not.'

'So, come on, tell me what's really going on because I know you, Son. You're hiding something.'

Billy didn't want to go into the events of the previous evening. He was drained, and how could he even make sense of it, let alone relay it to Dottie? 'Can we just go home?' He leaned forward to open the glove compartment, looking for a tissue.

Dottie spotted the knife tucked down his jeans and instantly pulled it from its holster. 'What the hell are you doing with this, Billy?' She held up the weapon before throwing it into the open glove compartment and slamming it shut.

'All right,' growled Billy. He paused momentarily, catching his breath and thinking of how to explain what happened. 'On the way home from Bluewater, we came to a sharp bend and a car raced towards us. It looked like a Ford Escort. Ross braked hard, and I looked, and I was sure I saw Danny driving. He's the lad who Willow went off with at the shopping centre. Anyway,' he said, pointing to a wheat field, 'something caught my eye. I looked across the field and I thought I saw something moving. I wasn't sure if it was a person, ya know, or an animal, or . . . well, it was dark. Anyway, I got home, went to bed, couldn't sleep, and decided to come back here in case it was Willow, and she was lost or hurt or . . . anything.'

Dottie didn't interrupt. She nodded for him to go on, but he stopped.

'Okay, I understand, but tell me this: why return with a knife? Because I can't imagine there being any fish around here to gut.'

Billy chewed his lip, his face flushed with embarrassment.

She knew that look. It was rare for him to look like that. Then her voice softened. 'It's okay, Billy. You know I've always got your back. You can tell me, Son.'

When he peered up, his face awash with a sense of sadness, she saw him again as a little boy – not the manly teenager he was now. 'Go on, love.'

'So, on our way home, we got pulled over by a copper, and when I came back, the same copper was still here. He drove towards me, stopped his car, and asked me what I was doing. I made up a lie, and he . . .' He paused and rubbed his forehead. 'He tried to get me in his car. He threatened me with a knife, like a big Army-type knife. He frightened the fucking life outta me. Anyway, I kneed him in the nuts, booted him in the face, and ran through the field. I doubled back, got my bike, and headed home.'

He stopped when he saw the look of absolute rage on Dottie's face.

'It's all right. He didn't hurt me.'

But Dottie was still picturing a police officer holding a knife to her son. She didn't need to ask what he thought the copper would do. She knew.

'I think he killed her.'

Dottie's eyes widened. She hadn't thought of that. '*What?*'

'Mottie, he was terrifying, and it takes a lot to put the shits up me, but he was like a monster. A big, fat, sweaty, bald monster.'

His description turned her stomach, but she couldn't hang around. There seemed to be police cars and bystanders all over the place. 'Let's go back and we can talk about it at home. I don't think we should be here.'

'I'm nothing to do with it, though, Mottie.' He suddenly fingered the scratches on his face. He wasn't stupid. 'She will have my skin under her nails. They will blame me. They will pin this on me. I'm an easy target. Plus, I'm a Murphy.'

CHAPTER EIGHT

It was eight o'clock when they arrived home. Billy saw the police car outside his house. He turned to Dottie, who seemed to be in a daze. 'Be honest, they will arrest me, won't they?'

'Listen, Billy, not all police are bad. You've just seen the worst of them,' she said, managing a small smile. 'And the best if you include Ray Clarkson. Of course, they will want to ask you questions, but one step at a time. We don't even know what's happened yet.'

'I don't want to go to prison. I don't even want to go to the poxy station.'

Dottie gripped his arm. 'Billy, you won't go to prison, and even though you don't act like it, you're still a minor. I doubt they will take you down to the station. But we need to go inside because you need to sleep. You look drained, love.'

'I only had probably an hour's sleep.'

'You look like it too.'

'Mottie, shall I tell them about the copper?'

Her eyes narrowed. 'I'm not sure. Although I want to kill him myself, the bastard.'

Billy dragged his heels as he walked in through the back door.

As soon as they entered the kitchen, they could hear voices in the lounge.

Letting him know he had her support, Dottie had her hand on his shoulder. Unlike Carrie, who was always hugging and kissing her kids, she wasn't really a touchy-feely type of person. Billy was much like her because he wasn't a tactile kid either.

Dottie stopped to indicate that he should take a seat at the kitchen table. If the police wanted to question Billy, they could do it there, where he could sit up straight at the head of the table. It wasn't a small table, but the kitchen was large enough to accommodate it.

As soon as he sat down, he began fidgeting, chewing his thumbnail, and taking deep breaths.

Carrie suddenly appeared. About to sit down next to her son, she saw him look up as two police officers appeared in the doorway.

Deciding there and then that Billy wasn't ready to be grilled by the officers, she spun around and waved them back into the hallway.

'Give my boy a break, would ya? Go in the lounge, and I'll call you in once I've had a chance to break the news.'

Billy expected an argument to ensue, but the officers merely smiled, nodded, and retreated to the lounge. As soon as they were out of sight, he felt his mother's warm, loving arms envelop him, her full breasts practically suffocating him.

'Ahh, my boy, I'm so sorry, darling.' She gently pulled away and kissed the top of his head before sitting beside him. 'She's gone, Billy. Poor Willow. They found her body early this morning. Some random walker, rambler, or whatever they're called, spotted her just before a bloody great combine harvester was about to run over her dear little body. Lucky he did spot her, 'cos she would've ended up—'

'All right, Carrie, spare us all the gory details,' Dottie quickly interrupted, her voice firm and steady.

Billy felt his chest tighten, and for a split second, he had to gasp for breath. He had already assumed that Willow was dead, but to have it confirmed, it put a complete stop to any ray of hope that she was still alive. And it also ended his image of her stomping home with her shoes in her hand and cursing Danny for leaving her in the middle of nowhere. His vision blurred with unspent tears, and his body trembled as waves of rage rose inside his stomach. He hated Danny for leaving her there. He would never ever have been so cruel.

'Are you okay, love?' asked Carrie, her voice soft and concerned, trying to gauge his reaction.

But Billy just stared ahead, his face a sickly grey colour, his eyes wide and intense.

'I'm okay, just angry with Danny.' He glanced at his mother before looking away, his gaze shifting to the floor. She could always tell when he had more to say or more to hide.

'While you were out, the police have been talking to Jesse and Ross. Now they just want to ask about the time you spent with Willow before she left with this Danny lad. Okay?'

'I told Lolly everything on the phone. I said she just went off with him after I tried to stop her. Shouldn't they be asking Danny what happened after she was with him?'

Carrie looked up at Dottie, who was standing in her usual crossed-arms stance, her brows knitted in a questioning expression. 'Apparently, they can't find Danny. He wasn't at his house. They found his car with the driver's door open, like he'd scarpered. I mean, right there, it sounds like a whole lot of guilt, if you ask me.'

Billy suddenly wiped his eyes and glared at his mother. 'What? The police are already looking for him? How did they know?'

Carrie nodded. 'Yeah, apparently, when Lolly reported her missing, he told them that Danny was, as far as he knew, the last person to see her.'

Billy needed time to think and to process all this information. It was beginning to befuddle his brain. And it made no sense. Why would Danny scarper if it wasn't him who had killed her? Why would he run? He was sure he saw him in that lane, and now her body had been found. He wondered if Danny had hurt her. But perhaps he'd been entirely wrong and the movement in the field wasn't a person after all. Could it have been a bush or a tree blowing in the wind? But, he acknowledged, it could have been an animal, most likely a fox.

But what if Danny had stabbed her, and she was running for her life? If only he'd gone searching to see if it was her, while Ross and Jesse were changing the tyre, she might still be alive right now.

His mind raced as he bit his nail again, trying to work out the sequence of events.

His thoughts then focused on that copper who had tried to molest him. What was he really doing there? He was becoming more and more convinced that he was the actual killer, although he only had intuition on his side. And what did he have to give him this? He was only fifteen. But in his gut, he knew that that policeman was a wrong 'un. He just knew he was. But there was that little niggle at the back of his mind that was telling him to be a little more rational in his thinking. It could be, he conceded, that because the copper merely frightened him, he was putting two and two together and coming up with ten. But, what about the knife? The copper had threatened him with it.

'How did she die?' he asked, his voice quivering.

'The detective said they believe she was stabbed.'

Billy looked over her shoulder. 'Where is Lolly?'

'He's at home.'

'And Cas? Has anyone told Cas?'

'Lolly told Cas she was missing before he reported to the Ol' Bill that she hadn't come home. He had to check to ensure she hadn't gone to Cas's place. Apparently, she goes over there to ride her horse if she's got the hump. Poor cow, so young an' all.' Carrie welled up, tears brimming in her eyes.

The two detectives had now entered the kitchen. One was an older man with substantial square shoulders, his hair grey at the sides but with a friendly round and open face. The second detective was a slight man with dark gelled hair and beady eyes. He looked as though he would rather be anywhere but here.

'Sorry to intrude, but the sooner we get a statement, the closer we may be to catching our . . . the person responsible,' the older detective said, lowering his tone.

Billy nodded. 'I'm ready.'

Dottie leaned against the sink. 'Are you sure, Billy?'

He nodded again. 'Yes, I'm sure.'

'Great. I'm DCI Andrew Keldon, and this is DI Paul Gurney.'

Billy nodded once more.

Carrie rose from her chair and invited the two detectives to each take a seat. 'How about a coffee? And some toast or biscuits?'

Keldon smiled. 'That sounds great. Coffee and biscuits for me, please, and my colleague will have the same.'

As Keldon spoke, Billy noticed the detective's teeth, which might have been perfect had they not been stained with nicotine. It was obvious that the man was a heavy smoker. The yellow stains on his right fingers were a dead giveaway.

Keldon took out his notebook. 'So, Billy, I've had a quick chat with Jesse and your cousin Ross. Basically, I want your account. What time you arrived at the shopping centre, who you spoke to, what you did, and . . . where you've just been this morning.'

Billy sat up straight, feeling the weight of the moment pressing down on him. He began by recounting the altercation with Joey, Stuey, and Atlas Carson. As he spoke, he noticed the detective writing hasty notes, which made him pause and feel a pang of anxiety.

'So you have an ongoing issue with the Carsons, do you? And did they say anything to Willow?' Keldon asked, his tone probing.

Billy could tell where this line of questioning was going. It was a wild goose chase. 'The issues with the Carsons are nothing. They're just slanging matches, really, not anything to worry about.'

Keldon was impressed with how Billy was conducting himself and by the way he spoke. He did so calmly and clearly, and in those respects, he was very different from his brother. 'So did they make threats or . . .?'

'No, they are just idiots, really, showing off,' Billy replied, trying to keep his composure.

'And Danny Slade, when did you meet him?'

'He arrived when the Carsons were acting lairy. He seemed to enjoy the potential fight, and when I walked away with Willow, she looked back. She knew him. He knew her. You probably need to ask him about their relationship. I don't know any more than that,' Billy explained, feeling a knot tighten in his stomach.

'We will, as soon as we find him. And you wouldn't happen to know if he had any plans for Willow? For example, where he intended to take her, would you?'

Billy shook his head, his mind racing with memories of the night.

'Okay, so after she walked out of the restaurant, you tried to stop her from leaving, did you?'

Billy nodded again, feeling the weight of guilt pressing on his chest.

'Hmm, and your brother and cousin told us that Willow clawed your face. Is that right?'

'I tried to stop her from going, and she . . . yes, she clawed me. I don't think she meant to. She was just very animated, and her nails caught me,' Billy said, his voice trembling slightly.

'I think you must have been pretty angry that she was going off with another lad when she was on a date with you,' Keldon suggested, his eyes narrowing.

Billy smirked, mockingly. 'Oh, I see, Detective, so . . .' He paused and sighed. 'You think because she went off with Danny, I'd be so angry that I'd hurt her?'

'Oi, that's enough of that! You'd better not be trying to pin this on my boy! 'Cos I'm not having a bar of it. Do you bloody understand me? Your lot have caused us enough grief to last a lifetime, as well you know!' snapped Carrie, who was ready to rip into them.

Dottie grinned inside, knowing Carrie would verbally tear each of them a new arsehole if they upset her boys.

Gurney glared back. 'We're merely collecting the facts.'

'Did you leave school with a colouring book to show for it, 'cos that ain't merely collecting facts. That's insinuation. I left school with fuck all, and I clearly know more than you,' Carrie retorted, her eyes blazing.

Keldon put his hand up to calm the situation.

But Carrie was angry and upset, and, in any case, she had no time for the police.

'Look, we do know what your family went through, but we are not Brian Colt.'

'Then, if you know what we were subjected to, you wouldn't be insinuating shit, would you?' Carrie shot back, her voice edged with fury.

Again, Keldon held up his hand. ‘Okay, like my colleague has just said, we need to establish a few facts. At the moment, Billy here is a significant witness, and I hope it stays that way. So let me do my job, and we will be out of here in a sec. Billy will remain a significant witness, while we gather more evidence from everyone else who was there before Willow left with Danny.’

‘All right, but if you two start making out that my Billy looks like the bad guy to suit yourselves, to add another nicking to your CVs, I will launch you two out of my home, and you’ll only question him when his brief is with him. Got me?’

Dottie flicked the switch on the kettle and turned away to hide her grin. *Good ol’ Carrie. Say it how it is.*

‘Okay, so, Billy, how long after Danny left with Willow did you leave Bluewater?’ Keldon asked.

Billy had to think because he wasn’t sure. Ross had marched through the Centre in the hope that the sports shop was still open. That took a while because they ended up searching for any shop that sold trainers. Then he bought a can of Coke. They watched a few souped-up motors gather in the car park, and Jesse spoke with one of the drivers.

‘I don’t know exactly. Maybe forty-five minutes to an hour. I wasn’t paying attention. Oh, but the copper that pulled us over, he’ll have the details. Ask him,’ Billy said, trying to maintain his composure as he bit his nail yet again.

‘Copper?’ said Keldon, twisting his head to face Carrie. ‘The other lads didn’t mention being pulled over. What was all that about, I wonder?’

‘It was just routine,’ Billy replied, quickly. ‘The officer just asked us where we were going and stuff like that. My cousin showed him his licence, and he waved us on.’

‘Where was this?’

‘The lane towards Crockenhill.’

Keldon frowned and looked at Gurney. 'Radio through to the station, would you?'

Gurney looked as concerned as Keldon. 'For sure,' he agreed, before getting to his feet and walking out of the back door.

'Do you recall when this officer pulled you over?'

Billy shook his head. 'No, sorry. But it must have been latish because it was very dark. All I remember is that he was driving a jam sandwich and was on his own.'

The detective suddenly jolted as if he'd had an electric shock. 'You what? Are you sure it was a police car with the red stripe?'

But it was Dottie who answered. 'Billy would be sure. He has a keen eye for detail.'

Keldon smiled. 'Thank you.'

But Billy wasn't done. 'What's so surprising about the officer driving that car?'

'Nothing,' Keldon replied, quickly, before he rose from his chair.

'Here, I've made the coffees,' said Dottie, wanting Keldon to retake his seat and answer Billy's question honestly.

'Oh, er, thank you,' he said, taking the hot drink and politely lowering himself back onto the chair. The freshly brewed coffee was just how he liked it, and for a moment, he sat back and savoured the taste. When an array of expensive biscuits was placed under his nose, he suddenly realised how hungry he was.

He had barely been out of bed this morning when he'd got the call that a girl had been found murdered. A quick swig of coffee after brushing his teeth had left him with a nasty taste in his mouth. So now, as he munched on a chocolate-covered shortbread, he sat back and enjoyed the snack. He needed it because his head was pounding. The weight of the case, the early morning call, and the tension in the kitchen all contributed to the throbbing in his temples.

When Gurney returned, he smiled at Carrie. 'Ooh, coffee. Is that for me?'

She nodded. 'Yeah, don't choke on it.'

He chuckled. 'You didn't poison it, did ya?' he asked, trying to lighten the mood and get her back onside.

'Nah, I'm all out of poison and middle fingers, so enjoy your drink and help yaself to a biscuit.' Her tone lightened, and she even added a smile.

'So what happens now?' Billy asked.

Keldon would never have gotten into that kind of conversation with a kid under normal circumstances, but there was something about this Billy Murphy lad that warranted respect.

'Well, Billy, we will need to bring Danny into the station for questioning, and you will also have to come in, only for a formal statement, as, at the moment, you, as I said, are a significant witness.'

'Is Danny a suspect?'

'I can't answer that, but we will need to speak to him, since, at the moment, he was probably the last person to see Willow alive.'

Billy's eyes unexpectedly welled up. He bit his top lip to stop the emotion. 'Did she suffer?'

Keldon put on his best sympathetic expression. 'No, Billy, I don't think so,' he replied, gently, hoping to offer some comfort.

Billy nodded, but the reassurance did little to ease the knot in his stomach. He looked at Carrie and Dottie, seeing their concern but feeling that he was all alone in his grief and anger.

The room fell silent, each person lost in their own thoughts.

Keldon and Gurney exchanged glances, knowing the complexity of the case was only just beginning to unfold.

The silence left Billy wondering if he should tell them what happened when he returned to the field.

But it was as if Dottie knew what he was about to say. Swiftly, she said, 'So, if that's it, I think Billy needs to get some sleep. Worry can take it right out of you.'

Keldon nodded. 'Oh, before we go, where have you been this morning?'

Billy shrugged. 'I didn't want to hear the news that Willow was dead. I didn't want it spelled out to me. I heard Mum tell my dad that the police were waiting for Mr Price at his home.'

'Why would you think they were going to say she was dead?' Keldon asked.

'I'm not deaf, dumb, or stupid. I guessed,' Billy replied.

Gurney finished the last of his coffee and tilted his head at Billy. 'You had feelings for Willow, didn't you, Billy?'

Billy glanced at Carrie and then back at the detective. 'I was annoyed that she'd gone off with Danny. Of course I was. I really liked Willow a lot. A helluva lot. She was sweet, really, and the sad thing is, now I won't be able to tell her how special she was.'

Tears tumbled down Carrie's face. 'Ahh, Billy boy, come here.' She pulled him up from the chair and wrapped her arms around him. 'We all know how much you loved her.'

Seeing as Keldon hadn't had the answer to his earlier question, he asked, 'So where did you go, Billy?'

Pulling away from his mother, Billy turned to face them. 'I just went for a bike ride.'

'Okay, Billy, we'll be off, and when you are ready, please come to the station, so that we can take a formal statement from you.'

Billy nodded and watched the two detectives grab an extra biscuit and walk along the hallway and out of the front door. The muscles in his body relaxed a smidgeon before he yawned. 'I need my bed.'

Dottie was the one who hugged him and whispered, 'Well done, Son.'

CHAPTER NINE

A loud bang woke up Billy. He jerked bolt upright, his skin slick with sweat, his breathing rapid, and his mind spinning. He had been dreaming and Willow had haunted his dream, her face smeared with blood, her eyes filled with a mix of sadness and fear. Because she was pleading for his help. After a moment of panting, he forced himself to slow down his heart rate. Taking a few deep breaths, he reminded himself that it was only a dream, albeit an especially unpleasant one.

He pricked his ears listening for any sounds coming from his family but the house seemed quiet. He was sure he'd heard a bang. When he looked at the clock, he realised that it was one o'clock in the afternoon. He shouldn't have been surprised because his head hadn't hit the pillow until nine o'clock that morning.

Sliding out of bed, he wandered out of his room and down the stairs. The moment his feet hit the bottom tread, a cold chill washed over him. It came back to him: the police had told him they hadn't found Danny.

'Shit!' he muttered, hurrying to the kitchen. It was more in hope than expectation of finding his parents or Dottie there, who could drive him to where he wanted to be.

To his surprise, Dottie was there. She was sitting at the table. 'Sorry, Billy. The wind caught the back door, and slammed it behind me. I didn't mean to wake you. I thought I'd come over and get started on the business accounts.'

'It's okay. I had to get up anyway.'

'That was a quick sleep. How are you feeling?' she asked, before a concerned frown flickered across her brow. 'What's up, Billy?'

'Mottie, I think the reason the police can't find Danny is because Cas has hunted him down.'

'How? Why? I don't understand.'

'Danny passed us in that lane, I'm sure of it. And I'm convinced now that I saw Willow out there. She was running across a field, which means she was alive when he left her. The last person, as far as the police and Lolly are concerned, to see her alive is Danny. Come on, Mottie, think about it. Where is Cas? He would have been here with Lolly, surely. Mottie, have they said that they've arrested Danny yet?'

Slowly, she shook her head. 'No. In fact, I heard your dad tell your mum when he got off the phone with Lolly that the police are still searching for this Danny guy and—'

Before Dottie could continue, Billy ran back upstairs.

She knew he had a point, and knowing Cas, it was precisely the kind of thing he would do. Cas doted on Willow, and if he got his hands on the person responsible for hurting her, there was no doubt in her own mind that he would kill them. Her hands shook. It was so unlike her. But the thought of Cas going after Danny, who might not even be the killer, worried her deeply.

Billy reappeared in no time fully dressed. 'Come on, we need to get to Cas's place. I could be wrong, but what if I'm not?'

Dottie gave Billy a confirming nod, and they left the house. Typically, Dottie was a careful driver, but today, she told Billy to buckle up as she tore through the streets like a racing car driver. As soon as they hit the A21, she put her foot down even harder and hammered it all the way to

Wadhurst. She knew the way, having been to Cas's barbecues before.

Dottie had known Cas since she was a child. She used to hang out with his daughter Tara and Ray Clarkson's daughter Jenny, but as an adult, she had never been too friendly with Cas. There was something about him she didn't like. Maybe it was his gangster bullying tactics. It was no secret what Cas was or how he had made his money. It was all done through illicit means. But it wasn't so much that the man had such a lot of front. It was the fact that he still spoke to her as though she was a child and because he never seemed to feel any fear or unease around her – unlike most people. Her violent history didn't seem to bother him. It was as if slaughtering one's parents was just like having cereal for breakfast. It was nothing too shocking or noteworthy.

Billy was out of the car and pressing the intercom on the gate before his mother had even turned off the engine. He pushed the button again, holding it there, as he glared through the massive iron gates at the two cars parked outside the garage. One belonged to Cas and the other to Keith. Receiving no answer, he turned to his mother, with a look of frustration etched clearly on his face. 'They're deliberately not letting me in, the bastards.' He looked at her car, then back at the gates. 'Mottie, can you pull up alongside these gates? I'm gonna climb over.'

'Wait,' Dottie said, grabbing his arm. 'If they're doing what you think they are, Cas might become so enraged that he could hurt you, if you get in the way.'

'Mottie, what if they kill Danny, and I could have stopped them? I know he didn't murder Willow. Well, I don't think he did.'

Dottie sighed and then she nodded, before returning to the vehicle and parking it up against the gate.

Billy wasted no time. Jumping onto the boot, and leaping onto the roof, he practically launched himself over the wall and landed with the agility of a monkey.

For a moment, Dottie stood there feeling helpless. Her thoughts weren't for Danny. She was more worried about her son. Quickly, she pulled a knife from the glove compartment, slid it down the back of her trousers, and clambered onto the roof of the car. Cautiously, she straddled the top of the gate before swinging her legs over and plunging to the ground. Because she didn't attempt a dive roll as her feet hit the drive, she suffered momentary pain in her feet and legs. However, seeing Billy racing up the drive to Cas's front door, she ignored the throbbing and raced after her son.

By the time she'd caught Billy up, he'd gone around to the back of the enormous house and entered via the impressive walled garden with French doors leading into Cas's study.

'Cas! Keith!' Billy's voice echoed angrily as he tapped his foot impatiently.

Billy and Dottie would have heard a pin drop in the silence that was only broken by the tick-tock of the grandfather clock out in the hallway.

'I don't think they're here, Billy,' Dottie whispered.

'Oh, they're here,' Billy replied, his voice low but firm. 'Both of their cars are in the drive, although Cas normally keeps his in the garage. So something's off.'

Dottie watched her son with pride. He was no longer a boy, that was clearly evident. His determination and sharp instincts belied his years.

'I'll check upstairs while you take the other rooms down here,' she suggested.

But Billy shook his head. 'No, they're not in the house,' he said, turning on his heel. 'They're out at the back.

There's a barn, some stables, and other outbuildings. I bet that's where they've taken Danny.'

'I can't hear anything,' Dottie said, straining her ears to pick up any sound.

'Mottie, wait here. I'll go and check it out,' Billy urged.

'Not on your nelly, Billy,' Dottie retorted, refusing to let him go alone.

He didn't argue. Together, they hurried back outside through the French doors, through the opening in the walled garden, and headed towards the stables.

Billy's stride was purposeful, almost aggressive.

Suddenly, Dottie grabbed his arm. 'Wait,' she said, feeling the tension in his muscles. 'Why are you so angry?'

'Because I shouldn't have let her go. I should have forced her to come with me.'

Dottie observed her son. *Was he tormented by guilt?* She sighed. 'You couldn't have stopped her, love. She was a determined young lady.'

Running across to the stables, they encountered a sudden loud banging noise echoing through the stillness. When they reached the stables, their eyes were drawn towards Keith. There, they saw him struggling to control a large seventeen-hand horse, its stress evident, as it kicked and bucked violently. The banging continued, with the horse's hooves striking the walls of the stables.

At first, Dottie and Billy were too stunned to understand what Keith was doing until they heard Cas's voice, harsh and unforgiving. 'That's it, boy. Kick him again. *And* again.'

'Jesus!' Dottie cried out, horrified.

It took Billy another moment to fully grasp the situation. This was Willow's horse. She'd always said that while the horse was gentle outside the stables, it became uncontrollably dangerous inside. Realising what they were doing, Billy's fury ignited. He had to stop them.

Without a second thought, he ran forward, grabbed the reins from Keith, and shoved the unsuspecting man aside. Using all of his strength, he pulled the horse out of the stall and released it into the back field. The horse bolted, kicking and bucking, before it disappeared into the distance.

'What in the cunting hell are you fucking doing?' Cas shouted. He was on the other side of the stall, standing on a ledge to peer inside.

But neither Dottie nor Billy could respond. They were mesmerised by the scene before them.

Lying still on the floor, they could see Danny. He was covered in blood. A deep, crescent-shaped gash was embedded in his forehead, and his left cheek was so swollen, it looked disfigured.

The brutal reality of what had just happened hit Dottie and Billy like a ton of bricks.

Billy's heart pounded in his chest, but he couldn't tear his eyes away from the horrific sight. Cas's words barely registered as the gravity of the situation sank in. Because Danny had been mercilessly beaten, not by Cas's hand but by Willow's horse.

Billy watched on as Keith brushed himself down. For the first time, Billy saw a weaker side to the man. He clearly hadn't been firmly on his feet to have fallen down like that, having not even noticed them there.

Billy had no time to react when Cas stormed over to him.

The look of rage on Cas's face was a shocking sight. Normally jovial and magnanimous in most people's company, Dottie and Billy couldn't believe the transformation. Cas's snarling expression looked like that of Jack Torrance in *The Shining* as he stormed across the yard.

With his eyes narrowed and his nostrils flared, spittle flew from the sides of his mouth. 'You, ya bleedin' faggot, should've looked after her,' he yelled, before he pulled his fist back and punched Billy hard on the forehead.

Like Keith, who had been on the receiving end of Billy's temper, Billy hadn't expected that, and he went flying to the ground.

Dottie saw red. No one touched her boy. In an instant, she ripped the knife from behind her back, and, with the speed of a striking viper, she grabbed Cas by his thin ponytail and shoved the knife under his chin, her face just centimetres from his. 'You dare hurt my son, you fucking bully. And just so you know: I hate bullies.'

Billy scrambled to his feet, and with Keith's help, they managed to pull Dottie away from Cas, although she still gripped the knife tightly.

'I will slit your throat, Cas, and believe me, I won't even flinch.' Her voice was icy with conviction.

Billy's eyes widened. He'd heard the story about how his mother had killed her parents, but seeing her like this – her face transformed into that of a cold-blooded killer – it shook him to his core. There was no doubt in his mind that she would have killed Cas.

Stepping back in amazement, Cas's demeanour and personality changed in an instant to that big-hearted loveable grandfather.

'I always thought you were a sweet girl, Dottie. Cor, you're a right nightmare, ain't ya.'

Cas then looked at Billy. The lad had that seemingly unfazed look on him, and it then became clear that he possessed the same ruthless charm as his natural mother. He'd sensed it from the first meeting three years ago when Billy had hidden his pain and held himself like a man – not a scared child, like most twelve-year-olds would have been.

But, instantly, his jovial countenance was replaced by one of fury. 'You put that fucking tool away, and fuck off, Dottie, you stupid tart. My grandbaby's dead and that cunt lying in horse shit killed her. Now, fuck off. I've got work to do.'

Billy rubbed his forehead. 'I deserved that. I shouldn't have let her go. But you punch me again, and I'll not forgive you a second time.'

''Ere we go, cocky bollocks.'

'Shut your mouth and listen, Cas,' spat Dottie, tapping her fingers against her arm. 'Listen to him.'

Cas turned to face Billy.

Billy pointed to the lad curled up on the ground, who, to his relief, was still alive. 'I came here to tell you this: I don't think he killed her.'

'Bollocks!' Cas's eyes flicked to Danny, his expression hardening again.

Quickly, Billy raised his hands to stop him from acting on his anger. 'Listen, I don't like that prick either, but I'm pretty sure I saw him driving home. I think he passed us on the country lanes.'

'What? Alone was he?' Cas demanded, impatience lacing his words.

'Yes, but like I said, I don't think he killed Willow,' Billy insisted. 'I think . . . I think I saw her. I think I saw someone, anyway. Whoever it was, they were running across a field.'

Cas clenched his fists. 'So why didn't you go after her, eh? Eh? You saw her, and you left her to be slaughtered by whoever.' He took a step forward, his body tensing as if he was ready to launch himself at Billy again.

However, Dottie stood in a threatening stance. And the knife was still in her hand.

'Put that fucking thing away or I'll forget I'm a decent bloke.'

'Cas, please listen to me,' begged Billy. 'I didn't know it was her. My eyes were playing tricks with me. I've replayed that scene a hundred times thinking I must have been wrong and that all I saw was an animal or a bush blowing in the wind. So, at the time, I was confused. But now, I'm not. I'm pretty sure it was Willow. Hurting Danny, though, won't bring her back.'

'Hurting him, hurting him? I was in the process of tenderising the meat on him before I killed the scrawny little cunt.'

'It won't help us find out who really did this, though, will it?'

Glaring at Billy, Cas's chest heaved with anger, but, eventually, the truth of Billy's words seemed to reach him. Slowly, the fight drained out of him, leaving only a man overwhelmed by grief and rage.

Finally lowering her knife, her right hand trembling slightly, Dottie ensured that her eyes never left Cas.

'Well, the cunt deserved a good kicking for leaving my baby in that field, and that's the truth of it,' Cas spat.

Still rubbing his forehead, Billy asked, 'What did he say happened?'

Cas rolled his eyes, his shoulders sagging with frustration. 'He said she stormed off after they'd had a row, and he drove around for fifteen minutes but couldn't find her. But that's probably a load of bullshit.' He paused, his gaze hardening as he pointed from Billy to Dottie. 'And I'll tell you this: if it turns out that he *did* kill my Willow, I'll come for you two as well, for stopping me.'

Tightening her grip on her knife, Dottie held her ground, her eyes continually locked on Cas. 'If you find out he did it, I won't stop you from annihilating him. But until then, you need to keep your head on straight, Cas. You go off half-cocked, and you'll lose any chance of getting real justice for Willow.'

Billy nodded in agreement, still feeling the sting of Cas's punch but now more concerned about the bigger picture. 'We all want to find out what really happened, Cas. But beating Danny to death won't get us any closer to the truth. I for one don't believe he killed her.'

CHAPTER TEN

Keith was still stunned by Billy's strength. Being literally pushed over by a fifteen-year-old also made him question his own agility. *Were his days of fighting coming to an end?* he asked himself. He had actually thought about this some months ago. His bones ached, something that had never happened to him before. And it seemed that with his strength weakening, so his desire for violence was diminishing. It was a far cry from when he'd been a youngster, when even at the tender age of five he'd had to fight in order to survive.

***

His mind quickly recalled his younger scrapping days when he'd forged a relationship with Cas. It had all begun when Cas approached him after watching him brutally beat up one of Cas's men in a back-alley brawl.

He could still picture that particular night.

Cas was dressed in a long coat that was opened to show a fitted suit with a bright-pink shirt. He'd appeared from the shadows as cocky as hell. Wearing his own inimitable style of apparel – or what he considered to be a cut above the rest – he was not only comfortable in his own skin but he didn't give a shit about what people thought of him. With a cigarette perched at the corner of his mouth, he slowly clapped and chuckled. 'So, I see, you've fucked up my supposedly strongest man – good and proper an' all.'

Keith recalled the intense moment as if it was yesterday. He didn't react to Cas's obvious signs of approval. Instead, he silently looked on as Cas stopped laughing and blew out a thick plume of smoke, unaware at that moment that Cas was sizing him up.

Having heard of Cas's reputation and seen him across a bar once, he had never actually spoken to him. He knew, though, that he couldn't just stand there dripping in blood and shaking in his boots. He had to respond. 'He knocked me pint over and refused to replace it. He got lairy, offered me out, so I gave him what he asked for. So do you have a problem with that? Only, I don't see it is any of your business.'

'Quick with your fists and your mouth, eh? And yeah, mate, it *is* my business. He's one of my men.' Cas pointed to the man lying out cold on the ground. 'And now, I bet he won't be able to walk and talk at the same time. Jesus, I thought I was gonna have a good day! But you just went and pissed all over my chips.' He threw his hands in the air. 'For fuck's sake, now I'm gonna have to get me own hands dirty. Fuck it! I hate getting my best suit mucked up!'

Keith recalled clenching his fists, ready to go another round, this time with Cas. But he was wrong.

When Cas turned on his heel, seemingly about to walk away, he suddenly spun back, stepping forward into the light of a streetlamp.

Keith saw the cheeky grin spread across Cas's face before he noticed him reaching into the deep pockets of his long coat and whipping out a wad of cash.

Cas repeatedly slapped the large chunk of cash against his open palm. 'Who do you work for, eh? . . . And what's your name?'

'I work for no one, and my name's Keith.'

'Wanna work for me? I could use you. 'Cos, look at that cunt. He thinks he's Hong Kong Phooey, but he's as useful as fucking special fried rice without all the prawns and shit.

S'posed to be part of the Triads. My arse.' He frowned. 'He's made a bit of a mess of your face, though, mate.'

Keith didn't need to be told. His face had been cut to ribbons.

The Chinese guy had unexpectedly pulled out a cutthroat razor, and, in a flash, he'd swiped his cheek a few times before he'd even managed to get a punch in. But once he launched his right hook – something of a speciality of his – and caught the man on the chin – he didn't stop and wouldn't until the man was practically paralysed from the neck down. For two reasons: one, he knew his face, which although not strikingly handsome, was butchered, so his chances of a Saturday night shag were over anyway, and two, he didn't like men taking liberties. Toe to toe meant fist to fist, not fucking knives. Still, the wannabe Triad was in a sorry state by the time he'd finished with him.

'So, tell me, Keith, how come you didn't leg it? I mean, you don't look to be tooled up. Most geezers would run if some cunt flashed a knife at them.'

'I'm not most geezers, and dying doesn't scare me. I won't walk away if there's a point of principle involved.'

At that moment, as they stared at each other for a second or two, an unspoken connection was forged. Years later, Cas admitted to Keith that he had admired and respected him from that day. He realised that Keith wasn't just bluffing. Unlike most people, who claimed not to fear death, Keith had actually meant it, which set him apart from all the other wannabe heroes.

Amused by Cas's quick wit and fairness in the face of what most people would describe as a horrific situation, Keith began to warm to the man. From a very young age, he'd learned that people could be 'smiling knives,' but he also knew how to distinguish those who weren't. At that moment, when their eyes locked, he didn't see Cas as that kind of person.

And Keith knew what he was looking for. He'd had a lifetime of experience. His own family had been the cruellest people he'd ever known, so fighting to survive, literally from the age of five, was all he knew. He'd been offered money to fight before and had always believed he had nothing to lose. So when Cas had flashed a wad of notes under his nose and offered him a position as his right-hand man, he'd grabbed the opportunity with both hands. The main part of the job was roughing people up, a role he actually enjoyed. Fighting was all he knew, so getting a regular wage just to be on standby and follow Cas around was a doddle.

***

But now, after being knocked down by a mere shove from a fifteen-year-old, he wondered if he still had a job. The thought of starting over made him shudder. Over the years, his relationship with Cas had become tight. He was Cas's right-hand man, all right, and trusted above all else. He even had his own pad in the attached annexe, with a free run of the grounds, which included a stunning rose garden and breathtaking views.

He glanced at Cas wondering if he was thinking the same. Was this the end of his employment? But what he saw instead was the anguish etched across his face. The poor man had doted on his granddaughter, and from this day, Keith knew Cas would change. He would either age rapidly, giving in to becoming a pensioner, or he would go insane with anger. But as much as Cas was a violent gangster, he did have a fair side. However, today hadn't been one of his fair days. Today, he had wanted to torture and kill Danny.

When Cas discovered Willow had gone off with Danny Slade, he knew exactly where to go. The Slade family was familiar to him. The old man Vic Slade had been a face on the scene many moons ago, and Cas knew he had sons, one of them being Danny.

He and Cas were outside the Slades' house within minutes, only to find Danny sitting in his car and counting a few pound notes while listening to music. He hadn't expected to be bundled into the back of a car with a sack over his head, with Cas demanding to know where Willow was.

They drove Danny back to the house and handcuffed him to a post in the tack room, intending to release him, once Willow was home safe and sound. Cas also planned to give him a little reminder about treating a girl with respect and bringing her home properly.

Unable to sit still and wait, Cas drove to his daughter's house on the off chance that Willow had gone there without telling him or her father. But as soon as he arrived, it was clear that she wasn't there. It was a wild idea anyway. Everyone knew that Willow hated her mother for leaving her, so, in reality, that would have been the last place she would go. However, by the time he reached Tara's house, Lolly called to say that the police had found Willow's body. Now, they were searching for Danny Slade, the last person known to have seen her alive.

He'd almost begged Cas not to kill Danny outright. Instead, he'd urged him to get the truth out of him first. Lolly would want to know what had happened to his daughter in her final minutes, and killing Danny wouldn't get them any answers.

Initially, Cas had agreed and had started to question the terrified lad, who had pleaded and sworn blind that he hadn't hurt Willow. It wasn't him.

But as Cas's frustration peaked, he dragged Danny into Goliath's empty stall. It was Willow's beloved horse, who no one could handle, except her. Goliath loved to be ridden, but no one dared enter his domain when he was inside.

Danny had no idea what torture Cas was going to inflict on him, but he could only guess it would be messy. Why else would he have been dragged to a stables? He couldn't even move his lips. His eyes bulged in fear, and he held his hands to his ears.

***

In a momentary flashback, Keith saw himself at five years old. His father, a big man with whisky breath and a vile temper, towered over him with a leather belt raised high above his head.

He was demanding that his son get into the stranger's car. Struck by terror, he couldn't move. Just like Danny, fear had compelled him to freeze on the spot, cowering in the corner. His voice became strangled, his cheek throbbed from the sting of the belt, and his skin was red and burning from the beating. While he crouched down in agony, all he could see was this stranger standing behind his father and chortling with glee.

***

Keith snapped out of his haunting recollection when Cas bellowed to him to bring Goliath into the stall. Just the name of the horse could instil fear in anyone. And seeing the sheer size of Goliath and knowing he was being brought there for a reason when it wasn't for a riding lesson would terrify anyone, especially a teenager being accused of murdering a gangster's granddaughter.

As he led Goliath happily into his stall because it usually meant his mealtime or treats, he then saw the horror on Danny's face, and the wave of nausea hitting him.

Cas had turned into the circus ringmaster by standing on the ledge of the stall and peering over as if he was about to feed a live antelope to a lion.

Cas's sudden high-pitched voice made him wonder if his boss had indeed gone as mad as the horse.

The first kick caught Danny's arm, and his scream was so loud it nearly pierced Keith's eardrums.

Cas yelled, 'Go on, there's a good boy, Goliath! Kill the bastard!'

***

Amid the noise and chaos, they hadn't heard Dottie or Billy until they were upon them. Keith certainly didn't see Billy until he was pushed to the ground and the reins snatched away from him. By the time he'd got to his feet, the horse was in the distance, still bucking, while Danny squirmed around in the horse muck, probably not as badly injured as he'd first thought.

Keith studied the boy. There was some blood coming from his forehead, and his face was swollen, but he was conscious.

But what surprised Keith was what happened next. After Billy had convinced Cas not to kill Danny, it wasn't Dottie who had gone to Danny's aid but Billy.

'Can you get up, Danny?' Billy asked.

Danny used Billy as a crutch to get to his feet, his arm around Billy's shoulder, gripping him as if his life depended on it. 'Thank you,' he whispered.

'Do you need to go to the hospital?'

'I just want to go home.'

Suddenly, Cas was in Danny's face, jabbing a finger deep into the lad's swollen cheek. 'If I find out you killed my baby, I'll do worse than let Goliath kick you to death. I'll torture your sorry arse for a month. Believe me, you'll be begging to die. Understand?'

Danny's nails dug into Billy's shoulder as his body tensed up. He wasn't taking the threat lightly. He was genuinely terrified of Cas.

Billy looked at Cas and nodded. 'He won't say a word, will you, Danny?'

Danny frowned. 'I don't understand why I was brought here.'

Billy removed Danny's arm from his shoulder and turned to face him. 'You came here of your own free will looking for Willow. You got kicked unconscious by her horse. Right?'

Danny nodded. He would have agreed to anything, just to get away, if he could.

Dottie shook her head. 'Hold up! The police know you left your car outside your house. They found it with the door still open because we all assumed you'd scarpered. So, they will know that's a lie.'

'Oh, 'ark at fucking Miss Marple 'ere,' said Cas, still annoyed that he'd backed down to a woman.

'Well, Mr Corleone, what the hell do you suggest?'

Cas rolled his eyes and gave Dottie one of his cheeky grins. 'Fair enough.'

'The battery will be drained now,' said Danny. 'I left the keys in the ignition, the lights and the radio on. Me battery always dies.'

'Good, so you say you flagged down a random taxi to take you to my place and went fucking nosing around and got kicked by a horse!'

Danny nodded again. His face was even more swollen.

'Are you sure you don't need the hospital? Because you look like the Elephant Man,' said Billy.

'I just want to go home.'

'They'll arrest ya, Danny, so you'll spend hours in a police cell. Hospital's your best bet for now,' said Billy, shaking his head in dismay.

Danny nodded once more. 'Okay.'

‘If you so much as squeal like a piggy, I’ll hunt ya down, and—’ hissed Cas.

‘I won’t, I promise,’ Danny said, as he gently fingered his swollen cheek and dented forehead.

‘Hmm, ya’d better fucking not.’

Feeling embarrassed, Keith led Danny to his car, leaving Billy, Dottie, and Cas alone. He wanted his own space to give himself time to think and to make plans for his future. He was no doubt out of a job. But as much as he liked Cas, he wouldn’t give the man the satisfaction of firing him. He would leave quietly, probably in the dead of night.

***

‘If I find out—’

‘Cas,’ Billy interrupted, ‘I’ll kill him myself.’

Dottie hoped that these were just teenage fighting words, thinly veiled threats, but the look in her son’s eyes made her wonder.

‘You’re convinced he didn’t hurt her . . .’ Cas paused, choking on a sob lodged in his throat. ‘I need a drink.’ He stormed off across the grounds, towards the open French doors.

Dottie and Billy followed.

As soon as they reached the house, Dottie stopped Billy. ‘Shall we just go home? Let’s leave the man to grieve.’

But Billy was stunned, almost indignant, his eyes suddenly dark. ‘No, Mottie, I’m not letting this go. That copper is responsible. It had to be him, and I can’t do this without Cas’s help. He has the right to know.’

Dottie didn’t argue; it was futile. If there was one thing she knew about Billy, it was that when he was determined, he would follow through regardless of anyone else’s opinion.

By the time they caught up with Cas, he had already poured himself a large brandy and was sitting at his desk. His eyes were red and his expression sullen.

'Want one, Dottie?'

She smiled, compassionately. 'No, I'm driving. Cas, um . . .'

He looked up. 'Go on, spit it out. I'm not stupid, Dottie. Billy has another reason for believing that the lanky cunt didn't kill my Willow. So speak.'

Dottie and Billy were both shocked. They had underestimated Cas's ability to read people, to see through their personas and body language, and to know when they were holding something back.

'I went back, Cas, to a field, to see if it was Willow, who I thought may have been the movement in the field. I thought I might find her walking home . . .' Billy paused, struggling to control his emotions. 'I expected her to come traipsing back with that stroppy head on. You know what I mean.'

Cas nodded, his face stern and cold. 'Go on.'

'This copper stopped me. He tried to get me in his car.'

Cas placed his glass down on his desk and inclined his head. '*What?*'

Dottie walked over to the drinks cabinet while Cas's eyes followed her.

'Sorry, Cas, I *will* have that drink.'

He nodded. 'Sure, love, go ahead. Knock yourself out.'

'He pulled out a knife, tried to get me in the car, and he said he'd find something to nick me for, if I didn't get in.'

'How did you get away?' Cas asked, rolling his eyes, as if this was some fabricated tale.

'I kicked him in the bollocks, ran through a field, doubled back, and rode home.'

'Are you sure you weren't dreaming? Coppers don't pull out knives. They might pull out a truncheon or slap handcuffs on you, but a knife?'

Billy nodded. 'I know it sounds mental. I don't blame you for thinking I'm nuts. But listen. The copper pulled the three of us over when we left Bluewater. He checked my cousin's licence and let us go. It was the *same* copper, all right.'

Cas shrugged. 'So?'

'I told the detective that we were stopped by a copper, but I didn't tell them I went back and saw the *same* copper. I left that bit out.'

Billy could tell Cas was getting impatient.

'But get this. When the detective asked me about the car, I said it was a jam sandwich.'

Again, Cas shrugged.

'They asked me if I was sure, and then one of the detectives went outside to radio through.'

Billy had now caught Cas's attention; he could see his eyes widen.

Cas leaped up from his high-backed chair and hurried from the room without explanation.

Dottie frowned. 'What is this about the police car?'

'Well, evidently something, because he had the same reaction as the detectives.'

When Cas returned, he sat down, swigged the last of his brandy, and glared at Billy. 'You're either fucking lying—'

'He's not, Cas.'

Cas nodded. 'Or some cunt's playing policeman or this copper ain't from Kent because Kent just replaced their fleet with new Battenburg markings. As soon as you said *jam sandwich*, I thought, what? I'm sure I've seen the new police cars, and my pal just confirmed it.' He stared into space for a minute. 'What did the copper look like?'

‘Five foot seven or eight, fat, like big belly fat, rolls of fat around his neck. I think he was bald, and he had a mole on his left cheek.’

Snatching a pen and a notepad, Cas hurriedly wrote down some details.

‘Accent?’

‘Southern. I think I detected a slight Romany twang. I could be wrong, though.’

‘Did the detectives ask you for a detailed description?’

‘No, Cas, not really.’

‘Wankers. I bet they didn’t, ’cos they think it’s one of their own.’

‘What was the number plate?’

‘I don’t know.’

‘You what? You daft prick.’

‘Cas, I was crawling through a wheat field with a nutty copper trying to find me.’

‘Hmmm, well, for future reference, always clock a number plate. Right, now fuck off home. I’ve got work to do.’

CHAPTER ELEVEN

Arriving back at Cas Ferrier's mansion, Keith sat still in his black Mercedes S-Class, which, as it happened, was the same one he'd had since first setting eyes on Billy Murphy. Why Billy had come into his thoughts he wasn't quite sure. But it seemed that the young lad had made a huge impression on him. Recalling the conversation they'd had when he drove the boy home in Cas's Bentley Azure three years ago, Billy had shown extraordinary strength of mind. So, he mused, perhaps he shouldn't have been so surprised that now Billy was much older, he also had the physical strength as well. But being pushed over by someone nearly fifty years younger than him was not something he wanted to dwell on. It had been a wake-up call all right, that was for sure.

Shaking his head in disbelief that he seemed to be having serious doubts about his ability to be the master of his own destiny, he stepped out of his car. The only sound breaking the heavy silence of his grief was the gravel crunching under his feet as he walked across the drive to his annexe at the side of the main house.

Though attached, the annexe had its own front door. Opening the door quietly, trying not to disturb the night, guilt clung like a shadow. He'd planned to pack his bags and slip away unnoticed. He had enough money, and at least his self-respect would remain intact.

But as soon as he stepped into his small tidy living room, he stopped dead. Sitting in his favourite armchair was Cas, with a drink in one hand and a cigarette in the other. Cas's head was tilted back, his eyes focused on some distant point on the ceiling, until, slowly, he sat up straight and turned his gaze towards him.

'How did it go, mate?'

Keith didn't like the way Cas said *mate*. The tone was stern, almost dismissive, and *mate* was tacked on out of habit rather than out of affection.

'I left him at the entrance to A&E,' Keith replied. 'I warned him you'd remove his whole family if he even thought about grassing you up.'

Cas nodded slowly, then he downed the rest of his drink. 'You know, Keith, I would've given Willow the world. She was the apple of my eye, and now my life will never be the same.'

Keith felt his eyes welling up, but he brushed the tears away and poured himself a drink. He wondered if leaving now, for the sake of his dignity, was really the right thing to do. 'I know how you feel.' When the words left his mouth, he wished he could take them back. Cas, it seemed, was in one of his argumentative moods.

'You have *no idea* how I fucking feel, Keith. None whatsoever. You've never had kids, let alone a beautiful, kind, loving, sweet granddaughter like mine.'

Keith's right hand trembled as he picked up a glass and tried to pour a generous measure from the fine bottle of brandy that took pride of place on the sideboard. With his glass half full, he gripped it to hold back a rising tide of emotions.

'You wouldn't know a fucking thing about grieving for a child, so don't you ever tell me you know how *I* fucking feel.'

In a flash, Keith slammed the glass down on the sideboard, and the brandy splashed everywhere. Turning sharply to face Cas, his eyes filling with tears, his mood shifted dramatically.

'I've worked for you for most of my life. I've stood by you like a brother and cared for your family as if they were my own.' He wiped the snot from his nose with the back of his hand, but the tears didn't let up. 'I loved Willow as much as you did, whether you believe it or not. Who did you hand Willow to when she was born, eh? Eh?' He poked himself in the chest. 'Me! When Tara couldn't cope, you said you'd babysit, but who was it really doing the babysitting?' He jabbed his chest again. 'Me, Cas, fucking me. I changed her nappies, I fed her, I had her sleeping on my chest, and what the fuck did you do?' His chest heaved with each breath. 'I'll tell you what you did. You went out on the piss. You bought her everything she needed, but you didn't look after her like I did. Willow was *my* world, Cas. You may have bought her the horse, but it was me who taught her to ride.'

Suddenly, Cas's face changed. With the weight of reality pulling down his features, he slumped in the chair. There was no point in denying it: Keith had never spoken a truer word.

But Keith hadn't finished. 'Cas, I get that you're angry, frustrated, and grieving. I know you loved her, but don't you fucking tell me I don't know what it feels like to lose someone like Willow,' he said, his voice steady but still laced with emotion. Watching Cas closely, he searched for any sign of understanding in the man's hardened expression. But there was none.

A moment of silence existed between them. It was a heavy pause that felt as though it had stretched out for ever.

Finally, Keith broke the tension by pouring another drink and refilling Cas's glass. The clink of the bottle against the glass was the only sound in the room.

Cas stared into his drink before speaking, his voice low and almost hesitant. 'She wasn't even mine. You do know that, don't you, Keith?'

Taken aback by what seemed like such an odd question, Keith blinked, now totally gobsmacked. '*What?*'

'Yeah, it's all in that black briefcase I keep in my bedroom. But I used to keep it in the study before that Carson prick nicked it and Billy returned it. I can see now that you never looked through it, did you? You only knew what the DNA results were for that cunt Brian Colt. You never looked at Tara's, though, did you?'

Keith was stunned. 'No. But why would I look at your private paperwork?'

'I dunno. Maybe to see if I was going to leave you anything in my will. I mean, if it was the other way around, I've no doubt I would have had a butcher's.'

Keith rolled his eyes, trying to shake off the absurdity of the situation. 'I would never expect that. I'm just your employee, Cas, nothing more.'

'See,' said Cas, pointing a finger at Keith, 'see, right there, that really hurts me, Keith. That comment cuts me like a knife because I don't see you as just *my employee*.'

Cas's expression softened, and a rare genuine smile, which was tinged with sorrow, now played about his lips. 'I saw what happened today. Billy took you down.'

'Well, not exactly. He didn't actually take me down, did he. He pushed me over, but—'

'You would never have gone down like that a few years back, Keith.'

'I know, Cas. That's why I've decided to resign. I was going to leave, but I thought I'd hang around for a bit, just to make sure you're okay, and then I'd go.'

Cas nodded slowly, his gaze dropping to the floor. 'I thought as much. I saw the look on your face at the time. It wasn't so much a look of anger but a gutted expression, if you know what I mean. So I kinda guessed you would question your ability to do what you're paid to do.'

Keith nodded in agreement. At this moment, his self-worth was the last thing on his mind.

'I like to think we've been proper mates,' Cas continued. 'Like brothers, because that's how I see us, Keith. And just so we're clear, I haven't asked you to graze your knuckles for fucking what . . . ten years now.'

Keith sipped his brandy, the warmth of the drink spreading through him, as he listened.

'We're a bit like an old married couple, me and you,' Cas said, with a chuckle. 'Christ, when was the last time I put anyone on their arse, eh? I'd break a fucking bone or need a hip replacement. I even worry about farting too hard, in case I end up paralysed from the waist down. All this getting old ain't bleedin' fun. And you're the same. I see how you walk sometimes, like you've shit yourself. No doubt it's arthritis.'

Keith couldn't help but smile slightly at Cas's attempt at humour, even amid their heavy conversation. He nodded again.

'I know you loved Willow,' Cas said. 'I know you did. I'm just angry. I'm sorry. I shouldn't have taken my anger out on you.'

Keith's eyes widened in surprise. Not once had he ever heard Cas apologise. Not like this. In fact, not in all the years they'd known each other. The sincerity in the man's voice actually felt rather touching.

'I mean it, Keith,' Cas continued. 'I've been a bastard, and I know it. But I need you to know that I appreciate everything you've done for me and my family. For Willow, especially. Granted, she had some of her mother's traits. She could be a cow – like Tara – and she was wild.' Cas huffed and then gave a short laugh. 'And I had the fucking audacity to tell Billy to take care of her.' He sipped his brandy. 'You know what, Keith? That Billy came suited and booted as though he was taking her on her first date. The lad showed up with all good intentions. It wasn't as if he was itching to get into her knickers, like all the other lads.'

'She wasn't like that, Cas. She was a good kid. Yeah, she was a mouthy little thing, but she was a genuine person.'

Cas shook his head. 'Nah, she wasn't. I'm not gonna pretend she was the Virgin Mary, not to you. I heard her chatting to some bloke on the phone, and I didn't like it one bit. She was too womanly, too provocative.'

'*Really?*'

'Yeah, I pulled her up on it, and she looked me up and down like I was nothing to her, like a bit of shit, and she said, "Oh, fuck off, Grandad. It ain't like it was in your day. Us women . . ." His voice went up a notch. '"We're independent and can do what we want. It's all changed. So, if I wanna go with a boy, I fucking will. We're not like the women in your days, all subservient in long dresses and big hats."' He sighed. 'She thought I was a hundred years old. Anyway, I realised then that she was never going to be tamed. As I said earlier, she was wild. So that got me thinking. I just needed to somehow protect her, but short of getting her a bodyguard, what do you do? And now . . . well, now she's gone.'

Keith didn't say a word. He knew what Willow was really like. He'd caught her in the barn snogging the face off of the livery hand. And she'd been only fourteen at the time. He'd punched the teenage boy in the face and booted him down the drive but he'd never told Cas because he didn't think it warranted taking the boy's life.

After finishing the last of the brandy, Cas pushed himself out of the armchair, a small sad smile tugging at the corners of his mouth as he looked at Keith. 'So, don't you be packing your bags. I've got too much work to do, and I need my right-hand man, but not for any violent activity, mind you.' He winked, the tension between them easing slightly.

Keith nodded. 'Can I ask, did you always suspect that Tara wasn't yours?'

Cas sighed, his smile fading as he considered the question. 'Yeah, I did. I mean, look at her. She's tall and blonde. But her mother wasn't, was she, God rest her soul. She was a short arse with jet-black hair. And me? I've always been of average size with what you'd call a handsome disposition. So, yeah, it played on my mind, but her mother's dead and buried, so I left it at that. I raised Tara as if she was my own, even though she turned out to be a proper cow. But she was *my* cow.'

Cas's face grew grave, his usual bravado replaced with a rare moment of vulnerability. 'Tara never really loved Willow, you know. I watched how she was with her. Yeah, she dressed her in pretty dresses and posed as the perfect mother in front of people. But behind closed doors, she wasn't. Poor Lolly, he was a good dad to Willow. I suppose he made up for Tara's bastard ways.'

Taking a deep breath, Cas's voice faltered as he continued. 'I was with Tara when we got the call that . . . that my Willow was dead. And I swear to God, I expected Tara to collapse in hysterics. To react as though she was devastated. But she didn't. She cried a few crocodile tears and let that new fella of hers, the ugly wanker, hug her. She didn't even let *me* hug her, though. Everything with her is for show. I drove back, Keith, gutted. In fact, I was so fucking gutted that I felt like I'd lost *both* my girls in the click of my stubby fat fingers.'

'Listen, Cas, stop thinking about that,' Keith said, trying to steer the conversation more productively. 'Let's focus on finding the cunt who's responsible—'

'Oh yeah, some copper or a cunt in a costume, probably, is a likely suspect,' Cas said.

'*What!*' Keith screeched, his eyes wide with shock. 'And you didn't think to tell me when I walked through the front door?'

Dismissively, Cas waved his hand. 'Well, I'm telling you now, ain't I. Anyway, I've been on the blower to my pal in the nick, ol' Robson, and he's doing some digging for us. I told him I wanted every bit of information flying around the station regarding my . . . I mean *our* Willow. So that's your next job, Keith.'

Keith nodded, his mind already turning to the task at hand. 'Go on.'

'Yeah, take a monkey around to his missus. The address is on my kitchen table. Tell her I'll have the other half for her tomorrow.'

Keith's lips tightened into a thin line as he absorbed the instructions. He stood up, ready to leave, but he couldn't help but glance back at Cas, who was already reaching for another drink.

'Cas,' Keith began, his voice firm, 'I may not be as strong as I was, but if I catch the bastard, you know what I'm going to do, don't you. I will kill him.'

Cas shook his head. 'Not before I spend a good few weeks torturing the cunt.' He winked. 'Like we used to, back in the day. Ain't that right.'

CHAPTER TWELVE

12 July

The following evening was solemn. Sunny sat in the kitchen with Carrie. Sitting next to them were Billy and Dottie. Nellie and Charlie were in the lounge watching a movie quietly with the volume kept low, out of respect for the situation.

Billy could only manage a slice of toast and a glass of milk. His stomach was in knots as he tried to process everything that had happened in the last forty-eight hours. Of course, he had to explain things, as Dottie had urged him to. She hated keeping secrets from Carrie.

Carrie had immediately gone into her usual animated angry self, fuming that some copper, or whatever he was, had tried to haul her son into a car.

Sunny, staying calmer, pulled Carrie back onto her chair, urging her to listen and not launch a single-handed rampage through Kent to find the bloke herself. Once he managed to keep her seated, the conversation turned to what to do next, especially since Jesse and Ross had gone off to do some investigating themselves.

Everyone had assumed Danny was responsible, so they had been on a mission to find him and bring him to justice.

But things changed when Billy told his parents where he'd been and what he'd been up to. When Billy told them about how he and Dottie had witnessed Danny sustaining injuries from Willow's horse, at the direction of Cas, Carrie and Sunny were flummoxed. Billy then told them that had he and Dottie arrived at the scene just a minute later, Danny would have been carted off the estate in a hearse, not an ambulance.

'Seriously?' Sunny said. 'Cas was gonna kill Danny? Jesus Christ, no one knows if Danny killed her or not yet. Fuck me, Cas is a proper maniac.'

'That's what grief does to you, though, Sunny,' Carrie replied. 'That old man wants blood. It's his granddaughter, for Christ's sake. I'd be the same if it was my Nellie.'

'It was almost certainly not Danny, though,' Billy insisted. 'I saw him driving back, like I told you, and I'm sure now I saw Willow running across that field. And then, with the copper trying to drag me into his car, I'm ninety-nine per cent sure it wasn't Danny who killed her. It was the copper. You should have seen his face. It scared me.'

Carrie was almost out of her chair again, her mind racing with the thought that some fat paedophile had been trying to hurt her son. 'Seen his face?' she screeched. 'I'll fucking slice the bastard from ear to ear before I cut his bollocks off with a rusty blunt knife!'

'Carrie, sit down, will ya, and drink your tea,' said Sunny, who had spent most of the day consoling Lolly. He was now emotionally exhausted by it all. 'I don't want you going off as well.'

'Well, then, I'd better call Jesse and tell him to come home before he finds that Danny kid and drags him to the police station,' Carrie said, her tone calmer. 'I tell ya what. It's knocked our Jesse sideways hearing that Willow was killed, and that worries me. 'Cos, thinking about it, I'm not sure if he really would drag Danny to the station. I reckon, by the look on his face, he might do the boy some damage.'

Billy frowned. 'Jesse?'

'Yes, love. Your brother seems to have taken it bad. I guess he would, like you, Billy, 'cos you were all mates, weren't ya? You've known her for a few years now, so, of course, it would upset him as well.'

Billy chewed the inside of his lip, replaying Jesse's reaction when Willow had thrown a strop at Bluewater. Jesse had told her straight that she wasn't a good person. He had been so cold towards her. Yet he'd also confessed to him later on that in the recent past, she had been the one who had come on to him. He wished Jesse had told him at the time, not weeks later, or not at all, because what did it matter now, now she was dead?

'Do you mind if I go up? I'm tired. I'm . . . er . . .'

'Sure, Billy boy, you get a good rest. It's all been a right nightmare,' Carrie said, blowing him a kiss. 'Shall I bring up a nice cup of hot chocolate with squirty cream and a few chocolate sprinkles?'

Billy raised an eyebrow. 'Mum, really? I'm not Charlie or even bloody Jesse. I'm fine, thank you.'

Carrie nodded and blew him another kiss. But as soon as he was out of sight, her expression hardened. 'If I get my hands on that copper, I swear I'll kill him, 'cos I've had a lifetime's worth of dealing with the fucking lot of 'em.'

'I'm going home, Carrie. Spud's been left on his own for too long. I might go back to find he's turned my back garden into a rescue centre for Great Danes,' she said, gently stroking Duchess, Jesse's dog.

'All right, love,' said Carrie, getting up from her chair and hugging Dottie. 'Stay safe, my girl.'

Dottie, who rarely embraced anyone, returned the hug. 'Billy's grieving, Carrie, but you know what he's like. He won't openly show it.'

'I know, Dot, he's so reserved, that one.'

No sooner had they said their goodbyes than Carrie noticed that Dottie had left her phone behind. She was about to hurry after her when Jesse and Ross came charging in through the back door. The sound of it slamming shut echoed throughout the house.

Jesse's hair was wild, with strands sticking to the sweat on his forehead, and his right cheek was already swelling with the deep purple of a bruise. His right eye was starting to swell as well, promising a shiner by the morning.

Ross stumbled in behind him, looking even worse. He had blood still dripping from his nose and a deep cut above his brow.

Sunny shot up from his chair. 'Jesus! What the hell happened to you two?'

Carrie was already on her feet, her heart pounding as she rushed to Jesse. She grabbed him by the chin and turned his face from side to side to assess the damage. 'Who did this, eh? I'll bloody—'

'Mum, leave off,' Jesse cut in, his voice rough and tired. 'It was just a fight, that's all.'

'Just a fight?' Carrie bellowed. 'Look at the state of your face! So much for modelling for Hugo Boss. He'll have to look elsewhere.'

The room was filled with a charged silence, the air heavy with worry and unspoken threats. Even Duchess, lying quietly at Sunny's feet, lifted her head, sensing the unease.

Jesse tutted and gently removed his mother's hand. 'I'm fine, Mum.'

'And what about you?' she asked, turning her attention to Ross and taking a closer look at his battered face. 'You might need stitches, boy.'

'A plaster and a drop of Dettol will soon fix me, Carrie,' Ross replied, with a forced grin, although he knew she could tell he was smarting with the pain.

With his patience wearing thin, Sunny tapped his foot impatiently. 'So, then, what happened?'

Before either of the boys could respond, the screeching of tyres could be heard on the drive. It was followed by the abrupt sounds of car doors opening and slamming shut. The noise sent a jolt of adrenaline through those sitting in the kitchen.

Sunny's instincts kicked in, and he bolted into the lounge. Without glancing out of the window, he ushered Charlie and Nellie upstairs with a sense of urgency that left no room for questions. His expression darkened as he hurried back into the hall and turned to face Jesse, who now looked not only battered but terrified, his bravado clearly gone.

'What the fuck's going on, Jesse?' Sunny demanded.

Jesse's eyes darted towards the front door. The noise outside was growing ever louder, and the unmistakable sound of heavy footsteps could be heard approaching the house.

'Jesse! Who the hell is outside that fucking door?' Sunny asked again. This time, his voice sounded more like a growl.

Carrie's anger boiled over. She nearly knocked Jesse and Ross out of the way as she barged down the hallway. Instinctively, she grabbed a golf club from the umbrella stand, her grip tight and her knuckles white.

'I'm opening the front door, and the first person across my threshold will get a mouthful of metal,' she snarled.

Sunny grabbed her arm. 'Don't answer the door. They could have a gun.'

He turned back to Jesse. 'Who are they?'

Jesse's face was a turmoil of guilt and fear, his voice barely above a whisper. 'The Slades. I don't know their first names . . . they're all Danny's brothers. Older brothers. They're much older than Danny, Dad. I mean, they're in their twenties. The Carsons told them that we have Danny.

They reckon we dragged Danny from his car and took him away. Someone told them we were at Bluewater, and they came after us.'

Jesse stopped talking as a loud bang echoed through the house, rattling the front door on its hinges.

'Don't let 'em in, Dad! The big one had a knife,' pleaded Jesse.

Ross, still catching his breath, chimed in, 'It took three of them to muller me and Jesse, and I've never run from a fight, but we had no choice. We flew out of the Bluewater car park, and I drove like Michael Schumacher to get here. I thought I'd lost them.' He glanced at Sunny, guilt etched on his face. 'I'm sorry, Sunny. You don't need this grief.'

Sunny shook his head. 'It ain't your fault.'

Suddenly, Billy's distinctive voice cut through the tension from behind them. 'I'll tell them where Danny is.'

Jesse spun around, his eyes wide. 'There you are! Fucking hell, Billy! How do you know where he is?'

'Keith drove him to the hospital,' Billy replied.

Another loud bang, this time more forceful, was followed by a voice demanding they open the door. The next sound was another screech of tyres as more cars pulled up abruptly, the noise adding to the chaos.

From upstairs, Charlie called down, 'Uncle James and Uncle Dylon have turned up. Oh, hang on. And Spud.'

Carrie's heart eased slightly knowing Charlie must have called the cavalry, and since they lived only minutes away, they had arrived practically on the doorstep before the Slades could force their way in.

The tension in the house shifted as James's deep, gravelly voice hollered, 'Get the fuck away from that door or I'll use each and every one of you like a bowling ball!'

A surge of relief washed over Carrie once she knew her brothers-in-law James, a mountain of a man, and Dylon, who was not much smaller, were out there. Having seen James in action before, she knew that few men would stand a chance if they took a clump from him.

With this new level of confidence, knowing she had solid backup, Carrie yanked the door open before Sunny could stop her. She gripped the golf club tightly, ready to swing it, if need be. She only needed a minor reason. After all, the bigger reason was standing right behind her with a bruised face.

Sunny's immediate instinct was to pull her back, as he mumbled under his breath, 'Here we fucking go again.' His wife was a firecracker with an overeager protective nature, especially if anyone threatened her family. She was already fired up because Jesse had been beaten up.

To their surprise, standing on the doorstep was a woman, her presence instantly commanding attention.

Behind her, James, Dylon, and Spud were already forcing the men back. Of course, the young men looked fearful. They would know precisely who James and Dylon were; they had a reputation for taking no prisoners.

James already had his hand around the thickset tall lad's throat, while Dylon had another one in a headlock. Spud had his right knee firmly digging into the back of the third lad, with him pinned to the ground.

Carrie pulled her arm free from Sunny's grip, her eyes locking on to those of the woman's. They eyed each other in silence, the tension between them thick like two predators coming face to face.

Now assessing the woman, who was probably a good ten years older than herself, Carrie observed that she was still attractive for her age, but she was now clearly worn down with it all, almost certainly from years of stress. Her hair, pulled back tightly, was thinning, though dyed jet black to maintain a semblance of youth. Her high cheekbones added to the sternness of her appearance, giving her a harsh no-fucks-given look.

'Who are you?' Carrie demanded, her voice laced with a readiness to fight. Yet an uneasy feeling crept over her.

Even the woman's narrow catlike eyes had a hardness to them. A cold glint that spoke of a life that had been anything but easy. A jagged scar marred her left cheek, and her bottom lip bore the lumpy remnants of old scar tissue. Carrie clocked the woman's elongated earlobes with slits where quite possibly her Creole earrings had likely once hung, which had probably been torn out during a fight. Dressed in well-worn faded jeans and a shirt that was no nonsense, no frills, and nothing pretty, and with sturdy boots on her feet, the woman sparked a vague recognition in Carrie's mind.

'Where's me son Danny?'

'Your son ain't fucking here, so why don't you spin on your cowboy boots and get off my property before I launch you off it. Coming here with a poxy posse, who do you think you are, eh?' Carrie shot back, her voice as sharp as a blade.

The woman, responded with a sneer. 'I knew you'd have a gob on ya. But I ain't afraid of you, Carrie Ann Verne, or should I say Carson? I want me boy, Carrie, and I'll search your house from top to bottom unless you hand him over.' She turned to her left, casting a venomous glance at James, who had now kicked one of her lads towards the kerb. 'And I don't care that you've got the Murphys ready to fight your battles. They're scum an' all. So just hand him over.'

Carrie's foot tapped with barely contained rage, her grip tightening on the golf club, ready to swing it. But something about the way the woman curled her bottom lip, and that familiar snarl, jolted her memory. A cold feeling crept over her. Goosebumps coated her arms and her blood felt as though it was turning to ice.

'Donna Carson,' Carrie murmured, her words trailing off as fear replaced her anger. She swallowed hard.

Donna nodded slowly, her bottom lip curling further into a vicious grimace. 'That's right, Carrie. Remember me now, then, do ya? But I'm Donna Slade now.'

Carrie knew exactly who Donna was. Everyone did. But everyone also assumed she was rotting in prison for the brawl in Catford, where she'd blinded a man, given two women the Glasgow smile, and sliced another woman from throat to stomach. Though, miraculously, she'd survived. Donna had a reputation for being one of the hardest women in South East London.

'I thought . . .'

'Yeah, you and the rest of them thought I'd die in prison. Well, you were all wrong. I got out years ago. But, believe me, I'd do time again. Now, where's me boy?'

Before Carrie could respond, Billy stepped forward. 'He isn't here. Like my mum said.'

Donna's eyes darted from Carrie to Billy, narrowing, as she assessed him. 'I see you're a Carson.'

'I'm not. I'm a Murphy, and I'm not interested in dredging up old shit about my family history. Your son is in Pembury Hospital. He got kicked in the head by a horse. Now, call your sons off, and my advice would be to phone the hospital.' Billy didn't flinch as he held her unwavering stare.

Donna glanced over her shoulder to the tall well-built man in his mid-twenties who bore a striking resemblance to Danny. He was now standing a safe distance away from James.

Billy guessed he was a relative.

'You got ya phone, Kieron? Call the hospital, will ya? See if our boy ain't there.' She spun back around, glaring at Billy. 'You don't wanna be lying, 'cos one of me boys will 'ave ya, or I will, and your muvver knows I will, don't ya, Carrie?'

But before Carrie could respond, a cold familiar voice cut through the tension behind Donna, causing Billy to grin.

'Well, fucking well, if it isn't Donna Slade,' came the voice of Dottie Ellis, as she swanned up the path, moving with stealthlike grace.

Even Carrie was stunned that someone like Dottie would know a person like Donna, but then it dawned on her. They had probably met in prison.

The look on Donna's face was priceless. As she slowly turned to meet Dottie, the blood drained from her face, and her cocky demeanour vanished. It was replaced by the wide-eyed fear of a deer caught in headlights.

'Giving my boy a bit of stick, are you, Donna?' Dottie's voice was cutting.

Donna looked at Billy, then back at Dottie. Confusion flickered in her eyes as she tried to piece together the relationship between Dottie and the boy.

Carrie noticed the change in Dottie's expression. It was a look of death that she recognised all too well. It was the same look Dottie had had when she'd cold-bloodedly killed Albert Carson, and, she guessed, it was probably the same expression she'd shown when she killed her parents. It was a look that meant business, one that could make the hardest of souls think twice about crossing her.

Billy's chest swelled with pride as he watched Dottie, his natural mother, reduce this hard-faced woman – who had clearly made Carrie feel uneasy – to a crumbling mess with just a single glare. The woman who had stormed in with her posse, demanding answers and throwing threats, was visibly shaken, her bravado instantly stripped away.

Dottie took a step forward, her presence alone enough to make Donna flinch. 'Now, Donna, are you going to listen, or do I need to remind you why I'm the last person you want to mess with?'

Donna didn't reply. She simply nodded, the fight having gone out of her.

Still gripping the golf club, Carrie found herself in awe of Dottie's ability to command fear and respect in equal measure.

'Billy said your son was in the hospital. So what are you still doing here on Carrie's doorstep?'

Donna stepped back, still shocked that she was face to face with Dottie. Half of Holloway Prison had feared the girl. There was always that dark stare that spoke volumes. She was a killer, the type of psychopath that had no fear, and, once again, here she was, as bold as brass, with that death stare and her cool-as-a-cucumber tone. It was like the calm before the storm.

Then the pieces fell into place. Her Aunt Ginty had consistently moaned about how Carrie and Sunny had adopted Jimmy's two sons and brought them up as their own, even though one of them was actually the son of a woman called Dorothy Ellis. She had never listened much when Ginty droned on and on about how hard done by she was and how she was so alone since her sons were inside because of the Murphys and Cas Ferrier, the reckless and ruthless gangster. Even her husband knew of Cas and had crossed paths with him a few times back in the days of pavement work. Robbing security vans had been their bread and butter until Cas had moved on to bigger things, while her husband had settled for selling knocked-off gear. And, of course, she hadn't heard the last of her husband being done out of a substantial amount of money over the pub robbery a few years back.

Donna glanced back at her son. 'Did you call the hospital?'

Kieron nodded, biting his bottom lip. 'He's there.'

Donna, though visibly nervous, couldn't resist a final jibe. She looked back at Carrie, and for a moment, her lip curled into a smirk. 'Shame about Willow being murdered. Poor Cas must be devastated, losing a family member like that.'

'What the hell is that supposed to mean?' Carrie snapped, taking a step forward, nostrils flaring, as she squared up to Donna.

'Nuffin, I was just saying, that's all,' she replied, before looking Dottie up and down and then scooting back along the garden path towards her sons.

Billy smiled inwardly, but as he turned and saw the state of his brother's face, rage exploded within him. In a flash, he launched himself off the steps, yelling, 'Which one of you cowards did that to me brother's face, eh?'

'Just leave it,' Jesse called out, rushing to pull his brother away.

The three young men responsible averted their eyes, not out of fear of Billy but because of the inevitable reprisal from James.

'If you wanna fight, we'll fight, but let's make it a fair one.' Billy's mouth foamed at the sides, his eyes darkening with fury. 'Come on, then, you fucking shitbags. Three on two ain't fair in my book. How about three on three? Yeah, come on. Who wants to have it?' He ripped his T-shirt off, much to the surprise of Carrie and his uncles.

But the real surprise came when a thoroughly diminutive lad, who was still a good foot taller than Billy, suddenly stepped forward. 'I beat up ya skanky cunt of a bruvver, and he went down like a sack of shit.'

'Leave it, Nobby,' Donna called after him, as she walked back towards the car.

Ignoring her, Nobby lifted his fists. 'Come on then, you fucking mouthy bastard!' he shouted, as he charged towards Billy.

But Billy was ready. In one swift, brutal motion, he delivered two vicious punches. That was all it took.

Not only did the sound of Nobby's jaw cracking echo through the air like a gunshot, but he went down hard, his body hitting the ground. As he tried to scramble to his feet dazed and disoriented, he now tried to make sense of what had just happened.

But Billy wasn't done. He followed up with a savage kick to Nobby's ribs, the impact driving the air out of his lungs and leaving him gasping on the ground.

James stepped in, pulling Billy away. 'Enough, Billy boy.'

'For fuck's sake, you're a total embarrassment, Nobby,' Donna scolded, as her son struggled to his feet. 'Now, get in the car, you useless twat.' Her voice was sharp with disappointment.

As he just about managed to stand up, Nobby shot Billy a sideways glance.

'Want another kicking, do you?' Billy raged. 'Touch my family again, and I'll hunt you down, Nobby Slade. Your brother Danny owes me big time, and, believe me, I'll be calling it in. Now, fuck off. All of you.'

Dottie watched the Slades all hurry away. Her eyes bored into Donna's back, before she turned to Carrie. 'I only came back for my phone.'

'Well, I'm glad you did. Will you stay for a cuppa?'

Dottie shook her head. ‘You see to Billy, love. I must get back and take Sherry for a walk.’

CHAPTER THIRTEEN

James was still gripping Billy when he shot a look at Sunny, with frustration evident in his eyes. 'Why didn't you stop him?' he snapped. 'He could have caused a bloody war on the front lawn. Did you hear the boy's jaw break, or was I hearing things?' With a shove, he directed Billy into the house. 'Go and get cleaned up and calm down.'

Sunny pointed towards Jesse and Ross; his tone was defensive. 'Have you not seen the state of these two? Three of them on two! Come on, James, they're men. Jesse's still a boy. To be honest, I'm glad Billy *did* hurt that Nobby. He's a grown-ass man, and it might make them think twice about coming back for more.'

As they all walked inside and gathered in the kitchen, Carrie took Ross and Jesse to the bathroom, where she cleaned them up. She tried to convince Ross to have stitches, but he flatly refused, claiming he wasn't going to be a model, so a few scars wouldn't bother him. They might even give him some street cred, he joked.

Charlie, who had been watching the events from his bedroom window, came down the stairs and announced that he had called their nan and grandad in case they needed further backup.

But Sunny rolled his eyes. 'For fuck's sake, I just wanted an early night.'

James could tell that there was something else bothering his brother. Still, he decided to let it slide, knowing that Sunny had been with Lolly earlier and that alone could have drained him.

Eager to avoid a late-night drinking session, which would probably happen if he waited for Luanne and Jed, his in-laws, Dylon decided to head home. Too much of Jed's latest batch of booze, and he would be swaying home and suffering for it by the morning.

As Dylon left, James put his arm around Sunny's shoulders. 'I guess this is a taste of what our dear old mum went through with us as teenagers.'

'I hope they get decent jobs and live good lives, James. We've walked a fine line, and we ended up okay, but what if they don't? What if they end up inside, like Jimmy?'

Spud jumped in. 'That won't happen for two reasons. One, they have you and Carrie as parents – not like fucking Ginty. And two, they're smart boys. They know right from wrong. So, keep that thought in mind, okay.' He patted Sunny's shoulders. 'Anyway, I must dash. I've got to open up the boxing club for the new starts tonight.'

James paused, then he slightly grinned. ' I'm wondering if Billy should take up boxing professionally. I mean, he can't half punch.'

'Not a bad idea. I'll see you later, mate,' said Spud, as he hurried out of the back door.

Sunny nodded, but his face remained solemn.

'Are you all right, mate?' James asked, pulling away slightly to look Sunny in the face.

'Yeah, yeah, all good.'

'No, I know you're not. Come outside,' James whispered.

They walked out of the back door, checking that no one was around, before Sunny spoke, in a low voice, 'Did you see Billy's face?'

'Yeah, I did,' James replied, his tone cautious.

'The red mist . . . it's not just that. He has a dark side, James – like Dottie has.'

James shrugged. 'So? He's a good kid. He's a bit reserved and quiet at times, but he's loyal. Very loyal. He'd fight the world for his family.'

Sunny ran his hands through his hair, clearly struggling with his thoughts. 'I know, but . . . I sometimes worry . . . Sorry, James, I'm tired, I guess.'

'Tell me, Sunny, what's really going through your head?'

'It's Billy. Even though he's only fifteen, he's as clever as fuck. And he's ruthless too. I've heard things. Jesse's told me how Billy takes no prisoners. He can really mess people up. You saw it for yourself. He clearly broke that lad's jaw and wouldn't have stopped if you hadn't pulled him off.'

'Yeah, but we were all like that,' James said, poking Sunny in the chest. 'You too, Sunny.'

'But he doesn't have *my* blood in him. He's got Jimmy Carson's blood, the same as Jesse has. But there's not an ounce of Carson in their characters, right?'

'Thank fuck for that,' James muttered, shaking his head.

'But look at what happened tonight. You saw how Carrie looked nervous when she saw Donna Slade, right? That woman's a hard and nasty piece of work. But see, Dottie, she didn't give a shit. It was as if she was holding a shotgun to Donna's face. But it wasn't a shotgun: it was a look. A dark sinister look. Christ, the woman practically shit her pants. And I see that same look in Billy.'

'So,' James said, his tone growing more serious.

'You know me, James. I'd protect my boys over everything.'

'What are you getting at, Sunny?'

'Billy went back down the lane in the dead of night . . . to find Willow.'

There was a moment of silence before James nodded. 'And you think that maybe he had something to do with it?'

Sunny sighed, heavily this time. 'I don't know, James. I'm tired. I'm devastated for Lolly, and I'm scared for Billy. I love that kid, but . . . what if?'

'I'm gonna stop you right there,' James said, firmly. 'You just said it yourself. You're tired and stressed. Get some rest, and you might have a clearer mind in the morning. And I'll leave you with this thought: I did a lot more damage than Billy at his age, but would you ever think I'd do something like that to a young girl, eh?'

Sunny shook his head, conceding the wider point that James was making.

'And Billy ain't Dottie, either,' James added.

'No, I suppose not,' Sunny replied, though the worry lingered in his eyes.

***

It was now well into the evening. James had followed his brother Dylon home.

Thirty minutes later, Luanne arrived first at Carrie and Sunny's having been given a step-by-step rundown of the confrontation by Donna Carson – now Slade – over the phone, courtesy of Charlie.

Luanne couldn't get to her daughter's house fast enough. She'd never trusted Donna Slade. And she still wasn't convinced that Donna had changed, despite hearing that she was out of prison.

Jed greeted everyone with a wide grin. He was holding up two headless chickens and a demijohn filled with his latest batch of homemade wine. Once jet black, his wild hair was now a thick wiry grey, but the mischievous spark in his eyes remained.

Luanne flicked the kettle on before embracing everyone, and then she looked at her daughter. 'What a mess, eh? Poor Lolly must be beside himself with grief. I'll make up some proper homemade dinners for his freezer.'

‘Aww, Mum, that’s kind of you,’ Carrie said, kissing her mother on the cheek.

Already settled at the table, Jed held up the dead chickens with a satisfied look before Sunny pursed his lips in utter disgust and rose to take the poultry back outside into the garage.

‘Boy, don’t leave them out there! The foxes will have ’em. You need to pluck ’em and cook ’em for Sunday roast. You don’t get much fresher than those mullered today,’ Jed called after him. ‘Now, sit down and try me wine, son. Best I’ve made this year. Luanne will tell ya. She loves it.’

Luanne leaned into Sunny’s ear when Jed wasn’t looking and whispered, ‘Not even my rubber plant likes it, but it did unblock me sink.’

‘How’s the lads?’ Jed asked, glancing around to see where they were.

Carrie flicked her thumb over her shoulder. ‘They’re up in their rooms, no doubt bragging about their war wounds.’

‘Has Ross been behaving himself? His muvver reckons he can be a right handful.’

Carrie waved her hand. ‘No, he’s been good. Jesse has been like a pig in shit, having Ross driving him around all over the country.’

‘Donna Slade was here, then,’ Luanne said, her jovial tone disappearing. ‘Charlie, bless him, filled me in. I swear to God, that boy will be a news reporter, if he ever gets off his games machine thingy.’

‘She turned up as bold as brass. I had no idea she was Danny Slade’s muvver. Still as rough as old boots. I thought she was gonna have a ruck on me doorstep, but when Dottie got in first, the woman backed off,’ Carrie replied.

Luanne’s face tightened as she took a seat next to Jed. ‘Donna’s dangerous, Carrie. Don’t underestimate her. If you think Ginty’s bad, believe me, she’s like a kitten compared to Donna. Although she's been keeping a low profile for years. But I know that bitch. She'll wait until the time's right, if she wants to start trouble.'

'But she only came looking for her son,' Carrie replied.

'With all her lads as backup, right?' Luanne said, recalling the details Charlie had given her.

'Yeah, but if she knows what Sunny and his brothers are like, she might've thought she needed backup. Besides, she ain't no spring chicken,' Carrie reasoned.

'You don't need to be a spring chicken to have a knife down your knickers, do ya? You just need the balls to use it. Besides that, do you think she was here as some kind of payback for what happened to the Carsons? Ginty won't go quietly to her grave. She'll go kicking and screaming, while forming an alliance with as much of the remaining family as she can. Donna was always her favourite, though I reckon that was because she had a ruthless reputation that suited Ginty just fine. She revelled in the fact that her niece was one of the hardest women in South East London.' She paused for breath. 'Now, see, the fact that Willow was murdered, and Danny might be in the frame for it, it will be a royal headache for Donna.' She sighed heavily. 'And knowing that Willow was seeing Billy boy, 'cos 'alf the gypsies in Bluewater apparently saw them, will 'ave the Carsons making up all kinds of shit. You know what a bunch of filthy liars they are. Ginty's the biggest liar of them all. Gawd knows what she's gone and told Donna.'

'I did hear that Ginty wants nothing to do with Billy and Jesse. I guess she knows there isn't a chance in hell that she could turn them against the family 'cos that was her plan. But it backfired, and now, apparently, she has disowned them, as if they give a rat's arse. And it wouldn't surprise me if she was in Donna's ear'ole brainwashing the woman,' Carrie replied, keeping her voice low.

Luanne nodded in agreement.

'Well, Donna and her butt-ugly sons soon scurried away like sewer rats. Fuck 'em,' Carrie said, trying to sound resolute.

Luanne shook her head, her expression serious. 'Like Ginty, Donna holds grudges, Carrie. Billy boy's proper humiliated her son up, by the sounds of it. Charlie reckons Billy broke the lad's jaw. I'll tell you this for nothing. She won't let that go. So be careful, Carrie. Donna's a sly bitch who not only carries a knife but a grudge as well.'

The room lapsed into silence, the gravity of Luanne's warning weighing heavily on their minds.

Carrie's defiant attitude wavered as she considered the implications. Donna wasn't someone to take lightly, and if she was holding a grudge, things could get a lot more dangerous.

'Anyway, how's Billy? He must be gutted. He liked that girl, didn't he?' Luanne asked, trying to steer the conversation to something more personal.

'Liked her?' said Jed. 'He couldn't keep his eyes off her. Every family do we had, he was looking for her. And as soon as she arrived, he was the first to greet her with a soppy smile. A rare smile, in Billy's case. I . . .' He paused, wiping his eyes. 'I thought they'd get wed. Our poor boy is grieving, and you know what teenagers are like. He'll hide it and suffer in silence.'

'He's definitely been quiet, that's for sure,' Sunny added, his voice tinged with concern.

'What's that supposed to mean?' Carrie snapped. 'He's suffering, can't you see that?'

A sudden cold atmosphere descended on the room, thick with tension, which was abruptly broken by a loud knock at the front door. Carrie glanced back at Sunny. 'Don't tell me the poxy Slades are back.'

‘Sounds like the Ol’ Bill’s knock, that does. I’ll go,’ Jed said, taking his place as the head of the family. Storming through the hallway, with Carrie and Sunny close behind, he pulled open the door. Sure enough, DCI Andrew Keldon and DI Paul Gurney were standing on the doorstep.

‘This had better be urgent, ’cos it’s gone ten o’clock,’ Carrie said, thinking they were there because of the earlier disturbance with the Slades.

‘Can we come in?’ Keldon asked, with a smile.

‘As long as you ain’t here to arrest anyone,’ Carrie replied, eyeing them warily.

Keldon shook his head. ‘No, not at the moment, anyway. We need to have a chat with Billy.’

Jed stepped forward, holding up his hand. ‘No, you don’t. What’s this about? Our Billy’s just a kid, so you talk to us first.’

Keldon, recognising the traveller’s accent and understanding the need for tact, nodded, choosing his words carefully. ‘I understand. I’m happy to talk to him with his parents present, or—’

‘Yeah, I know your game,’ Jed interrupted. ‘You’ll cart him off down the station, make him feel like shit, interrogate him, scare him, and leave him hating all coppers. This family’s been through enough with your kind. In case you didn’t know, one of yours is in jail for what he did to my daughter and my son-in-law. A proper nightmare, that was.’

Keldon offered a reassuring grin. ‘I know, but we’re not all like that. Look, I’ve already met Billy. He’s a bright lad. I just need to eliminate him from our inquiries, that’s all. But we do have questions regarding the latest update.’

Jed shrugged. ‘Don’t know what you’re talking about.’

Keldon turned to Sunny, his expression serious. 'You've probably already heard the news, right? And I understand you're friends with Laurence Price?'

'To your first question, no, I haven't, but, yeah, I am friends with Lolly,' Sunny replied, a deep frown creasing his forehead. 'I suppose you'd better come in.'

As soon as Keldon and Gurney stepped into the kitchen, they immediately sensed the tension in the room.

The family gathered around them, their protective instincts on high alert.

Keldon quickly sized up the situation, realising that these weren't the type of people who would leave them alone to do their job. Their sense of loyalty and defence was like a pack of wolves encircling to protect one of their own.

Billy, Jesse, and Ross gingerly walked into the room, having been alerted by Charlie that two men, most likely police, were at the door. One was wearing a mac. The other detective was in a cheap suit and he looked like a wino. They knew there would be questions from the police – but the nature of those questions wasn't known.

Keldon turned his attention to Billy, trying to keep his tone neutral. 'Do you mind if we have another chat?'

Billy shrugged, but Keldon couldn't help but notice how pale he looked. 'Are you okay?' he asked, concerned.

'Just tired,' Billy replied, subdued.

'Okay, look, Billy, we need to ask you a few questions, but I'm wondering if you'd like to have just one of your family members present rather than everyone,' Keldon suggested, expecting Billy to choose his mother.

'It's fine, just ask. These are my family. We have no secrets.'

Gurney, unable to hide his irritation, let out a sarcastic laugh. 'That's not how it works, mate.'

Billy's eyes flared with anger as he shot a look at Gurney. 'I'm *not* your mate. If you want questions answered, then ask. What difference does it make if my family's here?' His posture was defiant, with his hands on his hips and that fierce intensity burning in his eyes.

Gurney, now exasperated, threw his hands up in resignation. 'Okay, did you have a sexual relationship with Willow?'

'Now, hold up a minute,' said Jed, stepping forward. 'You can't ask questions like that. It's none of your business.'

But Billy, more composed than anyone expected, raised his hand to stop his grandfather. 'No, I didn't. I'm not that type of person. I respect women, and in case you ain't noticed, I'm only fifteen.'

Once again, the room fell silent. The family's collective tension didn't ease, but there was a sense of pride in how Billy was handling himself.

Keldon nodded, feeling that by getting too pushy it might only escalate the situation.

'Thank you for being straightforward, Billy,' Keldon said, his tone respectful. 'We just needed to clarify a few things, that's all.'

The family's protectiveness was unwavering, and any further probing would need to be done with caution.

Gurney had taken a thorough dislike to the boy. He didn't like being outsmarted by anyone, and so he could quickly get into an argument with a teenager instead of handling himself like the adult he was. 'Come on, you can be upfront about it, Billy. Loads of lads have sex at your age. Besides, in a few weeks, you will be sixteen,' he snorted. 'It's okay. We wouldn't be looking to charge you with having sex with an underage person, because Willow was already sixteen.'

‘You don’t get it, do you,’ Billy began, his voice steady and his demeanour surprisingly mature for his age. ‘Just because some teenagers have sex doesn’t mean we *all* do. And just because you seem to think I shouldn’t be concerned about having sex with a girl because she’s over sixteen, it says more about you and your morals, Detective, than it does about me. And that, Detective, is a shame.’ Billy’s words were calm but they carried some weight that put Gurney on the back foot.

Momentarily taken aback by the boy’s composed and articulate response, Gurney shifted uncomfortably on his chair. He wasn’t used to being challenged so directly, especially not by someone so young.

Keldon, on the other hand, found himself appreciating Billy’s straightforwardness. It was rare to encounter someone who could speak their mind so clearly, especially under pressure. Knowing that Billy wouldn’t hide behind evasive answers or get caught up in unnecessary bravado would make his job far easier.

‘Fair enough, Billy,’ Keldon said, nodding in acknowledgement. ‘I appreciate your honesty. It helps us understand things better.’ He paused and looked around him. ‘So I can see you haven’t heard the latest news from Laurence Price, then?’

In a moment of realisation, Billy’s eyes widened in shock. His hands flew to his mouth as he braced himself for the news. ‘Oh my God, was she raped?’ he asked, his voice trembling, as tears welled up in his eyes.

Keldon exchanged a glance with Gurney before delivering the devastating news. ‘Billy, we can’t be sure at this stage, but she was found naked.’

‘Oh, no, no!’ he cried.

‘But . . . the other issue is the fact that she was also pregnant. We estimate about three months.’

The collective gasp from Luanne and Carrie echoed in the room as the family stared at each other in utter disbelief. The shock played out on their faces.

'She was pregnant? Really?' Billy asked, his voice barely above a whisper.

Keldon nodded, solemnly. 'So, Billy, you can understand why we need to find out who the father is. We need to eliminate you completely from the investigation.'

Billy's face crumpled as the weight of the situation bore down on him. 'But . . . she never said . . . she never told me. I-I . . . I never knew,' he stammered, his tears now freely falling. He looked down at the floor, overwhelmed by grief, before looking back at the detective. 'I-I never . . . I never . . .' His voice broke as he choked on his words.

Seeing her son in such a state, Carrie immediately wrapped her arms around him, glaring at the detectives with disgust. 'Enough, now. Can't you see me boy's heartbroken. Best ya leave,' she snapped.

Keldon looked at Gurney, who clearly didn't like Billy. 'Sorry, love, no can do,' Gurney said, his tone hostile. 'He has to come with us. You can bring your solicitor, but we need his DNA.'

'Now, hold on a minute. You can fuck right off with your DNA rubbish. Me boy's told ya he didn't sleep with Willow. The baby obviously wasn't his, and there's no way you or anyone else is getting his DNA on record, not without a warrant. So, off you trot,' snapped Carrie.

Jed stepped forward, solidly positioned between the detectives and his daughter and grandson. 'If you've got any more to say, you say it to me,' he growled.

Seeing that the family were united in their refusal to allow Billy to be harassed further, Keldon hesitated, sensing the situation could quickly escalate if not handled carefully.

'We're not here to cause trouble,' Keldon said, with a conciliatory tone. 'We just need to follow procedure. This isn't about accusing Billy. It's about making sure we get to the truth.'

'Well, me boy don't lie,' Carrie said, her voice firm and final. 'Now, it's late, we're tired, and you're not welcome, so—'

Already nearing the end of his patience, Gurney couldn't resist a smirk.

It caught Carrie's attention. Her eyes narrowed as she fixed her gaze on him. 'Got somat to say, 'ave ya?' she challenged, her head inclining slightly, as she prepared for whatever was coming.

Gurney replied with a tone that was more demanding than suggesting. 'I think it's better if you come down to the station, Billy, because we need another statement from you.'

Billy kept his stance steady, but unease washed over him. 'I *gave* you a statement. I told you everything I knew. Maybe you need to speak with Danny Slade. Like I said, when you came to speak to me before, he was the last person to see her.'

Keldon's eyes sharpened. 'Was he?'

'What?' Billy asked, caught off guard by the shift in tone.

'Tell me, Billy, do you own a push bike?' Keldon's question hung in the air, heavy with implication.

Billy's heart sank. He knew then that someone had told them he'd returned to the lane.

The tension in the room increased considerably now, the family sensing the growing pressure on Billy.

'Every bleedin' teenager has a push bike,' Luanne snapped, her frustration boiling over. 'Jesus, it's like asking if he owns a pair of trainers.'

'I do,' Billy admitted.

Keldon nodded as if the confirmation was expected. 'We need to take another statement, Billy. I can see you're tired, so please come to the station in the morning. We can take the DNA there, and you can make a statement. You want to help us with our inquiries, don't you?' Keldon's tone was patronising, a calculated attempt to coax compliance, but it only served to rile up Sunny.

'Help with your inquiries?' Sunny echoed. 'What you're doing is trying to pin something on a kid who's already grieving. And he ain't giving you his DNA. Now, you've overstayed your welcome. Next time, come with a fucking warrant.'

CHAPTER FOURTEEN

13 July

The morning was oppressively muggy, with thick clouds hanging low in the sky and threatening a downpour. It proved to be a welcome relief to Billy, since he woke up with a stinking headache.

The revelation that Willow had been pregnant had plagued his dreams. He couldn't get his head around the idea that someone, who had always been so honest with him, could have kept such a dark secret. But now it was clear: she had only told him what she wanted him to know.

It seemed as though she had destroyed him twice over. Firstly, by not mentioning she was seeing anyone else, and secondly, by flirting with him to the extent that she had made him fall deeply in love with her.

He imagined he would have been the one Willow would have trusted enough to lose her virginity to because he had cherished her, and she knew that. He would have forgiven her for going off with Danny, as long as she came back to him. He had convinced himself that her acting out was just a reaction to her mother leaving the family home and thereby abandoning her without a second thought. Willow had confided in him how much it hurt to realise her mother didn't love her. Knowing that made him want to protect her even more.

But in thinking things through, he was beginning to wonder now how much of her grievances were just excuses. That really, she didn't care about her mother at all. In effect,

Tara's actions were simply a good reason for Willow to get away with doing as she pleased.

Rolling over, Billy was about to reach under the bed to retrieve the necklace he had bought for Willow. But instead, his hand brushed against something warm and soft. He looked down and saw Duchess, the family's massive gentle dog lying beside him with her head resting on the bed.

Billy couldn't help but smile. Duchess was technically Jesse's dog, but she had a way of gravitating towards the family member who needed her the most. Right now, it seemed she sensed that person was him. Her big soulful eyes seemed to say she understood his pain, and at that moment, he felt a small but much-needed comfort in her presence.

The smell of bacon pervaded the room. So much so, it was making Billy's mouth water. Despite the hollow feeling in his stomach, the familiar aroma of his mother's cooking had a way of whetting his appetite. His mother always worried if one of her kids didn't eat, and she was probably deliberately cooking up a full breakfast, knowing he would have a tough day ahead, and that he wasn't in a good enough place to cope with any further dramas.

After a quick shower, he slipped into a fresh pair of jeans and a crisp ironed T-shirt before heading downstairs and mentally preparing himself for the trip to the station. As he entered the kitchen, he paused and looked at his mother, who was standing at the stove with a spatula in her hand and flipping the lard over the eggs. The morning sun caught her profile, which highlighted her soft features.

'There's my big boy,' she greeted him, with a warm smile, her voice full of affection. It was how she often referred to him, a term of endearment that never failed to make him feel special, even at fifteen. 'Full English fry-up, babe?'

Billy had intended just to ask for toast, but the sizzling in the pan and the salty smell in the air were too enticing. He nodded and took a seat at the kitchen table.

Carrie pulled a plate from the oven, already piled high with sausages, bacon, and mushrooms. She added two perfectly fried eggs and a generous ladle of baked beans before placing the plate in front of him with a touch of pride.

He smiled at her. 'Thanks, Mum.'

Sitting across from him, she cupped her slim fingers around a large mug of coffee.

Billy paused momentarily, taking in the sight of his mother's face. It was filled with such love and concern, he never doubted for a second how much she cared for him. Even though he wasn't her natural-born son, he had never felt any less loved than Jesse, her biological child. And he was like her in many ways, with thick dark hair and round expressive eyes, which often betrayed his emotions.

But looking in the mirror, he saw only Dottie's eyes staring back at him, a constant reminder of his biological roots.

His mother's voice broke his thoughts. 'Are you sure you want to go to the station and do this DNA thingy?'

Billy sighed, setting down his knife and fork. 'Mum, listen, I never slept with her. The baby isn't mine.'

She waved her hand. 'Babe, I know it's not, because you said so, and you've never lied to me. I'm more worried about what the police will say, now that they know you went back to the lane just a few feet away from where she was killed. They'll want to know why you hid that from them.'

Understanding her concern, Billy nodded. 'I'll tell them the truth. It worried me, thinking it could've been Willow running across the field, and that's why I went looking. But

I didn't mention it earlier because that copper tried to get me in his car with a knife at my throat, and with the history of rogue coppers – like that prick Colt – I didn't think they'd believe me.'

Carrie nodded reassuringly, her eyes softening. 'Good lad,' she said, reaching across the table to give his hand a gentle squeeze.

Although it was a simple gesture, it meant the world to Billy to know his mother believed in him, no matter what.

***

By the time Billy was seated in the interview room, Clive Clemence, the family's long-time solicitor, had arrived with a beaming smile and a tatty briefcase in his hand. Known affectionately as 'Clemmy' by the family, he was also a close friend of Ray Clarkson, who was not only ex-police but also another dear family friend.

Clemence was in his late sixties and had stubbornly refused to retire. His appearance was more reminiscent of a history teacher than a lawyer. It was an impression that would lull people into a false sense of confidence.

Keldon and Gurney, however, knew better than to underestimate Clemence. They were well aware that the man was no fool and that they would have to tread carefully, especially since Billy was a minor and there of his own accord.

The interview went smoothly, with Clemence not interrupting once, largely because Billy was so articulate in recounting his version of events. He handled himself with a maturity that surprised even Keldon, who found himself looking at Billy not as a boy but as a sharp, perceptive young man.

After a moment of silence, Keldon leaned forward, locking eyes with Billy. 'And this copper, as you called him.

Was he real, or was he something you made up to suit your narrative?'

Billy's glare hardened. 'I told you the truth.'

Unable to resist bringing Billy down, Gurney smirked and said, 'A jam sandwich was taken out of service in Kent only recently, so your description is . . .' He tapped the side of his head, his tone dripping with condescension. 'Probably from what you're used to seeing the police driving.' He folded his arms and leaned back, clearly enjoying the moment.

Billy could feel his anger rising. He had been honest, and now this smarmy detective was questioning his integrity. But he forced himself to stay calm, returning Gurney's smirk with one of his own. 'I—'

Clemence gripped his arm. 'You don't have to respond to that.'

But determined to have his say, Billy gently pulled away. 'Oh, but I will.' He turned his attention back to Keldon, pointedly ignoring Gurney. 'I told you the truth. I'll admit I left out returning to the lane because I didn't think you'd believe that a copper would try to get a teenager into their car for some pervy move and use a knife to do it. I mean, you lot don't carry knives, do you? But you are all equipped with a built-in chip that says we protect our own.'

As Keldon opened his mouth to respond, Billy held up a hand. 'Sorry, I haven't finished. You see, I started to sense something was off when you,' he glanced at Gurney, 'suddenly went out into my garden to use your radio to check on some information following my description of the car. And I'm not stupid. I know you found it odd that we were pulled over by a copper in what I now know to be an older model car, currently replaced by the new Battenburg vinyl.' He paused, raising an eyebrow, waiting for a response.

Clemence, sensing the moment, spoke up. 'I take it you're looking for a police officer driving a former police car in connection with the girl's murder.' He spoke as if the conclusion was evident. With that, he began to pack up his briefcase, fully expecting the interview to be over.

Not wanting to lose the upper hand, Gurney quickly replied, 'We need a DNA sample.' His tone was sharp. He expected resistance, but, to his surprise, Billy nodded.

'Of course,' Billy replied, calmly. 'As long as it's wiped clean from your database as soon as it clears me of being the father of Willow's baby.'

Gurney was caught off guard, his attempt at a final provocation having failed spectacularly.

For his part, Keldon respected Billy's maturity and straightforwardness, even if it complicated matters for their investigation.

Clemence, ever the professional, stood up, his demeanour relaxed. 'You heard my client. We'll cooperate fully, but on the condition that the DNA sample is used strictly for this case and it is removed from all records once it has been established that Billy isn't the father of Willow Price's baby.'

Keldon nodded, knowing there was no room to argue. 'That's acceptable.'

As soon as Billy and Clemence had left the station, Keldon pulled Gurney into a side room. 'That kid isn't stupid. Now it means we have a serious problem on our hands, especially if the press get hold of this.'

'Let's just hope that the DNA shows the baby *was* Billy's. Because then he'd have a motive to kill her, especially if what they are saying is true. Namely, that she buggered off with Danny when she was supposed to be out on a date with Billy.'

Keldon rolled his eyes. 'Come on, let's bring Danny in and see if we can get him to talk.'

'But you heard what his mother had to say. Her precious son can't remember a fucking thing,' he said, mimicking Donna's voice.

'I know Donna Slade. She will protect her boys, even if one of them did murder that young girl. She'll swear black is white, if it stops any of her sons from going to prison. We're bringing him in. Horse kick, my arse. His story is all a load of bollocks. Danny Slade doesn't even own a horse.'

CHAPTER FIFTEEN

14 July

Danny's cocky wink and half-smirk even had Keldon, the more reserved of the two detectives, riled up. It had been four days since Willow's murder and now he was faced with the frustration of the doctor's note. It clearly stated that the lad was suffering from amnesia, likely caused by shock or injury, which left him with concussion and limited memory. Whether this condition was temporary or long-term remained uncertain, but one fact was clear: he was not fit for a formal interview.

Despite this, Danny agreed to undergo a DNA test, shifting the focus away from him as a potential father. He complied willingly, without hesitation. However, when informally questioned – i.e. not in a full interview – he seemed to toy with their frustration. His smile deepened, with a cruel twist to it when they asked the more probing questions, such as: *Why would Willow jump out of his car and run?*

That question hung in the air like a jagged knife. Danny didn't blink, his gaze unflinching. Then, with a sickening lopsided grin, showing utter contempt, he shrugged as if it meant nothing to him.

Keldon's fists clenched under the table. He wanted to lean across, grab Danny by the throat, and shake the smugness out of him, but he managed to resist doing so. Instead, he stared at the injuries to Danny's left cheek and forehead, which were left exposed. There was no gauze, not even a bandage.

Keldon knew it was for show. And if he was honest, it looked brutal. The deep gash throbbed. It was purple and raw. He had been kicked by a horse, so he said. But that only led to another question that was put to him: *Whose horse?*

Again, Danny shrugged, but, this time, Keldon saw it. A flicker of something different appeared across his face. Was it panic? It was fleeting, almost imperceptible, but the widening of Danny's eyes, and the way they darted for a split second, gave him away. Fear. *There it was.*

There was nothing more they could ask. Every time Danny didn't want to answer, he would just wave the doctor's note under their noses. He was still taunting them and grinning as if he held all the power.

After a PC took his DNA, Keldon and Gurney escorted him outside the police station, only to find half the Slade clan waiting in a tight, hostile knot.

Keldon's stomach clenched, the moment he saw Donna. She hadn't changed much. She was just older and meaner, with eyes that burned with the same unsettling darkness as Danny's.

Her presence alone made the hairs on the back of Keldon's neck stand on end. He remembered all too well how Donna had nearly savagely bitten his finger off years ago when she was arrested for GBH. Now, she turned slowly towards him, that familiar smarmy smile curling her upper lip, just like Danny's had.

'I told ya, didn't I? That me baby boy don't remember a *fucking thing*, but you still dragged him into the station,' she sneered, jabbing a gnarled finger in his direction. The thick gold keeper ring she wore had practically fused into her skin, a grotesque symbol of defiance. 'Once that DNA comes back and proves me boy ain't the farver, I want it in writing that you've taken him off your records. I know my rights.' She lifted her chin, her voice rising with every word. 'And by the sounds of it, Willow was a slapper, spreading her legs for any Tom, Dick, or Harry. That Murphy boy was shagging her too, so I heard. Dirty cow. And let me remind you of this, Keldon: *me boys don't mess with dirty gorgers*. It ain't our way.'

Gurney, who rarely held back his contempt – even on a good day – couldn't resist a good old dig at her. 'Your boys have shagged their way through the whole of Kent, Donna. And they still do. Even once they're married. And what the hell would you know? You weren't in their lives, were you. You were behind bars. So reel your neck in. You can take your foul mouth and your boy and piss off. Or I'll nick you for disturbing the peace.'

Donna's eyes flashed with fury, but she kept her composure. Her voice snapped venom. 'Bollocks. I'm just stating the facts about that girl.'

'The *dead* girl,' Keldon cut in. 'In case you've forgotten.'

Nonchalantly, Donna shrugged. 'As long as you don't try pinning it on me boy, 'cos he didn't do it.'

Keldon held back, refusing to stoop to her level. Instead, he smiled coldly, locking eyes with Danny. 'Don't leave the country, Danny. You're still a significant witness . . .' He paused for effect. '*For now.*'

With his family now surrounding him, Danny smirked and raised two fingers, in a mocking gesture.

Gurney rolled his eyes. 'Childish.'

But Keldon's attention was elsewhere. His frown deepened as something caught his eye. 'Nice watch, Danny,' he said, staring at the gleaming Rolex on Danny's wrist.

For a split second, Danny froze, his smirk faltering just long enough for Keldon to see it. Then, just as quickly, he yanked his sleeve down, covered the watch, and turned away without a word. His mother and brothers followed, tossing low, muttered expletives over their shoulders as they scurried away from the police station.

As soon as the Slade family had gone, Keldon shook his head in disgust. 'They're one vile family,' he muttered. 'You can tell Donna's blood runs straight back to the Carsons, even though she's a Slade now. Those lads of hers. Just like her side of the family. Funny thing is, I actually admired the old man, back in the day. He was a bit of a face, a real gangster if you like. And Donna – believe it or not – used to be a looker. Yeah, *used* to be. She had that Spanish flamenco dancer vibe, you know. But now? Now, she's withered into the spiteful creature she always was underneath. Jealousy's in her blood. She'd knife a girl across the face and not blink, if she caught them looking at her ol' man.'

Gurney nodded, lighting up a cigarette. 'I never knew her that well, but, yeah, I heard the stories.'

Keldon extended his hand, pointing to the deep scar that circled his finger. 'She bloody well nearly bit this off once. She was like a wild animal. She's ruthless.'

Gurney exhaled a cloud of smoke, shaking his head. 'Can't believe how cold she was about a dead teenager. No heart, a right horrible heartless bitch.'

Keldon let out a dry, bitter chuckle. 'She hates all females. Always has. The story goes that her mother abandoned her when she was young. She spent a few months in foster care as a teenager. There, she was pinned down by the girls in the family while their brother raped her. The social worker was a woman and made Donna stay at the foster carers' home, not believing a word of it, until Donna ran away and screamed blue murder to her father.

Apparently, he returned to the foster carers, collected her belongings, and she never went back.'

Gurney raised an eyebrow. 'Yeah? But is that really true?'

Slowly, Keldon nodded. 'That's what came out in the court case. It's the reason why the judge reduced her sentence on appeal, because she had psychological issues.'

Gurney took another long drag of his cigarette. 'Did *you* buy it?'

Keldon shrugged. 'Hard to say. Every bastard's got a story. Some are exaggerated, some are true, and some are even spun out of pure desperation. But something must've happened to Donna. She's got a hatred for women that runs a mile deep. Not all of 'em, though. She gets on with Ginty Carson well enough.'

Gurney snorted, stubbing out his half-smoked cigarette. 'I'd hardly call Ginty Carson a woman. She's more like a prime menace and looks more manly than most men. Even her gruff foul-mouthed voice is like a geezer's. I suppose Donna is just like her. Another one raising monsters.'

'It's questionable. Even if what she'd been through was true, how could she be so cruel about a young dead girl? Christ, if that was my daughter, I'd be . . .' Keldon said, his voice trailing off, as he scratched his brow with his thumb.

Noticing Keldon's distant stare, Gurney asked, 'What are you thinking?'

Keldon's eyes narrowed. 'Willow's grandfather is none other than Cas Ferrier. The man's got horses, a whole farm, in fact. Which always tickles me since he looks like he's just stepped off a private jet from Hawaii. But, yeah, he owns horses. I reckon Cas got to Danny before we could, and I don't think he's the kind of guy to ask nicely over a cup of cocoa. Nah, Cas would've tortured him first and asked questions later.' His mind returned to the interview, recalling Danny's reaction when asked about the horse.

Gurney nodded, his bottom lip jutting out as he lit another cigarette. 'Well, if Cas grilled Danny, he must've been convinced the kid was innocent. Because we both know Cas. He'd have buried the lad in pieces across the country, if he thought otherwise.'

'Exactly,' Keldon agreed. 'Which means whoever killed Willow either didn't know she was Cas's granddaughter or they didn't care. And, clearly, they didn't care they were pitting themselves against the dangerous Laurence Price either. He's got a reputation, too, though not quite like Cas's. But Danny must've known Willow was related to Cas.'

Instead of heading back inside the station, they decided to grab a coffee at their favourite café a few hundred yards away. Their hands were tied for the moment. Even though they were investigating the possibility of the culprit being a Kent copper, the details of the car were off-limits. The Chief Superintendent had made it clear that that particular piece of information never left the station. It would destroy their reputation. Still, both Keldon and Gurney had to admit that even though Gurney didn't like Billy, he seemed to be telling the truth about the man who had tried to force him into the car.

CHAPTER SIXTEEN

It had been over three weeks since Willow's death. Billy had continued to be subdued, even more so than his usual reserved self. Every so often, he would sneak outside and come back in reeking of cigarettes.

Carrie noticed, and although she wanted to stop him, the grief in his eyes was so deep she didn't have the heart to lecture him over smoking. Instead, she offered him his favourite food, a bacon sandwich or a cheese toastie, and whenever he passed her, she stole a quick hug or a kiss.

Sunny watched as Billy slid in through the back door, head down, barely looking up for a brief nod.

Carrie's instinct was to grab her son and try to alleviate the pain, but Sunny quickly shook his head and winked. Once Billy was out of sight, he said, 'I knew he liked her, but I didn't realise he *loved* her. He's proper upset, Carrie. You can't take his pain away.' He chuckled gently. 'But you might make him into a little porker with all that comfort food.'

Carrie sighed. 'I swear to God, whoever killed that girl needs to hang.'

Jesse and Ross entered the kitchen. They were beaming. It was such a stark contrast to Billy's expression that it felt almost insulting to his grief.

'Ross is taking me to Brands Hatch. We won't be back 'til late, so don't bother with dinner for us, Mum. We'll grab a burger from one of your vans, Dad,' Jesse said, giving Ross a playful shove. 'A proper dirty burger.'

Before they had the chance to leave, there was a fierce knock at the front door.

Both Carrie and Sunny said in unison, 'Copper's knock.'

Suddenly, a flicker of alarm spread across Jesse's face. 'What do they want?'

Carrie waved her hands. 'I won't know until we answer the door, will I? Anyway, it might not be the police. I hope it ain't that rough ol' tart Donna again.'

Pulling off her apron, Carrie stormed down the hallway. *It certainly wasn't family*, she thought. They would have come in through the back door. As she opened the front door, two silhouettes appeared against the sunlight. It was Keldon and Gurney.

'Sorry to disturb your Sunday, Mrs Murphy. Can we come in?' Keldon asked, with one foot about to cross the threshold.

Carrie stood with her hands on her hips. 'That depends. As long as no one's getting dragged down to the station or arrested.'

'No, no one's getting arrested. But we do have more questions.'

Reluctantly, Carrie nodded. 'Better come in, then.'

As they stepped into the hallway, Carrie noticed beads of sweat on Keldon's forehead. It didn't surprise her at all. When she'd opened the front door, it had felt like stepping off a plane into the heat of a tropical country.

'A cold drink?'

'Yes, please. Water would be perfect,' Keldon replied, appreciatively.

They followed Carrie into the kitchen, where Sunny was already seated at the table, a deep frown creasing his forehead.

Before the officers could speak, Jesse opened the back door, ready to leave, but Gurney stopped him.

'No, lad. We need to speak to you.'

Billy appeared in the doorway, having overheard the commotion from inside the lounge. 'What do you want to know now?' he asked, assuming they were here for him.

Gurney kept his eyes on Jesse. 'We need to ask your brother a few questions.'

All eyes turned to Jesse, whose face had turned very pale. His eyes were wide with fear. Carrie recognised that look, as did Billy.

Billy knew every smirk, grin, side-eye, and expression his brother had, but, this time, he stayed quiet. He knew Jesse couldn't have murdered Willow. His brother had been with him that night. Yet, the atmosphere in the room was emotionally charged.

Carrie glanced at Sunny, totally puzzled, while Ross stood with his head tilted in confusion.

But it was as if Jesse was expecting this.

And then, Billy saw it. That look. He knew it well: it was guilt.

Feeling uncomfortable in the eerie silence, Carrie hurriedly snatched two glasses from the cupboard. 'Take a seat, officers,' she said, filling them with water from the new filter jug. She handed one glass to Keldon and placed the other in front of Gurney, who had now seated himself and was retrieving his notebook from his jacket pocket.

Keldon was less relaxed than Gurney. He knew what he was about to say would upset the family.

'The DNA results have come back on Willow's baby,' Keldon began, speaking slowly, to let the information sink in. He turned to Billy, whose hands were now on his hips, his eyes firmly fixed on Jesse.

'Billy, your DNA was significant. Although you said you didn't sleep with Willow, the match was so close that our specialists believe the father may be a close relative.' He then turned his attention to Jesse. 'So, we're asking if you would take a DNA test too, Jesse.'

As the shock reverberated through the room, Carrie threw her hands to her mouth.

'You must've got that wrong,' Sunny spat, now furious. 'Go back to your so-called specialists and tell them they don't know their arses from their elbows!'

Keldon shook his head. 'Mr Murphy, they rarely get these things wrong. They checked it twice, and the match is with someone closely related to Billy.'

Billy stepped forward, towards his brother, his voice a deadly intense growl. 'Did you sleep with Willow?'

Jesse didn't have to answer. His face said everything. Everyone in the room could read him like a book.

'Billy, listen, mate, I'm sorry. It just happened. I didn't think . . .'

Suddenly, Billy ripped the chain from around his neck and threw it onto the table, where it landed with a heavy clink, an inch away from Jesse.

For a moment, there was silence, with everyone staring at the necklace – with the gold heart – which was engraved with the word *special*.

'I'm . . . I'm sorry,' Jesse stammered, the words sticking in his throat. They weren't from fear of Billy turning violent but because of the wider consequences. 'Look, Billy boy, I never knew you really liked her like that . . . I mean, it was just . . . I had a drink. She was—'

'She was meant to be *mine*.' Billy's eyes burned with a fierce intensity. 'You knew how I felt, Jesse. *You* knew! Of all people, *you* knew how much I loved Willow.' He slammed his hand down on the table, making everyone jump. 'You've ruined everything, Jesse. Everything we had, everything I had with Willow – you've ruined it. Even my memories of her . . . they're fucked now, all because my own *brother* slept with her.'

Tears filled his eyes, but no one could find the words. No one knew what to say. And neither did Gurney, who had no genuine care for people. He had a preference for dogs.

Duchess got up from her bed and nudged Billy's hand. But ignoring the dog, he bent down and snatched the necklace, before turning and bolting from the room and running down the hallway and out through the front door.

'Billy!' Carrie called after him.

But Sunny grabbed her arm. 'Let him go. He needs to . . .' He turned to face Jesse. 'He needs to get his head around the fact that his brother, his *best mate*, slept with the love of his life.'

Jesse hung his head in shame.

For the first time in her life, Carrie felt a surge of anger towards her son. In a swift, sharp move, she slapped him hard on the back of the head. 'You nasty, nasty bastard, Jesse. How the hell could you do that to Billy? You knew—' She jabbed him hard in the chest, her voice shaking with rage. 'You *knew* how much . . .'

She had to pause to catch her breath, trying to control her temper.

'That's enough, Mrs Murphy,' Keldon said, rising from his chair.

But Carrie wasn't having it.

In a flash, she pushed Keldon back onto his chair. 'Mind your own business. This is my son. My *family*!'

Keldon nodded, realising he had overstepped the mark.

'Jesse, you know how deep our Billy is. You've crossed a line he may never forgive you for.' Her voice cracked with emotion. 'I raised you two to love each other, to have each other's backs. But you.' She shook her head. 'You've wrecked that. You stupid, stupid boy.'

Seeing the devastation on Jesse's face, Sunny leaned across and gently pulled Carrie away. 'He knows, Carrie Ann. He knows.'

'He should've known *before* he got into her knickers! Jesus, didn't I raise you right?'

'All right, all right, come on, Carrie,' Sunny said, trying to calm her down. 'Let's leave the detectives to talk to Jesse.'

Carrie walked out of the kitchen with tears streaming down her face.

Sunny got up from the table and followed her. Putting his arm around her, he pulled her close, whispering softly, 'You raised them good and proper, Carrie. But look. They are almost grown up. They have to make their own decisions. You know what young ones can be like, always pushing boundaries. And as for Jesse . . . well, if Willow – God rest her soul – was that way inclined, he may not have thought it through. Not about Billy, and certainly not about getting her pregnant.'

'Oh, my poor Billy. Did you see his face? Devastated, he was, like his whole world had just crumbled. Sunny, I've never seen him like that. He looked so dark . . . so, so hurt. I wish he'd come back.'

'He'll be back, love. He's probably gone to Dottie's for a few days to clear his head. It'll be very strained between him and Jesse, but give it time. I know you'll want them to be best mates again overnight. But betrayal like this? Well, it'll take a long while for Billy to get over this.'

Carrie wiped her eyes and returned to the kitchen, where Jesse sat with the two detectives at the table. He barely raised his head, his shame written all over his face.

Ross stood awkwardly in the corner, and when he spotted Carrie, he smiled.

‘I’d best go. I’m heading back home tomorrow. I’ll stay at Aunt Luanne’s tonight.’

With a sharp nod from Carrie, Ross slipped away through the back door.

Normally, Carrie might have persuaded him to stay since Jesse had been thoroughly enjoying his cousin’s company – and, of course, the car – but, right now, she didn’t care about what Jesse wanted. She was still fuming, and her heart ached for Billy.

Without a word, she turned on her heel and walked out of the kitchen again and into the lounge. She couldn’t be around Jesse right now. His usual flippancy, which had often been a blessing – cutting through tense moments with a quick joke – was useless today. This wasn’t something he could laugh off, and Billy certainly wouldn’t.

The knot in her stomach tightened as she thought of Billy’s heartbroken expression. She had never seen him look like that before. Upset, even tearful, yes, but never white with heartache. She wondered: was it the loss of Willow that had really crushed him or was it the loss of his brother? Because the bond between Billy and Jesse had always been one of deep love and trust. Billy would have trusted Jesse with his life. But now? Now, that belief was shattered, and Billy was gone. Something inside was telling her that their life would never ever be the same again.

***

Cas sat at his desk in his study as the evening drew to a close. He didn’t want to face yet another night of lying in bed and imagining what he would do to the man who’d killed his granddaughter. Keith had already retreated to his annexe, and as he yawned, he stubbed out his last cigarette in the ashtray. He stood up to close the French doors, but then something made him wonder if there was someone outside. Walking through the garden and out through the opening that led to the stables, he stopped and then sighed. The door to the stables was wide open. He was sure he'd shut it earlier.

Before he reached the entrance, he hesitated, scanning the area for a pitchfork. It was just in case he was met with any unwelcome visitors. With the tool in his hands, he cautiously stepped inside. Something didn't sit right. Willow's horse, usually the last to settle for the night, wasn't peering over his stall as he normally did.

Feeling his heart pounding in his chest, Cas approached the stall slowly. Willow's horse was always a handful, so he had to be careful when opening the door. With his hand on the latch, he peered over cautiously and then blinked twice, struggling to believe what he was seeing. It was dark, but he could make out the outline of a young man lying on the floor with Willow's horse lying beside him.

Cas quickly ran to the main door and flipped on the lights before hurrying back, still gripping the pitchfork. He swung open the stall door and stepped inside, mindful of the horse's unpredictability. His eyes settled on the boy, who was clutching a half-empty bottle of vodka.

'Billy Murphy, what the hell are you doing in my stables, boy?' Cas barked.

Billy groggily opened his eyes and tried to sit up straight, but his vision was blurry, and his head was pounding.

Cas glanced at the horse, which still hadn't moved. 'Oh, for fuck's sake. You haven't gone and gotten my horse drunk, have you? You silly twat.'

Billy struggled to his feet, a sudden wave of nausea hitting him. His mouth filled with water, and he staggered outside, zigzagging, before collapsing in front of an old metal trough and about to throw up.

Cas swiftly shut the door to Goliath's stall and the one to the stables and followed him out.

Billy was now heaving into the trough.

'All right, all right, lad. Give me that bottle before you end up with alcohol poisoning – and me having to explain it to the cops. How'd you even get here?' He grabbed Billy's arm to steady him.

'A cab,' he replied, before heaving again.

'I never took you for a prize prat. Fancy getting drunk on neat vodka at your age. Jesus, you should've started with a pint of cider, not vodka. That stuff will rip your insides out. Come on, I bet you feel better, now that you've filled up my trough.'

Billy shook Cas off. Then, leaning over with his hands on his knees, he spat out the foul taste in his mouth.

Cas, who had momentarily lost sight of how fiercely independent Billy was, turned and started walking towards the house, not waiting for the lad.

'Come on, boy. I'll get you some water.'

Billy didn't respond at first, but then he managed to follow, clearly struggling to put one foot in front of the other.

Born with no patience whatsoever, Cas held the French doors open, grimacing, as he watched Billy stagger towards him. As soon as he was inside his study, he guided Billy over to one of the huge sofas.

'And don't fucking shrug me off,' Cas grumbled. 'I've got valuable antiques in here. Not sure what they are, but they're worth a lot of money. So let me help you before you break anything.'

This time, Billy didn't resist. He allowed Cas to help him to sit down, where he collapsed. However, he tried to keep his eyes open. 'Jesse . . . my own brother . . . Jesse, of all the blokes in Kent . . . My own brother . . . Can you even im-imagine?' His words were slurred, barely recognisable. He ran his hands around his neck as if he was searching for something. 'The poxy necklace . . . I've lost that as well, now.'

Hearing Billy mention Jesse in this negative context gave Cas a nasty taste in his mouth. A sudden chill ran through him and he shook Billy's arm. 'What *about* Jesse? Did he hurt my Willow? Was it him?' Cas's voice sharpened, urgency creeping in.

Billy looked at Cas in disgust as he pointed a finger. 'I'll never speak to him again.'

Cas's mind was racing at such a rate, he was now jumping to the worst conclusions. 'Did he hurt my Willow?' he demanded, once again, louder this time.

Billy's eyes sprang open, a frown crossing his face as confusion and disgust washed over him. 'Hurt her?' His head swayed. 'Nah, he never hurt her . . . I bet she even liked it.' He shook his head, his expression hardening. 'But he ain't no brother of mine now.'

Trying to remain calm, Cas decided to make some strong coffee and toast to help sober Billy up. He needed to understand precisely what the boy was talking about. No sooner had he put the kettle on than his mobile rang. It was Lolly. The call was brief, to the point, and very bitter.

Lolly informed him that although the DNA test from Billy was a close match, it was not strong enough, suggesting the father of Willow's baby was either his brother or a very close relative. So the police had been to see Jesse at the Murphys' home. He had admitted to having unprotected sex with Willow three months before her death. Protocol deemed that Jesse would be given a DNA test to confirm what the police already knew.

Cas kept his voice steady, not letting on that Billy was at his home.

After ending the call, he returned to the study and sat down next to Billy. A tear rolled down his cheek as he watched the young man struggle with his emotions.

CHAPTER SEVENTEEN

Peter and Sandra O'Malley had been bursting with anticipation during the lead up to the fifth of August, which was the day their granddaughter Elizabeth turned eighteen. Together, they proudly watched her beam with excitement. Her hands were still shaking as she held the keys to her new Nissan Micra – not a brand-new car, but new to her.

'Oh, Grandad, Gran, I don't know what to say. It's so generous.'

'Yes, well, your mother would have wanted you to be safe, and it's a safer option than taking buses everywhere. You're just like her. Now, you be careful. No speeding or acting foolishly, do you hear?'

Elizabeth nodded, as she did with every rule her grandmother set. She wouldn't dare argue; unlike her late mother, her gran was stricter and much sterner, though it all came from a good place.

'And red is my favourite colour too!' Elizabeth sang, her voice a sweet chirp.

'Yes, well, it wasn't so much the colour I chose. It was more about the safety. Anyway, as a little runaround, it will do you just fine,' her grandfather said. 'Now, get used to it. Drive around the block a few times until you're ready for the main roads. I'm going back inside and leaving you to it. And happy birthday.' He kissed her cheek and walked back along the garden path, gently closing the front door behind him.

‘Oh, Gran, it’s perfect,’ Elizabeth said, as she peered inside the driver’s door. ‘Oh, look, even one of those air fresheners!’

‘It needed a good wash, but it’s all set now.’

As she watched her granddaughter step into the driver’s seat, Sandra noticed a man walking towards them. They lived in a cul-de-sac, and she knew every face in the neighbourhood, having lived there most of her life. The man was grinning peculiarly as he approached, and she expected him to say something, because he looked as if he knew her. But the way he slowed down and stared at her made her blood run cold. Then, for a moment, he stopped and said, ‘Nice car.’

Meeting his gaze, Sandra knew she had seen someone very sinister like that before, but for the life of her, she couldn’t remember where. She wasn’t familiar with many men, apart from her neighbours and the local shopkeepers, as she tended to keep herself to herself. Her husband preferred it that way too. She had no idea who this man was, but one thing was certain: she didn’t like the way he was glaring at her granddaughter, not one little bit.

Sandra watched the man retreat down the road; he walked slowly and deliberately, his footsteps plodding as if every move was mechanical. Her instincts told her not to look away until he was out of sight. As he rounded the corner, her attention shifted back to Elizabeth, who was adjusting the mirrors and checking the unfamiliar controls inside the car with a grin plastered across her face, blissfully unaware of her grandmother’s concerns.

With a forced smile, Sandra hid the chill that lingered from the strange encounter. ‘Well, go on then, Lizzie. Take it for a spin around the block. I’ll be waiting right here,’ she said, her voice wavering only slightly.

Elizabeth nodded eagerly. Starting the engine with a proud little rev, she waved as she pulled away.

The car had barely disappeared around the bend when Peter rejoined his wife.

'She's off, then?' he said, with a touch of pride.

'Yes, she certainly loves it,' Sandra replied, nervously glancing down the street where the stranger had disappeared.

Unaware of his wife's unease, Peter put his arm around her. 'Are you okay, love?' he asked. 'Only you're shivering.'

'Yes, sort of, Peter, but I have just had the oddest feeling. There was a man—'

The unmistakable sound of screeching tyres halted her words.

They both froze.

Moments later, Elizabeth's car appeared back in view, stopping sharply in front of them. Her face was pale, and her hands were gripping the steering wheel.

Sandra rushed over as Elizabeth shakily rolled down the window. 'Gran, I . . . I nearly hit someone. He stepped right out in front of me. I swear, he was just . . . waiting there.'

Sandra's heart sank. 'Was it the same man who just walked by here?' she asked, softly.

Elizabeth nodded, her eyes wide with confusion. 'Yes . . . Gran, maybe, but he just stared at me, like he knew me or something.'

Sandra's fingers tightened on the edge of the car door. She took a deep breath, trying to keep her unease hidden for Elizabeth's sake.

'Come inside, love.'

As they walked up the path, Sandra kept an arm protectively around her granddaughter, casting one last glance over her shoulder. The street was empty now, but that unsettling feeling hadn't left her.

However, she had to shake it off before her husband sent her to the psychiatrist again. She didn't want to go back on tablets. She'd needed them at the time, of course, when her dear daughter Shirley had just dropped dead. An aneurism, they'd said. So being a single parent, the job of raising Elizabeth was left to them. She was only ten years old at the time.

The next evening, Elizabeth's anxiety over the man on the road had faded, and she was eager to get out and enjoy a bit of freedom away from the confines of the house. The journey from her estate to her friend's house in Beckenham went without a hitch, and with each mile, she gained enough confidence so that it felt as though she'd been driving for months. Once there, she and her friend, who was much more worldly-wise than herself, celebrated with two glasses of wine.

By the time she left, it was past midnight, and she hadn't given the two glasses of wine a second thought until she saw the police car in the rear-view mirror flash its lights. Her heart raced, and the only thought in her head was how disappointed her grandparents would be. The realisation struck: if she was breathalysed, she might fail, and her licence would be gone, and her car along with it.

She pulled over on an empty road with no houses, shops, or other structures and waited as the officer approached. Shaking with embarrassment at the thought of her grandparents' displeasure, she slowly opened the window and looked up at the big, burly officer.

'Step out,' was all he said.

Too afraid to argue, she did as she was told. Then, he must have smelled the drink on her breath.

'Have you been drinking?' His voice was harsh, and she hadn't expected an officer to sound like that. But how many police officers had she known? None.

She stepped out and stood with her head down.

'I said, have you been drinking?'

She nodded, too afraid to deny it.

'Right, you'll have to come with me.'

Again, Elizabeth didn't question him. She followed the officer to his car, where he opened the back door, and she climbed in automatically. But as they drove off, she noticed something unsettling: the inside of the car didn't look like a police car at all – not from what she'd seen on TV. The only part resembling a police vehicle was a partition. Yet, on closer inspection, it wasn't standard. It was crudely fitted, with old rusty screws holding the Perspex screen to a wooden frame.

The smell of cigarettes and stale drink reminded her of the inside of an old pub. Surely this wasn't a police car? It couldn't be. She looked towards the front hoping to see a radio – anything that gave her some idea that he was a genuine police officer, but there was nothing. In fact, the more she looked for any clue, the more her heart raced. The officer, or whoever he truly was, suddenly drove through a lit-up area, which illuminated the inside of the car only for a second, but that moment was enough for her to see the bloodstains all over the rear seats.

Her gaze drifted to the rear-view mirror, where she caught sight of his face – and on closer inspection, she now recognised him. Her stomach churned. It was the man who'd stopped in the middle of the road and glared at her the night before.

She attempted to open the door but found it locked. Child locks! Fear crept up her spine and paralysed her. Then came the thought that she would be another teenager gone missing, like the girl who had been on the news for the last week.

'Just like your muvver, you are.'

Elizabeth didn't answer, too afraid to speak a word.

'Your grandmuvver was the old bitch who told my muvver that I should be shot. Yep, that's what the old bag said, and d'ya know what happened then, all 'cos of her?'

Elizabeth locked eyes with him in the rear-view mirror, her heart beating practically outside her chest. She shook her head; her mouth wouldn't move.

'Me dear ol' muvver had me sectioned. They only allowed me home on the odd occasion. In that hellhole, they treated me like an animal, they did. The ugly porter fucked me up the arse, he did. Ya know, he fucked me on a regular basis, but I got used to it, see. But I tell ya what I didn't get used to. It was being tied up, trussed up, and tied to the bed, or those straitjackets. Now, they are a proper nasty bit of kit, those fuckers are.' He stopped for breath and glared before a beaming smile slid across his face. 'Well, see, now since your grandmuvver made that happen to me, I thought, well, I might as well repay the favour, and by the time she gets your body back, she'll know what I did to you. So now sit back and relax. We're gonna have a little bit of fun. And I warn you: don't you go all hysterical on me like the last silly bitch. Fuck me, you would've thought I was killing her.' He chuckled. 'Well, come to think of it, I suppose I was.'

CHAPTER EIGHTEEN

It was the seventh of August, almost a month since Willow's death. The ache of her absence lingered, though having Billy stay with him for a week had, in an odd way, helped Cas navigate his grief.

Billy's presence had been a distraction, but it was time for Billy to speak to his mother.

Cas wandered into the stables. 'Right, boy, you can leave that horse and come back inside. We need to talk.'

Billy rolled his eyes. 'Cas, I'm not going back.'

'All right, but I can't have a spoiled brat wrapped around me for ever.'

Irritably, Billy yanked the bridle off the horse and stormed towards Cas. 'Spoiled? Really? And how's that, Cas? Do tell me.'

'Well, your mother's been on the blower every day asking when she can see you, and you keep saying you're not ready. You ain't some silly tart. You're a grown lad, and you're breaking your mother's heart. Carrie's a good 'un. She doesn't deserve your cold shoulder. Now, get in the car. I'm taking you to—'

'I ain't going back.'

'Cor, cut me off, why don't ya? I was *saying*, before you rudely interrupted, that I'm taking you back *to talk*. Then, if you're still sulking, you can come back and get under my feet for another week. Ya silly twat.'

Billy took a deep breath, trying to rein in his frustration. 'All right.'

'She's a kind mum, you know,' Cas added.

‘I know!’ Billy snapped. ‘Both my mums are good people, and I *do* care. I’m just.’ His voice, thick with sadness, dropped almost to a whisper. ‘I’m gutted, that’s all, and I can’t go near the house while he’s in it.’

Uncharacteristically, Cas put an arm around Billy’s shoulders. ‘I get it, son, I do. But don’t let your mum hurt like she is. You’re arsehole lucky, mate, to have a good mum. Even two. Me? I never had a mum. Well, not one who wanted to keep me.’

Billy stopped in his tracks, his eyes searching Cas’s face. ‘Really? I know you said you grew up in care, like with Mr Clarkson, but I didn’t know. I’m sorry, Cas. Yeah, I guess you must think I’m acting spoiled.’

‘I dunno, maybe not,’ Cas replied. ‘Anyway, your mum’s at home alone, and your brother—’

‘He *isn’t* my brother. I have a little brother called Charlie. Jesse is nothing to me now.’

Theatrically, Cas rolled his eyes. ‘Come on, Billy. You and Jesse were inseparable. I’ve heard the stories. You two had a special bond. Sometimes, we hit bumps along the way, but that doesn’t mean you can just disown your brother for ever.’ He held up a hand to stop Billy from interrupting. ‘I know you’re angry now, but you don’t understand, ’cos you’re still a kid, how precious having a brother is. Yeah, he messed up, and I could thrash the fucking living daylights out of him meself, but,’ he said, lowering his voice, ‘I knew what my little Willow was all about. And Jesse? If I’m honest, well, he was just doing what lads do when given half a chance. Believe it or not, this handsome face was once a teenager, and I would’ve done the same.’

Billy shook his head. ‘I’m *not* you, Cas. And Jesse isn’t who I thought he was. We had a pact. There were lines we never crossed. He crossed that line big time. Everything else is irrelevant. I believed my brother cared about me, that it was me and him against the world. That's all gone, Cas. All my hopes for the future? Well, they're gone too.' He threw his hands up in frustration.

'One day, you'll look back and think I was hurt and being only fifteen, I overreacted.'

Billy stared at Cas as if he was completely out of touch. 'You have no idea, Cas. No idea what *I* feel. Jesse knew what Willow meant to me. He knew about the plans I had for us. How I was going to propose to her when I turned eighteen, the kind of house I wanted to buy for us, and the car I was going to get her when she passed her driving test.'

Cas stood there, realising for the first time just how deeply Billy had cared for Willow. He also realised then how much Jesse had betrayed that trust. A lump formed in his throat as he looked at the boy – a boy who might have loved Willow as much as he had.

Unexpectedly, he reached out and pulled Billy into a long comforting hug. 'You're right, son. I had absolutely no idea.'

***

Before they drove over to Billy's home, Cas got on the phone to Carrie to give her the heads-up that her son was coming over to see her.

The drive to Billy's house was steeped in silence. Replaying everything Billy had told him, Cas realised just how much he'd misunderstood the situation. He only hoped both brothers could work things out, but the coldness in Billy's eyes when he mentioned Jesse made him think it might already be too late.

As they pulled up outside, Billy turned to Cas. 'Will you wait for me?'

Cas nodded. 'Yeah, of course I will.'

***

Cautiously, Billy opened the back door, now feeling like a stranger in his own home. It felt odd, almost as if he didn't belong anymore. Something in his head kept telling him that he was an outsider, maybe because he had walked out while Jesse stayed. Still, he owed his mother some kind of explanation for his absence.

As he stepped into the kitchen, Carrie rushed at him, flinging her arms around him. 'I've been so worried about you.'

Gently pulling away from her, Billy gave her a small smile. 'I'm okay, Mum, but I can't live here.'

'What?' she shrieked. 'Of course you can. It's your home! Your family! Look, Billy, I know what Jesse did, and I don't say it's okay – for one minute – but this is *your* home, *our* family. We can talk about it.' Her voice trembled with desperation, and her eyes searched his face, pleading for him to change his mind.

But Billy shook his head. 'Mum, maybe one day I'll come home, but, right now, I just can't be in the same house – the same room even – as Jesse.'

Just then, Jesse came into full view from the hallway. His mother had told him to apologise, to explain himself, because she desperately wanted Billy back home. He knew he was in the wrong, but he figured he could coax Billy around like he always did whenever he messed up. A cheeky grin, a playful wink. It had always worked before.

So, as he stepped into the kitchen, he smiled, arms outstretched. 'Come on, Bruv, let's hug it out.'

The mere disregard, masked by one of Jesse's famous grins, sent Billy over the edge. He imagined Jesse laughing at him, treating the whole thing like a joke. The red mist descended as rage took control. With flared nostrils and rapid breathing, he grabbed the nearest chair and swung it with such force that Jesse didn't have time to react.

The chair smashed into Jesse's ribs, sending him crashing across the kitchen. He landed hard against the cast-iron range, crumpling to the floor and clutching his ribs.

Carrie screamed. She was about to intervene, but there was no time to do so.

Billy pounced, fists flying and laying into his brother effortlessly, as if this was a mere warm-up before a serious bout in the ring.

Stunned and in pain, Jesse knew he had to get up fast, or Billy would tear him apart. His brother was harder and stronger, and they both knew it.

Jesse, who was now already hurt, could barely keep up. He scrambled to his feet and tried to dodge the punches, but Billy was relentless.

Carrie screamed for her sons to stop but she knew that screaming wouldn't be enough. She tried to step between them, desperate to prevent Billy from pulverising his brother. Blood sprayed, and bone-crushing punches echoed in the kitchen.

Carrie's heart pounded as she saw Jesse's swollen face, with blood pouring from his nose and split lip.

In a frantic attempt to stop the fight, Carrie grabbed Billy, but as he pulled his fist back for another blow, his elbow struck her square in the chest. She staggered back, winded, and collapsed to the floor.

At that point, the fight stopped. Billy froze, the rage draining from him as he stared at his mother, who was struggling to breathe on the floor. His eyes darted back to Jesse. There was no doubt he'd done a number on him. He was so battered, his eyes were badly swollen, and blood was streaming from his nose and mouth. Then, he looked across to his mother again, who was now dazed.

‘No! No!’ Billy bellowed, the sound rising from deep inside him. Panic surged as he turned and bolted down the hallway and out of the front door.

As promised, Cas was waiting in his car outside. As he looked up, he saw Billy, as pale as a ghost, hurtling towards him. Behind him, Jesse stumbled out, barely recognisable, his face swollen and bloodied.

Billy yanked the passenger door open and jumped in. ‘Please, just get me away from here.’

Cas was on the point of demanding answers, but taking one look at Billy and the wreckage of Jesse in the doorway, something told him that this was not the time. Without a word, he floored the accelerator, tearing off like a getaway driver.

‘What the fuck just happened?’ Cas demanded.

‘I don’t know, I don’t know. I just lost it with him, and I’ve hurt my mum. I caught her when I threw a punch.’

Cas slammed on his brakes and began reversing along the road. ‘You silly little twat, is she all right?’ He slammed on the brakes again just as he arrived outside the house.

But it seemed that Carrie was okay. She was at the door trying to pull Jesse back inside. When she saw Billy in the car, she stared for a moment, and huge tears fell down her cheeks.

Realising Billy was in the car, Jesse tried to get to him.

But Carrie stopped him. ‘Let him go, Jesse.’

There was a look in her eyes that said so much. She knew Billy wanted to leave. She understood: he had been so betrayed, and no amount of *sorry* would ever bring him back. Her two big boys were for ever separate. And as Cas drove away, half of her heart went along in that car. She loved her Billy too much to make him stay in the house with her other son. Would Billy ever look at him again?

***

Carrie would have been in the bathroom patching up Jesse if anyone else had hurt him. But this time, she let him clean himself up. Nursing a mug of tea while her throat felt tight with heartache, she sat in the kitchen all alone. Seeing her eldest son – her big boy – so hurt, it had ripped her apart.

She glanced at the clock, knowing that Dottie would be coming over soon to see Billy. They had all assumed that he would find a way to work things out once he was back home. She never expected her two sons to fight like that – to see Billy tear into Jesse, not just to hurt him, but to destroy him. And Jesse fighting back just to stop himself from being killed.

CHAPTER NINETEEN

The Slades sat around a table in the dimly lit back room of The Black Bear, a run-down pub. Vic Slade swigged his rum and Coke and flicked his finger for one of his sons to pass him a cigarette. Sitting beside him with his jaw still wired shut was his youngest son Nobby, who had lost a ton of weight. He could barely eat anything but baby food. He handed his father a premade roll-up, avoiding eye contact.

Opposite them sat Donna, who was sour-faced, her nails tapping irritably on the table. Anyone walking into the room might have thought that they had stepped back in time to a Western saloon.

'I tell ya, Vic,' she spat, after a long pause, 'Irvin is a thick git.' She shook her head. 'And I hate to say it, but our Danny is a fucking idiot as well. I can't believe I raised such a thick bunch of bastards.' She spat on the floor, disgusted by the vile taste in her mouth.

Vic, hard-faced and cunning, looked just as rough as his wife. His stint in the nick and his hard life had left him with deep scars, physical and otherwise. He glared across the table. 'You didn't raise them, well, not all the bloody time,' he muttered, waving his hand dismissively. 'Anyway, the plan's shot to shit. So, what do we do now?'

As Donna opened her mouth to speak, Vic cut her off before she could get a word out. 'Woman, I wasn't asking you. I was thinking out loud, airing my thoughts. You know what I mean. Keep your mouth shut. You've been warned enough. If you want to stay part of this family, you need to reel your fucking neck in. You're already on thin ice for moving Ginty into the house. I can't have much more of her rabbiting on about the poxy Murphys. She's doing me head in.'

He held the roll-up between his fingers and glared at Nobby. 'Well, it ain't gonna light itself, is it?'

Hurriedly, Nobby lit the cigarette, still nursing his wounded pride after being beaten up by Billy Murphy. He avoided eye contact with anyone, the humiliation all too fresh.

Vic took a long drag and exhaled slowly, his mind ticking over. 'So, practically all of your lot are behind bars because of Cas, that so-called Governor, and the Murphys—'

'And Carrie Ann Verne,' interrupted Donna, almost as a reflex.

Vic waved his hand, brushing the name away, as though it was nothing. 'That silly tart. I ain't worried about her.'

'She's got a mouth on her, though. Not like a proper traveller girl, mind. She's ditched the old ways. Stuck two fingers up at them, the nasty bitch.'

'I don't give a shit. The Murphys ain't my main concern. But Cas Ferrier is.'

Vic's eyes slowly scanned the room, taking in each family member seated around the table. His sons were big men. Luke, the eldest, had the sly eyes of a bastard who couldn't be trusted, and everyone knew it. Kieron, his second eldest, had fists the size of hammers but not much going on in the looks department, with one tooth in his head and a heavy jawline. Nobby, the next oldest, was tall but lean and still looking beaten down by his recent humiliation. Danny, the youngest and the most handsome member of his brood, had the potential to make something of his life, as well as to give the family something to be proud of.

But then, looking at his sons once more, Vic wondered if any of them were a match for even one of the Murphys.

They all knew what had happened to Jimmy and Atticus Carson. The brutal beatings they took at the hands of the Murphy boys, left them disabled and locked up, thanks to Cas grassing to the police. It went against every code they lived by, and the grudge had never really died.

The feud between the Carsons and the Murphys might have been verbally laid to rest three years ago, but Vic had Ginty bleating in his ear that it wasn't over. Not that he cared much for the Carsons himself – he'd never really liked them. And his only issue with the Murphys was their loyalty to Cas. His hatred for Cas and his right-hand man, Keith, ran deep, so the Murphys' allegiance was just another thorn in his side.

'Vic, Aunt Ginty will be here in a minute. What are we gonna say?' Donna's voice wavered slightly, sensing the tension.

'Fuck Ginty, Donna. I'm not interested in the Carsons—'

'Vic,' Donna interrupted, once again, her tone firmer now. '*I* was a Carson. *They're* family. Ginty was like a muvver to me. I owe her.'

Vic jumped up from the table, his face twisting in fury, and hurled his glass at her. 'I *told you* to shut it! When I say I don't give a shit about that old bag Ginty, I mean it! She's practically outstayed her welcome as it is.'

The glass bounced off his wife's arm, landing harmlessly in her lap, but, nevertheless, the violent gesture hung heavy in the air, like a pungent smell.

Meanwhile, Luke rose from his chair to fetch his father another drink as if nothing had happened. This was all routine in their household. Donna and Vic always fought like cat and dog. It had always been the case. In fact, violence between them was as regular as breathing.

Although since Ginty had moved in, their father had toned down his temper.

'All right, Vic, but don't take it out on me,' Donna muttered, her voice heavy with sarcasm. 'I didn't fuck up the plan, did I.'

Vic rubbed the back of his neck, pacing furiously. His eyes flared, his tone carrying the sting of unrestrained anger. 'That *cunt* robbed me of my future. My money. And this: this was my chance to get some of it back.' He slammed his fists on the table, making the glasses rattle. 'But now, it's all fucked!'

Kieron, who was seated at the far end, grunted. 'I don't know why we don't just go in and rob the prick.'

Vic stopped pacing, turning to glare at his son. 'Don't you *lot* ever listen to a word I say?' His voice was dangerously calm before he erupted again. 'Do you know what Cas would do if he caught you?'

Kieron shrugged. 'Oh, leave off, Dad, he's an old man now.'

'*Old man?*' Vic shrieked, his face twisted with rage. 'That *old man* would shoot you in the legs first, drag you to some cesspit, and leave you to fucking rot! I've seen what he's capable of. I've known him to take a bloke, tie him up in a sewer, cut his legs to ribbons, and leave him to die in his own filth. The poor bastard was eaten alive by rats before infection even finished him off. *That* is who you're dealing with. You really think his place ain't alarmed? Booby-trapped even? He's not some soft old man, Kieron. He's a *very* dangerous cunt.'

Kieron shrank onto his chair, now also feeling humiliated and stupid. His father had a way of making him feel small.

Vic Slade might have seemed like he had mellowed with age to the outside world, even turned into a recluse.

But behind closed doors, he was the same violent, ruthless man he had always been.

'Go ahead, rob him if you want,' Vic snarled. 'But don't say I didn't warn you when you end up in pieces.' He glared at his sons, daring them to challenge him even more.

Luke returned with a fresh glass of rum and Coke, setting it down in front of his father. 'Danny's called. He's on his way.'

Vic nodded, snatching the drink and taking a large gulp. 'Good. Let's see what this prick has to say for himself.'

'Listen to me, Vic, it ain't Danny's fault. Come on, the poor boy had his head practically caved in by the bloke's horse.'

Now thoroughly exasperated, Vic threw his hands in the air. 'See what I mean about that cunt's level of violence? He didn't just *beat up* Danny, did he. No, he got a horse to kick the fuck out of him! That's the kind of sick bastard he is.' He shot a glance at Kieron, and then back at Donna. 'And that's another reason why I'm not interested in the Murphys. Danny told me that Billy stopped Cas from killing him.'

Donna shook her head, her face twisted in a grimace. 'I bet that was a set-up. I've heard that Billy boy's living with Cas now. So, although I'm no genius, I reckon Cas was always gonna let Danny go. Billy just happened to be there, and it was all part of the act.'

She tutted loudly, her voice laced with contempt. 'Danny doesn't owe Billy fuck all for that. And it sure as hell doesn't make up for what the Murphys did to Jimmy and Atticus. So, fuck 'em. All of 'em. And our Atticus is sick, Vic, proper ill.'

Vic stared into his glass momentarily, with Donna's words swirling around in his mind. He hated Cas with every fibre of his being, but even he couldn't shake off the feeling that something didn't sit right. As far as anyone knew,

Danny had been the last person to see Willow alive. The police knew it, and so did Cas. Cas had every reason to kill Danny, and yet he hadn't. That fact alone made him suspicious. A cold shiver ran down his spine, turning his blood to ice.

'Christ!' Vic muttered, his voice barely above a whisper.

'What is it, Vic?' Donna asked, her eyes narrowing, as she saw the fear written across his face.

'I'm not sure, but I've got a bad feeling about all of this. No one knows about Irvin but fingers are being pointed at Danny.' Vic took a deep breath. 'If Cas thinks Danny killed his granddaughter – *his granddaughter* – let that sink in. He wouldn't care whether Danny did it or not. The fact is that Danny was the last one to see her alive and he didn't bring her home safe . . . Cas would kill him for that alone. But if he really believes Danny's guilty . . . it wouldn't end there. He'd make our boy suffer in the worst way possible.'

The room fell deathly silent, all eyes on Vic.

'How?' Donna asked, impatience and fear dripping from her voice.

Vic's face went pale, the hard look in his eyes dissipating, now replaced by raw fear. 'In the worst way. He'll start by killing his family – one by one – until Danny is the only one left. Then, he'll hunt him down like an animal. Like a fucking poacher in the Serengeti.'

Luke screwed up his face. 'Bit dramatic, don't you think?'

'*Dramatic*?' Vic yelled, slamming his fist on the table. 'Believe me, it wouldn't be the first time! Some idiot hurt Cas's best mate years ago, and Cas killed the bloke's bruvver right in front of him! He doesn't play by any rules. If he thinks Danny's responsible for Willow, he'll make him pay in ways you can't imagine.' Beads of sweat peppered his brow as he let out an exasperated sigh. 'Shit.'

The tension in the room rose another notch. It was matched by spirals of cigarette smoke that were not only thick, but suffocating those present.

At that moment, the side door creaked open. In walked Danny. He was still bruised, but his cocky grin, which was spread across his face, spoke volumes.

Vic's glare turned icy. 'Wipe that fucking smirk off your face, you dickhead,' he snapped, pointing to a chair next to Luke. 'Sit your arse down.'

As Danny sat down beside his brother, Donna wrapped an arm around his wide shoulders. 'How are you feeling, Son?'

'Yeah, I'm fine,' Danny muttered, though his eyes were fixed on the door, which swung open again.

Standing in the doorway, dressed like a bloated Michelin Man in an ill-fitting tweed suit, was Irvin, Vic's brother. A ridiculous wig was perched on his head, and his lips, which were slathered in ChapStick, stretched into an even wider grin than the one Danny had when he entered the pub. 'I'll have a gin and tonic,' he purred, licking his lips and aiming the order directly at Donna.

With a huff, Donna rose from her chair and stomped towards the bar, muttering under her breath.

Vic stared at Irvin in disbelief, his patience already wearing thin. 'What the *fuck* are you doing here? I told you to stay the hell away for now! Jesus, you're a bloody nightmare. And what the fuck is that on your head? You look like a clown.'

'Charming,' Irvin replied, smoothing down the wig. 'I look like a gentleman. This suit's a *Barbour* and it cost more than your entire wardrobe, Vic.'

Vic glanced nervously at the door, his voice dropping to a hiss. 'No one followed you, right? You're not stupid enough to bring heat here, are ya?'

Irvin waved a hand, dismissively. 'Relax, ya daft sod. No one's followed me. For fuck's sake, it's been a month, so don't shit yaself. Anyway, where's my money?'

'Money?' Vic's eyes narrowed, fury bubbling up again. 'Fucking money? You idiot, you should be paying *me* after the mess you've made, not the other way around. You fucked up, *big time*.'

A grin crawled across Irvin's face. 'It was an accident, Bruv. I couldn't help it.'

Vic glared at him, shaking his head in disgust. 'I swear to God, they should have kept you locked up in that funny farm. I don't know what possessed me to fight for your fucking release and to pay to have your papers doctored. You're a proper lunatic.'

Luke chuckled, watching Irvin with a bemused expression. The boys had always found Irvin a source of dark comedy, but they had never underestimated him. His father was right: Irvin should have stayed locked away. In and out of mental hospitals since the age of seven, his erratic behaviour was legendary. Dangerous, too. Luke knew that his father was hoping Irvin didn't get on the drink because he was a living nightmare with a drink inside him – totally unpredictable.

''Ere,' Irvin said, his grin widening. 'I just saw ol' Ginty outside. Might give her one later. She looks like she could do with a good old-fashioned fuck. It would wipe that miserable look off her face.'

Vic cringed, his nose wrinkling in disgust. 'Leave off, Irvin. She's *old*.'

'Old, young, boy, girl – dead even, I ain't fussy.' Irvin shot back with a laugh. 'I'd fuck a sheep if I could catch one. Now, where's your missus with me drink? She'd better not be putting poison in it.'

Licking his lips, Irvin eyed Donna as she placed the glass in front of him. 'Cheers, darlin'. Don't worry, I can taste poison a mile away,' he said, with a wink, reaching for the glass.

Donna kept her distance with disgust written across her face. She wiped her hands on her shirt as if touching Irvin's glass was enough to contaminate her.

Watching the exchange, Vic finally snapped. 'You're unbelievable, Irvin. You waltz in here like you've just come back from holiday. Please tell me you ditched the burner phone?'

Irvin's grin turned ugly, his eyes narrowing. 'You think I'm fucking stupid?'

Vic felt uneasy, but he dared not show it. Instead, he glared at Irvin. 'Watch your tone. You need to remember who you owe: *me*. You'd still be rotting in that nuthouse if it weren't for me. So watch it. And as for me owing you money, that wasn't a given. I said you could pay me back for getting you out, so maybe, just maybe, when I get the money off Cas, you could have a few quid.'

Irvin grinned, his smile deranged. Swallowing his drink in one go, he slammed the glass on the table and turned his gaze to Danny. 'State of your head.'

Vic responded before Danny could speak. 'Cas's horse did that. Because *you* fucked up the job, Irvin. The last person to see that girl alive, according to the police, was *my* son. Look at the fucking state of him. And now, Cas is out for blood.'

Irvin shrugged, lazily waving his empty glass in the air. 'So? The bloke's a cunt.'

Vic rolled his eyes, exasperated, once again. 'A dangerous one, Irvin. A *fucking dangerous* one.'

'Oh, come on, Vic, it was a stupid plan, anyway.'

'No, it wasn't,' Vic snapped, glaring at his brother. 'Danny had the girl eating out of the palm of his hand.'

He looked at his son, signalling for him to explain.

Danny hesitated, glancing between his father and Irvin. 'The plan was going just fine, I knew she'd be at Bluewater. She had a thing for me, even though no one knew it. She wasn't my type, but I knew I could get her away from that mug Billy Murphy. I messaged you as planned.'

He paused, looking at his father for approval. Vic nodded. 'Go on, Son. Tell him.'

Danny took a deep breath. 'So, I drove her to the place. The field with the lay-by, as agreed. Got her out of the car by saying I didn't like smoking inside. Then I gave her the bag of charlie, as we planned. I knew she'd snort it: she'd done it before. That's when *you* were supposed to show up, Irvin, with your fake police car and blue lights. I'd act panicked, say I was gonna get nicked for the coke, and we'd both split.'

Irvin's left eye twitched, his voice dripping with sarcasm. 'Yeah, and *that's* where it went to shit, didn't it? She shot off across the field, and instead of sticking to the plan, *you* let her run.'

'*You* were supposed to stop her!' Danny shot back. 'You were supposed to pull up, drag her into your fake police car, and hold her until you heard from Dad. But I watched you when she bolted. You laughed like it was a game.'

Irvin's face twisted into a scowl. 'She wasn't supposed to run, was she? I was supposed to pull you both over, get her in the car, and pretend I was taking her to the station. But *you,* you let her go, not me. So how's that *my* fault the plan went tits up?'

Danny's face reddened. 'Because you fucking killed her.'

The words hung in the air, for what seemed like an age, before they then faded.

Irvin leaned back on his chair and slowly removed his wig, wiping sweat from his brow. 'Hot in here, ain't it?'

Luke finally spoke up, his voice tinged with curiosity. 'Why'd you kill her?'

Irvin tutted, chuckling to himself. 'You know what I'm like. She fought like a wild animal, even when I had a knife to her jugular. Then she kicked me in the bollocks – twice. That's when I lost it. I suppose, I went a tad over the top.'

Exhaling heavily, Vic rubbed his face. 'Great. Now we've got no kid to barter with, and the police will be after *you*, or Danny, or both.'

Before Irvin could respond, the side door swung open, and in strolled Ginty.

'I was waiting outside. I didn't realise your lot was in the back room. Fuck me, it's hot. I'm sweating me tits off.'

Donna, who had remained quiet until now, gestured to the chair beside her.

Ginty plopped down, her outfit – a too-tight vest and tube skirt – leaving little to the imagination, even at sixty-five.

'So what's happening, then?' Ginty asked, wiping her brow. 'Heard through the grapevine that Jesse Murphy's the farver of Willow's baby. Caused a right stir between the bruvvers, hasn't it? Well, bollocks to the lot of 'em. They denied our family, so I've resigned meself to the fact that they ain't my grandsons. They're dirty scumbags, those Murphys.'

Vic's jaw tightened, his simmering anger now aimed at Ginty. 'Oi, I'm not interested in the *poxy* Murphys! I want Cas to pay what he owes me. Don't give a shit if the Murphy boy *was* dating Cas's granddaughter. That means *fuck all* to me. So, shut it, Ginty.'

‘Oi, Vic, no need to speak to Aunt Ginty like that,’ Donna piped up.

Without warning, Vic shot up from his seat, stormed around the table, and slapped Donna so hard, she fell off her chair.

Ginty, who had seen Vic’s violent outbursts before but never against Donna, was on her feet in an instant, swinging for him. But being off balance, she missed completely and tumbled to the floor beside Donna.

The room fell silent. Vic stood over them, breathing heavily, his face flushed with rage. No one dared to move or speak.

Irvin’s lips lifted into a smile as he surveyed the chaos. ‘Well, this has just got very interesting.’

‘Shut your mouth, Irvin, you idiot. Now, fuck off. Get out of here, and stay low. Where’s the car?’

‘Out front.’

‘You what, you bellend?’

‘Don’t shit yourself. I took the vinyl strips off and changed the number plates back. Jesus, you have no faith in me.’

‘Just go, will ya? And stay the hell away. If anyone recognises you from that night, we’re all poleaxed – including Danny. They’ll never believe he’s innocent, will they? You’re his bloody uncle, for Christ’s sake.’

‘I’m not getting nicked for this right now,’ said Danny. ‘Me lawyer reckons Billy Murphy told the filth he was sure he saw Willow running across the field after he saw me driving away. Apparently, I nearly ran them off the road. And then, for some ridiculous reason, Irvin, after you killed Willow, you pulled over the Murphys. Why the hell did you do that?’

Irvin laughed. ‘You said to make sure someone sees the police car, so I pulled them over, and they were shitting themselves. I must be a shit-hot actor 'cos they thought I was the genuine article.'

Vic sighed. 'You prick! You were only supposed to pull Danny over and make it look like a routine stop. And then hover around a bit for passing cars to see a copper's motor. But no, not you. You murdered the girl and then thought you were in a fucking episode of *Z Cars*. And I meant make sure the police car was seen. I didn't mean get out of the motor and show off your ugly mug and to none other than the Murphys. Cas was supposed to think some bent copper was holding his granddaughter for ransom. We wanted the Ol' Bill looking for a dodgy copper, not a lunatic in fancy dress.'

Irvin nodded, chewing his lip. 'I'd better lay low. Billy Murphy will definitely recognise me – he's a proper bastard, that one.'

'And how would you know?' Danny asked, frowning deeply.

'He came back to the field when I was looking for a place to dump the body and I thought he might have seen something. So I figured I'd finish him off too. I'd fuck him first, then, well . . . whatever.'

'And what do you mean by whatever?' snapped Danny, now feeling confident with the backing of his father.

'Well, yeah, I was in the mood and thoroughly enjoying meself. Christ, can't a fella have a bit o' fun these days, without everyone getting hysterical.'

Vic shook his head in disbelief. 'Why the hell I fought for your release, I'll never know. You are insane. Just go. Fuck off and take that dead rat you carry around on your head with you.'

CHAPTER TWENTY

21 August

Cas had been out all morning visiting Lolly. By the time he returned, his eyes were bloodshot. He stormed through the kitchen like a bear with a sore head. All that could be heard were the sounds of cupboards and drawers being opened and slammed shut as he attempted to put together a makeshift late brunch.

Keith kept his distance. When Cas was like this, he found that it was best just to let his boss get his anger out of his system. So keeping his thoughts to himself, he focused on dealing with an old mate who had a deal for Cas to look over.

Billy had set up his laptop on a table between the red and green sofas at the other end of the study to where Cas had his impressive antique oak desk with the oxblood leather inlays.

Billy had already sussed out that Cas was basically very conscious of his poor upbringing, and so he totally understood why Cas felt the need to overcompensate by going all-out to show off his wealth.

But now, he was getting frustrated trying to block out all the noise in the kitchen. He was doing some research on a particular investment he had in mind. The stock market had announced that a new IPO – Ebay – was going to launch in late September, so it had piqued his interest. He was eager to find out what the launch price would be.

He was about to do some further digging when his concentration was ruined by even louder sounds coming from the kitchen. It was no use. Finally, switching off the laptop, he got up, and walked across to the French doors that overlooked the beautiful rose garden.

Eventually, Cas appeared in the study.

'Are you all right?' asked Billy.

Cas slumped down on the red sofa. 'No, I ain't all right.' His sigh was loud and heavy. 'Those two poxy detectives have as much drive as a fucking snail on holiday. I swear to God, blokes like that are the reason we have instructions on shampoo bottles.'

Solemnly, Billy clasped his hands together. 'Still no news, then?'

Cas shook his head. 'They called a meeting with me and Lolly just to tell us they have no update. Oh yeah, and the wankers told me not to take the law into me own hands. They have reason to believe I had something to do with Danny's injuries. Well, fuck 'em. If they can't do their job properly – and, clearly, they can't – then what the fucking hell do they expect a man to do.'

'So, they still don't have a suspect?'

'Not a fucking clue.' Cas clenched his fists and looked at his watch. 'It's the fucking twenty-first today. Which means it's been six weeks. The useless bastards.'

Billy raised an eyebrow. 'And I bet they're not in any hurry to consider that it might've been one of their own.'

Cas shot him a look that was contorted with anger. It wasn't aimed at Billy, but life itself. 'I swear to you, Billy, if I get my hands on the bastard, I'll do time. I don't care. I'll torture the cunt.'

He got up. Running his hands through his hair as he paced the room, he continued. 'Even me mate down the nick – who I pay well to keep his ear to the ground – says they've drawn a blank. They reckon the copper wasn't actually a copper at all, just someone impersonating one.'

'You believe that?'

Cas shrugged. 'I don't know what to believe anymore.' He paused, sucking in a deep breath, which made a whistling sound through his teeth. 'Anyway, they came to Lolly's to let him know this: they're releasing Willow's body.'

He got up and went over to one of the casement windows that looked out on to the wide sweeping drive to hide his face as emotions welled up.

Billy, not one for hugging anyone, if he could get away with it, let Cas have his space.

After a moment, Cas turned back, wiping his eyes. 'And . . . my daughter, the selfish cow, wants Willow cremated and done with as soon as possible. Says she needs closure. *Closure?* My arse. I'll have *closure* when the cunt responsible is dead.'

'She wanted to be buried,' Billy said, quietly.

Cas wiped his eyes again, frowning. '*What?*'

'Willow told me a long time ago that she wanted to be buried, and her grave covered in pink roses.'

Cas blinked. 'What the hell did you two *talk* about?'

'Everything, Cas. We spoke about everything.'

Cas bit his lip, now trying to hold back his tears. 'No wonder her phone bill was so high.'

'Every night, we'd talk for hours until she fell asleep. I could hear her purring like a kitten.'

Cas turned away, his voice cracking. 'She must have loved you, Billy boy.'

Billy looked down. 'I'll never know, Cas, will I.' He cleared his throat and shifted the conversation. 'Anyway, do you want help with the funeral?'

'You knew her better than I did. You should be part of it.' He knew Billy wanted to help. Of course he did. It was his way of grieving too.

CHAPTER TWENTY-ONE

It was close to a week since Ginty had been held captive by Irvin down in the cellar of the old farmhouse somewhere in Sussex.

Today, he had brought her upstairs into a living room that also served as a kitchen-cum-bedroom. The minute he removed the wrist and ankle zip ties, which were cutting into her skin, she felt the blood return to her hands. She couldn't stop the pins and needles effect, though. That hurt like hell, but at least she could have a moment of comfort.

But not for long. The stench up here was vile. In fact, it was beyond anything she'd ever smelled before. And it wasn't getting any better. Her nose wasn't adapting to it at all. The foul smell wasn't coming from the piss bucket that Irvin allowed her to use downstairs: this was far more potent.

Ginty was told to sit on a chair near the bed. There, she remained seated, the terror crawling up her spine as she watched Irvin. After her first attempt at speaking landed her with a few slaps and a punch to the mouth, she stayed quiet.

However, having spent days on her own, the frustration of having no one to talk to and with so many thoughts in her head had her dying to tell him what was on her mind. It was important. So important, in fact, that she just went for it.

'Irvin, listen, love,' she said, finally, her voice trembling, although it was laced with an attempt at sweetness, 'I wouldn't grass, mate, o' course I wouldn't. I was just . . . fucked off. You know how it is. I wouldn't go to the Ol' Bill. It ain't who I am. Never has been, never will be. I hate fucking grasses. I mean, look at Jimmy and Arthur rotting like cancer in prison, all because of those snitches. So, to me,' she said, as she wiped her sore lips, which were now bleeding, with the back of her hand, 'what you did to Willow is kinda payback to that Cas geezer. So, nah, mate, I wouldn't say a word to no one. I'm on your side. Donna knows I wouldn't upset you, Vic, or the boys. I mean, Irvin, we're practically family.'

Her words almost tripped over each other as she continued. 'Me and you. So what d'ya say, eh, love? I can fuck off, get outta your hair, and with me mouth closed and not saying a word. And you don't have to stay in this . . .' She looked around. It was a dilapidated, damp, and mouldy building, that was for sure. An old metal bed with a heavily stained mattress had been pushed into the corner. An old butler sink was chipped and barely hanging on to the wall. Above the sink was a dripping tap. And next to the sink there was a camping stove, which was perched on an old cabinet. 'This place. I'm sure you've got a nicer home to go to, sweetheart.'

Irvin didn't look at her. He was at the stove frying an entire pack of bacon as if it was one solid slab. He hadn't even bothered separating the rashers, the edges curling and hissing in the pan. The sound alone was enough to fray her nerves, but his humming – some eerie, off-key tune – made her blood run cold. His back was to her, but even then, his presence filled the decaying room like a shadow creeping through every crack in the walls.

She felt trapped, not just in this crumbling farmhouse, but in a nightmare she really hadn't seen coming at all. It had all seemed like a joke, a sick little suggestion over drinks with Vic at the Slades' place. 'Kidnap Willow', she'd said, just for something to say. It didn't matter whose family. She just liked to be in on anything that would give her a voice – make her feel like the head of the family – because that was how she'd always seen herself. However, her almost throwaway suggestion wasn't even meant to be serious at all . . . until it was.

They had all looked at her as if she'd just cracked the 'Enigma' code, and before she knew it, they'd discussed the plan and then executed it. At first, she thought it was just the drink talking, but it wasn't. Now, she was here, having been a willing participant in something that had spiralled far beyond what she could ever have imagined. Her stomach twisted with unease, but it wasn't because of what had happened to the girl. No, she felt nothing for her or that Cas Ferrier bloke. But her stupid mistake had landed her here, at the mercy of a man who was about as human as the derelict walls closing in around her.

Her throat tightened. It wasn't just about the kidnapping, although this situation was terrifying enough. It was about everything she'd lost – her grandsons, her Jimmy, her Arthur, and her home. In her mind, the Murphys had taken it all. She'd thought that Vic and Donna would help her to win back some of her former life. But now, in this cold filthy room, she knew how wrong she'd been. Donna, for all her bravado, was not only dominated and suppressed by her husband, but she was living under his threat of being expelled from the house and the boys' lives again.

Irvin turned away from the stove with a twisted grin plastered across his face. His eyes, cold and piercing, locked onto hers, and she froze.

That stare – God, it reminded her of Dottie Ellis. It was like the dead-eyed gaze of a psychopath. She had only seen it in one other person, and like Irvin, he also gave her the chills. That was Danny Slade, Donna's pride and joy.

'Do you think I care, ya silly fat bitch,' he said, slowly. 'I couldn't give a shit if you are on my side or not.' He laughed, the sound sharp and jarring, before returning to his grotesque slab of bacon.

Ginty nervously shuffled to the edge of her seat, her hands gripping the arms of the mouldy old chair, as she tried to rise. She had to do something – anything. 'Shall I make that sandwich for ya, Irvin?' she asked, her voice small and shaky. 'Me boys always loved a nice bacon sarnie from their ol' mum. They reckoned—'

'Sit down,' he snarled, his words as sharp as the knife he held.

It was as if he'd pushed her back onto the chair himself. She collapsed onto it, her heart racing. 'I-I was only trying to help ya, Irv,' she stammered.

But he was looking at her again, with his signature predatory gaze. 'Don't you call me *Irv*. Me name's *Irvin*,' he growled, his eyes raking over her, as though she was prey.

The way he looked at her made her skin crawl. Licking his lips, he stared at her breasts, revealed by her low-cut top.

Watching his gaze, she realised that she needed to pull his attention away from any idea that he could have sex with her. She was too old for all that malarkey. It had been years since anyone had touched her, and she wasn't going to let it happen now.

'You've gotta be the same age as my Albert would have been,' she said, quickly, giving him a little reminder of how old she actually was, although he would have to be blind not to know that. However, her words tumbled out before she could think. 'You two probably knew each other. What school did you go to?'

Irvin chuckled, but the sound was more unsettling this time. He stabbed the bacon with the knife, as though he was killing it.

'I never went to a normal school past the age of seven,' he said, his voice dripping with something darker. 'They locked me up when I was a kid.'

The sight of the knife in his hand sent a jolt of fear through her. She couldn't tear her eyes away from it. Her tongue stuck to the roof of her mouth, her pulse thundering in her ears, as the realisation of just how dangerous he was hit her. This wasn't some game she could talk her way out of. She was trapped, and Irvin held all the cards. After all, he was the one holding the blade.

***

What gnawed at her mind wasn't Irvin playing with that razor-sharp knife but Vic's words when he locked the car doors and drove her to the derelict farmhouse. 'You, Ginty Carson, might've thought it was a joke when you threatened me.'

The words still echoed in her head.

'Out of the goodness of me heart, I was gonna sort you out. Ya know, get you a place. There was a caravan at the Streatham site with your name on it. Your sons 'ave got mates there. You'd have fitted right in. They'd have looked after you, made sure you had gas, food. Treated you like the bloody queen of the gypsies. But no, you sly fucking bitch. You sit there, like a tower of lard, with ya fat fucking legs firmly squashed under my table, pretending to be part of our plans. And then you have the bare-faced nerve to threaten me when I asked you to leave! So, I've had enough of you.'

His voice rose to a scream, one hand gripping the wheel, the other jabbing at his chest. 'Me! The one who took you in when your whole family kicked you out. You took Donna's kindness for weakness. And you think I wouldn't be pissed off when you started your whining and then threatened to grass me, me bruvver, and me boys, if you had to leave?'

He swerved, narrowly avoiding a car, as he screamed into the rear-view mirror, his eyes locked on her, his mouth foaming with rage. 'Well, I've found you a new home, and it's exactly what a nasty piece of work like you deserves!'

The silence that followed seemed like hours, but it was only a minute or two before he grinned into the mirror again. 'I'm sure me bruvver will make you feel so at home you won't want to go anywhere. He'll think all his Christmases have come at once. Like a cat with a mouse.'

Her blood ran cold. She knew what he meant. Irvin was a raving lunatic, and she'd heard him talk about killing Willow just as if it was a joke, a game he enjoyed. And then there had been Danny, who was sitting next to her, grinning like the Cheshire Cat, his eyes wide and excited as though he was getting off on it.

***

Irvin stabbed at the bacon with such savage precision, it looked as though he was slicing through some haunting memory from his childhood.

'Irvin, please, love, listen to me,' she pleaded. 'I'm an old woman now. I ain't got much time left. Me bones rattle when I walk. I'm half the woman I used to be.'

'Shut it, girl,' he growled, not even glancing her way. 'You're twice the size of most women. But it don't matter to me if you're old, fat, thin, or even dead. I'll still fuck ya, then fuck you up.'

She swallowed hard, trying a different tactic. 'Oh, I see. Irvin, I didn't know you felt that way about me.'

Slamming the bacon onto a chunk of bread, he then made a sandwich. When he turned to face her, a cruel light burned in his eyes. 'I never said I *liked* you. A screw's a screw. I don't give a shit what hole I put it in. Now, get your kit off and bend over that bed. I love to eat and fuck – two pleasures in one go.'

Ginty's heart pounded, her pulse racing. She widened her eyes in disbelief, but there was no way she was going to let this happen. 'I'm telling you now,' she said, with force in her voice to inject as much authority as she could, 'over my dead body will I bend over for you!'

Again, Irvin's eyes flashed angrily as they appeared like dark projectiles. 'Dead body?' he snarled, yanking her hair and nearly tossing her off the chair as he might a rag doll. 'Fucking dead body?' His fury melted into laughter, starting with a chuckle that rolled into a belly laugh. It was so jarring, it made her skin crawl.

Ginty scrambled to get up, but pain shot through her shoulder as her arm gave out beneath her. She yelped, and just like that, his laughter stopped. In one swift movement, he seized her by the arm and flung her onto the filthy bed. The stench burned her nostrils as she landed face-first on the rancid mattress. His strength was terrifying – he had the power of ten men. But no matter how scared she was, she wasn't going to let him rape her.

She desperately tried to fight him off by attempting to turn to claw his eyes, but he was faster. Her dress – cheap and poorly stitched – ripped open at the back as he viciously tore at it, the fabric giving way easily. She wriggled, now desperate, but it was as futile as a worm trying to escape a bird's beak. If she had been twenty years younger, a move like that would have had her wanting more, but this wasn't welcomed at all.

She could feel his breath by her ear, and as she turned to the side, she could see his fat dirty fingers gripping the greasy lump of bacon squashed between two slices of bread.

Seconds later, she jumped and squealed when she felt him rip her knickers off.

And now, with his victim powerless, he allowed his weight to hold her down, realising she couldn't breathe. Letting go of the sandwich, he used both hands to rip her buttocks apart.

She screamed in pain, feeling as if he was ripping her in half, before she felt something huge and long force its way inside her. As he groaned and moaned, moving back and forth, it took her back to the time when she was a child. To a time when her grandfather had raped her mercilessly, just as Irvin was doing to her now.

***

She'd only been ten years old. No one believed her when she told her parents that her grandfather had beaten and raped her to within an inch of her life. Her perceived lies led to her being made a virtual outcast. So instead of living with her family in the caravan, she was forced to live outside where she slept in the bender tent.

For years afterwards, she was shunned by her own community, while being allowed to live within the confines of it. She was forced to improvise by sleeping under what amounted to a hessian throw over a few picked bendable branches. Not once did she have the luxury of sharing the warm fire or sitting at the family table. Instead, she was thrown the scraps as if she was a dog.

However, that all changed when eventually she met her husband-to-be. He turned out to be her saviour. As soon as she was married, her grandfather passed away, and she was returned to the bosom of the community. Having her own children, she stood no nonsense by building a reputation for being a hard woman, one who not even men would mess with.

***

Now, déjà vu had returned, or so it seemed. This time, it was Irvin using his grubby hands to paw at her body.

When Irvin was done and he'd climbed off her, he snatched his sandwich and began munching down on it like a starved dog.

Ginty continued to lay there in the same position. She didn't care anymore. He had removed her last ounce of dignity. As far as she was concerned, she had lost everything now, and so she wondered if her death would be a welcome relief from constantly fighting the world and facing rejection at every turn.

Suddenly, she felt something thrown over her.

'Get that around your fat arse. You're putting me off me food.'

Ginty got up slowly, her body aching, as she wrapped the filthy matted blanket around herself.

The strength Irvin had used to toss her onto the bed had shifted the entire metal frame closer to the wall.

She glanced down, about to push herself up, when she noticed the hand.

At first, she thought her mind was playing tricks on her. Maybe it was one of Irvin's sick jokes – he was always into props, showing up at Vic's house in strange costumes and always pretending to be someone else. Donna had even nicknamed him 'the impersonator'.

But then, her senses hit her all at once – the hand wasn't a joke. It looked grey, waxy, and far too real to be a toy. This was the source of the foul stench that had lingered in the air and was now unbearable.

Irvin caught her staring at the hand. His burst of laughter made her jump. 'I told ya, Ginty. When you said: "over my dead body", it fucking cracked me up, see?' His eyes gleamed with twisted pride as though he had pulled off the ultimate prank.

Ginty felt as though she was trapped in a nightmare. Nothing made sense. Surely this couldn't be real, could it?

With a sick grin, Irvin bent down, grabbed the corner of a plastic sheet, and pulled the body partly out from under the bed to reveal the gruesome remains of a girl.

Just moments ago, Ginty had almost made peace with her fate, ready to accept whatever came next. But the sight of the girl's decomposed body jolted her out of that numbness, striking her with sheer horror. The girl was little more than a skeleton, her mouth frozen in a permanent scream and her sunken eyes giving her a grotesque hollow expression.

Ginty couldn't move, couldn't breathe. The shock was too much.

Meanwhile, Irvin stood there chewing his sandwich as though it was the most casual thing in the world. To him, the dead girl was no more than a discarded doll – a mere afterthought.

But Ginty couldn't tear her gaze away. The girl's foot was detached from her body, and a rusted chain was still locked around her ankle. Her stomach churned. Judging by the way the foot was severed, the girl had probably tried to cut it off in a desperate attempt to escape.

This was no joke, no prop. This was the monstrous reality in which Irvin thrived.

CHAPTER TWENTY-TWO

4 September

The church was only a mile from Cas's house, nestled in a well-kept graveyard tended to by proud gardeners. It took only a few minutes for the mourners to arrive. Most were Cas's old mates, a few of Lolly's, and, of course, the Murphys.

With the September midday sun shining brightly, it was the kind of day that would have been perfect for a wedding. But today was far from glorious. Today was Willow's funeral. The grieving faces all around Billy made him feel worse than he did already.

Lolly stood alone, his face set like stone, betraying no emotion.

On the other hand, Cas appeared visibly shattered, as he personally guided the hearse up the drive, lost in his thoughts.

Keith walked across to Billy and stood beside him. They both watched as the procession followed in behind. The weight of grief hung heavy in the air as they all faced the grim reality of saying goodbye.

Billy inwardly smiled when he saw that no expense had been spared. The stunning oak coffin with ornate gold handles was covered in perfect pink roses, just as Willow would have wanted. He was pleased Cas hadn't forgotten the crucial details, even in his grief.

Billy's eyes then shifted to Tara.

What a sight she was. Walking behind the hearse, she was draped in an overly dramatic black dress suit, a large hat, and sunglasses. To any onlooker, she could have been the wife of a mafia boss. The man beside her, though, tall and imposing in an Armani suit, looked more suitably dressed for a fashion show than a funeral. But his presence was clear: he was there to show off – to mark his territory as Tara's new man. Lolly was a 'yesterday's man', or so it seemed.

But neither Lolly nor Cas cared. Tara hadn't been near her father in days, never bothering to check on him or see how he was coping. She had used Cas for years, taking everything he gave her – gifts, money, attention, the whole caboodle. Now, with her tall Italian boyfriend on her arm, she had turned her back on everyone else.

Carrie held Sunny's hand tightly, with Dottie and Spud just behind them, gripping each other's hands. Behind them were Luanne and Jed, both there to show their faces and keep an eye on Billy.

Ever since that night Billy had witnessed with his very own eyes his brother's betrayal, he had stayed away from the family home. He was living at Cas's place because he needed space to grieve. He wasn't ready to go back to his immediate family, not even to live with Dottie and Spud. And the last thing he would have done would have been to create a situation where he might be seen to be driving a wedge between his two mums. They didn't deserve that.

The service was short and bittersweet. As they gathered around the grave, ready to lower the coffin, Carrie quietly moved to stand beside Billy. She reached out, tugging gently on his arm.

He turned to her, giving her a sad smile. 'I'm okay, Mum.'

She nodded, though her eyes brimmed with tears. ‘Come home soon, Billy boy,’ she whispered. ‘We miss you so much.’

Jed nudged Luanne to look at their daughter, who was clearly heartbroken over Billy’s absence.

‘He’s hurting, Jed,’ Luanne said, softly. ‘Jesse hurt him badly. He needs time, but Jesse’s still his blood. They’ll work it out one day. I know they will.’

‘I’m not so sure,’ Jed muttered, under his breath.

As the coffin was lowered into the grave, Billy’s throat tightened. He couldn’t speak. The love of his life had finally gone, and he would never know exactly how she felt. But he knew one thing: he had always loved her. Loved her with all his heart.

Looking up, his eyes locked with Jesse’s from across the grave. For a brief moment, they shared a glance. Billy could see the sadness in his brother’s eyes, but he wasn’t here to forgive. This was Willow’s day. He was going to focus on her.

But something had caught his eye. It wasn’t the sadness in his brother’s eyes but a number of bruises on Jesse’s face. They looked fresh and painful, so they couldn’t possibly be from that fight weeks ago. Those would have healed by now.

However, Billy pushed the observation aside. It wasn’t his concern.

With his face so crestfallen, Jesse mouthed, ‘*I’m sorry.*’

Billy looked away. He didn’t want to hear it.

Finally, as the dirt and flowers were thrown onto the coffin, the mourners began to drift away.

Carrie gripped Billy’s arm. ‘Please, Son. Come home,’ she pleaded.

'Not yet, Mum. I can't . . . I can't be anywhere near him.' His eyes flicked back to Jesse, who was standing on the other side of the grave.

'He needs you, Billy. We all do.'

'Nah, you don't. And he doesn't need me either. He's got all of you.'

'No, you don't understand, Billy. Jesse needs *you.*'

Billy glanced back at Jesse, his eyes lingering on the bruises. 'What, to fight his battles for him?' he muttered, pulling away from his mother. He turned to leave, but his father stepped in front of him.

'Don't just walk off, Billy. Can't you see you're breaking your mother's heart? And Dottie's, too. They're not crying for the dead. They're crying for the living. For *you*, Billy.'

Billy's eyes narrowed. 'Then blame Jesse. It's all his doing, not mine.'

With that, he stormed off, despite hearing Jesse call after him. But he wasn't ready to face him. Not today, and maybe not ever. In fact, he was so overwhelmed by the coffin going into the ground that he needed to be alone.

Alone to think. He wouldn't forget the moment he first saw Willow in the prison car park, when his family had come to see his father, who was being held on remand. What an absolute stunner she was. From that very first moment, he now believed he had been in love with the girl. And despite the hurt and humiliation she had caused him recently, in his heart, he knew he still loved her.

Growing up in his house with all the family around and the back door opening and closing every five minutes with friends and extended family, in and out, Billy had never really experienced his own space.

Now, staying at Cas's, with his own room and the large country manor house often empty, he realised that he actually liked the quietness. He also appreciated, though, that he'd only been living there for a few weeks. Maybe his view on the lack of company might prove to be wrong in the future. But at present, it suited him just fine.

As he headed away from everyone climbing into their cars to return to Cas's for the wake, Billy suddenly bumped into Danny. He stopped dead, and at first, he didn't recognise him until the recollection became clear. 'What are you doing here? The funeral's over.' His voice was cold and a tad harsh, but he wasn't up for any sweet small talk.

'I, er, I wasn't sure I would be welcomed, but I wanted to pay my last respects.'

'Yeah, sure,' said Billy, about to march on.

'Billy, thanks,' said Danny, looking awkward.

'For what?'

'Putting Cas straight. Telling the police you saw me drive away, and then you thought you saw Willow afterwards.'

'I want the murderer caught as much as anyone. I didn't see the point in going along with everyone assuming it was you. Now, that would be stupid, wouldn't it.'

Danny nodded.

Billy looked him up and down. 'Not dressed for a funeral, are ya, Danny. Willow had at least deserved you wearing a black tie today.'

Danny swallowed the rebuke and tilted his head to the side. For a lad of fifteen, Billy was, it seemed, tough-minded and so straight talking, it was as though he was talking to a grown man.

'Bill?' Danny said, as he watched Billy walk away.

Billy turned to Danny. 'I ain't Bill. My name's Billy.'

'Sorry, the force of habit of shortening people's names, Billy. I am sorry for what happened. I was only gonna have a bit of a laugh with Willow, nuffin more.'

Billy shrugged. 'It doesn't matter now, does it. She's dead.'

'It matters to me, Billy. I like you.'

'You don't know me, Danny, and, as it happens, I don't know you either.'

'Ah, but we're a lot alike, me and you,' Danny said, desperate to find common ground.

'Are we?' Billy's voice was dripping with sarcasm.

'We've got the same taste in girls.'

The second those words left Danny's mouth, he regretted saying them, especially when he saw Billy's face tighten with anger.

'What are you? Some kind of sicko?' he hissed. 'Now fuck off, Danny. I can't see how you and I are alike at all.'

'Listen, Billy,' Danny said, quickly, trying to regain the initiative, 'I know I owe you for saving my arse. But I thought I could help you out.'

Billy raised an eyebrow. 'Help me out? What makes you think I need your help?'

'The Carsons,' Danny replied, cautiously, testing the waters.

Billy shook his head. He was now even more irritated. 'What the hell have they got to do with me? They're all wasters, not my scene. Dirty pikeys, the lot of them. And just so you know, none of them could take me on in a fight, so I don't need your help. I don't even know if *you* can swing a punch.' He grinned, his mood darkening. 'But you and your family know I can fight, so get lost.'

Danny's stomach churned. The Carsons were his relatives – Ginty was a Carson, and so was his mother. It stung to hear Billy talk about them with such contempt, but he was determined to stay on his good side. Billy had money, power, and a knack for turning nothing into something. So he wanted a piece of that luck.

'I get it,' Danny said, trying to keep things cool. 'But listen, Billy, the Carsons are hell-bent on revenge.'

Billy waved a hand, dismissively. 'They're a bunch of wankers,' he said, but then he was irritated that he was swearing like Jesse. He didn't want to turn into his brother.

'And you don't care that two of them bashed up your bruvver? That they slyly caught him alone and beat him up bad?' Danny asked, pushing his point.

'Oh, I see,' Billy said, with a cold laugh. 'You're offering your *relationship* with the Carsons as some kind of protection for me. Fuck off, Danny. Like I said, I've never seen you handle yourself. And just so we're clear, if your idea of payback is calling off all your cousins, then don't bother. I wouldn't mind a good ruck with the pikeys. I'm probably in the mood for a tear up.'

But, once again, not thinking, Danny made a grave mistake. 'Your mum's a pik—'

Before he could finish, Billy gripped Danny's throat and began to squeeze the life out of him. 'Shut your mouth about my mother,' Billy growled.

Realising he had gone too far, Billy released his grip.

Now wide-eyed and choking, Danny gasped for air. 'All right, sorry. I didn't mean no harm.'

Billy loosened his tie, now feeling a little guilty for overreacting. He rubbed his neck, trying to cool down.

'Look, sorry, all right?' Danny coughed.

'Go away, Danny,' Billy said, his voice cold and final. 'There's nothing you can do for me. I don't need mates – least of all some relation to a Carson.'

'I'm a Slade,' Danny protested, weakly.

'Yeah, and your aunt is that fat bitch Ginty,' Billy shot back.

'Not my choice, though,' Danny replied, trying to save face. 'I've heard you're not talking to Jesse,' he continued, trying to shift the conversation, 'but I thought you should know. It was the Carsons who did it. They were masked up, apparently. And they won't stop. They will come after your bruvver.'

Billy shrugged, his face indifferent. 'Tell Jesse, then. Why are you telling me?'

Clearly not grasping how sharp Billy Murphy was, Danny was left feeling how badly he had underestimated him.

'I will,' he said, 'but I wanted to talk to you first and try to find a way to pay back the debt. I was hoping the heads-up about your bruvver might be part payment.'

Billy laughed. 'Oh, behave. I'm not in the fucking mood to talk about debts,' he said, before walking off again.

'Wait up. Listen,' Danny called after him. 'I've got some business we could start. You and me. It could be big.'

'You're like a blue-arsed fly buzzing around. Just leave me alone.'

'I will, but hear me out.'

'You are beginning to become a right fucking pest, and here I am swearing now.'

'Nah, straight up. Me and you in business together.'

'Why me?'

Danny placed his hands on his hips and smiled. 'I can trust you, Billy. There ain't many I can.'

'Are you sure about that?'

Danny winked, tilted his head, and slowly bit his bottom lip. 'Behind those devilish eyes there is a straight-up, straight-talking man of morals. Every quality I respect in a person. Come on, Billy, what d'ya say?'

An uneasy feeling came over Billy. 'Don't look at me like that, you fucking weirdo!'

Danny showed the palms of his hands. 'I weren't doing anything.'

Billy protruded his bottom jaw. 'Just tell me, when and where are these cunts gonna set about Jesse?'

Danny frowned. 'Jesse?'

'You just said they were going for my brother again.'

'No, not your bruvver Jesse. They've already given him a larruping. They're going for Charlie.'

Billy staggered backwards. The thought knocked the wind out of his lungs. '*What?*'

'So you ain't heard, then?'

'Heard what?'

'Atticus Carson died two days ago in prison. Even after three years, he never fully recovered from his injuries. They want blood, Billy.'

CHAPTER TWENTY-THREE

Staying well back from the burial, Danny remained partially hidden behind an oak tree, with his phone pressed to his ear. His eyes had been locked on Billy the whole time. He admired Billy's stature, his air of mystery, and how manly he was for someone still in their teens. Now he grinned as he watched the lad run towards the road because for all Billy's tough exterior and dark daunting stares, his Achilles heel was his family.

Nobby's groaning down the phone suddenly gripped Danny's attention. He was irritated by his brother's constant moans, although even without the wired jaw, his voice wasn't that attractive.

'Nobby, stop banging on about how you're gonna do over Billy. You'll get your chance,' Danny muttered. He heard his brother tutting on the other end of the phone. 'Just stick to the plan, all right? Or Farver will boil our heads in a bag.'

'Fuck the ol' man. I'm sick of him going on about this thing with Cas. And now, since you messed up, Danny, we're all running around at his orders.'

'Just stick with the programme, Nobby, and let's work out our own plan to take out the Murphys. But later, Nobby.'

'Good, 'cos I fucking hate those Murphys. They've got way too much clout for two pretty boy gangster wannabes,' spat Nobby.

'Oh, come on, Nobby, be truthful. Before Billy broke your jaw, it was your idea to search for Jesse. You, Luke, and Kieron battered the bloke and his cousin because you're jealous of Jesse. Always have been. And I know how you wank over the photo of Bronte, but she likes the Murphy bruvvers, and you, Nobby, hate the fact she don't like you.'

'Yes, she does.'

'Yeah, like a mate she feels sorry for.'

'Fuck those bruvvers. Billy and Jesse are no-good pretty boys. They ain't nuffin special.'

As far as Danny was concerned Billy *was* something special. As for being a pretty boy – well, no. That was a better description of Jesse.

'Nobby, listen. Once we've sorted the business for Farver, we can use the feud between the Carsons and the Murphys to our advantage. We started with a game plan. Let's finish with one that benefits us, not our farver. Just me and you,' Danny replied.

Danny could hear his brother chuckle. 'Me and you? Danny, no one trusts you. You're a psychopath.'

Danny could easily influence two of his brothers, Nobby and Kieron, but not Luke their eldest brother.

Luke barely spoke to him, having long ago concluded that he actually was a psychopath.

***

As soon as the funeral was over, the mourners made their way to Cas's grand mansion for the wake.

Carrie was one of the first to get out of the car, and she hurried to catch up with Cas. She was quiet as she walked beside him. It was hard to know what to say, really. But she didn't want him stepping into that house alone. Seeing that coffin being lowered into the ground had really affected her. After all, Willow was the same age as her boys, so it broke her heart.

'Thanks for coming, Carrie. Would you be a doll and make everyone a cuppa? Unless, of course, they'll want the hard stuff, like me.'

Carrie gently put her arm around his shoulders. ''Course I will, Cas. Anything else you'd like me to do? I can rustle up some sandwiches, if ya like.'

Cas paused before putting the key in the door and facing her. 'You're a darling, you are. I got a load of food delivered yesterday. It's all in the fridge and already made up. Just needs putting on the tables.'

'I'll do that for you.'

He stared at her for a second. 'I'll talk your Billy round to coming home, Carrie. I'm not trying to keep him as some kind of replacement for Willow. You know that, don't ya.'

'Gawd above, Cas, that never entered my mind, love. I'm just pleased he's with you. It could be worse. He could be on the streets.'

Shaking his head and opening the front door, Cas said, 'Your Billy's way too smart to ever spend a night out in the cold.'

Then, he stopped short as he looked at the door of the study.

'I am sure I closed that door before I set off for the funeral,' he said, as he hurried along the hallway and pushed it open. But then, he suddenly stopped dead. 'What the bloody hell has gone on here?'

Carrie peered in, confused, until she saw what he was talking about. Papers were strewn everywhere. She instantly closed the door behind them, not wanting the mourners to see what had happened because now they were piling in through the main door.

Holding an empty drawer from his oak desk, he looked up at her. 'Cunts. Fucking cunts!' he said, shaking his head and looking around.

'Shall I tell everyone to leave?'

'Do us a favour, see if the drawing room has been ransacked, yeah? If not, usher them in there, and if you and

Dottie could dish out the grub, tea, and whatever, that would be a help.'

Carrie gave him a comforting wink but she forgot to shut the door behind her before scooting to the drawing room, where it looked spick and span. She grabbed Dottie. 'Dot, listen, Cas has been burgled, right? We need to get the mourners in here. You pour the hard stuff, and I'll make the tea while Cas sorts himself out.'

Dottie's mouth dropped open. 'No way! How cruel! How could someone do that while he's at a funeral?'

'I know, it's bollocks, ain't it. Let's get these people back out as soon as possible.'

Sunny followed Carrie into the kitchen. 'What's going on? Cas just slammed his study door shut. Is he all right?'

'He's been robbed, poor bloke. It's terrible. I'm getting the food organised. I need to get the mourners fed, watered, and fucked off, so we can help Cas. Where's Billy?'

'I thought he came back with Cas. I dunno. He might've gone off alone to get his head together. His face was full of sadness, poor kid. Are you sure Cas was robbed? The place looks sound to me.'

Carrie removed the trays of sandwiches from the huge American-style fridge and handed them to Sunny. 'Someone broke into his study. Put these sandwiches in the drawing room on the side tables – they can help themselves,' she said, before filling the kettle for tea. 'Let's hope they don't linger. You know what it's like at these things. And did you see the look on Tara's face? It was like her shit don't stink. I swear to God, if I was putting one of my babies in that hole, you'd be dragging me off the coffin screaming my head off. And her boyfriend, ol' Mr Mafia, reminded me of one of those Christmas nutcracker soldiers. He was as stiff as a board. I thought Lolly was gonna lamp him one. I mean, it's a right liberty that the prick was even there and rubbing poor Lolly's nose in it.'

'I know. Never mind, I'll take these in, check on Lolly, and then see if Cas needs a hand.'

After Sunny had taken the sandwiches and drinks in to the mourners and had a quiet word with Lolly, he tapped on the door and entered Cas's study.

Keith was there picking up the papers strewn across the floor while Cas was rummaging through cupboards.

'Can I help? Have you called the police?'

Cas stopped what he was doing and spun around. 'Listen, I don't want anyone knowing I was robbed. Tell Carrie not to say a word. The culprit will cock up somewhere along the line. And if they brag, I will know, and I will cut their fucking fingers off and shove them up their arse. Can't a man even grieve in peace? I swear, whoever did this is one gutsy bastard.'

'I hate to state the obvious, but you've got cameras everywhere. Didn't they record who did it?'

Cas sighed. 'A man all blacked up, wearing a balaclava, by the looks of it, and the bastard tampered with the camera at the front of the house. As for the others, well, I'll need Billy to go through the footage. He's the techie in this house.'

'Big, small, fat, thin? Any clues?'

Cas sighed again. 'No, no real clues. But whoever it was must have known I was at my granddaughter's funeral. They could work out how long I'd be gone. And all my associates would obviously be there, too, so whoever robbed me knew they wouldn't be disturbed.'

''Ere, Cas, where's Walter Whistler and Dennis the Menace?' Keith asked, with suspicion.

'They're in Thailand. They've got a couple of birds out there.'

‘Are you sure about that?’

‘Yeah, yeah, and they wouldn’t rob me, never.’

Keith looked out of one of the casement windows, deep in thought. ‘Shit, we’d better check the livestock.’

Cas dropped a file he had in his hand. ‘Shit! Shit! Me fuckers! Me fuckers!’ he yelled, before he opened the French doors and ran across the garden and out towards the fields.

‘Fuckers?’ Sunny asked.

‘Heifers, but he calls them fuckers. They’re his new girls, ready to calf.’

Sunny got on his hands and knees and helped Keith pick up the mess the burglars had left.

Minutes later, Cas returned. ‘They’re all right. Jesus. My heart was in my mouth for a minute there.’

‘Shouldn’t you call the police?’

‘What for? They won’t do fuck all, the lazy bastards. I’ll find who did it, and I’ll personally incapacitate them.’

***

Now breathless, Billy ran as fast as he could towards the cars, but they had already gone. No one was there to give him a lift back, and he figured everyone assumed someone else was taking him to the wake. He quickly pulled out his mobile from his pocket and frantically dialled his father’s number. No answer. He knew they would keep their phones off out of respect during the funeral, and it would probably be a while before they realised he was missing.

He hesitated to call Cas’s house phone, but this was serious. His little brother Charlie was an innocent kid, not the type to get into a fight. No one had ever dared start anything with him, not when they knew he had two older brothers who would handle that for him.

Finally, Cas picked up, his voice sharp with irritation. ‘What?’

'Cas, it's me, Billy. Is my dad there? Please put him on.'

'Billy, where are you?'

'At the graveyard. Cas, please, just put him on.'

'Why ain't you here, Billy?'

'Never mind that. Just put him on.'

'Well, boy, I've been robbed, so best you get your arse back where I want you to look at my cameras for me, although the front one has been tampered with. But you're good on the computers. See if you can get a clearer picture.'

'Robbed?'

'Yeah, burgled, robbed. Took me valuables, the cunts. The dirty stinking bastards, robbing a man burying his granddaughter.'

'Cas, put my dad on, will you, please.'

'Why? Do you know anything about the robbery?'

'No!' Billy snapped. 'Cas, just put my dad on, will you, please.'

'For fuck's sake.'

A minute later, Sunny's voice came through. 'Billy, what's up?'

'Dad, listen. I'm still at the graveyard, and Danny Slade is here. He told me the Carson cousins beat up Jesse.'

'Well, we don't know who they were, Billy. They had balaclavas on. But, yeah, they hurt him badly. He's got some bruises on his face, but you should see his ribs. They're black and blue.'

'Dad, it was the Carsons. I bet it was Stuey and Joey, the bastards. Anyway, Danny said they're going after Charlie.'

'*What?* You mean your Uncle Charlie?'

'No, Dad. Little Char. They're out for his blood.'

There was a brief silence. 'Dad, are you there?'

'I'm here, Billy. I'm calling the house on my mobile now to check on Charlie and make sure he's home from school safe and sound. Misty was supposed to get Nellie and meet Charlie. . . . It's ringing but no one's answering. Right, I'm heading home now. Shall I pick you up on the way?'

'Yes, of course.'

'I'll have Jesse with me,' Sunny said.

'What for? If he's as bad as you reckon, he won't be up for a fight,' Billy responded.

'Listen, Billy, forget your grievance with your brother. I'm sick of it. You're smarter than Jesse, so shut up and focus. This is about little Char. Either you come now or stay away, Billy boy.'

'Pick me up. I'll be by the entrance to the church.'

Billy spun around and saw Danny grinning. 'What are you grinning at?'

'Sorry, I wasn't . . . I was just smiling. I admire you, that's all. Anyway . . .'

Billy stared at him as though he was mad. 'What? You're banging on about some load of bollocks after telling me my little brother could be getting his head kicked in? Fuck off out of my way,' he growled, shoving past Danny as he headed to the main gates.

By the time he stepped on to the pavement, Sunny had already skidded to a halt in the car.

As Billy jumped into the front passenger seat, he immediately noticed Jesse sitting in the back. It was strange: Jesse never sat in the back. Rationalising it, he guessed his brother was trying to exercise some kind of humility.

'What else did that Danny bloke say?' Sunny asked, glancing at Billy. His face was pale, and clearly, fear had taken over.

'They want blood because . . . Dad . . . Atticus is dead. He died from his injuries,' Billy said, the hesitation showing in his voice.

'What fucking injuries?' Sunny asked, gripping the wheel tighter.

'The injuries inflicted by James at the prison visit three years ago – apparently. But it seems that Atticus blames you for what happened to him.'

'Well, lucky it was three years ago and not under a year, or me brother would've been done for murder,' Sunny growled. 'At least that's one down.' He pressed down on the accelerator even harder. 'If they've hurt that little boy, I'll kill every single one of them.'

Billy was itching to speak to Jesse, but he was still angry. Yet, his father was right. They had to put their grievances aside, at least for now.

'Billy, call your Uncle James or Uncle Dylon. Anyone! Find out if Charlie's all right. He should be home by now. Tell James to drive past the school.'

Billy quickly made the call, and without delay, James said he would leave right away to check on Charlie.

'I swear to God if they—' Sunny started, his voice filled with rage.

'If they hurt him, Dad, I'll hunt them down. One by fucking one,' Billy finished, his voice cold. He twisted to face Jesse, who was looking sheepish. 'And you didn't see who it was who bashed you up?'

Jesse shook his head. 'No, they took me from behind, got me on the ground, and kicked the shit out of me. I would have pulled their balaclavas off, but I couldn't get up.'

Seeing Jesse's battered face and the lost-boy look in his eyes stirred something inside Billy, but his mind instantly flashed back to Willow, and any empathy with Jesse ceased.

He turned around and looked ahead, not wanting to engage with Jesse.

'I'm sorry, Billy,' Jesse said.

'Just because I am in a car with you don't mean I want to talk about it, so shut up. I'm here for Charlie, not you.'

Sunny wanted to say something, but he was angry with Jesse for upsetting Billy, and he wasn't too impressed with Billy for beating up his brother. Worse, he couldn't bear to see his wife so heartbroken by it all. The house hadn't been the same since Billy had moved out, and he blamed him for that too.

Taking half the time to get home, Sunny shot up the drive, almost taking out the front wall of the garage in the process. Seconds later, Sunny and the boys hurried through the side gate and entered the house by the back door.

There was silence. Sunny called out, but there was no sound of anyone being in the house. Fear engulfed him as he ran upstairs to see if Charlie and Nellie were there, but the house was evidently empty. As he ran downstairs back to the kitchen, he faced his sons, who were anxiously seeking good news.

But seeing the frown on their father's face, both boys feared the worst.

Sunny glanced at his watch. It was four forty-five. The youngsters should have been home from school ages ago. A sudden screech of tyres outside had them all running back out to see who had arrived.

James pulled up in his Range Rover, got out, and shook his head. 'I've been all over, Sunny. I can't find them.' He looked over Sunny's shoulder. 'Where's Carrie?'

'She doesn't know what's been going on. I've left her at the wake with Dottie and Spud.'

James nodded, knowing how fiery both women could be.

Seeing the despair on Sunny's face, James tried to reassure him. 'Look, let's not panic over Charlie. Misty isn't here, and neither is Nellie, so my guess is they're together somewhere. She could've taken them to the shops, the park, anywhere.'

'But why not leave a note or something?' Sunny asked, still anxious.

James smiled. 'Really, Sunny? Why would she leave a note? As far as she's concerned, she's picking the kids up from school and looking after them. I bet she's taken them on the bus to McDonald's. And the threat that the Carsons will hurt Charlie is just hearsay. They wouldn't have the fucking balls.'

'James, did you know Atticus is dead?' Sunny asked.

'No,' James replied, with a furrowed brow.

Billy stepped forward. 'Apparently, he's dead, and the Carsons want blood. They beat the hell out of Jesse.'

Sunny looked at James. He frowned and turned to face Jesse. 'But you said in the car that you didn't see who it was – they had balaclavas on.'

'Danny Slade told me,' Billy quickly replied.

James looked at Sunny. 'Aren't the Slades related to the Carsons? It's strange for someone to grass on his own family.'

'The Slades are only related by marriage. Donna Carson married Vic Slade, and apparently, ol' Ginty's living there at the moment. And there's not much love lost. Jed told me that Ginty moved in with Atticus's wife and was turfed out within a week – she pissed them all off. Then she moved in with those fuckwits Stuey and Joey. Their mother, ol' Ivy Rose Carson, had Ginty there for a month before she asked her to leave. So Jed says. Anyway, he likes to keep his ear to the ground. The old travellers love a good gossip, and Jed ain't no different,' said Sunny.

'I'm not surprised. That woman has a knack for kicking over her own sandcastle everywhere she goes,' James replied, shaking his head.

'So Ginty has managed to alienate most of her family. Since Ginty lives with Donna, perhaps she's formed an allegiance with them. She may even have turned on the Carsons. Perhaps,' Sunny added, 'she got Danny to warn us about Charlie being on the hit list because the cousins beat up Jesse, her grandson, as she might still refer to him.'

'Are you kidding? That bitch loves no one but Jimmy and herself. I'd like to think, though, that she's not out for revenge. But who knows what goes on in her head?'

No sooner had James said those words than a cab pulled up. All eyes were on the back passenger door. Everyone was desperate to see Charlie get out intact.

However, as soon as the door opened, it was Misty Jacobs who got out first and turned around to help someone. It was clear that it was Charlie because Nellie had already hopped out of the car from the roadside.

Instantly, all four of them hurried to assist, and as soon as they saw the state of Charlie, Billy's temper soared. 'Who did it, Char?' he demanded.

Sunny flung his arms around his youngest son and hugged him. 'What happened, my boy?'

Charlie was quiet, his face covered in gauze and his eyes bruised and swollen. Even his mop of black curls looked sticky and dull, from all of the blood.

Sunny looked at Misty, who appeared distraught.

'Oh, Sunny, I didn't know what to do,' she said. 'I got Nellie, and we were walking towards Charlie's school when I saw him walking towards me swinging his bag. Then, two men on a motorbike wearing balaclavas stopped. One of them got off . . .' She paused to catch her breath, as Charlie took over.

'He asked if I was Charlie Murphy. I couldn't move or speak. Then one of them hit me across the face, and I fell. I don't know why they went for me. I don't think I've upset anyone. Misty threw her bag at them, and they jumped back on the bike and rode off. We didn't get the number plate. I couldn't see properly for a bit . . .'

'Are you okay, though, Son?' Sunny asked.

Charlie nodded, but he looked far from okay.

'I took him straight to the hospital. I didn't know your numbers by heart. I'm sorry, Sunny, I'm so sorry,' Misty said, full of apologies.

James, who towered over Misty, suddenly put his arms around her. 'You did well to fight them off, girl. If you hadn't, they might have done worse. Misty, did you recognise any of them? You lived with the Carsons for a few years. Do you think it could have been one of them?'

'I couldn't say. I only saw the back of them. Why do you think it was them?' Misty asked.

'Atticus is dead. It could be revenge,' James replied.

'Oh shit, yeah . . . But targeting a little chavi? That's pushing it too far. Who in their right mind would do that to him?'

'Someone, as you say, who is not in their right mind,' Sunny said. 'And listen, Misty, I don't blame you.'

'The doctor reckons he'll be okay,' Misty added. 'A couple of stitches but no head injury.'

'Stitches?' Jesse piped up.

'Yeah, whatever they hit him with cut his sweet little face,' Misty said.

Billy and Jesse exchanged looks, both with rage in their eyes. Whoever did this would pay with their lives.

CHAPTER TWENTY-FOUR

Nellie leaned against Misty as she stared up at her father. 'Will these bad men come for me too?'

The question rattled everyone present.

Sunny ground his back teeth, trying to stay calm. 'Of course not, princess. It was all a mistake. Some horrible men got the wrong person, that's all.'

Just like her mother's expression, Nellie raised a single eyebrow, letting her father know she didn't believe him.

'Take the kids inside, Misty, would you, love?' Sunny said, softly.

Misty nodded, still feeling somchow rcsponsiblc, cvcn though it was in no way her fault.

The Murphys had been good to her over the last three years, especially Carrie, who had made sure she had everything she needed. After all, Carrie, Dottie, and herself had all suffered at the hands of the Carson family, namely Jimmy and his rotten mother, Ginty.

Billy's phone suddenly rang, and when he looked at the number, it was his mother.

'Mum's calling me. Does she know what's going on?' Billy asked.

Sunny shook his head. 'No, I left her to it. I jumped into me motor and got here as fast as I could.'

James shook his head, too, smirking. 'You're unbelievable. Carrie's gonna be raging all the way here when she finds out. Bet you'll be in the doghouse for a month.'

Sunny nodded for Billy to answer the call.

Billy didn't waste any time by immediately telling her what had happened. To him, the whole family needed to know the score. And to be made aware that any one of them could be a target next. 'Mum, ask Spud to check his brakes and tyres, would you?'

'Have they really hurt our little Char?' Carrie asked, sharply.

'It's okay, Mum. But whoever did this made a point – they wanted us to take this threat seriously.'

'I dunno, Billy, if it's the Carsons. They haven't got the brains.'

'Mum, have you forgotten how they recklessly blew up the burger vans and put you in the hospital for a few weeks?'

'Yeah, but Jimmy and Arthur are inside. Lenny and Albert are dead! The rest of the Carsons ain't capable of anything serious – they're all fuck-ups.'

'Please, Mum, just ask Spud to check,' Billy insisted.

'Of course, Son. And tell your farver I'm fuming with him. Look, I'll be home soon.'

Billy ended the call and looked at his father. 'Mum's annoyed.'

'No shit, Sherlock. I could hear her from here,' Sunny muttered.

James called Dylon to tell him to meet him at Sunny's place. There was serious business to attend to.

Meanwhile, Jesse had been unusually quiet. He retreated into the house and hurried upstairs.

As the men gathered in the kitchen, Billy noticed Jesse's absence. Quietly, he left the room, and as he approached the staircase, he could hear the low mutterings of his father and uncles, who were all plotting their revenge.

Gingerly, he crept up the stairs, feeling like a stranger in his own home. Although he hadn't been around for a few weeks, he wanted to know why Jesse had snuck off. It wasn't like him at all. Usually, Jesse was eager to have a say, and he was excited when their uncles made plans to protect the family. He and Jesse were always included in family discussions, being considered old enough to contribute.

Billy pushed open the door to what had been their shared bedroom. Although there were enough rooms for them to have their own, they preferred to share. He immediately noticed Jesse's demeanour – he was hunched over on the bed, his hands covering his face.

Slowly, Jesse glanced up, his eyes red from crying.

Under normal circumstances, Billy would have comforted him, but, right now, he wasn't ready for that. 'What's going on, Jesse?' His voice was steady but firm. He had already noticed the guilty expression on Jesse's face. His brother could barely look him in the eye.

'What's going on, Jesse?' Billy asked again, his voice rising with impatience.

The lack of an answer angered Billy. 'I asked you what's going on!'

Finally, Jesse peered up, tears streaming down his face. 'It's all my fault.'

Billy put his hands on his hips, his anger bubbling. 'How?' he demanded.

'I . . . I was upset. I was so upset. I never meant to hurt you. I just wasn't thinking. I mean . . . Willow—'

'I don't care about Willow right now, for God's sake! Our little brother's been attacked, and you're banging on about Willow!' Billy snapped.

Jesse wiped his eyes, his voice trembling. 'No, listen. I was upset that I hurt you. When you left, I was angry – angry with myself, angry with you for leaving, and . . . I went out with my head all messed up. I went to Bluewater to see Bronte, to see if she could take my mind off it.' He looked down. 'Funnily enough, she doesn't like me in that way . . . She likes you.'

Billy's expression hardened. 'Jesse, just tell me what happened.'

Jesse nodded, wiping his eyes again. 'I was going to take Bronte for a burger when your mate Clint came up to me, warning me that practically all the Carson clan were at the Centre.'

He wiped his eyes once more, frustration evident in his voice. 'Look, I was in a bad mood, all right? Clint told me the Carsons were living in Kent because Atticus was in a hospital there. They moved him out of prison to die in the hospital.'

Billy's stomach dropped. 'Oh shit. So, what the hell did you do to them, you divvy?'

Jesse could tell Billy was pissed off now, just by the way he was mimicking his accent, which was much more like their mother's, while Billy spoke more like their father.

He sighed heavily, knowing he had messed up.

'I went to where they usually hang out. I saw Stuey, Joey, that fat lump Atlas, and a few others. Before I even got to them, they were looking cocky. I think they're related to Atlas. I dunno.' He paused and ran his hands through his thick black curls. His eyes then filled up again. 'I didn't think, did I. I was angry, right? They were standing there with this cocky attitude, like they owned the place. Joey had this smug look on his face. He was leaning back with his arms crossed, like he was some sort of hard nut just because his bigger cousins were there. Stuey, you know what a weirdo he is. He was acting all casual, hands in his pockets, like he was part of some gang. It pissed me off how relaxed he was, like nothing I said could touch him. And then, there was that fat prick Atlas, just standing there like a brick wall, barely moving, glaring at me, like I was nothing. I mean, I could beat up any one of 'em. The lot of them looked like they were untouchable, like they were daring me to start something just because they had some other blokes with 'em, a load of pikeys. They were so cocky, it made my blood boil. And when Stuey . . .' He looked up, his voice thick with anger. 'You know what he's like, a wind-up merchant. He pointed to Bronte and said to me, "If you don't wanna fuck her, I will." And he laughed. Then he said, "Where's your sidekick? Fell out, did ya? Looks like he gave you a right mullering. The state of ya face."'

Billy's chin jutted forward. 'Yeah, and what did you say?'

'I wanted to rip his head off, Billy. Bronte was pulling me away, but I laughed in their faces and said, "Where's your Uncle Atticus? Is he dodging the coffin? I hope he dies a painful death."'

'You've got to be kidding me, Jesse.'

'No. Anyway, as soon as they ran at me, I knew I'd messed up, so I grabbed Bronte's hand, and we legged it through the Centre. Obviously, security was called, and they turfed the Carsons out . . .' He looked down.

'What is it, Jesse?' Billy asked, sensing there was more to the story.

'Joey wasn't turfed out because he'd already gone into the men's room. He came out of the same exit as me, and when he started giving it large, I ran over and landed a good one on his chin and knocked the wanker out.'

Billy shook his head. 'And who are these cousins you mentioned? And were there any other geezers?'

'I dunno. But they all had that Carson look about 'em. Oh yeah, and that prick Nobby. The one you battered for hitting me.' He shook his head. 'I've been a proper punchbag lately. What with the Slades, although they didn't do much damage. Then you. And now these two blokes in balaclavas. It's a miracle I haven't got brain damage.'

'Debatable,' Billy mumbled, under his breath. 'And when exactly did they attack you?'

'A few nights ago,' said Jesse. 'But, like I told you, they were wearing balaclavas, and they jumped me from behind. I couldn't see who they were and then they got on a motorbike and rode off.'

'But you reckon it was the Carsons?'

Jesse shrugged. 'Must've been. I pissed them off, and Danny told you it was them. But I'm telling you, Billy, they had quite a big gang. I reckon all the pikeys came out of the woodwork to join together.'

'Do you think they want the feud to start up again?'

'If they do, Billy, there's a lot of them. I dunno how we'd even call a truce.'

Billy flared his nostrils. 'You are so stupid, and they've gone after our Charlie, for fuck's sake! He's just a kid.'

'They fucked me up too, Billy,' Jesse said, hoping for some sympathy. In a flash, he lifted his top.

Billy stared at the purple bruising. 'Shit.'

'Yeah, I nearly shit myself too. I thought I was gonna die. I thought they were gonna kick me to death.'

Billy curled his lip. 'Perhaps they should have,' he said, coldly, but then he wished he hadn't, when he saw the epitome of hurt in his brother's eyes. 'You'd better get back downstairs and tell Dad what you've done.'

***

Spud brought Carrie and Dottie over to Carrie's house at high speed. Carrie almost fell out of Spud's car before storming towards the house. The moment she pushed open the back door, everyone sat upright as if they were standing to attention.

'Why did you leave me at the wake, eh?' Not waiting for an answer, she said, 'Where's me baby boy?' Aiming her wrath at Sunny, she gave him such a glare.

For his part, Sunny had already been expecting a backlash. Rarely did they fight, and he just hoped this time he could take the sting out of her anger.

'He's in the lounge with Misty. He's okay. Well, he's got cuts and bruises.'

'Cuts and fucking bruises? He's not even eleven.'

Striding angrily across the hallway, Carrie entered the lounge where she found Misty playing a board game with both the youngest children.

Instantly, Charlie got up and ran to his mother for one of her hugs.

She had a tendency to mother both Charlie and Nellie because they were *her* babies, so seeing the oversized gauze on Charlie's face sent her raging. She assumed the feud between the Carsons and the Murphys was well and truly over. She understood that a couple of the cousins – Ivy Rose Carson's two sons Stuey and Joey – had fought with her sons, but it was nothing too serious. They were mild and tended to toss names at each other, rather than cause serious damage. She knew the strength of her sons; they would have turned Stuey and Joey inside out. They probably had over the years.

Now, though, everything was a long way from fine, as far as she was concerned. Those Carsons had crossed the line wearing balaclavas, with two of them kicking the living shit out of her Jesse.

Her eldest boys were fighters in the ring, where any fight should have remained. But she was fully aware that Billy and Jesse were also fighters outside the ring. She knew they had a reputation. The whole of Orpington did. Besides, Jesse was almost sixteen, so he could take it, and she assumed it would be a situation that would right itself once Billy was back home and they were joined at the hip again. However, hurting Charlie was a step way too far.

She kissed her son on the top of his head. 'Are you all right, my little Char?'

'Yeah, Mum, it's only butterfly stitches. Look, Mum, I'm beating Misty at Monopoly.'

Stroking his soft cheek, she felt her heart breaking, and now she wished they'd moved far away. Away from the Carsons and all of the shit that came with them.

Charlie pulled away and hurried back to the game.

Carrie stared for a while as her two youngest played so sweetly with Misty. 'Thanks, Misty.'

'I'm sorry. I wished I could've stopped 'em.'

Carrie shook her head. 'It's not your fault, love.'

Misty smiled. She so admired Carrie. Even when her best friend was in a mood, she still managed to look so beautiful, so refined.

As Carrie spun around, she almost bumped into Dottie who was eyeing up Charlie.

'Bastards,' she mumbled, under her breath.

Placing her hands on Carrie's shoulders, she whispered, 'What's under that dressing?'

'Stitches. And whoever did it will look like a patchwork quilt themselves, by the time I'm done.'

'Shall I get the knife, then?'

Carrie tutted. 'Well, I'll need an axe and a skip by the time I've gone through the fucking Carsons.'

Dottie pulled her hair away from her face and retied her ponytail. 'So where shall we go first?'

'Let's talk with the boys before we go off on a rampage, even though I am fucking ready to take a roof off right now!'

CHAPTER TWENTY-FIVE

Still fuming, and ready to smash down doors, Carrie stormed through the hallway, only stopping when she met Billy. Her temper instantly stalled, and she threw her arms around her son, with angry tears flowing. 'I'm so glad you're home, Billy. At least we're a united front.'

Billy didn't want to hurt her feelings anymore, not now. He hugged her back. Over her shoulder, he saw his other mother enter the kitchen.

Dottie stood there awkwardly as if waiting in line for a hug.

It hit him then that Dottie had always let Carrie dish out the first embrace, presumably because she saw herself as mother number two. Gently, he pulled away from Carrie and wrapped his arms around Dottie. She wasn't so tactile, but the warmth between them was solid. He whispered, 'I'm going to hunt them down, Mottie.' He knew she, of all people, would understand.

Dottie caught her breath and hissed, 'Don't worry, we'll get them, and we'll hurt them really, really badly.'

That was the difference between Carrie and Dottie. Carrie went in all guns blazing, straight in, feet first. Dottie, though, was cold and premeditated. She didn't make mistakes. Everything had to be precise.

The men were up on their feet, ready to move. They were planning to hit each Carson house in turn, starting off with Ivy Rose's home. She lived over the main road, a few doors down from where Ginty used to live before she did time in prison and ended up in a bedsit. Then, she had gone to live with Monty Doyle. But she had only lasted a few months with him before he threw her out. Ever since, she had been doing the rounds. Surprisingly – or perhaps not, in her case – she had no friends or family left to turn to at all.

Sunny grabbed Carrie, trying to make her look at him, but she was still pissed off that he had left Cas's house without her. 'Listen to me, Carrie. I'm sorry, but what's done is done. You can't just go off on your own mission—'

Quickly, she cut him off. 'Well, *you* did.' She pointed at James and Dylon. 'And you didn't include me in your plans, did ya? So move out of my way, Sunny Murphy, because this woman is on her own mission.' The expression on her face hardened. 'I'm going to find who hurt Jesse and my little boy, and then you can all do your worst. Now, excuse me.' She tried to pull herself free of Sunny's grip, but he held her tighter.

'Stop, Carrie. Look how angry we all are, but I can't be worrying about you as well as the kids. Let us do what needs to be done and end this feud once and for all.'

James appeared, his shoulders seemingly as solid as if they were made of steel. 'Carrie, we have to be sure. Come on, have you ever known the Carsons to hide behind balaclavas? As much as they're scum, would they really cut Char's face?'

Jesse crept into the room. 'I don't even know these cousins of Joey and Stuey. I didn't know Atlas or his lot. There were loads of them. It was like something from *The Hills Have Eyes*.'

'But why start a fight? They wouldn't do it just because Atticus died, would they?' Carrie snapped.

Billy nudged Jesse. 'Tell them.'

Jesse hesitated at first but then he rattled off what happened a few days before the attack on his youngest brother.

Carrie threw her hands up in despair. 'Can't you keep your mouth shut, boy? What the hell's wrong with you? And now our Char—'

'Come on, Carrie,' said Spud, who had been leaning against the sink. 'Jesse couldn't have known they'd go after Char. Christ, who could've imagined that? I mean, I'm not being funny, but look.' He gestured at James, Dylon, Sunny, and himself.

Carrie glanced at them. They were like bruisers, all of them. Apart from Sunny, who was a bit sleeker, James was a mountain of a man. No one would argue with him unless they had a gun. Dylon was much the same. Spud wasn't as tall as the Murphy brothers, but he was just as beefy.

Carrie sighed. 'Maybe they've got backup we don't know about.'

When the back door opened, it caught everyone's attention.

Jed and Luanne walked in. 'Stuck behind a bloody tractor on the A21. Put the kettle on, Carrie, there's a good girl,' Jed said, rubbing his hands together. 'Cor, those sandwiches were limp. I'd want my money back if I were Cas. Now, how's the young 'un?'

Carrie didn't argue with her dad. She flicked the switch. 'He's bruised and stitched up, but he'll be all right.'

'The culprits soon won't be, though. I'd stake my life on that,' Luanne chimed in, as she sat down next to Dylon.

The earlier tense atmosphere passed and the conversation resumed. 'What kind of backup?' Sunny asked. 'Who'd side with the Carsons, for Christ's sake?'

'The Slades?' suggested Jesse.

'Nah, not them.' Jed shrugged. 'I reckon old Vic's hoofed Ginty out too.'

All eyes turned to Jed, the man who knew all the gossip. No one needed the local rag; they had Jed and his pub talk.

'They kicked Ginty out?'

'Well, no one knows for sure, but Donna's been going around asking if Ginty was staying with friends. Apparently, Ginty went out a week ago and she ain't come back. So, knowing old Vic, he's probably told her to do one. Sly ol' bastard. Never liked him, meself.'

'So you don't believe that this was anything to do with the Slades, then?' asked Carrie, who was determined to get to the bottom of it.

'When, er, I was in the shopping centre, I didn't recognise all the Carsons, but they did look alike. And I could be wrong, 'cos at the time I was going off on one, and so I couldn't be a hundred per cent sure, but that Nobby was there, the one who beat me up a few weeks ago. He was the one whose jaw was broken by Billy.'

'Well, it was Danny who warned me about our little Char. He said it was the Carsons.'

'You don't think any of this was connected to Cas's robbery, do you?' asked Sunny.

Billy shook his head. 'I doubt it.'

'Look, I couldn't give a shit. I'm going to get some answers, even if it means I have to shake Joey and Stuey's muvver until her fucking arsehole falls out. It'll be better than us throwing daft questions back and forth.'

Sunny rolled his eyes. He was about to grab his wife again when she leaned back and pointed a finger in his face. 'Don't you dare, Sunny.' She looked at Dottie. 'This is women's work! Clearly!'

'Aw, Gawd 'elp us,' said Jed, as his youngest daughter shot past him, followed by Dottie.

Spud held up his hands. 'Well, don't look at me! I ain't gonna stop 'em. Best we can do is follow 'em, and if it gets out of hand we can wade in. I should think they will speak to Ivy Rose first.'

Luanne hopped up from her chair. 'I suppose I'd best go an' all. Ivy Rose is no pushover.'

'Luanne, you ain't a youngster,' said Jed, before he realised what he'd just said.

Like Carrie, Luanne brushed off her husband's efforts to stop her from joining her daughter. 'And I ain't in me grave none either, so you just let me be, Jed Verne.'

Shrugging his shoulders and then rolling his eyes at the other men, he said, 'I ain't about to argue,' as he watched his wife take a band from her wrist and tie her hair up in a ponytail before hurrying after Carrie and Dottie.

***

Still cursing and muttering under her breath, Carrie clambered into the family truck. Luanne and Dottie hadn't even settled into their seats before Carrie floored the accelerator, and the vehicle set off with the tyres screeching down the drive.

'Whoa, slow down, girl!' Luanne yelped, who was still fumbling with her seatbelt. 'We don't want to end up in someone's bleeding front garden!'

Finally managing to fasten it, she asked, 'Do you reckon Ivy Rose will say anything? They're her boys. She'll protect them, like you would, Carrie Ann. Just like you are.'

'Yeah, but talking to me might be in her best interest.'

Dottie glanced over, now intrigued. 'How?'

Carrie shot a look, her jaw jutted forward. 'It'll keep her teeth in her mouth and not down her bloody throat,' she spat, with venom accentuating every word.

Luanne sighed, her eyes meeting Dottie's. 'Let's just hope Ivy Rose talks, and quick. I wasn't planning on getting into a ruck today. Just had me nails done. Our Mary's got a cracking little business going.'

It seemed that with every road they drove along, Carrie's driving grew more and more erratic. All she could see was her little boy's swollen face etched in her mind.

'Carrie, be careful, love! Bloody hell, at this rate, we'll be lucky to get there in one piece.'

But Carrie didn't care. She was fuming.

It was six o'clock when they arrived outside the Carsons.

Carrie noticed how nothing on the street had changed. The charred outline of a burnt-out car still lingered, the remnants of a fire started in the middle of the road. She didn't see any old tyres lying around on the road or pavements today, but the memories of the old days still remained.

Luanne hadn't set foot on this road since leaving that life behind. Her eyes drifted across the street to the house opposite Ivy Rose's place. It once belonged to Ginty Carson, a home filled with dark memories.

They had hardly pulled up before Carrie was out of the motor and striding purposefully towards a rickety old gate that led into Ivy Rose's property. Dottie was not far behind.

Seeing the women march on ahead, Luanne quickly tied her hair into a tight bun, smoothed down her thin sweatshirt, and hurried after them. But they had stopped dead and were peering upwards.

Perched on a ladder was Ivy Rose, who was washing her windows as though her life depended on it. The front of her house was always immaculate, her doorstep gleaming, and the windows polished so they looked like new. It was a wonder the woman had any skin left on her hands with all the bleach she used.

Carrie didn't waste time. Grabbing the ladder, she shook it hard. 'Oi! Get down 'ere!' she barked.

Ivy Rose, a solid woman at five foot eight and easily sixteen stone, glared down. 'What the hell are you doing 'ere?'

'Come down, and you'll soon find out,' Carrie shot back.

With a scowl, Ivy Rose tucked a strand of her hair, which was clearly a box dye shade of bright chestnut, behind her ear and climbed down, her feet hitting the ground with a heavy thud. Tossing a cloth into the bucket of hot water, she folded her arms, her eyes sweeping over the three women. She paused when she reached Dottie.

'I don't know you,' Ivy Rose sneered. 'But I recognise you, Carrie Ann.' Her gaze shifted to Luanne, a sarcastic grin crossing her face. 'And you, Lu. What d'ya want? I ain't got time for a cuppa. These bloody windows won't clean themselves.'

Carrie's eyes narrowed. 'Where are your boys?'

Ivy Rose tilted her head. 'And why d'ya want to know *that*?'

The cockiness in Ivy Rose's voice was winding Carrie right up.

Seeing the red mist coming over Carrie's face, Dottie yanked her back, before instantly taking her place. 'I'm Dottie Ellis. You *do* know who I am.'

Ivy Rose's eyes darted between Luanne and Dottie. Of course, she knew who Dorothy Ellis was. Everyone did. It didn't matter that she didn't live on the street. After dating Jimmy, and being subsequently ditched by him, she went on to murder her own parents, making her the hottest gossip for miles. However, with that came a fear of Dottie. She was marked as a psychopath, and the stories around the estate grew legs, running wild at every makeshift bonfire. Dottie was known as the most dangerous creature on the planet.

'Yeah, come to think of it, I do know who you are.'

Ivy Rose stiffened, now standing her ground. She had to. It was drilled into her to never back down, especially with the neighbours probably curtain twitching, if they weren't already leaning halfway out of their windows. 'What d'ya want with me boys?'

Luanne held Carrie back even more tightly. They needed answers, and the way her daughter was going, they weren't likely to get any.

'We've been told it was the Carsons who beat Jesse up, and—'

Ivy Rose cut her off, waving her hand. 'Oh, fuck off! Joey and Stuey treat Billy and Jesse like family. They are family by blood, even though they call themselves Murphys! Yeah, they fight and argue, but my boys love yours. If you're accusing them of hurting Jesse, he must've been hurt bad, and . . .' She held up her hand again, noticing Carrie Ann's murderous expression. It was like that of a raging bull. The only thing, it seemed, keeping her from charging at her was her mother. 'Listen, Carrie Ann, they've had their squabbles, sure. But believe you me, my boys came back worse – black eyes, split lips, chipped teeth. Let's face it, they weren't exactly lookers to begin with, and now they're downright ugly. So, what's really going on?'

'They set about my baby boy.'

Ivy Rose's face twisted in shock, and her lips twitched in disgust. 'What d'ya mean?'

Carrie's breathing intensified. 'They attacked him in the street, cut his face – and he's only ten. A little kid. And my Charlie, he ain't some scruffy chavi with a chicken under one arm and a fist up with the other. He ain't like that.'

Ivy Rose staggered back, waving her hands in disbelief. 'Nah, no way, Carrie Ann. No fuckin' way.'

'They were *seen*,' snapped Carrie.

‘Wait there,’ Ivy Rose demanded, before she shoved the front door open and bellowed, ‘Stuey! Joey! Get your arses down here, now!’

Luanne hissed in Carrie’s ear, ‘Don’t move.’

Dottie stepped back, her senses insulted by the strong odour of wet dogs mixed with burned fat.

Almost immediately, the sound of thunderous footsteps hitting each tread in turn heralded the arrival of the Carson boys. Neither lad, it seemed, was fazed by any of the adults standing outside the house.

When Carrie, Dottie, and Luanne studied the boys’ faces, they sensed that neither of them appeared to be the type to have beaten up Jesse or hurt little Charlie. They would surely know the consequences.

‘You little fuckers,’ Ivy Rose snapped. ‘If the Murphy men take you to the woods and nail you to a stake, I won’t be surprised. What the blazes have you gawn and done now?’

Right on cue, Sunny’s car pulled up, followed by Dottie’s, with Spud behind the wheel and Jesse and Billy in the back.

Ivy Rose’s attention was quickly diverted to the cars, and panic crossed her face. ‘Jesus Christ, whatever possessed you to hurt the little chavi, eh?’ Fearing a Murphy reprisal, panic kicked in, and she backhanded both boys in one swift move.

Joey and Stuey couldn’t have looked more shocked as they clutched their cheeks.

‘What chavi?’ Joey blurted out. ‘What are you on about?’

Dottie watched the boys carefully, noting how baffled they seemed. Then, both their faces drained of colour as they looked down the path. Turning around, she saw Billy and Jesse marching towards them.

Joey, who was now thoroughly agitated, pointed at Jesse. 'Wait, what's going on? Who did that to your face?' With Billy by his brother's side, Joey guessed it wasn't Billy who'd done it. And it had been a few weeks since he'd last seen Jesse in Bluewater.

In the blink of an eye, Billy grabbed Joey by the throat, lifting him off the path. 'You did, you sly bastard.'

Dottie was surprised that Ivy Rose didn't try to stop Billy, but it seemed that she didn't have the strength, be it physically or morally to protect her boys.

Stuey yelled, 'Stop!' so loudly that Billy dropped Joey back onto the path.

'We never hurt Jesse! We didn't do it!'

'You were balaclavad up – the two of you– and you battered Jesse. Then, two of you on a motorbike cut up my little brother. You didn't have the guts to show your faces.'

Ivy Rose grabbed Billy's arm. 'Hang on, a minute. So you never saw Joey or Stuey? You're just assuming it was them. Am I right?'

Billy shook her off, his eyes blazing. 'You cut little Charlie's face,' he said, glaring at Joey.

Furiously shaking his head, Joey locked eyes with Jesse. 'Me, you, Stuey – we scrap, we argue. But I swear, I'd never hurt Charlie. On me muvver's life, I wouldn't. He's just a kid. Why would we?'

Jesse stepped forward. 'Because I beat you up in the bogs at Bluewater, Joey.'

Joey rubbed his chin. 'Yeah, well, I probably deserved that. We were takin' the piss outta your bird.'

'And I told you I hope Atticus dies a painful death,' Jesse shot back.

Joey shrugged. 'So? He ain't my dad. Yeah, we chased you, but it was just a bit of fun. We might've hurt you if we caught ya, but not Charlie. No way.' He looked down the path, giving a short laugh. 'Look at your uncle, your dad. They're bloody giants. I like me face too much to mess with you Murphys. It ain't in me to hurt a little chavi.'

Billy glanced at Stuey, who was far from handsome. It looked as though his eyes wandered off on their own accord, and his chipped teeth made him look like the shark in the film *Jaws*. Joey wasn't much better, although he clearly thought he was, with the thick layers of gel holding back his bushy hair.

'You were with that Nobby Slade at Bluewater. Was he in on it as well? 'Cos I beat that wanker up a few weeks ago.'

Joey shook his head so fast that Billy guessed he was being truthful. As much as he hated to admit it, he knew the Carson brothers well enough to guess when they were lying.

'We don't hang around with the Slades, especially that gay boy Danny.'

'What did you say?' asked Billy, now totally shocked.

Joey's face tightened, afraid he had said the wrong thing. 'Nuffin. We just kinda keep to ourselves. I mean, I'm not like that. And our cousin's little firm – I mean Atlas's – certainly ain't like that. I mean, they still live on a site in their caravans. They ain't gay.'

Ivy Rose slapped her hands on her hips. 'Me boys ain't that way inclined either, just so yous know.'

Luanne knew precisely what Joey was talking about. It was frowned upon in their community to be gay. Obviously, times were changing, and outside their close-knit community, it was more generally accepted. But not in the travellers' world. All the men were taught to fight and bring home the bread, while the women were taught to cook and clean. The gypsy sites were still very much that way, so the lads steered clear of any kind of association. Billy and Jesse had grown up differently. Their mother was ditching the old traditions, and the only significant one that remained was keeping a clean house.

Luanne sighed. 'I think we're barking up the wrong tree,' she said, trying to steer Carrie away.

'Thanks for the fucking apology,' said Ivy Rose, in her most sarcastic tone.

Carrie spun around. 'If I hear any different, Ivy Rose, I will personally string your two boys up by their bollocks and gut them like fish. I ain't gonna pretend I like you or any one of the Carsons, so after what they did to me and mine, you can fuck off with your apology.'

'You can't tar us all with the same brush, ya know.'

Carrie's eyes shot across the road, and she lifted her chin to what was once Ginty's house. 'If I find out this has anything to do with that old bag Ginty, I will come for her, and you can tell her that from me.'

'Yeah, well just so you know, Ginty's on the missing list, so maybe whoever had it in for your boys had it in for their grandmuvver as well.'

Luanne stepped forward, right in Ivy Rose's face. 'Don't you ever call that woman their grandmuvver, after what she did to our family. And if she *is* lying dead in a ditch, bleedin' good riddance.'

Unexpectedly, Stuey gripped Jesse's arm. 'Jesse, I know we've always had our – what's it called?'

Jesse shrugged him off. 'Feud?'

'Nah, not feud. More kinda like wind-up days. I dunno, but listen, right, me and Joey are on your side. Whoever beat up you and your little bruvver, well, we'll join ya, to give 'em a good ol' pasting.'

Joey was nodding. 'Too right we will.'

Billy didn't want to get friendly. Looking across to Dottie, he flicked his eyes to indicate that he wanted to talk to her alone. In fact, he wanted to be away from Jesse, the Carson brothers, and everyone else present.

Just from that look alone, Dottie knew what he wanted.

CHAPTER TWENTY-SIX

The plan was set – Atticus's family was next. Grief or not, the Carsons mourning Atticus wouldn't slow the Murphys down. Mercy wasn't on the table if Atlas and his crew had crossed the line. Everyone in their circle knew that grieving rules didn't apply when the living were still bleeding.

So when Dottie quietly asked Spud if she could use his car – hers being serviced – because Billy wanted some time alone with her, Spud didn't hesitate. He simply smiled, kissed her cheek, and handed over the keys. No questions asked. After all, he knew what had to be done. He assumed Billy wanted some time alone – after all, they'd only just buried Willow six hours ago. They should still be at the wake, reminiscing about the good times. Maybe even looking through photos of her. But, he conceded, family is about the living, and whoever had hurt Charlie had crossed a line. There would be consequences. And someone would lose a hand.

Spud then joined Carrie and Luanne. They were preparing themselves to confront the next Carson family on their list. A cold, hard determination was in the air; it was the kind that meant business. Grief had its limits, but revenge didn't.

***

'Do you think it was them?' Dottie finally broke the silence, glancing at Billy. Her knuckles were white on the steering wheel, her voice seemingly modulated to correspond to the tense mood of the moment. 'Those boys were shocked.'

Billy loosened his black tie and shrugged, his gaze fixed on the passenger window. 'I don't know. But, either way,

Dad will get Atticus's lot talking. That is if Mum doesn't first.' He shook his head with a half-smile. 'Mum's a nutcase. She was ready to give that Ivy Rose a hiding.' His voice suddenly cooled. 'But you weren't, Mottie, were you? You suss everything out first before you do anything. I've seen you. You would have made a good sniper.'

'Charming.' Dottie smiled, her voice calm. 'Well, I like to think before I speak or act. Your mum's more passionate – she'll fight the world before knowing her enemies. But we love her for it.'

'Yeah,' Billy murmured.

Once they were off the estate, Dottie pulled over to the kerb and turned to Billy. 'So what's really going on?'

Billy's thoughts kept circling back to Danny. Something about him didn't sit right. The Carson brothers had said Danny was gay. Fair enough: perhaps he was. But the thing was that when Danny had taken Willow for a ride, he was holding her hand and laughing as if he had bagged the top prize. It didn't make sense. If he wasn't into her, what was he playing at?

'Thinking about it now,' said Billy, 'it could've been Danny, you know.'

Dottie frowned. 'Danny? Why?'

'Well, the Carson brothers said he's gay, didn't they. So taking Willow for a ride, pretending to like her, doesn't add up.'

'I don't get it, Billy. What's that got to do with the Carsons hurting your little brother?'

Billy spun to face her, frustration reddening his cheeks. 'I'm not talking about the Carsons hurting Charlie.'

Dottie's eyes widened as the realisation hit her. 'Oh, right.'

Billy turned away, his tough exterior cracking as tears welled up in his eyes – entirely out of character.

Reaching over, Dottie gently placed a hand on his shoulder. 'It's all right, love. It's not your fault.'

Billy wiped his eyes quickly. 'The thing I cannot understand is this: why would he have taken her that day? Was it just to mess with me? Why take her, if she's not his type? Had he intended to hurt her? I know what she could be like when she was with me.'

Dottie had to admit she found the whole thing strange and searched for a reasonable explanation. 'When I was younger, lads got called gay for the slightest thing. They only had to say something that bordered on feminine, and then they were marked as gay. Maybe taking Willow off like that was his way of proving he wasn't.'

'I'd like to believe that, Mottie, but . . .' Billy's voice trailed off, struggling to put into words what he was actually thinking.

'But what?' urged Dottie.

'Well, when I saw him that night at Bluewater, he got under my skin with the way he was smiling at me. At first, I thought he was laughing, like taking the piss out of me because I was rowing with the Carsons. But after the funeral today, he had the same grin.' He shuddered. 'And it gave me a weird feeling. Don't get me wrong – I'm not gay, but I reckon he is.'

Dottie nodded, deep in thought. 'I see,' she said at last. 'But why was he at the funeral?'

Billy clenched his fists. 'That's what I'm trying to figure out. He shouldn't have been there at all. And, Mottie, if it wasn't Willow I saw running across that field, and it was just a wild animal or a bush blowing in the wind, then I've got it wrong, badly wrong. What a fuck-up.'

Dottie looked at the pain playing out across Billy's face. Clearly, he had evidently loved Willow.

'What if it was Danny who killed her? And that flash wanker mugged me off when I stuck up for him? I just feel sick now. I should've let Cas get answers the best way he knows how. I should've let Danny suffer. But I was acting like an idiot, and maybe part of me actually *wanted* to see her run off. Perhaps I even *wanted* to believe she was running across that field. I think I even had the hump with her. Shit, Mottie, I was hoping she was lost – all alone and cold – and wishing she had stayed with me.'

Dottie held his arm. 'Stop it now. You are a human not a machine.'

He took a deep breath. 'If I got it wrong, then, in reality, perhaps she wasn't running away at all. She was already dead. And so Danny must have killed her. But I was too busy believing someone else was the real killer. And, at the time, I didn't believe torturing Danny was the answer. Now? Now, I should've let the horse take his head off.'

'Well, for what it's worth, I don't think it was him who killed Willow. I know you are desperate to find the bastard who did, but I don't believe it was Danny. They still haven't found that girl on the news who's been missing for what seems like ages now or that other girl who went missing early in August, and they're both from Kent. I reckon there's a nutter on the loose, and it's probably that copper who stopped you or a bloke impersonating one. So, I shouldn't think Danny is connected. How could he be?'

'It was him who told me that the Carsons were going to hurt Charlie, but we never got there in time. He also said that it was the Carsons who had beaten up Jesse.'

Dottie chewed the inside of her lip as she stared out of the window. 'Billy, Cas was burgled.'

'I know. He told me. But if you're thinking Charlie's attack was a distraction, well, that doesn't make sense because Cas was burgled while we were at the funeral, and I ain't being funny, but there ain't no bigger distraction than a fucking funeral.'

'So,' replied Dottie, 'it seems to me we have three possibilities. One, Danny has been fed a load of lies about the Carsons. Two, the Slades want us to turn on the Carsons. Or three, Danny said it to cause a bigger distraction.'

'Well, either way, Danny's going to get worse than a fucking horse kick. I will take his head right off.'

Dottie's grip tightened on Billy's arm. 'No!'

Billy looked at her, surprised by the sharpness in her voice. 'You won't stop me, you know.'

'Billy, let me tell you something,' Dottie said, her tone softening. 'I'm not the gushy type. I leave that to your mum and—'

'You're my mum, too,' Billy interrupted, quickly.

Dottie smiled. 'I know. But Carrie . . . Carrie has done what other women wouldn't. She loves you as her own. I never expected her to love you as much as Jesse, but she has. There's no distinction between you two, and she's given you a life filled with love, with your brothers and sister.'

Billy nodded, sensing she was heading somewhere deep, so he gave her time to speak.

'I've been lucky enough to see you whenever I wanted,' Dottie continued. 'Carrie let me share the responsibility of raising Jesse too. I got two for the price of one. We both love you dearly.'

Dottie paused, staring off into the distance, her thoughts drifting. 'When I was in prison, all I cared about was you. I promised myself I'd always protect you, even if it meant risking everything again.'

The two of them were silent each with their own thoughts.

Dottie's took her back several years. She recalled the night Albert Carson had broken into Carrie's flat, intent on killing one of the boys. She'd been hiding, watching, and, luckily, she was there just in the nick of time that day. She managed to knock him out. She then proceeded to tie him up and pour alcohol and drugs down his throat to finish him off. The authorities found his body months later, but she and Carrie had kept that secret close to their chests.

'I don't want you going to prison,' Dottie said, pulling herself from the memory. 'You're young, clever, and mature beyond your years. Don't take the law into your own hands. Promise me you won't do anything stupid. If needs must, then you leave it to me.'

Billy stared at her, now, his thoughts conflicted. 'This is my fight, Mottie, not yours.'

But Dottie shook her head. 'Your battles, Son, are mine too.'

He was silent, contemplating what she had just said. 'Would you take me back to Cas's? I want to ask him what was taken to see if it had any relevance because I've got this gut feeling that the Slades are connected to this whole mess.'

'All right, Billy. I'll take you back, but I'm thinking that perhaps you're so angry with Danny because of all that has happened recently – the robbery, Charlie's attack, and more – can be laid at the Slade family's door, when, perhaps, that's not the case.'

Billy felt a tad frustrated that Dottie wasn't getting it. Perhaps, he conceded, Danny's expression today spoke more than words. Nevertheless, he was convinced that all these incidents were connected to the Slades.

It was seven thirty and still light by the time they arrived at Cas's home. As they drove up the drive, Billy went cold. 'Fuck!' he said, as he clocked the missing camera that had been attached to the wall by the entrance porch. Then, he saw that the front door was ajar.

'Wait!' Dottie yelled. She remembered from this morning Cas saying that the camera had been tampered with. But now it was actually missing, she wondered if someone else was at the house at this very moment.

But it was too late.

Billy had already pushed the front door wide open. It was never open. Never! As he hurtled through the house, Dottie was not far behind him, ready to protect her son if whoever had removed the camera was still in the house.

However, as soon as Billy reached the study, he stopped dead.

Dottie hurriedly peered over his shoulder.

Cas was lying motionless on the floor by his desk. Blood was pouring from a wound at the back of his head and it was now covering his thin ponytail with thick claret.

At first, Dottie thought someone had shot him from behind, in which case, there would not be a lot left of Cas's face. She pushed the shell-shocked Billy to one side and quickly rushed to Cas, effectively, but not intentionally, blocking Billy's view.

When she slowly turned his head, to her astonishment, Cas blinked and then moaned. 'The cunts.'

'Billy! Call an ambulance!'

Billy slapped his hands over his pockets, frantically searching for his phone. 'Shit, I can't find my phone.'

Dottie whipped hers out from her back pocket and threw it to him, before seeing to Cas.

'Don't move, Cas. We're here. We're getting help.'

Cas's eyes rolled back before they closed again.

'No, Cas, stay with us, please!' Dottie shrieked, her voice now strained and desperate.

She was slipping back into prison mode. To a memory from which she could never escape. It was the moment her best friend, Billy, was stabbed in prison right in front of her. Billy had been the only one who'd understood her back then, and when she died, her world lost its meaning. They'd made plans for when they got out, but, in the end, she'd been released alone.

'The ambulance is on its way. I told the 999 operator that Cas may have been burgled. So the police might turn up.' Billy's wobbly voice broke her from the memory. 'Will he be all right, Mottie?'

'I don't know,' Dottie replied, glancing over her shoulder at him. 'But he's alive, so there's hope.'

Billy's gaze suddenly swept the room. 'Fuck, where's Keith?'

He sprinted to the annexe, his heart pounding. The place was empty. Nothing was disturbed, but there was no sign of Keith.

Panic took hold as Billy ran from room to room shouting Keith's name, his voice echoing through the manor house.

Could Keith have done this? The thought hit him like a punch to the gut. The two men were close, like brothers, but different. Keith worked for Cas. Surely, he wouldn't turn on him . . . would he?

Billy's mind raced, questioning everything. The Slades? Maybe not. He'd met them and had even beaten up one of the brothers. They didn't seem capable of pulling off something like this. They were more like alley cats. They were too scrappy, with as much sophistication as an elephant enduring an enema. He couldn't see how the likes of them would have had the balls to take on Cas's firm. No, this was something else. Although, if they *had* taken him on, they had used the ideal time, since Cas had dismissed all his men for the day on account of it being the funeral, and his two henchmen were still in Thailand.

His thoughts snapped back to Danny. It was as if he was hiding something in the dark shadows behind those eyes, and then, of course, there was that strange, unsettling smile of his.

Billy chewed his bottom lip, his gut twisting. *Had Danny done this?* He was already believing now that Danny had killed Willow, so what else was he capable of? Cas had all but sent Danny to his death, and Danny had probably expected to die, until, of course, he was rescued.

The wail of the ambulance siren brought Billy back to the present. He bolted to the front door and waved the paramedics in before directing them to the study.

Helpless, he and Dottie stood back silently, just watching, as the paramedics moved swiftly and secured Cas onto the stretcher.

'We will be taking him to Pembury Hospital.'

Dottie nodded and watched as they navigated their way out of the drive and turned on the flashing blue lights.

As soon as the ambulance was out of sight, Billy knew the police would definitely arrive because if Cas died, not only would the culprits be done for robbery but also for murder. As it stood, though, it was a case of aggravated burglary.

'What if they've killed Keith?'

When Billy's voice wavered with real fear, Dottie could see the weight of the world on her son's shoulders. He was just a kid, after all, but the bond he had built with Cas and Keith was strong, and the worry etched on his face was undeniable.

She hated seeing him like this.

Before she could reassure him, Billy suddenly lifted his head and stared out of the French doors, beyond the gap in the walled garden, and across the field. His eyes widened in alarm. 'Oh shit!' Without hesitation, he bolted towards the stables.

Dottie was right behind him, clutching a letter opener she'd snatched from the desk, ready for trouble.

When Billy pulled open the main door to the stables, a deep sense of unease hit him before he even got close to Goliath's stall. The door was shut, but something was off. Goliath was a curious horse. He always had his head hanging over if the main door was open. But, this time, he wasn't there.

Billy froze for a second, dread creeping in. 'This ain't right, Mottie,' he muttered, under his breath, his eyes scanning the dimly lit space ahead of him. There was an eerie silence, as if he almost expected someone to step out with a gun.

Dottie gripped the letter opener tighter, her senses on high alert. She also felt something wasn't right. Her instinct was to stop Billy from going into the stall. It was as if she could foresee a horrific scene.

'Please, love, leave.'

Billy stared at the closed door. He couldn't peer over; his mind wasn't ready to see what lay on the other side. He stepped back and clocked the letter opener in Dottie's hand, and in that moment, he saw her for who she was: a woman who you wouldn't mess with. She had this blank look, blank but determined. Darkness screamed from her eyes, and her jaw snapped to the side.

He took another step back and turned so he couldn't face what lay behind that door.

But then, curiosity got the better of him. Turning back again and holding his breath, he watched as Dottie opened the door to the stall.

There was a second or two before she slammed it shut. The look on her face had changed dramatically. She was white with shock, her eyes glistening, her mouth open.

'What is it?' he asked, but she didn't answer right away. She staggered back, catching her breath.

'Mottie?' he said.

But she was bent over and gasping for air while swallowing down the vomit that was rising to the back of her throat.

He watched as she placed her hands on her knees and retched. His eyes glanced at the closed stall door, then back at Dottie, who was now throwing up. Fear momentarily rooted him to the floor. He desperately wanted to see for himself what was obviously so shocking. So he walked up to the stall.

But in between retching, Dottie screamed, '*No!*'

However, Billy couldn't stop. He knew that whatever was behind that door was probably as bad as it gets because unlike Carrie, Dottie could stomach most things, so what had she seen?

As he stepped forward ever closer, Dottie tried to grab him, but it was too late. He had already pushed the door open, and the sight before him literally sucked all the air out of his lungs, his eyes still locked on the gruesome scene, while his brain tried to process it all.

Everything seemed to turn to slow motion. So much so, the ringing in his ears made him unable to move or speak.

Billy's breath came in short bursts, and his feet almost seemed stuck to the floor as the terrible vision burned in his consciousness.

Dottie was right behind him. Her presence was a chilling reminder that the evil he was witnessing was genuine. It wasn't a dream. He couldn't unsee it. Even when he forced himself to blink, the sight did not fade. Blood. There was so much of it. The metallic odour assaulted his nostrils. And he needed to be careful where he walked because the floor was very slippery. Not that he had any intention of staying there a moment longer. Despite his legs wobbling beneath him, he couldn't take his gaze away. Something then changed within him. He felt a basic terror, but it was mixed with rage, raw and untamed.

Dottie finally grabbed him by the shoulder, trying to drag him away from the doorway. 'Billy!' she hissed. While her voice was sharp, it barely broke through the haze clouding his mind.

He blinked again, harder this time, before taking one shaky step back. The ringing in his ears grew louder; it was drowning out everything except the chaos swirling inside his head.

'What the fuck . . .' Billy managed to say.

'Don't look any longer,' Dottie ordered, her tone stronger now.

At that moment, as if the movie in his head stopped, the ringing sound ended, and reality grabbed him by the throat. If the killer was still here, lurking in the shadows, they had to get out.

Dottie gripped the letter opener, with her concern now emulating that of Billy's. What she saw far outweighed what she was capable of. She had been marked as a psychopath, but if that was the case, this was the work of a real one.

CHAPTER TWENTY-SEVEN

Dragging Billy back to the house, they left via the main entrance. Hurriedly, she opened the front passenger door to the car and practically shoved Billy in before jumping into the driver's seat. But before she could even put the keys in the ignition, a police car arrived and blocked the road leading up to the house.

Billy sat in the car trembling, his hands shaking uncontrollably, and his head subtly nodding with each throb of his pulse.

Dottie, on the other hand, had started to regain her composure. Her priority was to get Billy away from the nightmare inside that house and inside those stables as soon as possible, but seeing two officers climbing out of their car, she realised that it wasn't going to happen. Not yet, anyway.

The officers, both in uniform and in their mid-thirties, approached the car. One was noticeably larger, probably a regular at the gym.

'We've had a report of a burglary at this property,' the bigger officer said, opening his notebook. 'The owner, Mr Cas Ferrier, right?' He looked up. His round crystal-blue eyes seemed so calm, starkly contrasting with the chaos in Dottie's mind.

She forced a smile. 'I think . . . er . . .'

'Oh, yes, sorry, I'm Officer Tatler, and this is my colleague, Officer Fenley.'

Dottie returned his calm demeanour with a strained smile. 'I strongly suggest you call a detective and the forensics team,' she said, not wanting the young officers to face what she had seen.

But Officer Tatler rolled his eyes, dismissing her concern.

'We don't need to do that at this stage,' he said, with a tone of superiority. 'We'll take a look and assess the situation first. It's our job.'

His dismissive attitude got under Dottie's skin. However, she smiled again, although this time with a smug twist. 'All right, but don't say I didn't warn you.'

Tatler glanced down at his notebook. 'Who are you, and what are you doing here?'

'I'm Dorothy Ellis, a friend of Cas's. We found him on the floor in his study and then called the paramedics.'

Officer Tatler nodded. He then glanced at Billy who was sitting in the car with a thousand-yard stare on his face. 'And him?'

'He's my son.'

'Right. We'll need a statement from you both. Could you stick around?'

Dottie shook her head. 'No, I need to take my son home first. It's been quite a shock for him. But I'll give you my address before I go.'

'All right. Is the front door open?' He pointed to the house.

She nodded, watching as Fenley went up to the door, pushed it open, and peered inside. Reeling off her address, she waited for Officer Tatler to move his car so she could get past.

Once they were on the main road, Dottie glanced at Billy. 'Maybe it's a stupid question, but are you all right?'

By this time, Billy had stopped shaking, but his voice was cold and distant. 'I'm not sure. I don't think I'll ever get over what I saw.'

Dottie expected tears, but Billy seemed distant, staring blankly ahead.

‘I’ll take you home,’ she offered, gently.

‘No!’ he barked.

‘What? Where do you want to go?’

‘To Pembury Hospital, to see Cas . . . if he isn’t dead already,’ he muttered, his voice emotionless.

Dottie nodded. She really couldn’t blame him. Her son wouldn’t be able to process anything until he saw Cas for himself. She could only hope that he had made it through.

***

Fenley stepped into the house first, eager to have a good nose around. Growing up on a council estate with piss-stained lifts and junkies hanging about outside, instead of pretty plant pots and neatly trimmed hedges, the idea of a country manor with all the finery was like something out of a dream. He wasn’t good at identifying antiques, but the furniture in the hallway and in what appeared to be the drawing room looked old and classy. He wandered past the ornaments and artwork, muttering to himself, ‘Quite the collector.’

Tatler, who was already in the study, called out, ‘This must’ve been where the bloke was attacked. There’s blood everywhere! I think that lady, Dorothy Ellis, was probably right about calling in a detective. I’m not sure if the bloke would have pulled through with this amount of claret.’

A few moments later, Fenley joined him. He now peered down at the floor. ‘Shit. I’ll be shocked if the bloke survived. Mind you, we haven’t had a call to say it’s murder, and you know what the murder squad are like. They’d be crawling all over this, by now.’

Tatler chuckled. ‘If he ain’t dead, I bet he’s got one hell of a headache.’ He glanced up, startled by a movement outside. ‘Oh shit, that bloody thing made me jump!’ he exclaimed.

Staring at him through the French doors was the biggest horse he had ever seen.

Fenley followed his gaze. 'Is that blood on its chest?'

Tatler squinted, nodding. 'Possibly. Is the horse hurt?'

'Not sure. I'm no horse handler, but I can't see any obvious injuries,' Fenley replied, uncertainly.

Tatler shrugged. 'Could be someone else's blood, then. Maybe the owner's.' He pointed at the pool of claret on the floor. 'He could've fallen off the horse or been kicked by it and crawled in to call for help. There's probably been no robbery at all.'

'You could be right,' Fenley agreed. 'Nothing seems touched here. A few trays of wilted sandwiches, empty glasses. Maybe he had guests, but the place doesn't look like it's been ransacked.'

Tatler's eyes caught a sympathy card on the desk. 'Looks like he was holding a wake here. So maybe I am right: there wasn't a burglary here after all.'

Suddenly, the horse turned and bolted. Tatler sighed. 'Call in the horse handlers. I think we may need a detective too. Anyway, I'm going to check outside. I saw some stables at the back as we drove into the property.'

Stepping gingerly out of the French doors, ensuring the horse wasn't coming back, Tatler headed over to some outbuildings.

He had been more than surprised to see the horse nuzzle the French doors back at the house. But it had obviously found its own way from the stables to the courtyard. That made him think briefly about the intelligence of horses. *Had something made it come across to the house?* he wondered.

Now, he had his wits about him. He didn't trust horses, especially one that size. One kick from that beast, and he would be done for.

Reaching the first of the outbuildings, which were clearly stables, he noticed that the door was open. He then observed that there were four stalls inside but not a single horse in sight.

As he was about to return to the main house, he heard a noise behind him. Now thoroughly spooked, he spun around and froze. The colossal horse had returned and was staring at him. It made a few strange noises before casually walking past him to the far stall. It used its nose to open the door but it didn't go in. Instead, it just stood there, tossing its head and raising its tail.

Now intrigued, Tatler decided to give the stables a quick sweep. He didn't expect to find much. He put it down to Mr Ferrier having had a riding accident. But as he moved closer, keeping an eye on the horse, he realised that something was unsettling it, just by the way the animal was focused on the far stall.

Tatler stepped forward cautiously, to avoid a kick from the beast and peered inside. But before he could make sense of what he was seeing, the horse reared up, and its front hooves came crashing down. The force sent him staggering backwards. The pain shot through him as he collapsed onto the floor. He gasped, clutching his shoulder, but what he'd just seen instantly numbed the pain.

Propped up in the stall, was what he had first thought was a scarecrow or something for Halloween. But then, a horrifying realisation hit him – it wasn't a scarecrow or a jack-o'-lantern. It was a dead person. Blood covered the floor in thick clotted pools. The stench was unbearable. The body had been mutilated beyond recognition, clearly violently butchered. A pitchfork had been rammed through the man's neck and had pinned him upright. His stomach had been sliced open, and its contents spread grotesquely across the floor. He had been utterly disembowelled. But the worst part? The victim's eyes were gone, replaced by straw which had been stuffed crudely into the empty sockets.

Tatler could hardly believe what he was seeing. The scene before him wasn't just a crime – it was unearthly, like something out of a nightmare.

***

Within thirty minutes, Dottie and Billy had arrived at Pembury Hospital. By the time Dottie convinced the woman at the main reception desk that she was Cas's daughter, she was simmering with anger. Her smile was merely a mask, holding back the inner frustration to throttle the receptionist.

Finally, having waited for a couple of hours, they were directed to a room in the ICU. The moment they saw Cas, they barely recognised him. He looked so frail, so lost, lying there with drips and monitors hooked up to him.

Already in shock from everything that had happened, Billy couldn't believe his eyes. This was the same hospital he had come to when his mother had been hurt from Jimmy Carson blowing up the burger van with her practically inside it. He shuddered. 'He looks bad, eh, Mottie?'

Dottie nodded but tried to reassure him. 'All those tubes and beeps make it look worse than it is, though. He's alive, so thank the Lord for that. That old sod's too stubborn to let a knock on the head take him down.'

Just as Billy was about to move closer, the door swung open and in marched a police officer with a coffee in a Styrofoam cup in one hand and a sandwich in the other. He stopped dead in his tracks and eyed them suspiciously. 'Who are you, and who let you in?'

Dottie's temper flared at his tone. 'I'm family,' she snapped.

'Well, he's not supposed to have visitors. As soon as he comes to, we'll be questioning him.'

Billy noticed Cas's fingers twitch, and his eyes fluttered open. He gave them a weak wave.

But the officer saw it too and rushed to Cas's side, shoving both the woman and young lad aside. 'Mr Ferrier, Mr Ferrier!' he called out, urgently.

Cas managed a nod. 'Water,' he croaked, his voice barely audible.

The officer looked around in search of a cup and flask, but he was still trying to determine if the patient was supposed to have anything. He was flustered and clearly out of his depth. 'Er, I'll get the nurse,' he muttered and hurried from the room.

Billy almost laughed at the ridiculousness of it all. The whole situation felt unreal.

'Cas, who did it?' Billy asked, his voice full of determination.

'Nice,' Cas rasped. 'Not even a how are ya, Cas?'

'Sorry, how are you?' Billy asked, a little sheepishly.

'Well, I'm not fucking great, am I? I'm in hospital with PC Nosy Bollocks hovering over me. Now, get me strides – I need to get out of here and get home.'

Dottie glanced up at the IV bag. 'I don't think you're going anywhere, Cas. You're having a blood transfusion. You must feel awful.'

'I ain't on top form, that's for sure, but I'm breathing, ain't I?'

'Yes, but you need to stay put. If you're getting a transfusion, you're weak. You won't be able to stand up, let alone walk.'

Cas rolled his eyes. 'Who gave you a badge and called you Florence Nightingale? And look at you, Billy, you miserable bugger. I'm the one in the bed, not you. Smile, for fuck's sake.'

Billy pushed on. 'Who did it, Cas?'

Cas sighed, his voice gravelly. 'Dunno, mate. Two blokes – one big fucker, one skinnier. They had balaclavas on. Me, the daft old git, I opened the door thinking someone from the wake had forgotten something. Next thing, they've got a gun to me head and demanding money. I didn't argue. I just opened the safe and let 'em take what they wanted. I reckon I'm getting too old for all this bollocks.'

'Did they take much?' Dottie asked.

'Nah, just a few grand. They wanted other stuff, but I didn't give it to them. Anyway, as they marched me from the room, where the safe was, one of 'em clocked me with something hard. Knocked me clean out till you two showed up.'

He glanced behind them, frowning. 'Where's Keith? Gone for coffees, has he?'

Billy glanced at Dottie, unsure what to say.

She quickly filled the silence. 'We didn't see Keith. We came straight here.'

Cas's frown deepened. 'Straight here? I've been in this bloody bed for hours. What are you on about?'

'They wouldn't let us up until they had you stabilised and settled,' Billy said.

Just then, the officer re-entered the room. 'The nurse will be in shortly,' he announced, notebook at the ready.

But Cas had already closed his eyes.

'I think he's tired, officer,' Dottie said. 'He needs to rest.'

The officer raised an eyebrow. 'Did he say anything? Anything at all about who might've done this?'

'No,' Dottie replied, lying smoothly. 'Just mumbled about a drink – that's all.'

The officer, who Billy thought looked like a gormless version of Mr Bean, nodded. 'Not surprised, really. Nasty gash. Needed quite a few stitches. Lucky he's not brain-damaged.'

Dottie smiled, politely. 'Well, we'll be off. Hopefully, he'll wake up soon, and you'll catch whoever did this to the poor old man.'

Billy caught Cas opening one eye, glaring at them in disgust at being called a poor old man.

***

Once they were home, Dottie left Billy in the lounge while she made the call to Spud. When he answered, she was relieved to hear that the family were on their way back home, having driven halfway around the county in search of the Carsons. Apparently, it wasn't Atlas, his brother, or the cousin, who had been involved in the attack on Charlie. They had been in a car accident the day before and had only just come out of the hospital. With Atlas having two broken arms, there was no way he or any of them could have been on a motorbike. Spud said they were just as shocked as everyone else. Even Atticus's wife – who, it turned out, had no desire for revenge and didn't care that Jesse had wished Atticus a painful death. In fact, she admitted she'd hoped for the same outcome. She hated Atticus, calling him a bully.

After giving Dottie the lowdown, Spud must have sensed something in her voice. He assumed that his wife was planning to wait until he got home to tell him about what had happened at Cas's place. But it seemed that the shock must have got to her because instantly she blurted it all out, every gory detail.

Spud had always been her sympathetic ear – not just to her, but to all the Murphys – and he knew she loved him dearly for it. It gave her comfort to know that he was on his way home and wasn't keeping her on the phone asking a thousand and one questions. She was too tired for that, and it wasn't surprising, considering it was one o'clock in the morning.

Holding back her own feelings, Dottie threw her black blazer onto the sofa and kneeled beside Billy, who was sitting on the floor by the sofa and rocking back and forth. She wondered if maybe he needed to see a doctor. The shock must have been overwhelming for a lad of fifteen. It had certainly knocked the wind out of her.

'I'm going to make you a sweet tea, love.'

He stopped rocking and reached out for a hug.

Dottie pulled him close without hesitation, holding him tightly, like a young child. His body trembled as huge tears began to fall and gently splashed against her as he wept. She didn't tell him everything would be all right – she knew better. From this day forward, nothing would ever be the same.

'Keith was so good to me . . . I liked him,' he whispered, his voice catching. He pulled away, wiping his eyes. 'Only a real nutcase would do that to someone. Or someone so full of hatred, they'd turn into an animal to carry out something that fucking evil.'

Dottie nodded. 'Come into the kitchen with me, love. I'll make that tea. I wouldn't usually offer this, but I've got a Valium if you want – it might help with the shock.'

Billy followed her into the vast kitchen and silently sat at the table. 'No, no thanks, Mottie. The police will be here soon, anyway. They'll probably drag us down the station since, well . . . we were the ones who found him.'

Dottie poured the tea, stirring in a heavy dose of sugar. She had read somewhere that it helped with shock.

He took the mug from her and sipped the tea, only to screw up his face as though she'd handed him poison. 'I can't drink that. Just water will be fine, Mottie.'

'Are you going to call your brother? See how he is? I mean, they were all fired up, ready to front Atlas Carson and his lot.'

Billy shook his head. 'I'm not speaking to Jesse, Mottie, and I'm not sure I ever will.'

Dottie sighed, her frustration rising. 'So you're going to let a girl come between you two? Haven't you seen the worst life can get – back there in those stables?' Her voice grew sharp, now annoyed that he was still upset with Jesse after everything they'd just witnessed. His comment about never speaking to him again struck a nerve. 'I would've given anything to have had a brother or a sister. Don't get me wrong, your mum's like a sister to me, and I love her for who she is. But family is everything. I know that.'

Billy tutted and rolled his eyes.

'Billy Murphy, don't you ever tut at me again!' she snapped, making him sit up straight. 'You've no idea what I went through to ensure you had a life with Jesse. I could've fought to take you back – you were my flesh and blood – but I didn't, Billy! I didn't because I wanted you to have what I never bloody had. A family. A brother you could get into mischief with, share your secrets with, have by your side. And believe me, Billy, when I watched you and Jesse grow up as inseparable boys, I knew the pain I felt handing you over was worth it. It was all worth the tears, the sleepless nights, and the empty arms.'

Billy had never heard Dottie speak like that, and just for a moment, it hit him hard. Yes, she *had* sacrificed her own happiness for him. But the problem was that he was already drowning in his own guilt and grief to consider her needs. 'But you saw me whenever you wanted to, whenever you could.'

Dottie smiled, but it was a sad smile. 'I visited, and, believe me, those days I treasured. And when you were older, Carrie let you both stay with me, and I still treasure those times too. But it's not the same as seeing another woman raise your child. Don't get me wrong. I love her for it. But, still . . . I feel more like an aunt than a mum.'

Suddenly, Billy shot up from his chair and threw his arms around her, hugging her tightly. 'I never saw you like that, Mottie. I always saw you as my mum. I still do. I am happy having two mums – spoiled, I guess.'

As he pulled away, he noticed her eyes filling with tears. That was rare. She was the tough one with the deadpan face. She was the sensible one. She wasn't one to shower anyone with affection – not like his other mother.

Returning to his chair, Dottie's words circled in his mind. He just hadn't realised how much she'd given up. It was all because she'd wanted him and his brother to have each other.

'Billy, anger can be as fleeting as the blink of an eye, but love . . . love isn't fleeting. It goes deeper. And, believe me, there will never be anyone you'll love more than Jesse. That's why you don't want to speak to him – because he's hurt you. And when you love someone, that hurt cuts so much deeper.'

He knew she was right, but he was proud too. He wasn't like Jesse, who would scream, shout, and cry in public. He would hug, kiss, and laugh at himself. They were all the qualities he wished he possessed himself sometimes. In fact, when he thought about Jesse admitting to him that he'd slept with Willow, he'd never actually seen that expression of guilt on his brother's face before. It was an entirely new one.

'Mottie, I'm going to stay here tonight. I'm tired. I'll talk with Jesse in the morning.'

‘That sounds like a good idea, love. Go to bed, and if you need any sleeping tablets, let me know.’ She smiled. ‘It’s been a very rough ride, Son.’

Dottie then texted Carrie to let her know that Billy was with her.

When Spud arrived home, he found Dottie on the sofa, still fully dressed, with the phone by her cheek. He removed it and placed a blanket over her, instead of carrying her to bed. He didn’t want to wake her because he guessed she had taken one of her sleeping tablets. And after what she and Billy had witnessed, she might not go off to sleep again. He imagined this would give her nightmares. It sure as hell would have if he had been in Dottie’s shoes.

CHAPTER TWENTY-EIGHT

5 September

Tossing and turning, going over everything that had happened, Billy had taken for ever to fall asleep. So, by the time he climbed out of bed it was late morning. After throwing on a pair of jeans and a T-shirt, he slipped his feet into a pair of trainers, ready to head home and have it out with Jesse. As he searched for his phone, he realised he had left it in Spud's car. Quietly, he crept downstairs. When he entered the lounge and spotted Dottie asleep, his eyes drifted to the clock. It was gone eleven o'clock. All the events that happened yesterday must have really knocked it out of them. Picking up the keys from the hallway table, he snuck out of the front door.

***

As soon as he stepped outside, a gust of wind slammed the front door shut behind him.

Staring out across the road, he felt the cool breeze soothe his skin. He was on the point of approaching Spud's car, when he noticed what he thought was a familiar vehicle parked along the road. He didn't stare or make it obvious. Instead, he looked away as he calmly unlocked the car, reached in for his phone from the centre console, and then shut the door with ease, still keeping his eyes away from the vehicle up the road.

Casually, he walked back up the drive and into the house. Still, as soon as the door closed behind him, he ran up the stairs two at a time and headed straight for the central landing window. The large oval window stretched nearly from floor to ceiling, but Dottie had covered it with a long voile panel for privacy. His heart pounded as he peered out. Sure enough, it was a very similar car to that owned by Danny Slade. He didn't recognise the number plate, but those go-faster stripes down the side were unmistakable.

It hit him then that he was the one hiding. Why was he hiding? He should have been outside confronting the prick. Maybe the shock of what he'd witnessed yesterday had rattled him, but he didn't believe that what had happened had been Danny's doing.

A sudden surge of anger shot through him and he flew back down the stairs. Then, leaving his phone on the side table, he yanked the front door open again and tore off towards the car. His mind was racing. He was going to drag Danny out and demand answers. And he wasn't going to be kind about it either: a few hard punches, and he would have Danny telling him what he needed to know. The question he wanted an answer to was this: who had hurt his little brother? It wouldn't have been the Carsons. He and his family were sure of that now. Whoever was behind it might also have been the one or ones who'd broken into Cas's place. The fact that he'd mentioned they were wearing balaclavas couldn't have been a coincidence, surely?

Without looking for a suitable weapon, Billy charged towards the car, his rage bubbling at the surface. But just as he reached it, he realised there was no Danny sitting in the front seat and the go-faster stripes were silver not black. Before he turned to head back, now feeling stupid, another car screeched to a halt in front of him. He froze, momentarily stunned, as the driver's door flew open, and, to his horror, a huge, meaty-looking man was sitting behind the wheel . . . with a balaclava hiding his face.

Shock coursed through Billy's veins like iced water. Cas had said one of the men was big, and he was wearing a balaclava. Before he could catch his breath, the man was out of the car and lunging at him. Another man, also wearing a balaclava, got out of the front passenger seat.

Billy turned to run and yell out, but the sound stuck in his throat. He couldn't move fast enough. The man grabbed him, slamming something rough and foul-smelling over his head. Hessian. A sack.

'Struggle and I'll blow your head off,' the man growled. 'Now, you're gonna be a good boy and do as you're told, or your brains will be all over the fucking back seat of me motor and ya innards hanging out of your arse.'

Billy was bundled into the back of a car before it sped away. There were at least two of them – one held him down in the back seat and secured cable ties around his wrists while the other placed a rope around his neck to secure the sack. He didn't struggle; the threat was still hanging in the air – one wrong move, and he was sure they'd shoot him.

Within a few minutes, though, his reasonable side kicked in. His mind raced. He was smart enough to know that he had no chance of fighting back, not with a gun to his head. There had to be a reason for his kidnapping. Someone wanted something, and he guessed he would be their bargaining chip.

However, the gruesome vision of Keith's mutilated body shot through Billy's mind, and suddenly, he began to shake uncontrollably. Had Keith been alive when they gouged out his eyes? The thought churned his stomach, and water filled his mouth as the nausea hit him hard. The hessian sack around his head was tight – if he threw up, he could choke to death. Sweat coated his skin, and a throbbing pain pulsed through his temples. Desperate to hold back the vomit, he forced himself to breathe deeply, grasping for a distraction. Anything, in fact, to take his mind off the horror.

He began to picture his family gathered around 'the big table,' as his mother called it, for Sunday dinner. Grandad Jed laughing and insisting everyone try his latest home brew. The heat from the kitchen turning his mother's cheeks rosy red, and the smell of roast beef wafting through the house. He could almost hear Charlie pestering their mother every five minutes asking when dinner would be ready. And Jesse . . . Jesse, with dirt on his hands and that cheeky grin because he'd just taught Duchess a new trick.

And then it hit him. If he was killed, Jesse would never know that he really had forgiven him. He would never know that he still loved and missed him. The fear that had wrapped itself around his heart turned to searing anger.

His family would never know what had happened to him. They might find him like he found Keith, which terrified him more than death.

But if these men used their guns on him, he would be dead. No question. And if that happened, his death would be quick. At least, his family wouldn't have to wonder about that!

Sitting in the back of the car, his head down, hands bound behind his back, he could feel the body heat of the person beside him. Without another second to think, he threw his head back with speed and force and cracked his skull into the man's face. The yelp of pain told him he'd hurt the guy. Fuelled by rage, he did it again and again until the car screeched to a halt.

The back door flew open, and a deep, gravelly voice roared, 'You pathetic weakling! I knew I shouldn't have brought you along, you laughable prick. I could've managed this on me own. You're like a wet wipe wanker with that stupid grin on ya face. And I can't see how your farver thinks you're anything like me. You ain't nuffin like me. Now, get yaself cleaned up. You're making a mess of me motor! And put that balaclava back on.'

Billy barely had time to register the insult before the man leaned in, his foul breath – from all the stale whisky and cigarettes – managing to penetrate through holes in the hessian sack.

The man whispered close to Billy's ear, 'Try that again, and I'll fuck you up the arse and cut your bollocks off.'

'What do you want from me?' Billy asked, somehow keeping his voice steady, refusing to show from his body language a flicker of fear.

The man let out a sick, menacing chuckle. 'Me? I don't want anything from you. You're just collateral, nothing more and nothing fucking less.' His voice grew darker, almost playful. 'Although, I do like a young boy. Makes a change from shagging an old tart.'

Turning his attention to the other guy in the car, the kidnapper barked, 'Make sure he doesn't mangle any more of your face, 'cos I ain't dealing with your muvver, the soppy cow, fussing over her favourite baby. And I ain't gonna be held accountable to your farver either, Gawd love the ol' bastard.'

Billy's ears were ringing, his head throbbing from the impact, but he didn't care. He knew he'd seriously hurt the other guy – the weakling. Whoever he was, he'd definitely rattled him, and that gave him a small and bitter sense of satisfaction. Shame, though, he couldn't see his handiwork. But he'd heard the bloke's nose pop. One thing he did know was that the gun threat was an empty one.

As soon as the man with the gravelly voice drove off again, Billy planned his next move. He imagined the guy beside him was ready for another headbutt. So he braced himself for his next step. He wanted to get the driver to stop.

At least then he stood a chance of surviving if a member of the public, be they in a car or in the street, saw something. Maybe the police had the number plate of the kidnappers' car, and they were, at this very minute, checking one of the ANPR cameras.

Taking a deep breath, Billy spun, kicking his legs into the air. With his head pressed against the door and his back on the seat, he had just enough room to kick – and kick hard. He moved quicker than the guy could react, and he didn't stop once he started. He kicked relentlessly, driving the breath out of the bloke until, once again, the driver slammed on the brakes.

Billy tumbled into the footwell, struggling to get back up, but the door flew open before he could.

'Get out, you useless cunt!'

His plan had worked. He was turning them against each other. 'Gravelly Voice' was now barking at the other guy to get out. Did that mean he only had one to deal with?

Because this guy was big, Billy doubted he could take him down with only a couple of decent right hooks, but he still felt he had the edge, especially if the man was driving.

But that plan soon went to shit.

'You drive, 'cos you ain't capable of much else other than looking pretty. And if you weren't my nephew, I'd fuck you an' all.'

The other guy stayed silent, which only confirmed Billy's suspicion – he would recognise the voice if he heard it. *A pity, though, that he still had to contend with both blokes*, he thought.

The doors slammed shut, and they were off again, but, this time, Billy was face down in the footwell while both men were in the front. Slowly, quietly, hoping they wouldn't notice, he twisted around like a rotisserie chicken until he could sit up. He listened intently to the one-way conversation. Gravelly Voice was tearing into the other guy.

'What a fucking numpty. What are you gonna tell your ol' man, eh? That a kid with his hands tied behind his back still managed to smash you up?' He laughed, darkly. 'It's like losing to a one-legged man in an arse-kicking contest.'

Ten minutes later, he chuckled again, but then his voice turned cold. 'And your dear ol' dad thinks you've got my genes, my DNA, my fucking psychopathic way. I can't see it meself. You killed your cat – whoop-de-doo. Me? I set fire to the house with me muvver inside. She didn't die, but it was fun watching her running around waving her hands. And you, you dear little pudding, you only *shot* your moggy, not even cutting it up. See where I'm going with this? No comparison. But, oh no, your farver still says we're like two peas in a pod. Well, boy, I ain't happy with that, 'cos, see, I like to be special. I don't care much for having a double.'

He sighed before continuing, his voice softening just a fraction. 'He reckons you'll work well with me and get the job done. Well, I'd prefer your older bruvver, although the cunt turned inside out when I asked if he fancied doing a bit of work with me. I suppose you showed the most excitement, but looking at the state of you, that ain't saying much, is it – you useless fucker!'

While the big guy continued to berate the other, Billy carefully pushed himself up onto the seat. Slowly, deliberately, he fished around behind him for the door handle. *Bingo!* His fingers wrapped around it, and just as the car rounded a bend, he yanked the door open and threw himself out. The pain as he hit the ground was dulled by the adrenaline pumping through him, but it was there, nevertheless, sharp and unforgiving. He rolled and tumbled until, finally, he came to a stop.

For a moment, everything was still, but then he heard the car door open and the sound of footsteps pounding towards him. He hoped and prayed it was someone from a car behind, someone to help him. But the rough hands that hoisted him to his feet told him otherwise. No, there were no other cars. He had messed up, and he knew it.

'So, you're gonna play silly buggers, are ya? Well, not anymore.'

That was the last thing he heard before everything went black.

CHAPTER TWENTY-NINE

Dottie eventually woke up late into the morning. Assuming Billy was in the bedroom, she got up from the sofa, stretched her aching limbs and headed upstairs to run a shower. The vision of Keith's mutilated body still haunted her. It clung to her like a foul stench. The black trousers felt uncomfortable, and the blouse, which was something she hardly ever wore anyway, was already getting on her nerves. She needed a warm shower. Something to help wash away the tension from all the horrific events of yesterday.

Not that she would ever feel normal again.

Expecting the police to arrive at some point today, she wondered how she would get over having to relive the devastating sight of Keith's remains back at Cas's place. It had been worse than she had ever experienced and she should know!

As she popped her head into Billy and Jesse's bedroom, she was surprised to find Billy wasn't there, but she didn't think anything of it. Perhaps he had gone for a walk to clear his head and call his brother in private. She could only hope so.

Throwing her dirty clothes into the linen basket, she climbed into the shower, allowing the hot water to rinse away every ounce of that lingering smell of rusted iron – the kind that makes your teeth go on edge. She scrubbed, but the taste and smell of blood stayed with her. After barely three minutes, she heard the doorbell ring. Instantly, she looked out of the bedroom window and was horrified to see a meat wagon parked up on the road outside her house. With her hands shaking nineteen to the dozen, she called Spud to tell him that she would probably be carted away. The police van was a cold reminder of the time she was taken from the police station to the courts as a terrified teenager. Fortunately, Spud was only around the corner at Sunny's, where he was discussing business, among other things.

Hurriedly, she threw on a tracksuit, before tying her wet hair into a bun and darting downstairs to open the front door.

Standing there like two cocky twats were two men who she assumed were detectives and behind them were two uniformed officers. Unease crept over her in bucketloads.

Keldon smiled. 'Dorothy Ellis?'

She nodded. 'Yeah, of course. You know very well who I am.'

'Yes, right. I'm DCI Andrew Keldon, and this is DI Paul Gurney. Ms Ellis, Tonbridge Police have just informed us that you were at the Ferrier residence.'

'Yeah, I was, and I told that copper to get forensics and a detective down there. He said he'd be the judge of that and allowed me to leave.'

Keldon's face tightened. 'You didn't tell him about the remains, did you?'

Dottie's eyes flicked between the two detectives. She knew exactly what they were implying. 'You mean Keith Purdey's body? No, I didn't think I had to spell it out. I mean, telling the copper he should call a detective and a forensics team would have suggested something more than an aggravated burglary took place.' She swallowed, the vision there in the forefront of her mind. 'It was gruesome. Whoever did that was a raving lunatic.'

With his hands stuffed in his trouser pockets, Gurney grinned, snidely. 'Yeah, we know. But you were the person who found him. And you didn't stick around to offer a statement, did you?'

Dottie remained silent, her face deadpan.

'As you said, the work of a lunatic,' Gurney added, his eyes narrowing, showing his suspicion.

She knew that tone. She had been called a lunatic herself back when she killed her parents. But she said nothing and just smiled.

Keldon stepped forward. 'I think it's best if you come down to the station . . . and we'll also need to speak to Billy Murphy. Apparently, he was with you.'

She stared at them, her expression not changing.

Keldon scratched the back of his neck. 'Tell me, Ms Ellis . . . did you have anything to do with it?'

She shook her head.

'I see you've changed your clothes,' Keldon said, looking her up and down, his gaze settling on her wet hair. 'Had a shower, I presume?'

Dottie nodded.

'Why?' Gurney asked.

'Why does anyone have a shower and get changed?' she replied, dryly.

Keldon glanced at the two uniformed police officers behind him. 'I'm sorry, Ms Ellis. You'll need to come with us.'

It was clear that they weren't here for a friendly chat. The presence of the meat wagon made that obvious. It hurt her feelings thinking that they believed her to be anything other than a psychopath. It was the first time for many years that she'd had to relive that feeling.

Before anyone could move, a truck came tearing up the road.

Dottie grinned at the sight of Carrie pulling up so close to the meat wagon. It meant that the coppers would have to move their van to open the back doors.

The car doors opened, and Carrie, Spud, Jesse, and Sunny spilled out, heading across the front lawn towards Dottie's front door.

The two officers raised their hands as if they could stop the Murphys approaching, but Carrie being Carrie, she bulldozed her way past them and threw her arms around Dottie.

'Bloody hell, girl! What a shock! Are you all right?' She pulled back, looking Dottie up and down before turning to the detectives. 'What a terrible thing to happen to Keith, eh? So, do you lot have any idea who did it?'

Sunny gently pulled Carrie back, letting Spud step forward. 'What's going on, then? Carrie just asked if you've caught the bastard that mutilated poor Keith,' said Spud.

'Well, we need Ms Ellis to accompany us to the station,' Keldon said, glancing at the uniforms. 'We need a statement.'

They all knew what that meant – they weren't just there for a statement.

'Yeah, sure,' Spud said. 'But my missus is still in shock. I'll bring her down when she's feeling better. Right now, she's not up to it.'

Keldon stepped closer. 'No, we'll be taking her now.'

'Like hell, you will! Unless my missus is under arrest, you ain't taking her anywhere. If it's just a statement, I'll bring her down when she's ready.'

When Gurney moved forward, Spud did too. 'Oi! You step over this threshold without a warrant, and there'll be trouble. You lot never found out who killed Willow or those missing kids, did ya? Now, you wanna take my Dottie in for questioning. Well, it seems to me you're wasting taxpayers' money 'cos you can't tell your arse from your elbow, can you?'

'Look, it's just routine. She was the one who actually found Mr Purdey.'

Carrie saw the sadness in Dottie's eyes. The detectives were treating her like a suspect, all because of the crime she had committed as a teenager. It was time to give them hell.

'Yes, she found Keith,' Carrie said, her voice firm. 'And she called an ambulance for Cas. She stayed to give her name and address. Like her husband said, she's in shock, and turning up here with a bloody meat wagon like she's Jack the Ripper is disgusting. You ought to be ashamed. Call yourselves detectives? Dicks, maybe, but detectives? Nah, mate.'

Sunny stepped in, trying to calm the rising tension. 'Look, Dottie wants to help. She and Billy came back here in shock. I'm sure she'll give you a full statement when she's ready. She hasn't been arrested, so give it a few hours, and you'll get what you need.'

'The sooner we get the information, the sooner we catch the killer,' Gurney pressed.

'Well, how's that worked out so far for Willow, mate?' Sunny fired back. 'Do you reckon it's the same person who's killed Keith and Willow?'

Gurney frowned as if the idea was absurd. 'No, we don't. And, just so you know, Cas Ferrier and Keith Purdey . . . well, they're known in criminal circles. But, Ms Ellis, you were there, weren't you?'

'Yes, I was there. I called an ambulance for Cas, and we were there when the police arrived.' Dottie shook her head at reliving the moment yet again.

'Well, we want you in for questioning,' Gurney said, impatiently.

Spud's anger was reaching boiling point. He looked at the two uniformed officers, his voice sharp as he stepped forward, his size alone enough to intimidate. 'If you just want my missus for questioning, why the hell is there a bloody meat wagon outside my house?'

Keldon scratched the back of his neck, clearly uncomfortable. 'Look, okay, okay . . . she can come in our car. All right?'

But Spud wasn't having it. 'I asked you a question. Why've you got a meat wagon and extra coppers here, eh?' On the edge of losing it, he flared his nostrils.

Nervously, Gurney pulled his hands out of his pockets and raised them. 'We didn't know what to expect.' He laughed, to counter the awkward silence. 'We just thought—'

'Go on, spit it out,' Carrie cut in, pushing her way forward, her arms crossed and eyes glaring. 'Let's see how you talk your way out of this one.'

'All right, all right.' Keldon sighed. 'Let's start again, shall we. You can bring Dottie – sorry, Ms Ellis – down as soon as possible.'

Spud nodded and turned to Dottie. 'Is that all right with you, love?'

'Yeah, sure. I want whoever did that to Keith caught because, by Christ, that monster shouldn't be walking the streets.'

Gurney smirked, his tone dripping with condescension. 'I agree. Lunatics shouldn't be allowed to roam free, should they, *Ms Ellis*. They should be kept behind bars where they belong.'

That was it. That comment riled Carrie up even more. 'And people like you shouldn't be in charge of finding missing girls, 'cos you clearly ain't got a clue. All the gear, no bloody idea. That sums it up, don't it, you incompetent fuckers.'

Gurney was about to explode, but the wiser and more experienced Keldon quickly intervened. 'Okay, we've got the message loud and clear. But we will find these perpetrators and bring them to justice. Oh, one more thing before we go. Bring Billy Murphy with you as well.'

Sunny stepped in. 'I'll bring my son. And Clive Clemence, our lawyer.'

Carrie glanced at Dottie. She was looking distant and chewing her thumbnail. She suspected that her best friend was almost certainly going over that courtroom scene when she was a teenager and waiting to hear her sentence.

Hurrying to her side, Carrie hugged her tightly. 'It won't be like before. You were a kid then. You've got all of us now, okay? You're not alone.'

'I didn't kill him,' Dottie whispered back.

''Course you didn't! I wasn't even thinking that.'

'No . . . but they were.'

'Fuck those pricks. They ain't got a clue.'

As the detectives reached the road, Jesse, who had been keeping quiet up to this point, suddenly called out, 'What about the copper who stopped Billy? The one in the old-style police car? One of your own, was it?'

Gurney, who was already wound up, spun around, and glared at Jesse. 'Jesse Murphy. Seems to me, we should be asking *you* a few questions. Like how you got those bruises on your face?'

Carrie was ready to leap in front of Jesse, but Sunny held her back. 'Let him handle it, Carrie.'

Jesse straightened up, his eyes hardening in a dark stare. 'I don't see how that's any of your business. But if you must know, I fell down the stairs. Anyway, how about you answer *my* question. Did you follow up on the copper who stopped me bruvver the night Willow was killed? Or was he one of your own?'

Gurney's jaw clenched, the tension rolling off him. He was about to fire a retort back, but again, Keldon stepped in to calm the waters. 'Jesse, it was a terrible crime. We're still investigating. We don't believe the officer was one of our own. Still, we haven't ruled out the possibility it was an impersonator who killed Willow Price.'

'Or one of your own,' Jesse muttered, under his breath.

Gurney, who reckoned he could master lip-reading and was now apoplectic with rage, raised a finger and was ready to snap.

But once again, Keldon intervened. 'We're done here,' he said, looking at Dottie. 'See you shortly, Ms Ellis.'

***

Once the door was closed, Carrie hugged Dottie again. 'We have to go, love. Got to get back to Misty and the kids.'

'Where's Billy?' Jesse asked, hoping for a chance to make amends.

'I'm not sure. He wasn't in his room when I checked. He might've gone for a walk, though. He's pretty shaken up, Jesse.'

Jesse nodded, about to head out, when he noticed Billy's phone on the side table. 'Mottie, this is Billy's. He doesn't normally go anywhere without it. Did he say where he was going?'

Dottie frowned. 'No, he didn't. Maybe he just needed some time alone to think.'

'I'm gonna call Clemence now. Get this over and done with,' Spud said, giving Carrie and Sunny each a brief hug before they left.

'I'll stay here, Mottie, and wait for Billy,' Jesse added.

'Of course. The sooner you two sort this out, the happier we'll all be,' Carrie said, before kissing Jesse and closing the door behind her.

Jesse nodded and then made his way upstairs to the room he shared with Billy. After a quick look in the mirror, he wandered into the kitchen, where Sherry, the Great Dane, lay resting. She was Duchess's mother.

Dottie was staring out of the window, glassy-eyed, her gaze lost in the flickering garden lights that looked as though they were flames dancing in the dark. She didn't notice that Jesse had come into the kitchen and was now sitting on the floor in the corner with the dog. Her mind was elsewhere, miles away. That was until Spud joined her and placed a comforting hand over hers.

'You ready for this, love?' he asked, gently patting her hand.

'Yeah, I guess so.' She sighed heavily. 'I just can't stop thinking about what we saw. And poor Billy. That image must be burned into his mind. He might even need therapy, you know.'

'He's young. He'll be all right. Billy's a tough egg.'

'Maybe, but he's confused right now. He's starting to doubt what he saw that night when he thought he saw Willow. He's wondering if he made a mistake. He's linking everything back to Danny Slade. But that's impossible, surely, isn't it? All the news about those missing girls . . . it makes me think Willow was a victim of the same nutcase. Who's probably that copper impersonator. But surely not Danny?'

Spud glanced up at the clock. It was nearing midday. 'Where is Billy?'

Dottie looked at the clock as well, her frown deepening. 'God, I hadn't realised the time.'

'I'll go and look for him. I know where he likes to go,' said Jesse, as he got up from the floor.

Spud nodded. 'Take your bike and your phone. And tell him he needs to come home right away – whether he wants to or not. We've got to get Mottie to the station. You heard that twat barking orders.'

Jesse nodded. Heading for the back door to fetch one of his bikes, he was stopped by Spud. 'Be careful, mate. We still don't know who attacked you and little Charlie.'

'I'll take a tool this time,' Jesse replied, with one of his knowing grins.

Spud didn't argue. 'Just come home in one piece – and with your brother.'

CHAPTER THIRTY

It might have once been a home, wherever he was, but now it was just a shell of its former self. Although most of the windows were intact, with some boarded up, the place was a shambles. Mould crept up the walls, and the floorboards were worn thin, barely covering some of the exposed joists.

Billy's head felt as though it had been clamped in a vice. It was pounding with every heartbeat. Opening his eyes, he was at least grateful that the sack had been removed from his head. Before he could even focus, the stench hit him – old, stale, like rot and damp. Strips of stained wallpaper, which hung from the ceiling, were peeling away in long dirty curls. When a cold draught blew around him, he knew, instantly, he had been brought to a house of horrors. He was in hell. And then it all came flooding back. Keith's mangled corpse, the men in masks, and the clump to the head that had knocked him out cold. He tried to move, but he quickly realised his hands were still bound tightly behind his back, to the point that his shoulders were stiff and aching.

Slowly, feeling every painful throb, he rolled to his side to take in his surroundings. There was a partition wall, half demolished, leading into what used to be a kitchen. The walls were brown, the floor uneven, and there, perched on an old orange 1970s melamine unit, was a camping stove. Blood dripped from two large fish, their gaping mouths frozen in grotesque stillness next to a grimy sink; it was just like the one his grandad had in the garden for growing herbs.

He tried to get up, but he soon realised that his legs were bound as well and tied to one of the exposed floor joists.

Then he heard the heavy thud of boots stomping across the room.

A man came into view. He was cooking something, the sharp smell of onions filling the air. Still, there was something else, something far worse – a sickly stench of decay, rotting meat . . . or was it rotting human flesh?

The man wasn't wearing a balaclava this time, and as he started to turn, Billy snapped his eyes shut, playing dead. His heart raced as he listened, praying the man wouldn't notice he was awake.

Then, a voice, sharp and unexpected, made him jump.

'Who've you got in there? Another girl?'

'Shut ya mouth, you nosy cunt, or I'll strip the meat off ya and have you for dinner, you fat fuck!'

'All right, all right, keep ya hair on. But then, again, you ain't got any, 'ave ya.'

'Was that a joke?'

Billy risked opening his eyes just enough to see the man standing sideways and pointing a knife at the woman hidden by the partition. His stomach churned when he realised who the man was. It was him. The copper. The one he'd kicked between the legs and escaped from. The one who he now believed had killed Willow. His body shivered in a complete state of panic. Why had this psycho kidnapped him? And why had he brought him here? He shut his eyes again, his brain spinning and trying to piece it all together. Was it about Willow? The missing girls? Was he a witness, and now the man was tying up loose ends? That had to be it.

But how did all of this connect to Keith's murder? He couldn't make sense of it. Either way, he knew he was going to die. The way the man was toying with the knife, twisting it in his hand, made it very clear. This wasn't going to be a quick and painless death.

'Nah, nah, mush, I wasn't trying to be funny. Sorry.'

Billy heard the other voice again. He could tell it was a woman's. It was older, with a London gypsy twang. His blood ran cold. *Could she be someone he knew?*

'Listen, love, I'm not one for grassing. You know me better than that. I like to keep meself to meself. Never done you no harm, so what d'ya say? Untie me, and I'll turn them two fish into a nice fish pie.'

'Shut your great big gob. See, that's why I ain't married. You women are only good for one thing. You should all be born *without* a fucking voice.'

Ignoring the insult, she carried on. 'Never fancied getting wed, then, love?'

Billy knew then that she wasn't his wife.

He kept his eyes shut until he felt those heavy boots thud across the floor towards him. A sudden kick to the ribs made him yelp. He couldn't fake it anymore.

When their eyes locked, the kidnapper laughed. 'You're fucked up now, ain't ya, boy? Seen me face. No matter, 'cos when we've been paid, you're dead anyway.'

'Who've you got back there?' came the woman's voice.

'Mind ya own business, ya fat bitch.'

'All right, all right, I don't need to know. I'll be outta your hair. Mum's the word, I swear. Then, you'll only have to worry about the chavi, not me.'

'Don't talk about me hair again, all right, woman? I'm sick of those fucking jokes.'

Billy watched the man stomping back to the kitchen, swaying as he did so, before standing in front of the stove ready to fry the gruesome fish in the pan.

'What d'ya say, love?' the woman persisted.

He grabbed a bottle of whisky beside the cooker and took a swig. 'What do I say? I *say*, shut ya mouth, or I'll shove this bottle down ya throat.'

'So tell me, love. Why are you keeping me alive, eh? Was it your bruvver's orders? 'Cos if he's worried I'll grass – which I wouldn't – but if that's what's on his mind – why keep me here, sitting on this stinking chair, rotting and wasting away?'

Billy's fear was slowly being replaced by intrigue. He listened closely, trying to get a handle on the man's twisted mind. And on that female voice. He still wondered if he recognised it.

'I said, shut it.'

Billy caught the change in tone. It wasn't as aggressive now, so whoever this woman was, she seemed to have some kind of hold over him. The clues were in the way he was handling her.

'You're like me muvver. Now, if you wanna stay alive, stop banging on 'cos, you're giving me a fucking headache.'

But the woman was relentless. 'Did you fuck your muvver too, then?'

Billy braced himself, expecting her to get torn apart, but, to his shock, the man turned to her, calm and collected. 'You ain't me muvver, so I can fuck you and fuck you up, if I want to. But not yet. I'm cooking me fish.'

Sensing a shift in the man's manner, Billy spoke up. 'Er . . . have they paid the ransom yet?'

The man spun around, eyes wild. 'Not your concern.' Ripping a piece of fish from the pan and shoving so much of it into his mouth, the grease dripped down his chin.

Billy swallowed the bile rising in his throat. 'Who did you ask for money? 'Cos I can tell you if they'll pay up or not. I'm not worth much to many people, I'll tell you that.'

The man let out a sharp, bitter laugh. 'Won't pay up, will they not? They'll fucking pay, all right. This time, the cunt knows better. 'Cos I left him a real warning, and he'll know you'll get the same, if he don't pay what's owed. And if he tries that fake-money shit again, he'll regret it.'

'Fake money?'

Suddenly, the man threw the knife down and stormed towards Billy, spitting fish flakes as he ranted, 'Yeah, fucking *fake* money! New, crisp, straight-off-the-fucking-press money! The cunt stung me with fake notes from his safe!'

Billy's mind raced. The dots were joining up big time. Was he talking about Cas? But how was this psycho connected to him? Not all of the pieces of the puzzle were fitting into place just yet. But he reckoned in time they would. He stared at the man's grim expression and asked the one question gnawing at his mind. 'Was Keith dead before you gouged his eyes out?'

The man's demeanour changed instantly into a full-blown beaming smile. It was as if he had just won the lottery, and he was now parading the giant cardboard cheque in front of the television cameras. Except he wasn't holding a cheque. He was smiling over the most horrific detail of the worst kind of murder. 'Hard to tell. He stopped screaming after I gutted him. I'm good at that, ya know. Wanna taste some of me fish? Fucking lovely, fried with onions. You can't beat it.'

Billy couldn't believe what he was hearing. This man was totally off his trolley. How the hell was he walking the streets?

'Did you kill Willow?' Billy asked, his voice shaking.

The man nodded, still grinning. 'Yep.'

Billy's heart pounded so hard, it felt as though it might burst out of his chest. It didn't matter what he said now. He would be dead soon, anyway. But, he had to know one thing. 'Did she die quickly?'

That sick grin spread across the man's face again. 'Yeah-ish. Quicker than I wanted. Didn't get time to properly torture the pretty little thing. But she cried for you, though.'

Billy felt as though someone had reached into his chest and crushed his heart. 'Nah, she didn't cry for me. I'd be the last person.'

But the man's reaction threw him completely. There was something almost brutally honest in the way he spoke.

'No, she definitely cried out your name . . . unless Billy ain't your real name.'

'Oi, what?' A voice called from the kitchen, higher-pitched now, almost fretting. 'Billy? *Billy?* Did you say Billy? Billy who?'

The monster stepped back into the kitchen, now glaring at the woman. 'Shut up. You hate him, anyway. You've been banging on about how much you hate that family. They took everything from you. I thought you'd be pleased. But I detect a bit of worry in your voice.'

'Just tell me . . . Is that Billy Murphy you've got back there?'

'Yeah. You'll be pleased to know it is. Now, let me finish cooking our supper for me and you, love. Fish and onions and a nice bottle of whisky. Like a proper couple, we can listen to music. I've got a pucker radio.'

The silence was tense as the man continued cooking. Then he stopped and turned to her. 'You do hate the kid, don't ya?'

'Yeah, yeah, sure I do,' she replied, but it was apparent that there was a slight hesitation in her voice. 'I bloody hate the whole family – they're a bunch of cunts.'

That was when it hit Billy. He knew her. The other person behind that partition wall was no other than Ginty Carson. Unbelievable.

His mind whirled with confusion, and the smell of fish and onions – and something far worse – made him feel sick. He swallowed hard, trying to hold any vomit down. He then noticed that Ginty had gone very quiet. She had stopped pestering the man.

Something tickled the side of his nose. It was a tear, and that was when he realised he had been crying. The thought that Willow had cried out for him – after acting as though she didn't care – cut him deeply. To know he had been the last name on her lips . . . it felt like more than a punch to the stomach. And then there was Ginty, his natural grandmother, someone who once claimed she wanted to be a part of his and Jesse's lives. It seemed that now she couldn't care less if he was alive or dead. It was another stab to his already broken heart.

Behind the partitioned wall, the monster grabbed the bottle of whisky and the pan with the cooked fish.

''Ere, Ginty, taste this. It's good! I swear I'd give that Raymond Blanc a run for his money. I can cook like a top chef. Now, open ya mouth and taste it, you rude bitch.'

'All right, don't ram it down me throat.'

'See? Nice, ain't it?'

'Yeah, love, it's delicious. Now, how about you untie me wrists, so I can use a fork instead of you nearly taking me tongue out with that knife?'

'How about I fucking *feed* you?'

'Listen, love, I do enjoy your cooking, but, honestly, the smell in here's getting a bit much. Can't you just get rid of it?'

Initially, Billy had no idea what she meant. Until it hit him. The stench. It had to be either a dead body or a rotting animal, but whatever it was, it was something terrible. His stomach turned as he noticed a few sluggish flies buzzing about. He knew what they were. They were the death flies, the ones that swarm decomposing bodies. He shut his eyes, wishing he could wake up from this nightmare. It was so horrendous that even the worst horror films couldn't compare.

His thoughts were cut off by the sound of a car approaching the property. This was his chance. He waited, listening, as the monster stomped across the room and opened the front door. As soon as he heard it creak open, he screamed – again and again – hoping that whoever was in the vehicle would hear him and take down this evil bastard. But then . . . nothing. He stopped, holding his breath, now straining his ears.

That was when he heard them. Two voices. The second voice was harsh. It was like someone who was a heavy smoker. The two of them were talking further away, in another room.

***

'Listen, Irvin, I'm telling you – be patient. The bloke's got concussion. He's hooked up to all sorts. He ain't in a position to get us any money. The problem is, you great fucking oaf, you whacked him too hard. The nurse reckons he's in and out of consciousness, so we'll have to wait. No point going back now, now that the police are still there. You proper messed up Keith as well. I told you not to go OTT, but, oh no, not you. Ya see, it's one thing to carry out an armed robbery, but it's a whole other thing to go and act like a fucking mortician. Anyone would have thought he'd had a postmortem carried out. And in Cas's stables, no less. I'm starting to wonder if I should've ever got you outta that nuthouse.'

'So what now, then? I've gotta keep the little bastard' – he pointed to a room – 'alive, 'ave I?' growled Irvin.

'Yeah, ya 'ave. 'Cos, if that cunt wants proof, then we'll have to send him something that shows we've got the kid.

He ain't gonna pay up if the boy is dead, is he? And if it's you who's been knocking off those teenage girls, pack it in. Christ, this all started 'cos that prick didn't pay us what we're owed, and now, I've got that mobster breathing down me neck. Oh, and yeah, stop teasing me boy, and, for your information, he *is* like you. He found the whole fucking Keith thing funny hysterical, in fact. Ya both need to be in an institution.'

***

Billy braced himself, knowing that he would probably get another kick for screaming out like that when the monster returned. But what choice did he have at the time? He'd had to try.

'Billy boy, you all right, love?' Ginty's voice called out.

'Fuck off, Ginty. 'Course I'm not all right. Should've known you'd be mixed up with a monster like him.'

'Listen, babe, what I said, I didn't mean it. I don't hate you. Not at all.'

'You, Ginty Carson, are the type of woman who'll go wherever you get served a better deal.'

'You talk nicely, Billy boy. Proper intelligent-like. That makes me so proud.'

'Yeah? Compared to your sons? What, Jimmy the bully? A fucking pet cockroach would make you proud. And don't even try to call him my dad, 'cos he ain't. He's a scumbag, and he ended up behind bars where he belongs. I hate him even more, every time I see my mum's legs all scarred up.'

'I know, Billy boy. I know,' she replied, her voice sheepish, almost defeated.

Billy tutted. 'See? If Jimmy was here, you wouldn't be agreeing with me, would you, now? You'd be telling him how I'm a scumbag, how my mum and Dottie – my other mum – are wasters, slags, or whatever filthy names you'd come out with.'

'You're wrong, Billy boy. I might be old and long in the tooth, but I've learned a lot along the way. I watched you and ya bruvver, ya know. I saw you come outta school and saw you two race on sports day. You won, and Jesse came second, miles ahead of the others.'

Billy knew she wasn't making it up.

'I love your mum Carrie. Believe it or not, I really do.'

'Leave off. I know what you did to her. How you were cruel. You tried to stop her from getting a new place. You let those sons of yours beat her up. She even had to turn away from her own family because of the threats your sons made. But she was smarter than you. Oh, and before you think she told me all this, it wasn't her. It was someone else.'

'You're right, Billy boy, I did. I didn't want her moving out. I wanted her with me, like the daughter I never had. Don't get me wrong, I suited boys, not being so feminine meself, but I wished I'd had your mum as my daughter.' She chuckled, almost wistfully. 'She was feisty, not afraid of anyone. She was too young to want kids, but she was a good mum. She turned out to be a right proper travelling girl. Kept a clean home and raised you two right. I wanted her to want me like a second mum.'

'Jesus, have you even *met* my Nan Luanne? You could never be anything *like* her. She raised *good* people. Your sons are *scum*, Ginty. What that bastard did to my Aunt Dilly, even after they killed the man she was supposed to marry, was downright cruel. He would have been my uncle. I never met him, but, by all accounts, he was a good man. Dilly didn't deserve that, but she's with James now. And they're all fine, now they're well away from your lot.'

‘I know, Billy, I know. I ain’t blind, love. I can see how well they’re doing. Pretty girls, your aunties, though not as stunning as your muvver. And, yeah, I only say I hate her ’cos she hates me, that’s all. And before you say it, yeah, I don’t blame her, Billy. Now listen, I don’t know how to help you escape, but that Irvin? He’s fucking mental. Proper mental.’

‘I don’t need your help, Ginty. I wouldn’t trust you as far as I could throw you.’

‘I know, Billy boy. I know.’

CHAPTER THIRTY-ONE

As Jesse spent all day riding around the streets in the hope of catching sight of Billy, he kept going over in his mind what he would say when he finally got his brother alone. As much as he knew Billy was hurting over Willow's death, he couldn't feel the same. He couldn't grieve. Not yet. In fact, he wasn't sure when he would ever be able to mourn her loss. Because right now, he hated her. She was the one who had caused this rift between Billy and himself. She had pushed them apart. And she'd been the one who had seriously wound him up by calling him a chicken for not snorting cocaine.

But he was honest with himself to concede that it wasn't all her fault. He just hadn't been forceful enough to tell her to fuck off. If he had, he would have been standing next to Billy with his arm around him.

This rift, it was eating him up inside.

That moment months ago would probably live with him for ever. Every time he thought about it, he cringed with embarrassment. She'd had that smirk on her face when she'd taunted him and called him 'half a man'. Out of pure anger, he'd given in and snorted some cocaine. And the event was so mind-altering. It was a rush that he'd never gotten from necking vodka.

Prior to that, Billy had warned him about taking drugs. He said they were for muppets. He'd even dragged him to an estate once to show him a bunch of teenagers sniffing glue, just to hammer the point home. Well, it was a point well made. He'd never forgotten it, seeing those kids sprawled out and unable to string a sentence together. It had put him off drugs for life. Or so he'd thought at the time.

But that day, when Willow shoved the cocaine under his nose and he went for it, everything changed. Suddenly her teasing turned into something more. She was kissing him, her hands down his trousers. He hadn't been with a girl before. Sure, he'd dated and had a snog or two, but he'd never gone further than that. His mum had drilled it into him that no matter how careful you are, accidents happen, and before you know it, the girl has a baby in her belly. He knew she was right. And what was the point of letting that happen? They had their whole lives ahead of them. But that night, all that advice went out of the window. And Willow had got him so aroused, she wasn't taking no for an answer.

He was weak and gave in. Before he knew it, she was taking control, as if she'd done this a hundred times before. She knew exactly what she was doing when she pulled his jeans down and straddled him. Suddenly, she looked beautiful, irresistible. And it didn't take long before it was over. She climbed off, almost smug, as though she wasn't really into him. She was just seeing what she could get away with.

When the cocaine wore off, the guilt hit him like a truck travelling at one hundred miles per hour. He had begged her not to say anything to Billy.

But as soon as he'd pleaded with her, he knew she'd won. The smug grin said it all, really. So he ended up hating her. But he hated himself more.

For months, he worried that she would tell Billy. But just when he thought his secret was safe, she ended up dead. And his baby – their baby – was inside her.

***

Twelve hours had passed, and no one had seen or heard from Billy. Desperate to find his brother, Jesse headed towards the parade of shops where some local teenagers usually hung out. It was dark and after eleven o'clock, so he figured most of them would probably have gone by now, especially with the off-licence closed. But as he approached the dimly lit row, he spotted three teenagers huddled together and smoking. He hoped Billy was among the group, but as he got closer, he realised that one of them was Joey Carson.

Jesse's gut reaction was to turn around. This wasn't the time to get into another fight.

'Oi, Jesse! You all right? How's ya bruvver?' Joey called out.

Jesse's hackles rose immediately. 'What the fuck did you say?' He assumed Joey was being sarcastic.

Joey pushed himself off the railings, his hands up in defence. 'Nah, nah, mate. Listen, I was serious. I didn't hurt Charlie. Cor, it'd be the last thing I'd do. I've seen what ya farver's capable of, and besides, that ain't a bit of me. But I'll tell ya this for nuffin, right? Whether ya like it or not, we're cousins. But me and Stuey, we ain't nothing like ya birth farver. We ain't like Ginty's boys at all.'

Jesse eyed him, still wary, but his shoulders dropped a little. 'We're always fighting, though.'

Joey chuckled. 'It's what we do! Fuck me, Jesse, we've been scrapping since we were ten or eleven. I remember you with that bloody catapult. Ya nearly blinded us, ya did. Anyway, we never hurt you or ya little bruvver, and I'll fight whoever did, side by side with ya, like family.'

Jesse knew Joey was sucking up to him, but he nodded politely. 'Have ya seen Billy?'

Joey shook his head. 'Nah, I haven't seen him, and I've been here a few hours.' He stubbed out his cigarette. 'I'll help you look for him, though.'

'It's all right. I'll ride around. If you see him, tell him to come home. We need to talk.'

'No worries. And that offer still stands – to firm up, if you find out who did that to ya face and who hurt little Charlie.'

As Jesse rode away, something Dottie had said suddenly popped into his head. He hit the brakes, turned around, and cycled back. 'Joey, where does Danny Slade live?'

Frowning deeply, Joey approached Jesse. 'Danny Slade? I hope when you see that fucking gay boy, you give him a right good hidin'. Tell me when you plan to do it. I wanna put the boot in meself, after he told you it was us who hurt ya little bruvver.'

Jesse nodded, his mind ticking over. 'I wanna know who told *him*.'

Joey spat on the ground. 'Well, the prick might look like he can handle himself. But the fact is, he's a fucking fruit loop. Seriously, mush, he ain't all there. But I reckon you could take him. And I'd pay good money to watch that.'

Chewing the inside of his lip, now in deep thought, Jesse said, 'What d'ya mean, he ain't all there?'

'Where've you been, mate? Hiding under a rock?'

'Joey, I don't mix with the Slades. I don't even *know* this geezer. I've only seen him around, although I've had a scrap with his bruvvers. The ugly wankers they are an' all.'

Joey snorted. 'Yeah, well, they moved out over the other side of London for years, but when their ol' girl Donna got outta prison, they came back. Even Ginty lived with 'em for a while, though no one's seen her lately.'

'Yeah, yeah, but tell me about this Danny geezer. You said he ain't all there. What makes you say that?'

Joey's eyes narrowed. Then Jesse's words hit him. 'Oh, fuck . . . you're wondering about that dead girl, Willow, are ya? That business?'

‘No, I wasn’t. But his name keeps coming up, and I’d like a word with him meself. But if he’s not all there, I wanna be on me guard, know what I mean?’

Joey rubbed his chin, his face darkening. ‘Look, Danny’s always been a bit off, even when we were kids. Before the ol’ man took ’em to London, he’d have these mad outbursts, like proper losing it over nothing. But it’s worse now, since he came back. People say he’s . . . how do I put it? He’s got that look in his eye, like he ain’t all there, like something’s rattling around in his head, and not in a good way. You know what I mean?’

‘The lights are on, but no one’s home,’ Jesse muttered.

Joey nodded, his face tightening. ‘He can fool the best with his charm an’ all, but it don’t work on me.’ He glanced down, looking ashamed.

Jesse clocked it. ‘Tell me, Joey, what did he do to you?’

‘Nuffin’!’ Joey snapped back, quickly, but his body language spoke otherwise.

‘Joey, listen, whatever it was, I’ll keep schtum, all right? I swear on me muvver’s life, I won’t breathe a word. Now, what did the cunt do?’

Joey checked over his shoulder to make sure the other lads weren’t within earshot, before he leaned in, his voice low. ‘If you say a word, Jesse, I’ll – well, I’ll be upset. I’m trusting you, bruv, with my reputation.’

‘Go on, Joey,’ Jesse urged, his curiosity piqued.

‘Danny bought us all drinks, yeah? We didn’t say no, o’ course. We were drinking bottles of vodka pop, weak stuff, really, in the car park at Bluewater.’ Joey’s eyes darted around again. ‘Next thing I know, I woke up in the back of Danny’s car.’

Jesse frowned. ‘So, you got pissed?’

'Nah, not on bloody alcopops! I only had two, which wouldn't even get me dog pissed. Nah, I was out cold. The bastard drugged me.'

'What? Fuck, no way!'

'Shut up, Jesse! Only you know, and o' course, that bastard does too.'

Jesse leaned in closer. 'Did he . . . Did he fuck ya?'

Joey's head dropped, the shame written all over his face. 'Truth is, Jesse, I don't know what he did.'

The look on Joey's face was heart-wrenching, and in that moment, he forgot himself. He went over to Joey and threw an arm around his shoulders. 'What a sly bastard. Didn't you tell anyone? Not even the police?'

Joey shook his head, his voice low. 'Nah. You know what me family's like. They'd slaughter me.' He let out a short bitter laugh. 'Can't believe I'm even telling *you*. Bloody hell, why did I do that?'

''Cos, Joey, deep down, you know me and Billy – we've got rules and morals.'

'More rules? What d'ya mean?'

'No, divvy, I mean principles. You trusted me with something no one else knows, and I'll honour that trust.'

Joey stared at him for a moment, and then he nodded. 'Fanks, bruv.'

'Where does he live?'

'Blimey, you really have been living under a rock! He lives on the other side of the main road, not far from me, but up by the bridge. But I heard his ol' man, Vic, has part-ownership in some pub, a real dive, a run-down shithole in Swanley. Sometimes they stay there, above the joint. But I'm sure I saw Danny drive past me an hour or so ago.' Joey's excitement grew. 'So, you gonna pay the prick a visit? Want me to come an' all?'

'No, Joey, I'll handle that later. First, I need to find Billy.'

'Oh, all right. Well, if ya need me, bruv, you know where to find me.'

Jesse winked. 'Cheers, mate.' Then he shot off towards the main road. Fishing out his phone, he tried Dottie first, but there was no answer. She was probably still at the police station. He called Billy's phone, hoping he would be home already, but, again, there was no answer.

Just as he was about to shove his phone back in his pocket, it rang. It was his mother. His heart sank. He had hoped it was Billy.

'Jesse, are you with Billy?'

'No, Mum, I'm still riding around looking for him.'

'Shit. The police came by the house again. They said Dottie's still at the station, but they wanna speak to Billy. For fuck's sake, why couldn't he just stay put? This is doing me nerves in. Now I'm bleedin' worrying about Billy boy.' Carrie sighed, heavily. 'All right, love. Best you come home. I can't be worrying about both of me big boys now, can I?'

'It's all right, Mum. I'm on me bike, just riding around the estate. I won't be long.'

When he ended the call, he slid his phone into his back pocket and felt for the hammer tucked down the back of his jeans. Then, he ran his hand down his shin to check that the knife was still lodged in his trainer.

***

Jesse could ride his bike almost as fast as a slow car. He was fit, being used to cycling everywhere, and he knew where the bridge was. His mum had never liked him or Billy venturing to that side of the main road – the side she grew up on. But they had been there yesterday, and he could tell the place held bad memories for her. Still, he wanted to check out where this Danny lived.

It took him all of five minutes. Parked outside a three-bedroom semi was Danny's car. He assumed the house belonged to the Slades.

Jesse carefully checked his surroundings because this wasn't his manor, and he didn't know anyone here, least of all the Slades. Seeing the lights were on in the living room, he lowered his bike to the ground and crept behind the front hedge, crouching down now to peer through the window. A few men were inside, but he couldn't be sure who they were. However, standing there, hands on his hips, was Danny. It was definitely their house.

Not wanting to knock on the door and draw attention, Jesse snuck behind Danny's car and peered in. He hoped it was alarmed so that he could set it off and cause a distraction. But the chances were slim that this old banger even had an alarm.

As he tugged on the door handle, it opened easily. No alarm. 'Damn it,' he muttered. But just as he was about to close the door, something caught his eye and made him freeze. There, in the centre console was a gold necklace. He snatched it up, his heart pounding, as he stared at it. His blood ran cold. This was the necklace Billy had bought for Willow. It wasn't something you could buy off the shelf. Billy had had it made specially for her. But he hadn't given it to her.

More than that, Billy had kept it on him all the time. Even after their fight, when he'd thrown it down onto the table in a fit of anger, he'd still grabbed it before he left the house. Obviously, the necklace meant a lot to him. But why the hell did Danny have it in his car?

Jesse stood up and stared into the house through the window, not caring anymore if they saw him. He needed answers. Why did Danny have that necklace? When a dark thought crept into his mind, he suddenly had a terrible sinking feeling in the pit of his stomach. Could Danny be the reason Billy hadn't come home?

With his hand hovering over his back pocket, he contemplated whether to call his dad and Uncle James. They would tear through that house like a bloody tornado. Just as he pulled out his phone, the front door creaked open. To his surprise, Danny stepped out, carrying a box.

A voice from inside shouted, 'And tell him he can get more when the fucking shop opens!'

Jesse ducked down, out of view, listened, and waited.

Danny approached the car, opened the boot, and dropped the box inside.

Just as he was about to start the car, Jesse acted without thinking. He ripped the knife from his trainer and flung the passenger door open.

Danny gasped. 'What the fuck?'

'Hello, Danny,' Jesse said, calmly, holding the knife up. 'I've got this, see? And you're gonna drive. Go on.' He glared into Danny's eyes, seeing the fear flickering there.

'W-What's going on?' Danny stammered, his voice shaking.

'Drive, cunt. Just fucking drive or I'll ram this blade right through your neck.'

Danny glanced back at the house, then at Jesse.

'Don't even think about it, Danny. 'Cos by the time your arse is outta this car, I'll have cut your spine in half. You'll be paralysed from the waist down. Now, drive.'

Danny didn't hesitate. He started the car and pulled away. 'What do you want, Jesse?' he asked, the fear dripping from his voice.

'What are you doing with me bruvver's necklace?' Jesse growled, holding it up for Danny to see.

Danny's hand twitched, about to pull over, but Jesse bellowed, 'Drive, you prick! I never told you to stop. Now, where'd you get this?'

For a moment, something shifted in Danny's face – a grin, twisted and sudden. It was as though the fear had left him and had been replaced by something darker. Without warning, he swung the car, jerking it from side to side, slamming Jesse into the door and back against him. But all it did was rile up Jesse even more.

In a flash, Jesse grabbed Danny's head and pressed the knife to his throat, the blade biting into his skin.

'Arrgghh!' Danny screamed, clutching his neck, the fear flooding back into his wide eyes.

'Where's Billy?' Jesse snarled.

'I don't know!' Danny croaked.

'Yeah, ya do! Why the fuck would you have this, then, eh?' Jesse rammed the necklace under Danny's nose, knocking his head back against the seat.

'Blimey, mate, listen, I found it! At the cemetery. Billy must've dropped it. Look, you can have it back!'

'Where's me bruvver, Danny?' Jesse demanded, his grip tightening on the knife.

'I swear, I don't know!' Danny's voice cracked.

But Jesse's rage was building, hot and fast. He wasn't like Billy. His brother would have had a plan and kept his cool. But he wasn't Billy. He was alone, and with no one there to guide him, he had to make his own decisions. In a flash of fury, he drove the knife into Danny's thigh, not deep enough to stop him from driving but enough to make him feel pain and sufficient to make him take notice.

Danny let out a guttural scream, while his hands trembled and gripped the wheel. 'Argh! Fuck! What the hell, Jesse?'

Jesse leaned in close, his voice low and cold as he whispered in Danny's ear, 'Now you know I ain't messing around. Where's Billy?'

***

Danny had heard how tough the Murphy boys were, but it had always been Billy who carried the more ruthless reputation. But now, sitting in the driver's seat, bleeding from a stab wound, he realised it was Jesse who might be the one not to mess with. The pain hit him in waves – deep throbbing aches that made him feel dizzy. He could also feel his jeans getting wet, the blood seeping out and soaking through the fabric. His mind was spinning; he couldn't think straight. What the hell was he supposed to do?

He didn't have a weapon, he was stuck in a beaten-up old banger, and he'd left his family behind in the house. The only person who could help him was Uncle Irvin – and that psycho would probably be excited by it too. Feeling light-headed and sick, he knew if he passed out or pulled over, Jesse wouldn't hesitate to hurt him again. He didn't handle pain well and especially not his own. Sure, he loved seeing other people in agony and loved having control, but only if they couldn't fight back. He wasn't willing to risk getting beaten up himself.

Now running out of options, and fast, there was only one thing left to do – deliver Jesse to Irvin. With any luck, the mad bastard would gut Jesse like a fish. Irvin was good at that. Maybe he would take out those pretty eyes of his while he was at it.

CHAPTER THIRTY-TWO

Cas stared at Dennis Cooper, otherwise known as Dennis the Menace, and not without reason. Dennis was a wind-up merchant, who had a penchant for constantly toying with his victims, like a cat with a mouse. He had that charm that could fool anyone, and even as an older bloke, he was still seen as quite a looker – the grey fox version of Cary Grant. Cas's eyes flicked to Walter Whistler, whose name suited him because of the way he whistled certain words. Walter wasn't as handsome, but for a stout man, he always looked sharp. Even before a scrap, he would turn up in a stiff white shirt and tailored trousers.

'Yeah, sorry, mate. We only got back from the airport a couple of hours ago,' Dennis said, his voice low. 'Lolly called us right away. The Ol' Bill's taking statements from everyone who was at your granddaughter's funeral.' He shook his head and sighed. 'Keith . . . he was a good bloke. No man deserves that.'

Cas nodded. He was still in shock. The detective from Tonbridge, who was now collaborating with the Kent Police, had filled him in on what had happened. Not many things rattled him to the core, but hearing that his best mate had been murdered in such a humiliating way . . . it stirred something haunting inside. His inner monster was clawing to get out. As he looked at Dennis and Walter, who were more than on the payroll – they were actually trusted friends – he could already picture what he would do to the bastard responsible for this atrocity.

'Any idea why?' Cas asked, his voice cold, barely holding back the rage.

'Nah, mate. We've made a few calls, but everyone's as shocked as us. And, let's face it, if it was some wannabe gangster from your past, they'd let you know it was them. What would be the point, otherwise?'

Cas nodded, his mind racing, still imagining the brutal vengeance he would unleash. 'What else?'

Dennis shifted. 'We called our man, Robson at the station.'

'Go on,' Cas said, still reeling.

'They're questioning Dottie and they want Billy in for questioning too.'

Cas sat bolt upright. 'What the fuck for?'

''Cos they were in your house when the police arrived.'

Cas frowned. 'Yeah, and if Dottie hadn't brought Billy back to mine, I'd be dead. They called the fucking ambulance for me. They came to the hospital after the police arrived to check I was okay. But I wasn't with it, was I. I lost a lot of blood. The bastard tried to cave me head in. Mind you, that doctor, whoever he was, reckons I've got a hard head. I'm lucky. It was blood loss more than brain damage. I just needed a bit of topping up.'

'Do you reckon Dottie could be involved? And does Billy hold a grudge from all that business years ago?'

Cas shook his head, his jaw tightening. 'No way. That kid has been staying with me, and there's no way he would have done that if he held a grudge. Admittedly, he's got that look in his eyes. And if I was a teenager, which, clearly, I'm not, I wouldn't mess with him. I do believe that young Billy will be a right handful, and a fucking rich one too. Me and him, we get on like a house on fire. And Dottie . . . I know what she did to her parents, and she may have gone a bit OTT with her mum and dad, but there's a backstory. It sounds to me like they deserved it. And she has no reason to hurt me. I don't believe she would.'

Dennis grinned. 'She's got ol' Clemmy with her. Probably giving the coppers a hard time, I bet. She'll be out in a few hours, no doubt.'

'So, where's Billy?'

Dennis shrugged. 'Dunno, but you know what kids are like.'

Cas frowned deeper. 'So Billy's missing, then, is he?'

Dennis shrugged again. 'All I know is the police have been to his house and Dottie's place looking for him. No one's seen him. Do you reckon it's him?'

Cas yanked the cannula out of his arm, anger flashing in his eyes. 'No, I fucking don't. But we don't have a clue who did this to me. And those useless wankers that call themselves detectives out there are asking if *I*.' He poked himself in the chest. 'If *I* know who would want to hurt Keith, me fucking best mate!' He stopped, his voice breaking slightly, as he blinked back tears. 'I loved that bloke like a brother. You know what I mean?'

They both nodded. Cas was their boss, but they knew he had a bond with Keith that also went well beyond the payroll.

'Get me strides, will ya?'

'Hang on a minute, you're not fit to leave,' Dennis said, shaking his head. But he knew that if Cas was on a mission, it would take the whole of the British Army to stop him.

'I'm alive, ain't I? Now, fetch me clothes. I ain't gonna lie here when whoever did this could be out there hurting Billy. 'Cos, right now, I have no idea who would do this, or even how many people are involved. Fuck me, I thought I was being robbed. The bastards wanted what was in me safe, and you know me, I ain't that stupid. I gave them a few grand, that's all. I never thought they wanted to kill me.'

'You did *what*?' said Dennis, raising a questioning brow. 'You gave them a few grand?'

Cas nodded, deep in thought. 'All right, all right. So those notes were fake. But what I don't get is this. We're all at the funeral, yeah? I get back to me gaff, and right away, I go into me study – 'cos the door was open – and, straightaway, I knew I'd been robbed. Drawers ripped out, cabinets a mess, that beautiful desk fucked. But I had this feeling that they weren't just after cash. They were looking for something else.'

'After everyone had their sandwiches and had buggered off – 'cos, let's face it, I didn't make them feel too welcome – that's when I found meself totally unprepared facing two blokes, both wearing balaclavas, one of 'em a big bastard. The first thing they wanted was what was in the safe. I thought, bollocks, let 'em have it. They cleaned it out, but they were asking for paperwork. They kept saying, "Where's the briefcase?"'

He tapped his head. 'And what crossed my mind was that job we did years ago, remember? That time we nicked that pervy politician's briefcase after that tip-off about the diamonds.'

Walter grinned, a flicker of nostalgia in his eyes. 'Yeah, I remember. We got all those tapes – the dirty fucker – and he shit himself. I can still see the terror on his face. The paedo handed over whatever we asked for, including that briefcase *and* those diamonds. We kept our promise that we wouldn't hand over the tapes.' He chuckled. 'But we never promised to hold back the photos. He served a right tidy lump of bird. But, come to think of it, if he ain't dead, he could be due out now.' He threw his hands in the air. 'I dunno.'

Cas nodded. 'Yeah, right, so I thought they might be on about that. Anyway, when I said I didn't have a briefcase and that they had the money, the big one hit me from behind. What with – God knows. I just remember hitting the deck. And that was it until Dottie was trying to bring me round.'

'What about your black briefcase? Ya know, the one you keep your important papers in. The one Billy had got a hold of that time.'

Cas tilted his head to the side. 'What? The one with me will and the DNA results, and shit like that?'

'Well, you kept that in a briefcase, didn't ya?'

Cas nodded. 'Yeah, but surely they didn't mean that. There's nuffin in that. Well, nuffin they could benefit from. I mean, the paper ain't diamond encrusted. It's just personal stuff of Tara's, Willow's, and of course me will was there as well. But Tara will see all that when I die. Which reminds me, I need to get it all changed.'

'Well, who knows, Cas. But when we find them, it's game over. For them!'

As soon as Cas's feet hit the floor, he was up and already looking for his clothes.

Walter hurried over to the cabinet and started pulling out a bloodstained white shirt and black suit trousers. He paused, holding the clothes, a wave of rage hitting him hard. These were the clothes Cas had worn to bury his granddaughter. There was a line you didn't cross – and whoever did this had crossed it.

Suddenly, the officer on duty outside came bursting in and looked utterly flustered. 'What's going on?'

'I'm going home,' Cas said, buttoning up his shirt as though it was just another day at the office.

'No, no, you can't! You're not fit enough to go home. W-We need to keep you safe, we . . . er . . .' The young copper was clearly entirely out of his depth.

Cas shot him a look, his eyes narrowing. 'Listen, son, you're not a doctor – you're a copper. So, you do your job and leave my medical condition to me. They've topped up me blood, and I've had all the medication I need. Now, correct me if I'm wrong, but this ain't a police station, and I ain't in a fucking cell. So move aside.'

'But, but . . .'

'There ain't no buts. I'm not under arrest. I'm a victim.' He glanced at Walter and Dennis. 'Those words never left my mouth, got it?'

They both grinned.

'We cannot guarantee your safety once you leave here,' the officer protested.

'And I can't guarantee yours if you try and keep me here.'

'But—'

Cas moved in close. Giving the young man a wide grin and a cheeky wink, he said, 'Don't you fucking worry about me.'

The young officer's eyes bulged. He'd been briefed on Cas Ferrier and knew his MO. Seeing him earlier in that hospital bed, looking frail with wires and tubes attached, he'd clearly been fooled. Because seeing him now, upright and dressed in a suit, fire burning in his eyes . . . it was clear that this wasn't some weak old man. This was someone who'd probably survived so much more and it was clearly evident that revenge was on his mind.

'You can't take the law into your own hands, Mr Ferrier,' the officer added, but as soon as the words had left his mouth, he knew how stupid they sounded.

***

The Black Bear was in total darkness as Vic Slade quietly turned the key in the back door. He'd decided that this meeting should be between him and the Italian alone. There was no point in bringing his sons. They weren't clued up enough, and as much as his two eldest were a size and could be intimidating, they were weak when it came to the crunch.

Useless, really. Right now, he regretted ever getting involved with the man. But he still saw himself as a bit of a face, a bloke who used to have a reputation. In this new world, though, he was nothing, and the young Italian had turned what was supposed to be a simple loan into a serious debt. A debt that revolved around getting his hands on Cas's money and a briefcase.

The Italian would be arriving at any moment, and Vic needed to grovel and beg for more time. He was sure the money was coming because Cas would pay up once the boy's life was on the line. Danny had done the groundwork, figuring out that Billy was now living under Cas's roof. And knowing Cas, no one stayed with him unless he had a soft spot for them. Kidnapping Billy was their only hope now. Because that oaf of a brother had royally fucked up his previous plan. He'd got too impatient and whacked Cas over the head before they'd had the chance to properly squeeze him and get what the Italian actually wanted. Apparently, it was a black briefcase, not just any briefcase. Now, he had to clean up the mess and pray the Italian wouldn't blow his brains out before he could explain.

After pouring himself a stiff drink, Vic sat there, waiting, his nerves frayed to breaking point. Headlights passed by, now and then, but no one had pulled into the overgrown car park. He poured himself another drink, threw it down his throat, and lit up a roll-up. His eyes fell to his hands, which were shaking like leaves in an autumn gale, and to the prominent brown nicotine stains between his two fingers. What used to be solid, meaty hands now looked wizened, like a man much older than his years. *What a complete fuck-up.*

He gazed around the shithole of a pub, with bitter regret creeping in. The money he'd borrowed hadn't gone anywhere near getting the place done up. His dream of owning a thriving business was shot to shit. Stupidly, he'd given the money to his sons, thinking they would keep it in the family and fix the place up. But they weren't plasterers, bricklayers, or carpenters. Their only real skill was bragging about how they could do the work. Even Danny's cut of the money was used so stupidly on a gold Rolex that he thought he could resell it for so much more money – only to discover it was a fake. It was a very good copy, though.

He stared at the mess they'd made, the botched job they'd slapped together, just to make it half decent for the local pissheads. But even they had started to dwindle away. Now, his pub was a dumping ground for down-and-outs. The back room – his so-called office – was nothing but a joke. He hadn't had any real business to discuss in years until now.

A car finally pulled into the car park, and Vic's heart almost leaped into his throat. He ignored the glass on the table and opted instead to take a massive swig from the bottle.

The back door creaked open, and in walked the huge Italian. He was dressed in a sharp black suit, crisp white shirt, and a black tie, his hair sleeked back with gel. His skin was tanned and moisturised, like a bloody model. But in the looks department? Well, they were nothing special. However, he didn't need looks. He had his little mob, and one of them was with him now. A shorter bloke, with greasy slicked-back hair, was quick on his feet and moved fast like a coiled spring. This was in marked contrast to the boss, who moved more slowly as he eyed up the place with obvious distaste.

'A drink, mate?' Vic held up a glass, trying to steady his voice.

'No,' the Italian replied, flatly. 'I didn't come here to be sociable. I want the briefcase. And the money.'

Vic swallowed hard, his head pounding. 'Yeah, yeah, I understand, but, look, we've run into a bit of a problem.'

The Italian nodded slowly, almost too calmly. 'Oh, Mr Slade, I know all about the problem you've had. And I also know about the problems you're *about* to have.'

Vic opened his mouth, trying to explain. 'Look—'

'I haven't finished speaking.'

Vic lowered his head, bracing himself for the backlash.

'You borrowed fifty thousand pounds from me,' the Italian continued, his tone deadly calm.

Vic let out a nervous laugh. 'Well, come on, mate, you approached *me*.' The drink had hit the spot and raised his bravado. 'In fact, I wondered why you did, offering to lend me the money to do up this pub, when you—'

'Yes, yes, you are so right. I did approach you. But because you bragged in the pubs about how Cas Ferrier did you over for money, I knew you wanted revenge. So, of course, I was happy to help you.'

Vic swigged another mouthful, trying to keep his confidence intact. 'So, you had this planned all along?'

A grin twisted the Italian's face, turning it ugly, his nose screwed up to show his gumline. 'Look, you thought Mr Ferrier owed you for that robbery, and that would have been your repayment plan, wouldn't it?' He nodded, the grin never leaving his face. 'We both would have gained, so I don't see the problem from your side – except, Mr Slade, you didn't come up with the goods, did you. You had a choice. You borrow the money and you pay it back with a hundred per cent interest. And if you couldn't pay that, then you would get me that black briefcase and give me the original fifty thousand I lent to you. Simple deal. But, Mr Slade, it seems you have a problem with your side of it. So I hear.'

Vic's confidence was at rock bottom now. 'I just need an extension, that's all. Listen, Cas is gonna pay a hundred grand soon enough. I can guarantee it.'

The Italian shook his head slowly. 'No, that deal is no longer on the table. Now, I want that black briefcase and its contents. And, I want my fifty thousand back. You see, it's even more important, now that Mr Ferrier nearly died at your hands. Life is so very fragile, don't you think, Mr Slade? So, I want that briefcase, and I want it by tomorrow night.'

Without warning, the Italian pulled a gun from the back of his trousers and aimed it directly at Vic.

'If you don't deliver, I'll put a sunroof in your head. And the same for every member of your family. Don't think I won't use this gun, because I will. Oh, and by the way, I've just been told that Mr Ferrier has left the hospital.'

Vic nearly choked, hearing that news. 'Seriously? I thought he was dying!'

'We all did. This is why getting that briefcase is now more important than ever. You've got until tomorrow night.'

The timeframe rattled through Vic's mind – it was impossible, surely. He eyed the Italian up and down, trying to gauge his next move. 'Does Cas even know who you are?'

Vic knew he'd said the wrong thing, the second the words left his mouth.

Before he could react, the shorter guy knocked him to the floor. He hit him so hard that pain was shooting down his spine like a bolt of lightning. He was too old for this, far too old for fighting. He lay there, his bones screaming. He didn't even try to get back up.

The Italian loomed over him, pressing the cold barrel of the gun against his temple.

Vic squeezed his eyes shut. Waiting for the sound of the click almost made his heart stop.

But instead of a bullet, there was laughter. Cold, sharp laughter cut through the tension. The Italian straightened up, his face hardening, his voice dropping low. 'You breathe a word to anyone, and I'll come for every single member of your family. I'll hurt them so badly, they'll be begging God to end their lives.'

Vic didn't move. He couldn't. He lay there, staring at the man who felt more like the Devil himself.

In Vic's eyes, Cas Ferrier was nothing compared to this mobster. He was merely small fry.

CHAPTER THIRTY-THREE

High on adrenaline, Jesse's heart was pounding harder than ever before. Maybe it was the fact that Billy wasn't beside him this time to make the important decisions. So, every move – sensible, foolish, or downright daring was down to him. It was the first time in his life that he'd had to take responsibility for his own actions.

He needed to call home, but his phone was in his back pocket, and if he tried to reach for it, he risked giving Danny the chance to make a move on him. But now, someone was trying to phone him. He could feel his phone buzzing against his leg every so often. It was probably his mother calling to find out where he was. He hated letting her worry, but what he was doing was more important right now.

'Where is he, Danny?' Jesse growled, gripping the bloodied knife in his hand.

'All right, all right! Please, don't hurt me. I'm doing my best. Look, I'll take you to him.'

'I didn't ask how you're doing, you prick! I asked where he is!'

'I don't know the exact address, I swear to you, Jesse.'

'Yeah? So how the fuck do you know where he is then, eh?'

Danny swallowed hard; there was panic in his eyes. He didn't know what to say. Before he could think of a lie, Jesse jabbed the knife into his other leg. The car swerved, and he screamed in agony, his voice cracking. 'Please, Jesse! Stop! All right, I'll take you to him. He's . . . he's . . .'

The pain shot up to Danny's groin, and he glanced down, almost passing out. 'Please, Jesse, stop! You're killing me!'

'Oh, fuck off, Danny. You're hurt, but you ain't dying. But if you don't answer my question, *you will* be dead. Got it? I don't give a shit. Where's me bruvver, eh? Where is he?'

Jesse's scream echoed in Danny's ear, the sound making him wince, and almost forcing his eyes shut. 'Please, please, no more!' he begged, his voice shaking. 'I'll tell you the truth!'

'Start talking, or I'll stab your arms next.'

'Okay, okay!' Danny panted, trying to steady his breath. 'He's at an old farmhouse, all right? He's helping me uncle with a bit o' business. That's all, I swear to ya!'

'Drive then, you cunt, and if you're lying, I'll cut your bollocks off and stuff 'em down your throat. Now, tell me: what kind of business has your uncle got with me bruvver?'

'It's . . . it's about money – making money, honestly, that's all.'

'Oh yeah? So why in the middle of the fucking night? And why in an old farmhouse? You think I'm stupid, ya prick?'

Without thinking, Jesse dragged the knife down Danny's arm, slicing it open.

'Argh! You bastard! Please, Jesse! I'm telling you everything I know!'

'You're lying, and I hate liars. How did my bruvver get there, eh? 'Cos he don't fucking drive.'

'No, no, me uncle gave him a lift.'

Jesse's grip tightened on the knife. 'I'll ask you one more question, and if you lie again, I'll fuck you up for good, ya tosspot.'

‘Wait! Please, look – there, up ahead! The farmhouse! He’s there, I swear!’

Jesse looked ahead and saw a run-down cottage-style house with half the roof missing. The silhouette was eerie.

When Danny suddenly swerved off the main road and drove down an overgrown track, Jesse barked, ‘Turn off your lights!’

‘What? Jesse, I can’t see, if I do that—’

‘Do it!’

Danny flicked the lights off, and the car crawled forwards in the darkness.

‘Who’s in there?’ Jesse demanded.

‘Just Billy . . . and me-me uncle.’

‘If you’re lying—’

‘I’m not, I swear!’

‘If my bruvver’s been hurt, or if he’s there against his will—’

‘No, no, he’s just talking business!’

‘I didn’t know my bruvver knew your uncle.’ Jesse threw the test at him.

‘Nah, he don’t. I mean . . . er . . .’ Danny fumbled, his lie falling apart.

Wham! Jesse stabbed Danny in the arm, then again in the leg. ‘You fucking snake! You brought my bruvver here, didn’t ya. But what for, eh? And what about that necklace? You slimy bastard! What are you up to?’

Danny was rocking in the driver’s seat, now desperate to scream, his body racked with pain.

Jesse raised the knife again.

‘No, Jesse, please! No more!’ Danny cried.

But Jesse’s mind was racing, his imagination running as wild as he felt. He pictured Billy tied up and being tortured by Danny’s uncle – whoever the hell he was.

Just as he reached for his phone, Danny turned his head, a sick, twisted grin spreading across his bloodied face. He was laughing – laughing like a deranged psychopath.

Jesse froze. The transformation in Danny's face was unreal, as if he was seeing an entirely different person. That cruel smirk, curled lip, and those monstrous mocking eyes made his skin crawl, and, worse, it made him question his own sanity.

Gripped by panic, Jesse's first instinct was to run, but he couldn't tear his eyes off Danny. Reaching behind his back, he found the hammer tucked in his jeans. In one swift movement, he ripped it out and swung it hard into Danny's head.

The impact sent a shooting pain up Jesse's arms.

Danny stared, eyes wide, still grinning, daring Jesse to strike again. And he did. Again and again, until his face was covered in blood, his eyes rolling back into his head.

Jesse almost fell out of the car as he gasped for breath, desperate to get away from the sight of Danny's mangled skull. His heart raced as he bolted towards the farmhouse, but then he realised he'd left his phone behind in the car.

He didn't have time to go back. Part of him didn't want to anyway, because in the forefront of his mind was Danny's haunting face. He had to get to Billy because now he imagined that Danny had drugged him, like he'd done to Joey. His mind spun with dread. All he could do was pray that his brother was still alive.

As he got closer, a torchlight flickered in the window. Someone was waving it around as though they were searching for something. Jesse dropped to the ground, lying like a sniper on reconnaissance. There was no way Billy would be in that building of his own accord. The place was as creepy as hell. Why would he be sitting in the dark? And who the hell conducts business in the pitch black?

Crawling forward on his belly, Jesse inched himself closer to the dilapidated house.

Seconds later, he heard a deep, gruff voice that sounded as rough as old boots. 'Oi, Danny, is that you out there! Where's me grub, you little scrotum?'

The man's voice was slurred as though he'd had too much to drink. He certainly didn't sound like any businessman – more like a thug, one who had lived a hard, dirty life.

Jesse's gut instinct told him that this man wasn't friendly.

Staying low, Jesse gripped the knife tighter, thankful he hadn't dropped it in his haste to remain unseen. He listened intently, hearing the door close but not the click of a lock. Slowly, he crawled until he was right up against the house. Then, rising to his feet, he pressed his back against the wall as he caught his breath. Carefully, he slid along the side and peeped through the window. The faint glow of candles cast a hazy light in the room.

As soon as Jesse's eyes adjusted to the darkness, he scanned the room. Sitting on a chair was someone he thought he recognised. Surely, it couldn't be her, could it? Blinking quickly, he focused on the figure, and, sure enough, it was Ginty Carson. He ducked down, panic tightening his chest. Why the hell was she here? And tied up?

He didn't think he had been spotted – yet, but he looked again, more cautiously this time.

Ginty's eyes were wide and staring right at him. She had seen him. But she didn't scream or call out. Instead, she mouthed two words: *be quiet*.

Jesse ducked down again, this time his mind racing. So what had Ginty done to be tied up? Why wasn't she saying anything? Nothing made sense, but he had to trust that the old girl was on his side for now.

Creeping along the side of the house, he checked every available window that wasn't boarded up. One seemed to be a downstairs toilet, and just as he peered in, he spotted the man. He was a rough-looking thug with a bald head, rolls of fat around his neck, and shoulders the size of a doorframe. *But there was something vaguely familiar about him*, he thought. Luckily, the man hadn't seen him because he was too busy pissing into a bucket.

Jesse pulled back quickly, his heart pounding. He hadn't been seen, but he couldn't just charge in. He didn't know if Billy was inside or who else might be lurking. He needed to figure out what and who he was up against.

Thinking quickly, he decided his best move would be to continue covertly checking each window and mentally mapping out the layout of the house. He backtracked past the room where he'd seen Ginty sitting down on the chair at the far end. This time, the man was standing by what looked like a stove.

Ginty spotted him again, her eyes flicking left as if she was trying to signal that someone else was in the room next door.

As much as Jesse had been raised to hate her for what she'd done to their family, there was something different about Ginty now. She seemed so helpless, so old, so washed out. For a second, he stared at the tattered blanket that was partially draped over her. Her upper body, it appeared, was bare. Clearly, the man – if it was him – was not sparing her much dignity. But there wasn't time to dwell on her situation. He had to find Billy.

Careful not to make any noise, Jesse slid along the opposite side of the building, moving towards the window to the left of Ginty. The glass was filthy, but there was a small patch where he could just about see through. At first, it looked like an empty room – until he looked down.

Curled up on the floor, with his hands and feet bound by cable ties, was his brother.

Jesse's breathing hitched up a few notches, and his heart continued to pound as he tried to ascertain whether Billy was alive. It seemed that he stared at his brother's chest for an eternity, hoping and praying that he would see it rise and fall. *Please be alive*, he said, silently, his throat tightening. But when there was movement, he let out a shuddering sigh of relief. Billy was alive.

Jesse's mind raced as he watched Billy lying there completely helpless. The relief moments ago of seeing him breathing was only temporary because he had to get him out alive. He knew he had to stay calm, because if he charged in without a plan, he would risk getting them both killed.

Ducking below the window, he took some time to assess his options. Ginty had already spotted him, and she hadn't given him away. Yet. *That had to mean something, didn't it?* She was either trying to help him or she had another motive, or perhaps, she was just looking out for herself. Whatever was on her mind, he concluded he couldn't trust her fully, not yet.

Jesse crept around the house, trying to see if there was another way in. Perhaps there was an unlocked door or a window he could sneak through. The place was falling apart, so there had to be a window that wouldn't be adequately secured.

At the back of the farmhouse, the dark shape of a partially opened sash window caught his eye. Right away, he could see that the window belonged to the room where his brother was being kept captive and it was big enough for him to slip through. He hadn't noticed the window earlier, probably because the window pane at the front was so filthy.

Also, his mind was on seeing Billy trussed up like a turkey. He shivered. It seemed as if now was a silent invitation to venture into the belly of the beast. Slowly, he slid the sash window up, being careful not to make a sound. Then, reaching out, he pressed down on the weathered wooden frame. It creaked under the pressure, a groan that made his heart race even harder, but the frame didn't give his presence away.

Carefully, he hoisted himself through the gap, his trainers landing softly on the creaky floorboards. The smell hit him first – damp rotting wood and something far worse lingering in the air. *Was it death?*

With the knife still firmly in his grasp, Jesse moved slowly, each step more calculated than the last. His brain was firing on all cylinders while running through every possible option.

Just as he moved closer to his brother, the floorboards betrayed him, creaking under his weight. His breath caught in his throat.

'What the fuck was that?'

Hearing that voice scared the living daylights out of Jesse.

But Ginty, with nerves of steel, jumped in without missing a beat. 'That'll be Danny, no doubt, with your drink. Think you could pour me a few glasses, Irvin? Help me get some sleep, love?'

'Sleep? What the fuck is that?' Irvin grumbled.

Jesse let out a breath of relief. Ginty had just bought him some time, and he needed every second.

He glanced towards Billy. Although he was alive, he was badly battered. Jesse flashed him a quick smile and winked.

Billy's eyes widened in surprise, but even though he was tied up, Jesse could see the fight in his eyes.

'Where is that cunt Danny? Thought I heard him come in,' Irvin growled, his suspicion creeping back.

Jesse froze again, his heart hammering in his chest.

'It's the wind, Irvin. It's this bloody place,' Ginty voiced, a little louder than usual, clearly keeping him distracted with her rambling. 'Everything's creaking and cracking, love. A bit like me ol' bones.'

Deciding it was now or never, and with all the stealthiness he could muster, Jesse rushed over to his brother. He didn't hesitate to cut through the cable ties, despite his hands shaking from the tension.

'Jesse,' Billy whispered, 'give me the knife and go, mate. Just get out of here. He's a fucking animal. Believe me, I need to take this cunt by surprise.'

'No way,' Jesse whispered back. 'I ain't leaving you alone.'

'Trust me,' Billy insisted, 'I know what I'm doing.'

Jesse hesitated but then he nodded. He knew he could rely on Billy when he had that look.

Reluctantly, Jesse crept back towards the window, but when the floorboards betrayed him again with another creak, he didn't hang around. Diving out of the window, he landed hard onto the ground.

Outside, he could still hear the heavy thuds of the man's boots as he stomped into his brother's room. 'Oi! Are you trying to escape? 'Cos, you stupid fucker, you can't. You're stuck here with me!' Irvin shouted.

Jesse peered back through the window. He saw the brute kick Billy in the ribs.

Ginty was still trying to get Irvin's attention, by raising her voice, until, out of nowhere, she screamed.

The distraction caused Irvin to turn towards her.

At that precise moment, Billy sprang to his feet, moving like lightning. In one vicious motion, he drove the knife into

Irvin's side. The big man staggered, but he didn't go down. With a grimace, Billy yanked the blade free, and, without hesitation, he plunged it into Irvin's chest.

The giant swayed, his massive frame stumbling back until he crumpled against the stove, the knife still lodged in his chest.

Jesse vaulted back through the open window, ready to help, but, by the time he landed, the man was already on the floor, his life leaking out in slow shallow breaths.

Billy stood over the man, breathing hard, his eyes locked on Irvin's body.

'Come on, Billy boy,' Jesse urged, grabbing his brother's arm. 'We've gotta get out of here.'

But Billy glanced at Ginty, now in two minds about what to do with her.

She gave them a sad smile. 'Cut me free, boys, and get yourselves out of here. Leave this bastard to me.'

Hesitating only momentarily, Jesse knew they didn't have time to argue. He grabbed another knife beside the stove and started cutting the zip ties that had been used to tie up Ginty. His stomach twisted as he saw the raw, bloody marks on her wrists and ankles. The zip ties had been bound so tightly that they had embedded themselves into her flesh, so her hands were purple.

After being cut free, Ginty winced as she waited for the circulation to return. When it did, she gave both lads a wide genuine smile even through the excruciating pain. It was out of gratitude for sure but also respect for what they had done.

'I'm so sorry, boys,' Ginty whispered, a tear slipping down her cheek. 'Now, go. Give me an hour before you call the police.'

Staring at Irvin, Billy muttered, 'He's still alive.'

'Leave him to me,' Ginty said, her voice hardening. 'Go.'

Jesse glanced at Billy, his heart heavy with the weight of it all. 'There's another problem,' Jesse said, quietly. 'Danny . . . I killed him, Billy. I fucking killed him.'

Clutching the old blanket around her, to preserve what dignity she had, Ginty stood up. 'Good,' she said, coldly. 'He was just as evil as his uncle. Believe me, boys, under that bed is the body of a dear little chavi, the poor girl. And for all I know, there may be others in this place. Now, go. You've never been here. Do you hear me? Never.'

Jesse hesitated, his voice wavering. 'Are you gonna be all right, Nan?'

The word *nan* melted her heart. 'I will be now, Jesse, love. And you, Billy boy . . . You make your ol' nan proud. You're both too good for prison. I never made anything good in my life. My sons were bad, my decisions were bad. But you two?' Tears rolled down her cheeks. 'You're good lads, kind lads. I've seen ya from afar. I've heard the stories, and I'm proud. Not that I had any part in your lives, but, still, all the same, I'm proud. Look, I've never done anything for you boys, ever, but I can do something now. Now, go.'

'No, come on, come with us,' insisted Billy. 'This place, the smell. Just leave with us. We'll figure everything else out later.'

Slowly, she shook her head. 'No, this is something I can fix, and, believe me, I want to.'

Billy swallowed the lump in his throat, unable to speak, but he nodded. Grabbing Jesse's arm, together they left the house through the front door and fled across the field, the night swallowing them whole.

As they reached Danny's car, Jesse cursed. 'Shit, me phone. I've gotta get me phone.'

Jesse opened the car door and snatched his phone from the seat. His eyes caught sight of the necklace in the console

– a cold, cruel reminder. Slamming the door shut, he cast one last glance at Danny's bloodied lifeless face before he hissed, 'You bastard. Rot in hell.'

'Come on, Jesse,' said Billy, as he put his arm around his brother's shoulders.

'Billy boy, do you forgive me?'

Billy stopped and faced his brother. 'I realised, Jesse, it would take more than a woman to break us apart. I was pissed off and hurt, but you're my brother, and you always will be.'

CHAPTER THIRTY-FOUR

6 September

When they reached the main road, Jesse's phone buzzed in his pocket, and both boys stopped dead in their tracks.

'It's Mum,' Jesse muttered, as he stared at the phone.

'Of course it is, you divvy. Now, answer it, and tell her we need a lift home,' snapped Billy.

Jesse took a deep breath, trying to sound as normal as he could, considering the circumstances, to brace himself for the barrage of questions that would surely come.

'Finally, Jesse! Are you all right? We've been out of our minds with worry! Have you seen your bruvver? I'm worried near to death, boy!'

'Mum, yes and yes,' Jesse replied, trying to calm her down, but he suspected it was in vain.

'Oh, so you're with Billy?'

'Yeah, Mum . . . er, can Dad come and get us? We're, er . . .' He looked at Billy, who was bruised, tired, and not in the mood for any more questions.

But Billy was also frustrated, and he snatched the phone out of Jesse's hand. 'Mum, we're fine. Can you ask Dad to meet us at Blacksmiths Lane?'

'Are you sure you're all right? Where've you been? We've been so bloody worried! And the Ol' Bill want to question you. The wankers think you may have had something to do with poor Keith's murder!'

Billy sighed, rubbing his temple. 'Mum, please. I'm so tired. Can you just ask Dad to come and get us?'

'Of course . . .' There was a pause before their mother could ask another question, but Billy cut off the call and handed the phone back to Jesse.

'Now listen, Jesse, do we tell Mum and Dad everything, or what?'

He glared at his brother.

'Oi, Jesse, are you even listening to me?'

Jesse blinked. 'I can't stop thinking about Danny . . . He was a proper psycho, Billy. The way he stared at me, even with his head caved in, it was like he was laughing at me.'

'Yeah, yeah, I get it. But listen, for fuck's sake, do we tell Mum and Dad?' pressed Billy, growing more impatient by the minute.

Jesse nodded, slowly. 'I don't think I can handle this on me own, mate. It's too much. How the hell can we hide something like this?'

Billy nodded. 'I know, but listen to me. For now, we should just say nothing. Look, mate, we're knackered. We'll just tell them we're tired and need to sleep. And then we can talk about everything tomorrow, yeah?'

Jesse glanced around. The early morning light was creeping into the sky and making everything feel strange and surreal. 'Billy, it *is* tomorrow. And guess what else? It's your birthday. Happy birthday, Bruv. You're sixteen.'

Billy was too caught up in his own thoughts even to register the fact that he was now sixteen. Unlike Jesse, he was already planning their next move. 'Look, there's a phone box up ahead. We can call the police from there and let them know about Ginty and the farmhouse.'

Jesse followed his brother, but his mind was still on the events of last night. Danny's twisted grin, the old farmhouse, and Ginty's pleading eyes were all flashing like the trailer to a psycho thriller film.

Billy made the call quickly, ending it before the operator could ask any questions about who he was. 'Hope she's all right,' he muttered, more to himself than to Jesse.

'And I hope she keeps her word,' said Jesse.

***

When they finally reached the bottom of the lane, Sunny's car screeched to a stop. The boys wasted no time in clambering inside, and the moment the doors shut, Sunny sped off, his face tight with frustration.

'Your mother's been beside herself, you pair of little sods. The police have been knocking at the door. Twice, now, Billy. So, tell me, where've you been, eh?'

'Dad, please . . .' groaned Billy, leaning his head back against the seat, exhaustion written all over him. 'Can we talk about it later? I feel like shit. Please, I just need to sleep.'

Sunny shot a glance at Billy. And then he checked out Jesse in the rear-view mirror. Not only did Billy have a number of bruises, but, more shockingly, Jesse's face was splattered with blood. His eyes widened in shock. 'Oh God . . . don't say a word. When I get you home, just clean yourselves up and get into bed. Do I need to burn the clothes?'

Neither of the boys answered, both staring straight ahead, but Jesse gave him a slight nod. 'Yeah, Dad.'

The rest of the journey home was spent in tense silence.

***

When they finally pulled into the drive, Carrie was waiting by the back door, arms crossed, ready to give her sons a lecture. But Sunny was out of the car first and holding up his hand. 'Not now, love.'

Carrie's face softened, the exhaustion showing in the lines around her eyes. She had worn herself out pacing the kitchen all night, with all the worry about her boys.

Billy and Jesse walked in a few minutes later, stripped to their underwear, having left their clothes in a heap outside.

'Are you two all right?' Carrie's voice was gentle now, seemingly showing more concern than anger.

Neither of them could meet her eyes. They headed upstairs and straight into the bathroom without a word, leaving her and Sunny in the kitchen.

Sunny shrugged. 'I'm going to light a fire.'

'No, don't,' Carrie warned. 'If you burn their clothes, the police will wonder why you were even starting a fire at this hour of the bloody morning. Just give them to me.' She sighed, knowing exactly what needed to be done.

If anyone could get the blood out of their clothes, it was his wife. Not only did she know every trick in the book, but she had tested every cleaning product known to man. After all, keeping her family's clothes and home spotless had always been her thing, a part of her gypsy heritage.

'What have they done, Sunny?' Carrie whispered, as he handed her the blood-soaked clothes, her eyes widening at the sight.

'I don't know, love. I really don't know. But whatever it is . . . it's bad. Very bad.'

'I'm going to ask them what's been going on.'

'No, don't. Let them rest. They might need time to process whatever's happened. And if the police come again, I'll tell them Billy came home but went out again, so they don't file a missing person's report.'

'Yeah, good idea,' Carrie said, sliding her hand around his waist and leaning into him for comfort. 'I'm going to lie down for an hour or so.'

Sunny gave her a light tap on the backside as she headed towards the stairs. He made himself a strong coffee and sat at the table, the seriousness of the situation draining him. He only hoped that whatever his sons had been involved in, it wasn't tied to the old Carson-Murphy feud. That had to stop.

What puzzled him most of all, though, was Carrie's calm reaction. He had expected her to fly off the handle or panic at the sight of all that blood. But it was as though she had seen it all before. He couldn't shake off the thought. *What secrets was she keeping from me in her life?* he wondered. With exhaustion overriding any attempts at logical deduction of these early morning events, he fell asleep face down on the kitchen table before he knew it.

***

Billy was the first one up. Creeping downstairs, he glanced at the clock. It was almost midday. The house seemed eerily quiet. The youngsters were nowhere to be seen. He assumed they were at his nan's. Spotting his dad asleep at the kitchen table, Billy gently tapped his arm.

Sunny stirred, slowly lifting his head to show his face etched with sleep creases on his face and drool at the corner of his mouth.

'Coffee, Dad?'

Sunny stretched, rubbing his eyes. 'Yeah, go on, I'll have one. Are you all right, Son?'

Billy filled the kettle, avoiding eye contact. 'Yeah . . . I guess so.'

Sunny knew his boy well enough. Getting him to open up would be like pulling out teeth.

'Do you want to tell me what happened?' Sunny asked, cautiously.

Billy turned to face him, leaning against the worktop. 'Dad, me and Jesse – we don't keep secrets from you or Mum. But what happened last night might never need to be talked about.'

Sunny straightened up, now very alarmed. 'What do you mean by that?'

'In the next few hours, there will be some big news. And, hopefully, our names won't be on everyone's lips. So, can we just wait? If the police come looking for us, then I'll tell you everything.'

Sunny felt the blood drain from his face. He didn't like this. Not one bit. He had always secretly had his suspicions regarding Billy's mental state. In fact, on quite a few occasions, it had crossed his mind that Billy may have a dark side. 'Billy . . . have you or Jesse hurt an innocent person?'

Billy paused, deliberating on what his father had just asked him. 'If you're asking if we're the ones responsible for either Willow's and Keith's deaths or those missing girls . . . well, no, we ain't. And no, Dad, we haven't hurt an innocent person. But . . . can we leave it at that?'

Staring hard at his son, Sunny tried to read between the lines. 'Just answer me this, Billy.'

Billy nodded, bracing himself. 'Go on, then.'

'Have you done anything that would make me disown you?'

A small smile tugged at Billy's lips, though it didn't quite reach his eyes. 'No, Dad. I promise you. But you need to know this . . . you'd be so proud of Jesse. He saved my life last night.'

Sunny's eyes widened in shock. 'Really, Son? Well, that's supposed to be *my* job.' He chuckled, trying to lighten the mood. 'Guess that's one way of making up for the hurt he caused you.'

But Billy didn't laugh. Deep down, he wondered if he ever would again.

Jesse came down the stairs far less gracefully than Billy had, his hair sticking up in all directions, as he rubbed the sleep from his eyes. 'I'll have a coffee, Billy boy.'

Billy didn't answer. He just made coffee in three mugs and joined his brother and father at the table. Before any of them had the chance to take a sip, there was a loud bang at the front door.

Billy's face dropped. 'I hope this is the news we want to hear.'

All three hurried to the door, and as they opened it, there was a shared sigh of relief. Sitting on Jesse's bike was Joey. He smiled awkwardly. 'Er, you don't mind me callin', do ya?'

Billy was about to tell him to get lost, but Jesse stepped forward, cutting him off. 'Nah, you're all right. What's going on?'

Joey's gaze moved to Billy. 'So, you found ya way home, then?'

Billy stared, not saying a word.

'Well, anyway, listen – there was a raid on the Slades' house this morning. O' course, I was being nosy seeing what all the gavvers were up to and what all the noise was about. And that's when I spotted your bike, Jesse. I thought since me and you are talking now, I won't nick it. I'd bring it home for ya.'

Sunny was about to thank him, but Jesse jumped in again. 'It ain't my bike, Joey. Mine's in the garage.'

With his overeager smile, Joey climbed off and looked the bike over. 'Cor, it's a nice ride, though. I thought it was yours. I mean, last night you asked me where the Slades live, and then when I saw this bike just by their house, I thought it was yours.'

'Not mine. Come and have a look, Joey. Mine's in the garage,' Jesse offered, knowing full well he and Billy had the same make and model of bike. They also had others. A couple were even at Dottie's.

'Well, looks like I've got myself a nice runaround, then,' Joey joked, shrugging with a grin.

Sunny intended to retreat to the kitchen but he couldn't stop himself. So he listened to the conversation in the hallway, out of sight of the boys.

'So, what's all this about the Slades getting raided?' Jesse asked, leaning against the doorframe.

'Looks like they've all scarpered. Done a moonlight flit. But I heard the police mention Ginty Carson and those missing girls. Not that they'd tell us much.' Joey glanced at Billy. 'Glad you're home, Billy.'

'Yeah, Joey even offered to help look for ya,' Jesse added.

'Yeah, cheers,' Billy replied, sarcastically, before heading past his father and walking back into the kitchen. But his unease had worn off now. According to what Joey had said, if he was to be believed, the raid on the Slades could well be linked to Ginty taking the blame. If that was true, the police might not come knocking here after all.

'He's a bit moody, your Billy, ain't he?' Joey remarked, raising an eyebrow.

Jesse grinned. 'He can be, but listen, Joey. There's still the issue of who hurt our Char. Until we know for sure, your name's still in the hat.'

Joey's eyes widened in panic. 'Oh no, listen. Get Billy back 'ere. He needs to hear this an' all. When the police raided the Slades, we were all outside havin' a good ol' nose. I saw the forensics team go in, and when they came out, they were carrying see-through bags. Inside them were balaclavas.'

'Really?' Jesse raised an eyebrow, intrigued.

'Yeah, I swear on me muvver's life. Ask the police yaself, if you don't believe me.' Joey's voice was urgent as if sharing this information would clear his name.

'I reckon it was them who hurt you and your Charlie, 'cos I swear it weren't us.'

Jesse shrugged. 'I don't know anything about the Slades. Only that Danny was the last one to see Willow alive. Other than that, I don't know anything else.'

'Well, anyway, I s'pose I'd best be off. I wanna see if there's any more gossip. Fucking 'ell, though, what if those girls going missing was to do with the Slades? Fuck me, Jesse, we only live around the corner, and to fink, bruv, Donna is some relative of ours. It makes me wanna puke, it does.'

Jesse shrugged again. 'Anyway, Joey, thanks for bringing the bike over, even though it's not mine. And you're right: you got yaself a nice one there. Best respray it before whoever it belongs to wants it back.'

Joey looked at the paintwork. 'Yeah, a nice red should do it.' He grinned. 'See ya, then, Jesse.'

Just as Joey rode away, Spud pulled up in his car, and a tired-looking Dottie got out. Before she even said hello, she called over to Jesse. 'Is Billy back?'

As soon as Jesse replied yes, he could see Dottie's face light up. 'Thank God.'

Spud hurried behind her. 'Put the kettle on, Jesse. We've had a bloody long night.'

As soon as they were inside, Carrie came down the stairs, where she met Dottie in the hallway. 'Blimey, I thought I looked rough, Dot. How'd it go, love?'

'Let me get inside. I'm gasping for a decent coffee and some sleep. So Billy came home, then. The officers were incensed with rage that they couldn't haul Billy in. But I'm glad they didn't. They were proper nasty. I think Clemmy is going to put in a formal complaint.'

Hearing Dottie's voice, Billy greeted her at the kitchen door. 'All right, Mottie?'

She nodded. 'More to the point, are you?'

'Yes, I'm fine.'

Walking back to where he was sitting, Billy sighed heavily. He sensed there was going to be a lot said.

This time, Jesse made the coffee while casually recounting much of what Joey had shared, except the part about Ginty, because he wasn't sure he would even say her name again.

Having listened in to the conversation between Jesse and Joey, Sunny wasn't surprised that his son hadn't mentioned Ginty by name in this conversation.

Carrie sat there with her mouth gaping. 'Bloody Nora, what's been going on, I wonder?'

'Well, something drastic happened,' Dottie continued, glancing at Billy and Jesse. 'That bastard Gurney was practically accusing me of being involved in Keith's murder. He was digging up the past, and going on and on about my psychiatric records. He wanted them brought to the station for the CPS to make a decision. Cor, that Clemmy almost went for his jugular. Then, suddenly, another copper burst in and whispered something to Detective Keldon. All I caught was the name Ginty Carson, and just like that, they said the interview was suspended. Clemmy and I were left hanging around for ages.'

Jesse handed her a steaming cup of coffee, and then he passed one to Spud. 'Two sugars, yeah, Spud?'

Spud nodded, keeping his eyes on Dottie, not wanting to interrupt. Everyone in the room was on edge, waiting for what came next.

'So then Clemmy stormed out muttering to himself. He was gone about ten minutes, and when he came back, he looked like he'd seen a ghost. It was as though the blood had drained right out of his face.' Dottie paused, taking a couple of mouthfuls of coffee while everyone leaned in closer.

'The police were called up, to what they thought might be a domestic incident at an old farmhouse. When they got there, they found two dead men and . . .' she paused, 'the remains of those missing girls.'

Billy and Jesse glanced at each other, both recalling the horrors they'd witnessed.

'But that's not all! You'll never guess who else was there. Only Ginty Carson! She told them she'd been taken to the farmhouse where these men were going to kill her, after they'd planned to torture her for days, but, somehow, she'd managed to release her ties, and she turned the tables on them.'

Billy and Jesse slowly grinned at each other, the relief washing over them.

Carrie and Sunny, on the other hand, were utterly stunned.

'Did they torture her?' Carrie asked, wanting all the details.

Dottie nodded. 'That's what Clemmy said. So they've taken her to the hospital for tests. Apparently, she was raped as well. And she told the police that this bloke – his name is Irvin Slade by the way – who is the brother of Vic Slade – killed Keith. According to Ginty, it was Irvin and Danny who robbed Cas's place.'

'Bloody hell,' Sunny said, shaking his head.

'For now, the spotlight's completely off me. It's all about Ginty Carson. I'm still trying to wrap my head around it.'

Carrie looked over at Billy, her expression softer. 'You had your suspicions about that Danny, didn't you?'

Slowly, Billy nodded. 'Yeah, I did. So, did this Irvin confess everything to Ginty before she turned on him?'

Dottie shrugged. 'I don't know all the details yet. What I do know is that Irvin and Danny are dead, and the police have enough evidence to think they were responsible for the missing girls and for what happened to Willow too.' She gave Billy a sympathetic look. 'I'm sorry, Billy, love.'

Billy's face tightened. 'But why? Why kill her?'

Dottie shook her head. 'I don't know, but I'm sure it'll all come out soon enough. Sounds like this Irvin was a proper animal.'

Billy glanced at Jesse, who nodded, sharing an unspoken understanding. They both knew the truth behind the farmhouse nightmare. But, for now, it seemed like the ordeal had ended.

'Is Ginty at the hospital now?' Billy asked.

Dottie nodded, her expression now very weary. 'I should think so.'

'D'ya reckon she'll get done for murder?' Jesse jumped in.

Dottie shrugged, taking a sip of her now lukewarm coffee. 'Not if they tortured her. Perhaps she did it in self-defence.'

Carrie stood up, the legs of the chair screeching against the floor. 'I bet she's in the Princess Royal.' She grabbed her cardigan from the back of the chair, her movements swift and purposeful.

Sunny frowned, leaning back with his arms crossed. 'What are you doing, Carrie?'

'I'm going there right now,' she replied, sliding into her cardigan. 'She's a right ol' bag, but that ol' bag's got no one. I'm going to see if she needs anything. I don't even know what state the woman's in. I'll get her some nightclothes, a washbag – whatever else she needs.'

Sunny rolled his eyes, shaking his head. 'Seriously, Carrie, you can't stand the woman.'

Carrie shrugged, her hand already on the door handle, pausing only to glance back at her boys. 'Yeah, well, I'm not sure she deserved to be tortured, and who does she have, eh? No one!' Her gaze lingered on Billy and Jesse – both looking worn out by whatever horrors they'd been through. Blood on their clothes, secrets in their eyes. But she knew better than to ask any questions right now.

Pulling the cardigan tighter around herself, she grabbed her car keys, and was halfway out of the front door when Sunny stood up. 'I'll come with you, Carrie.'

She raised an eyebrow, turning back. 'Why? D'ya think I'm going to do something stupid?'

Sunny grinned. 'It wouldn't be off the cards, love, would it? And we've had enough dramas to last us a bloody lifetime.'

***

When Carrie stormed through A&E at the Princess Royal University Hospital, she knew immediately that Ginty was there. For a start, there were several police cars parked outside, and officers were loitering in the main corridor.

Spotting DCI Keldon on his phone right outside one of the cubicles, Sunny tried to hold his wife back, his grip gentle but firm.

'I don't think you can go in there, Carrie.'

But Carrie was too determined, too riled up, to be stopped. She shook him off with a huff. 'I don't care. I wanna see for meself if she's okay.'

Sunny rolled his eyes but stepped back. He knew better than to try and argue when Carrie was in this mood.

As she approached the screen, Keldon cut his call short, stepping in her way. 'Mrs Murphy, you can't go in there.'

'And why not?' Carrie snapped. Her patience now paper-thin, she certainly wasn't in the mood for this, not after what she'd heard about what had happened to Dottie.

'She can't speak to anyone until we have taken a formal statement. And how did you even know she was here?' He gave her a suspicious look, his eyes narrowing.

Before Carrie could respond, a frail voice came from behind the screen. 'Carrie Ann, is that you, love?'

Ignoring Keldon, Carrie pulled the screen aside, her breath catching in her chest when she saw Ginty lying there.

For a moment, she just stared, frozen, at the sight of the deep wounds around Ginty's swollen ankles. They were red and oozing, and Carrie felt her stomach turn. When she met Ginty's eyes, she could see the pain, the sickness, and the fight that was now slipping away. Her hair was wet and stuck to her forehead, her eyes were sunken, and her limbs were so swollen they were purple.

DI Gurney tried to tug Carrie back, but she shrugged him off too, spinning around with a glare. 'Get your bleedin' hands off me.'

Rushing to Ginty's side, she gently touched her arm. 'Well, what a fucking mess, eh?'

A sharp-tongued doctor, who was hovering nearby, now came over to his patient and adjusted a blood pressure cuff on her arm.

'Mrs Carson, if we don't get this cannula in, we will not be able to administer the antibiotics you clearly need.'

'I'm dyin', doc. Leave me be,' Ginty muttered, waving her hand weakly.

Carrie peered up at the tall lanky-looking doctor. 'What's it for?'

'Are you a relative?'

'Yeah, yeah, I am. So, then, what's it for?'

'She has sepsis. The infection is in her bloodstream. If we don't start the antibiotics, she could very well die.'

Carrie turned back to Ginty, a fierce look in her eyes. 'Let them do it, you stubborn old bag.'

Ginty's lips lifted into a faint smile. It was far softer than Carrie had ever seen before.

Looking almost peaceful for a moment, as though all the rough edges had been smoothed away at once, Ginty said, 'Carrie, gal, I ain't got nuffin' to live for now. Made a right pig's ear of me life. Those bastards I raised turned out rotten, not like your two boys . . . Anyway, my time's gone now, Carrie.'

'No, it ain't, Ginty Carson. You've got more fight left in ya yet. Now, who am I gonna moan about if you're six feet under? You've been the bane of my life, but someone's got to be. So let that doctor do his job and get you better.'

Ginty's smile wavered, a tear slipping from her eye. 'Even after all I've put you through, you still care?'

'Enough of the soppy talk. Let that doctor stick the needle in.'

Ginty turned to the doctor, giving him a slight nod.

'Bloody finally,' he muttered, getting to work.

Gurney tried to step in again, but Carrie spun on him this time, her eyes blazing. 'Lay your fucking hands on me again, and you'll be lucky you're already in a hospital. Back off. She needs support right now, not any of your stupid questions.'

Keldon leaned in, whispering to his colleague, 'Leave her. She seems to be the only one who will get Ginty to do as she's told.'

Gurney retreated from the cubicle, with his nostrils flaring in frustration.

Carrie stroked Ginty's arm, her voice far more gentle now. 'I'll get you a nice soft nightdress, Ginty, and a dressing gown. Might have to wait for your feet to go down before I buy you some slippers, though.'

Carrie and the nurse remained with the screen closed around them. Carrie's expression was the epitome of concern. 'Did he hurt you badly, Ginty?'

Ginty's voice broke, now barely a whisper. 'Me dignity, Carrie Ann. Me dignity . . . He raped me, the dirty bastard.'

Carrie's hand tightened on Ginty's arm, her anger bubbling over. Reaching over to brush a loose strand of hair from Ginty's face, she said, quietly, 'You need to get that dyed, Ginty. You look like a skunk with that streak of grey.'

Ginty managed a small sad smile. 'Maybe I'll go all grey. S'pose I should, for me age, like.'

Carrie sensed Ginty growing weaker, her voice fading. 'When you get out of here, you should come to mine for a nice roast dinner, eh? You'd like that, wouldn't ya?'

'Yeah, and some of Jed's home brew, just like the old days,' she replied, her eyelids drooping.

As soon as the nurse left the cubicle, Carrie leaned closer, her voice a hushed whisper. 'Ginty, I need to know one thing . . . Did my boys . . .?'

Ginty's lips twitched, her voice barely carrying. 'Don't ask, Carrie, please . . . I . . . I killed those two bastards.'

When Ginty's eyes fluttered and shut, Carrie's heart clenched in panic. 'No, no, you can't die, you old bat.'

The nurse returned. 'She's not dead,' she gently assured Carrie. 'She's exhausted. The IV's in, and we've given her something to help her rest.'

'Is she in a lot of pain?'

'Yes, she has suffered such severe abuse that we will have to stitch her up.'

Carrie's hands flew to her mouth, stifling a sob. 'Oh, dear God . . .'

The nurse's voice was gentle as she continued. 'Seeing Mrs Carson's smile through the immense pain she is in, all I can say is you must mean a lot to her.'

'We're arch-enemies, really.'

'Sure you are, but she is very, very poorly. We will know in a couple of hours if the antibiotics are doing their job.'

Carrie nodded, feeling the lump in her throat.

CHAPTER THIRTY-FIVE

A smirk pulled at the corners of Cas's mouth as he listened carefully to everything his contact in the police station had to say. 'Your missus spent the last bit o' bunce already?'

The officer on the other end of the phone laughed. 'Of course, she has, Cas. The cow bleeds me dry.'

'All right, I'll drop off another little bundle. Cheers, mate. Appreciate the heads-up.'

He ended the call and turned to Dennis, who was perched on a chair in Cas's study. 'Fancy a pint?'

Dennis raised an eyebrow. 'Too early for me, mate.'

Cas chuckled, his voice low and dangerous. 'Well, we're paying The Black Bear a visit. And let's just say . . . I'm planning to annihilate a completely fucked-up family.' He glanced at Walter. 'Get Lolly on the blower. Fill him in, would ya, and tell him to get over there. The Slades ain't gonna know what's hit 'em. Looks like the cunts have scarpered from their shit pit in The Crays, and the only place they have to run to is that poxy pub.'

'And the filth reckon they're responsible for killing young Willow, do they?' Dennis asked, crossing his arms.

Cas's grin faded a little. 'Yeah, that's what the copper told me. They think Irvin Slade and that scrawny little rat Danny did it. Irvin's some kind of nutter, who should never have been let loose, but the paperwork got botched or someone was slipped a backhander. Now, they've got half the force running around like cunting headless chickens trying to piece together what went down before the press sink their teeth into it.'

‘Why Willow, though?’ Dennis’s tone had shifted. This latest revelation was certainly unexpected.

Cas looked down momentarily as though he was carrying a weight he didn’t like to show. ‘I don’t fully know, but a while back, me and Keith did a job with Vic Slade and his oaf of a brother Irvin. It was when you were out of the country, if my memory serves me correctly. Anyway, they roughed up the barmaid, a dear friend of mine. We should’ve known then that Irvin was off his rocker. But I didn’t pay ’em. I just told ’em to do one. It seems that Vic and Irvin returned for their money after their first plan to use my granddaughter as leverage failed. But that psycho killed her, like he did with those other girls, presumably. And Ginty Carson? Before she was carted off to the hospital, she sang like a canary, giving the Ol’ Bill everything she knew. ’Cos, apparently, she heard it all and made threats to grass on the Slades, so of course they tried to shut her up for good. But the clever ol’ cow escaped.’

Dennis’s grin grew wider. He was like a kid on Christmas morning finding the biggest present under the tree.

Meanwhile, Walter adjusted his jacket, his face set in that cold, stern expression he wore when things were about to get messy. He cracked his knuckles before gripping a metal pole in one hand and a blade in the other.

Cas gave them both a nod, his voice a low growl. ‘I wanna pin these bastards down and squeeze the rest of the story out of ’em.’

Walter’s grip tightened on the pole, and Dennis’s eyes sparkled with anticipation.

‘The only thing I can’t get me head around,’ Cas muttered, pacing the room, ‘is that that job was a few years ago. And I’ve seen Vic a couple of times since. There’s been nothing untoward. Know what I mean? Just the odd sarky comment. So why the hell is he suddenly going to these lengths to get money outta me? And this whole briefcase business? . . . It leaves me baffled.'

Walter, who was leaning against the doorway, rolled a cigarette between his fingers. 'Like you say, Cas, you can always squeeze the facts out of him – before you kill him, o' course.' He cast a glance out of the French doors. 'You still got that cesspit out back, or are you on the mains now?'

Cas barked out a laugh. 'Still got the cesspit, mate. Never know when you might need it, right, but I don't fancy having the likes of the Slades littering me backyard, even if I dump them in the shit. Come on then, lads. We'd better move quick before the filth put two and two together and realise that ol' Vic part owns that pub. As I understood it, the place was condemned years ago.'

Dennis cracked his knuckles too, an eager glint in his eye. 'And you reckon he's there now?'

'Well, of course I do. What do you think I am, eh? A carrot short of a vegetable soup?'

Dennis sat up straighter, his chilled demeanour vanishing. After all, Cas still had a reputation for having a very dangerous, unpredictable nature, and they knew better than to let their guard down and act too flippantly.

Lifting a loose floorboard, Cas reached down and retrieved a gun. He brandished it with a wicked grin, the metal catching the dim light as he waved it in front of his two men.

'Vic'll get this right between his eyeballs, the fanny merchant,' Cas growled. 'Along with his family – minus the dead cunts, of course. Let's pay 'em a visit, shall we, gentlemen?'

'Hold up, Cas,' said Walter, looking concerned. 'D'you think you're up to it?'

'Up to it?' Cas's voice rose. 'Fucking up to it? Listen, I might have a bleedin' great headache, but not as much as that family will have – and that's *before* I start torturing them. Anyway, I've got me shooter, and it don't take a lot of strength to pull a trigger.'

They drove quietly, pulling up a few yards from the pub, where they found Lolly sitting in a car, eyes fixed on the run-down building, the overgrown bushes around him providing some cover.

Cas got out, but his legs wobbled beneath him, and he had to grip the car door, to take a few steadying breaths. Although he obviously wasn't back to full strength, that didn't matter – rage kept him upright.

Lolly marched over, his face like stone. He gave Cas a respectful nod, and then he acknowledged Dennis and Walter. 'And you're sure they were responsible for killing my daughter?'

Cas nodded. 'Yeah, but listen, right, and I mean it, Lolly. Don't you go in there and kill 'em straight off. There are questions I want answers to, right?'

Lolly's glazed eyes burned for revenge, but he gave a terse nod. 'I got ya, Cas. I'll wait, all right.'

Cas leaned in closer, his tone sharp. 'I'm serious, Lolly. For all we know, there might be others involved. And I don't want any cunt going unpunished.'

'All right, no problem. I hear ya.' But the murderous look in Lolly's eyes made Cas wonder if he was capable of containing himself until the time was ready.

'Good, right, well, park the cars down the road. There's a turning – a dirt track. I don't want passers-by clocking our motors.' Cas's voice was low but firm, leaving no room for debate.

Everyone climbed back into their cars, the engines purring softly, as they rolled away from the pub. They found the dirt track, rough and narrow, framed by overgrown hedges that brushed the sides of the vehicles. Now parked up and hidden away from the main road, the men were soon ready for action.

'Do you even know if they're here?' asked Lolly, turning his razor-sharp knife around in the direction of the pub.

'Well, I don't 'ave a crystal ball, but the likes of those scummy pikeys won't exactly have a nice villa in fucking sunny Spain to go to, will they? Nah, my guess is they're hiding in the shithole and quaking in their fucking dealer boots.'

The back door to the pub was locked, but the Slades' lack of carpentry skills had left it in a sorry state and easy to break down, which Lolly did in one swift kick. The men then entered the pub and found themselves facing a rotten, rickety old bar.

The sudden scurry of feet and chairs scraping the floor told Cas that someone was in the back room. He could hear the window being opened on the other side of the door, but he wasted no time. Signalling to Lolly to take over, he watched with satisfied anticipation.

With another fierce kick, the door was off its hinges.

There they were – the Slades – piled up against the back wall, looking like cornered rats. They were all trying to squeeze through a window that barely opened more than a few inches. Vic, Donna, Luke, Kieron, and Nobby froze when they saw Cas and the others, their eyes darting between them like trapped animals.

Vic tried to put on a brave front, stepping forward, but Cas could see his hands trembling.

'What are you doing here?' Vic tried to keep his voice steady, but it wavered. 'I mean, I heard you've been in hospital.'

Cas chuckled, a sound that sent a shiver through the room. 'Yeah, thanks to you, ya cunt.'

Lolly glared while turning the knife around in his hand. 'Right, then, who's fucking first?'

Vic looked back at his three remaining sons, their eyes wide, like frightened kids, and at the moment, he was ashamed of them. He glanced back at Cas. 'Look, it wasn't me, it was that mental bruvver of mine. I couldn't control the bastard. I'm sorry, Cas, but it wasn't me, I swear.'

Holding up his hands as if relinquishing any responsibility, the lack of any remorse in Vic's voice riled up Lolly so much that he lunged forward and grabbed hold of him.

Placing the knife to his throat, he said, 'You'd better tell us what happened 'cos we've just buried our little girl, and you, ya cunt, was involved.'

Out of nowhere, Luke decided to play the hero, thinking this bunch of old men would be easy targets. Stamping hard on a chair and snapping off one of its legs, he grabbed the makeshift weapon. With the chair leg gripped tightly, he charged at Walter, the shortest of the bunch, hoping that his brother Kieron, who had hands like shovels, would back him up and jump in.

But Luke hadn't thought it through. The moment he charged and glanced sideways, expecting Kieron to follow, all he saw was fear in his brother's eyes.

Kieron was now a frozen soul, almost shitting himself.

Luke realised he was left to face the consequences of his reckless move alone. As he swung the chair leg, Walter held the metal pole like a spear and rammed it hard straight into his forehead, causing him to stagger back, before Walter then held the pole like a hammer and whacked him across the legs so hard, he screamed in pain as the sound of his kneecaps popping echoed around the room.

'All right, please!' yelled Vic. 'I'll talk.'

'I fucking know you will, Vic! You're gonna tell me everything,' said Cas, now pointing the gun at him. 'And your little inbreds will sit the fuck down and shut the fuck up.'

He glared at Donna who had her arms folded across her chest, in complete defiance.

'Oh, and don't for one minute think I consider you as a bird. I don't. 'Cos, see, here's the thing, Donna! You knew they were going to kidnap my little granddaughter. You knew, didn't ya?'

Donna just stood there glaring, unblinkingly.

'Go on, admit it.'

She continued to stare, tapping her foot as if she didn't care.

'Ya see, any real woman would've stopped the whole charade in its tracks, but not you, you greedy bitch! Nah, you let them take me granddaughter, and that Irvin, the bastard, he fucking killed her. And you didn't even have the sweetness in ya breath to tell anyone. You went along with it, so if you think I'll be lenient 'cos you're a woman, then, sweetheart, you're very much mistaken.'

Knowing his family would soon be decimated if he didn't do something, Vic held his hands up in surrender.

But it seemed that one member of his family hadn't got the memo.

Dennis clocked Kieron slyly running his hands along the window frame and guessed he was ready to do a runner. So he rushed towards him. Pulling a knife from his back pocket, he rammed it into Kieron's hand and pinned it to the frame.

The scream coming from her son was so blood-curdling, it made Donna suddenly gasp and try to pull the knife out to give him a chance to nurse his wound. But the knife was in too deep. As she attempted to pull it out again, Kieron screamed even more. Sweat ran down the back of her neck as the effort was such that the veins stood out like knotted rope.

Dennis backhanded her. 'Fuck off!' he said, before he turned to Nobby. In one fast move that no one expected, he belted him across the face so hard, his jaw snapped again.

Vic looked around at the carnage that had taken place in under a minute. He knew then that Cas and his men were not taking prisoners. 'All right, listen, Cas, please. We needed the money. The mobster was gonna come for us. All of us. Right?'

Cas nodded. 'Now, we're getting somewhere because a little pipsqueak like yaself wouldn't dare hurt my family, unless, of course, you were desperate or fucking stupid. My guess is you're both. Start talking! Who's this mobster bloke?'

'He's Italian. He lent me money and wanted it back. But he knew I didn't have it, and I think he knew I would never have it.'

'How much and what was the money for?'

'Fifty grand, to do this place up.'

'Well . . .' said Cas, gazing around, 'I can see you've had the designer in. You're going for the dilapidated look, are ya?'

Vic stood there, his face flushed with embarrassment.

'And fifty grand wasn't enough?'

'Not enough to turn this into a thriving business, so I ended up owing this Italian a hundred grand.'

'Go on, cunt. This is getting interesting. I might have to pull up a chair in a minute.'

'He knew you knocked me for money after that pub job, all because me bruvver hurt the barmaid But then he said he could put that right, and we would both win. All I had to do was pay back my original debt of fifty grand, with no interest on the loan, and get me hands on your black briefcase.'

'Yeah, well, I know that, 'cos your mental bruvver asked me for it. But the twat never mentioned anything about a colour. He just said *briefcase.* Anyway, why did this so-called mobster want me briefcase?'

Vic shrugged. 'I swear to ya, Cas, I dunno.'

'What did this cunt look like?'

'Tall, about six foot, quite stocky, black hair swept back, a mole on his lip, a nasty sneer, and veneers. Bright-white veneers.'

Suddenly, Lolly glared at Cas. 'Fuck me, you know who that is, don't ya?'

Cas nodded slowly. 'Oh yeah, we know who that is.'

Lolly removed the knife from Vic's throat and stepped back.

Vic let out a deep sigh. 'Christ, I thought for a minute you were gonna muller me.'

Cas grinned. 'No, no, Vic, not just yet.'

Turning to Walter and Dennis, he nodded and then smiled.

Before Vic could even catch his breath, Cas's men were literally ripping his sons inside out. Blood was splattered around the walls. All he could do was watch the carnage while his sons screamed and cried out as they begged for mercy.

But it didn't come.

Dennis ended Luke's life with a knife through his chest.

Nobby was already writhing around the floor with both of his hands missing and his jaw detached from his face.

Walter couldn't handle the childish screams coming from Kieron, so he rammed the metal pole hard around the young man's head until he slumped lifeless.

Cas smiled as he watched Donna's absolute grief and fear. She now knew what it felt like to lose her own child. But not just one. He didn't bother to torture her. Instead, he shot her dead with a single bullet straight through the head.

Vic was the last one standing. He looked about, bewildered. There was no time for grief. Turning to Cas, he tried to say something, but Cas shoved the gun so fast into his mouth that he knocked all his teeth out. One bullet and it was all over.

Walter sighed. 'And I thought you were gonna torture the cunt.'

Lolly stepped over the dead body of Vic and headed outside.

'Nah, there's someone else I'm gonna torture, though. Can I leave you two to clear this up or make it look like Vic killed his family and then himself?'

'Yeah, sure, but, Cas, I want a raise for this.'

'Whatever, Walter, whatever, mate.'

***

Lolly drove in silence until he was almost outside the mobster's house.

'It's hard, son, to take it all in, and if you don't wanna do this with me, I will do it on me own. I've got enough fucking hate for the pair of us.'

'No, Cas, this is *our* war. Not yours, not mine. It's ours. Although, thinking about it, I guess, really, it's mine, ain't it?'

'All right, all right, no need to split hairs.' Cas sighed. 'She ain't mine, ya know, Lolly.'

Now dumbfounded, Lolly turned slowly to Cas. 'What?'

'Tara ain't mine. God knows who her father is, but he sure as hell ain't me.'

'And you know this a hundred per cent?'

'Yep, I had a DNA carried out on that twat Colt and Tara. It was kinda for confirmation. You see, I had doubts, being that she don't look nuffin like me or her mother. The results confirmed that was the case. So I just thought, ah, well, if I deny her, I would be denying Willow of a mother, and I liked the idea of family. Know what I mean?'

Lolly nodded. 'I know exactly what you mean. Can I ask what is in that briefcase?'

Cas looked out of the window and laughed. 'A few drawings, Tara's school reports, Willow's handmade Christmas cards. In fact, all the things I treasured the most, and, of course, a copy of me will.'

'Cas, ya know that bloke ain't Italian, don't ya?'

Cas spun to face him. 'You what? 'Course he is! Well, he fucking looks like it.'

Lolly shook his head. 'No, I did some digging, as ya do, and he's Eastern European, although he says he's Italian. His name isn't Luca. It's Luka Balakin, not Luca Barberi. See that house.' He pointed to the new property that stood proudly with the flash Jag in the drive.

Cas nodded.

'That isn't his house. He rents it, and the rent is overdue by six months. He hires that car too. All to look like he's worth a few bob.'

'So what made you do some digging, Lolly? Did you want Tara back?'

'No way!' replied Lolly, looking indignant, as if Cas had insulted him. 'If he was going to be in my daughter's life, then I wanted to know about him, that's all.' He paused. 'You ain't gonna like this, Cas, but when Willow said she didn't like him and would never go to his house, I didn't bother looking into him anymore. I didn't tell Tara what I discovered. I thought it was not my business. She wasn't mine to worry about. Now, I'm not so sure I made the right decision. If I had found out more about this bastard, maybe things would've turned out very differently.'

Cas nodded. 'I understand what you're saying, Lolly. But we can't turn the clock back, can we. Don't worry, I'll see you right, mate.'

After an hour or so, Luka appeared.

'Look, there he is,' said Cas, glaring. 'He's on his own, getting in the Jag. We'll follow the cunt.'

Lolly waited until Luka pulled off his drive and headed in the direction they had just left. With his face like thunder and his eyes blazing, he shot off after Luka, but he kept a safe distance.

Suddenly, Luka swerved off the main road and drove down a side road into an industrial estate, where he stopped outside a lock-up garage.

'Any cameras, Cas?'

Cas shook his head. 'No, mate. The place seems to be deserted, the warehouses are empty, and it looks like they're going to pull the place down.'

They both watched as Luka exited his car.

Without any orders from Cas, Lolly drove his car like shit off a shovel at Luka. Before the man even realised it, he'd crushed Luka's lower half and pinned him to a concrete wall.

Both Lolly and Cas leaped from the car to find Luka flopped on the bonnet, gasping for breath.

'Help, help, you've crushed my legs. Please help me.' He obviously hadn't seen who was driving the car until he looked up, and his eyes gaped into those of a stone-dead killer. Cas Ferrier.

'Fancy seeing you 'ere, Luka.' Cas dragged out the name. 'What did ya want me black briefcase for, eh? You slimy cunt.'

‘No, please, Mr Ferrier, please help me. Look, look!’ he screeched. ‘My legs are crushed.’

‘Oh, mate, that’s just for starters! Now, let’s try again, shall we. What can you tell me about my black briefcase?’

Knowing that the game was up, Luka’s eyes ping-ponged between the two men. Although the pain was now leaving him, he couldn’t feel any movement in his legs. He then knew that he was paralysed from the waist down.

‘The will.’ He turned to Lolly, furious that he had been found out. ‘You didn’t think I would be with a woman like her for free, did you? No, she has a rich father, and I wanted to see if she was named in his will.’

‘Oh, is that all,’ said Cas, mockingly. ‘Best let him go, Lolly.’

Lolly grinned, got back into his car, and reversed.

Luka instantly dropped to the ground like a sack of shit.

Lolly then got back out and snatched the keys that Luka had dropped the moment he was crushed against the wall.

As soon as Lolly unlocked the garage shutters and lifted them up, both Cas and Lolly stood back. ‘Well, fuck me, this is our lucky day, Lolly. It’s like an Aladdin’s cave.’

As Luka writhed around on the ground, unable to get to his feet, Cas and Lolly took in all the treasured things, from Rolex watches to antique grandfather clocks and oil paintings.

‘The cunt was a thief.’

Ignoring the irony of that remark, Lolly said, ‘Well, Cas, I’m going to put him in the boot of his car and take him somewhere to have a bit of fun. You’d best start filling up the motor. We can’t let this find go to waste, can we?’

Cas winked. ‘Me headache’s gone already.’

‘And you’ve got your smile back,’ said Lolly. ‘Cas, we’re still family, yeah? I mean, I ain’t got anyone.’

''Course we are. Now, get rid of that piece of shit.' He pointed to Luka, who was now unconscious. 'And then, we'll have a proper carve up of all this gear. Ain't that right.'

CHAPTER THIRTY-SIX

18 September

As the coffin was slowly lowered into the ground, Billy felt the weight of the world on his shoulders. He stared into the hole, remembering Keith for the man he was, not the last image he had of him. That came when the lights were off, and the house was quiet.

After his interview with the police, they suggested counselling. They told him that *no kid* should go through what he had seen without having some kind of help.

But he knew better.

He had seen horrors that those well-meaning strangers couldn't begin to imagine. What happened at the farmhouse had changed him: it had twisted something inside that couldn't be untwisted by sitting on a plush chair in some stuffy room.

He had his mother and Dottie. They were all the support he needed. Dottie understood him in ways his mother couldn't, while his mother filled the gaps with the warmth and love that Dottie lacked. It balanced out just enough to keep him from falling into some deep depression. But the nightmares were now a different story. They haunted his sleep, Jesse's too, because they both often woke up with cold sweats in the dead of night.

Billy lingered as the mourners began to drift away, heads bowed, and hands stuffed into coat pockets. However, he wasn't ready to leave Willow just yet. With a single rose in his hand, he walked towards the freshly turned earth beside Keith's grave and laid the flower where her headstone would one day stand. It was only right that Keith's grave would be beside Willow's. In some ways, it brought a sense of comfort. After a moment of silent contemplation, he stepped back, feeling the weight of the goodbye settle in his bones.

Unexpectedly, he felt a familiar arm slide around his shoulders.

'I know we never really talked about it, Billy boy, but I can tell you, whether you believe me or not, that Willow loved you.' Jesse's voice was soft-spoken as he tentatively broached this sensitive subject.

Billy turned, his eyes glistening. 'Did she?' he asked, but it wasn't really a question. It was more of a plea. Because he so desperately needed something to hold on to. He wanted to carry her memory with fondness, not have it clouded by doubt.

Slowly, Jesse nodded. 'She was definitely going through a rough patch. She was lashing out at everyone, even the ones she cared about most. But she loved you, Billy. I know she did.'

Billy swallowed hard. 'I'd like to believe that, Jesse. I mean, I want to believe it. I really do. But how can I ever really know?'

Jesse shifted from foot to foot. 'Look, it's hard for you to forgive me. I know that—'

'I *have* forgiven you, Jesse. So maybe . . .' he said, as he tapped Jesse's chest, 'you just need to forgive yourself.'

Although Jesse knew that Billy was right – that one day the guilt would stop – he couldn't be sure when that would be. He glanced down at the rose he'd laid earlier. 'Billy, Lolly's got something for you.'

Billy furrowed his brow, wiping his face with the back of his hand. 'Yeah? What's that, then?'

'Willow's diary.'

‘Oh.’ The word hung between them heavily, with everything it could mean.

Reaching into his pocket, Jesse pulled out something small, something he held out to Billy with care. ‘I’ve got something too, something I’d forgotten about. Mum found it in the washing machine after she’d cleaned our clothes.’ Delicately, he placed the necklace into his brother’s hand.

It was the charm that Billy had never quite managed to give to Willow.

Billy stared down at it, his voice barely a whisper. ‘I lost this in the stables when I got stupidly drunk.’ He kneeled down and pressed the necklace into the soil above where Willow lay. ‘She never got to wear it.’

Jesse crouched beside him, his voice gentle. ‘You know, if there’s such a thing as spirits, then I reckon she helped me find you. I reckon things happen for a reason. Maybe it was decided up there in Heaven.’

Billy frowned, glancing at his brother. ‘How d’you mean?’

‘When I went to confront Danny, it was a bit of a stab in the dark, but something caught my eye. I saw it shining in his car. I knew right then that the only person who’d have had that necklace, who wouldn’t have let it out of their sight, would be you. Remember, even after we fought, and you threw the necklace down on the kitchen table, you picked up the necklace before you rushed out of the house, didn’t you? In my mind, I suppose it was as if Willow had made it shine, or whatever, so that we would know Danny had something to do with your disappearance. That’s why I made him take me to you. I think there was more to it than just chance.’

Billy looked down, his tears dripping onto the freshly turned earth. ‘I would love to believe that, Jesse.’

‘I think you should read the diary.’

‘Have you, Jesse?’ he asked, as he stood up straight.

‘No, it’s not my place to do that. Only Lolly and you have that right.’

‘Did I hear my name mentioned?’ asked Lolly, as he carefully approached, not wanting to impose on what looked like a heart-to-heart between what had been a fractured relationship between the two brothers.

Billy wiped his eyes and turned to see Lolly.

‘Sorry, Lolly, we’ll leave you to, er, . . .’ said Billy, looking at Lolly’s single rose.

‘It’s fine, Billy,’ said Lolly, noting the telltale redness around the lad’s eyes. ‘Here,’ he said, as he pulled out what looked like a diary with gems all over it. ‘It’s Willow’s, but I want you to have it, if, of course, you want it.’

Gingerly, Billy took the diary and smiled. ‘Thank you, Lolly. If you don’t mind, I’d like some time on my own.’

‘I’m off to the hospital. Mum’s just had a call that ol’ Ginty’s hollering and hooting. She wants Mum to bring her up some decent grub.’ Jesse winked and walked towards the main gates where their parents were waiting.

Lolly laid the rose, said a few words, and also left.

Billy sat on a bench that was a few feet away from the graves of Willow and Keith. He fingered the gems on the cover of the diary before he gently opened it at the first page.

It began on the day they had met at the prison. Her handwriting was immature, but her words were sweet. She described how she’d first met Jesse and himself and how she felt so protected when the fight in the prison had broken out.

Billy smiled although tears stung his eyes. Then, she went on to describe how she was so excited to be going to their family party, and afterwards, she mentioned that she’d had the time of her life. She even wrote about how she wished she lived with his family – the Murphys – rather than with her own mother.

As he turned the pages, he could see he was entering into her world.

She'd written: *BB called tonight. Oh how I could melt into his words – I love this boy.*

He reread the words: *I love this boy.*

As he continued going through the diary, he knew from her excitement when he'd called or when she joined their family parties that she had indeed loved him. He laughed and cried as he read each page twice.

But then her writing changed. It suddenly became more detached and sometimes erratic. There had always been the odd note describing a cold and harsh side to her life, which, sadly, included the lack of care and love from her mother.

But then, in contrast, Willow's next comment showed how excited she was to plan a future with him. She wanted a commitment and a promise of marriage – not to escape from her mother but to reaffirm how much she loved him. It seemed from her entry, she could never love anyone like she loved him.

As he read on, the truth of Willow's struggles slowly came to light. These were evidently ones she'd kept hidden behind her upbeat phone calls. She'd always put on a brave face, never letting on that beneath the surface, she was drowning.

Then he reached the entry where she'd written about her mother walking out and how her life fell apart that day. Her mother's words had cut her deeply, so it seemed. She had cruelly told her that she'd made the biggest mistake of her life. She could have been free if it wasn't for her daughter. The wickedness in those words leaped off the page; they made him seethe with anger and sadness.

He shivered as a cool breeze bit into him, compelling him to pull his jacket tighter around him. If only she'd confided in him and told him what she was going through. He could have helped her, but she'd spiralled out of control, lashing out at everyone who cared about her and pushing them away.

Her entries grew darker and even more chaotic as she wrote about hurting her grandfather and then feeling a crushing guilt that only fuelled her anger. It seemed that one bad thing led to another, to the point where her life had become one downward spiral. Feelings of guilt led to anger, anger led to hurt, and then things just got progressively worse as she lashed out again and again. She confessed to having used cocaine to numb the pain, as well as drink, and the reckless flings, it appeared, could be explained as a genuine cry for help. Her words became jagged and harsh, almost fierce. He imagined her sitting up in bed in the middle of the night writing to herself, so trapped in her own cruel nightmare.

Billy had to stop reading to wipe away the tears that blurred the words on the page.

'Oh, Willow,' he whispered, 'I wish you'd told me. I would have understood.'

Then came the page that made everything fall into place. The night she'd slept with Jesse. She began the entry with *Oh my God, what have I done? I shouldn't have forced him, but my head was all over the place. I wanted to hurt Billy, to drive him away, because one day he'd walk out on me, like Mum did. I can't ever get married. I can't have a family because I'll be left alone. I can't handle the pain of rejection.*

Billy's hands shook as he held the diary close to his heart, the words cutting through him.

She had hated herself. Her mother's cruelty had drained all the good out of her by leaving her convinced she was worthless. She carried that hurt, building walls so high, she never let anyone in, not even him.

She hadn't just been fighting the world. She'd been fighting herself.

A lump lodged in his throat, as he turned to the last page. There, she'd written in big messy letters: *Dear God, please let Billy forgive me. I messed up big time and I only hope the truth doesn't come out or I may have destroyed a special bond between the two brothers. I just seem to hurt the people I love the most. If you do exist, God, then please forgive me because I have to make Billy hate me so that when I walk away, he won't hurt because I couldn't bear it. How could he ever really love me, when I can't even love myself.*

The words became blurred again now through his tears. She'd tried to push him away, not out of spite but out of some misguided sense to protect him. It was all because she believed that by making him hate her, she'd spared him the pain of loving someone who was so chronically damaged. Someone who couldn't even see her own self-worth.

Closing the diary, he leaned back on the bench and shut his eyes while he allowed the cool breeze to wash away some of the pain. He hoped that what Jesse believed was somehow true.

The sharp click-clack sound of a woman in high-heeled shoes made Billy open his eyes. And there walking along the path dressed in jeans and a pink sweatshirt with her long black hair blowing in the breeze was a girl he thought he recognised. She was proudly carrying some flowers. She didn't look Billy's way before she turned off and continued walking towards a grave under an oak tree. He watched her, as she kissed her hand and tapped it on the gravestone before placing the flowers in the vase.

He stared, not thinking of anything other than this girl, who seemed so graceful. Then he felt guilty for having read Willow's precious thoughts because he was now admiring another girl. He tucked the diary under his arm and rose from the bench. Before he walked away, he glanced over at the girl, who was now looking his way and smiling.

'Hello, Billy,' she said.

He paused, startled.

'Sorry, I shouldn't have disturbed you.'

Billy's cheeks blushed when he realised who she was. 'It's okay, Bronte, but you're a long way from Orpington.'

'Me dear muvver is buried here. I come every birthday and lay the lilies,' she said, as she walked towards him. 'I'm ever so sorry about Willow.'

He nodded. 'Yeah, me too,' Billy replied, as he retook his seat. Suddenly, his thoughts turned to Jesse's words. *Things happen for a reason.* He looked up at her sweet smile and huge eyes, and a warm feeling crept over him. 'Would you like to join me?' He patted the space next to him.

When she smiled, her whole face lit up. Instantly, she sat down beside him and allowed her hand to gently brush past his. 'Did Jesse say anything about me?'

Billy blushed again. 'He did, actually. He said, you, er . . . well, he said.'

'I liked you?'

'Yeah, he did say that.'

'Good, because I do, Billy. I know you're probably still grieving, but if you need some company, well, I would like to be that company.' She rose from the bench and kissed his cheek. 'You take care, Billy. Hopefully, I will see you soon.'

'Yes, Bronte, I think you just might.'

Printed in Great Britain
by Amazon

54673766R00216